HEIR OF BONE
AND SHADOWS

GRAVESTONE BOOK TWO

AMBER DARWIN

Edited by - Sara Berzinski

Cover Art by - Ashley Seney

WELCOME TO THE TEMPLE OF DUSK

"And thus, the heart will break, yet brokenly live
on."
Lord George Gordon Byron

AUTHOR'S NOTE

I WRITE GRITTY, RAW, sometimes disturbing gothic/dark fantasy/paranormal romance. The heroes do villain-type shit, and the villains are not always what they seem. Some find redemption, some never will. These characters are not human and won't always behave as you or I would expect, but I hope you see something in each of them that speaks to you. And through their struggles, I hope you find those jagged pieces of yourself and learn to love them for what they are.

Are there errors in this book? Probably. I'm human, and I'm pretty sure my editor is too? Although magic can't be ruled out with her.

This is the second installment of The Gravestone Trilogy. Adult fantasy (18+)

It contains scenes that may depict, mention, or discuss: abduction, anxiety, attempted murder, blood, death, emotional abuse, fire, kidnapping, murder, occult, PTSD, torture, war, graphic sex, gore, foul language, dysfunctional relationships, miscommunication, and cliffhangers. If any of these themes are damaging to your mental health, turn back now. This is not the book for you, and that's okay.

- If that just made you want to read it even more? Congrats! We're besties, and I need to know your favorite color. XO – Amber

CONFESSION

I FOUGHT EVERY IMPULSE that screamed to stay away from him; but, maybe somewhere inside my messy soul I knew there wasn't a path that didn't lead us to destruction. From the first moment we locked eyes, and he looked at me like I was the bane of his existence, to the next moment when he swept the air from my lungs with unexpected tenderness. And all the moments in between.

I think I always knew he would be my downfall, but I couldn't accept it. So, I let myself fall. How could I have known I was wearing a blindfold?

Now there's a cryptic prophecy hanging over my head, and a curse I don't know that I believe.

If Killian is capable of love, I'm in big trouble. But somehow, I doubt that's the case. How could it be, when he worked with my evil sperm donor to abduct me from the Earth Realm and deliver me to The Netherworld? When he invoked an old contract of betrothal without even speaking to me about it first. All the nights he put me away on the shelf like a pretty vase. Hot one minute, cold the next. I knew. But hearts are wild, unreasonable beasts. That's why they live in cages.

Deacon is a prisoner of the Academy and Rowena is missing. Faustus has allied himself with the only other monster in the Netherworld who could overthrow Killian, and that's my father. I think Kalliope is in danger, and Calypso is dead. So, here I am. Alone, broken-hearted, numb. The saddest tears aren't the ones that flow from your eyes, streaking down your cheeks and making a mess of your mascara. They're the ones on the inside. The silent screams trapped inside your throat. That's pain.

I tell myself, "Who cares?"

But my inner voice always responds, "You do, stupid."

- Vivi Graves. Heir of Nothing.

CHAPTER ONE

THE TEMPLE OF DUSK

THE AMBIANCE FEELS VERY 'forgotten history' on this abandoned estate. It's been untouched by civilization for ages and the vibration is palpable. There's a foreboding here. Maybe it's the leftover energy signature of the suffering that befell the Darkmoors. Or perhaps it's the general emptiness. The hollowed ghost of what had once been a beautifully manicured estate.

And now? Well... I guess it couldn't overcome the damage that's been done. That's something I understand a little too well. It's eerily fitting, really.

Have you ever had a dream that felt so real it made you question your sanity? I've become uncomfortably familiar with them over the last few days. Weeks? I don't know anymore. Time is an illusion here. Reality is fleeting. I don't sleep, because when I close my eyes and collapse into the endless dark...

Strong hands wrapped around my waist, fingers digging into my hips, setting fire to my insides. The overwhelming pull to be near him, to touch him, to feel him inside me. Weeks locked away in a gilded cage with only a false impression of freedom. Kisses on my neck, the way he made me come alive. My magic reaching into the earth and creating life, juxtaposed with the terrible destruction it orchestrated. My fingers caressed his beautifully broken face. A ballroom filled with Netherlings, watching my world crumble beneath a mountain of lies. Killian screaming for me like I was his entire world; how can someone fake that? Even a demon. My evil sperm donor's merciless face as he hid behind a legion and threw my sister to the wolves. Calypso's blood. Killian watching me walk away, doing nothing to stop me.

My blackened heart splinters, silent tears flow down my sunken cheeks. I'm living like a fucking ghost.

My eyes drift toward the cobwebs adorning the window in my less than impressive chamber. It's sparse; the wallpaper is flower printed and peeling. And this makeshift cot has a straw mattress that pokes holes in my ass, but the early morning light filters through stained-glass panes, casting a reddish glow onto the stone-covered fireplace and it's a desolate sort of beauty.

My dark thoughts drift to Kalliope. I was so sure my sister would see me, the real me. So confident she would leave the Court of Shadows behind.

That she would choose me.

Instead, she tried to murder me. In what I thought were my last moments, Calypso did what she was born to do. She protected me, traded her life for mine, and I'd do anything to take it back. I'd sell my soul to undo it. I can't think about Kalliope without thinking of Calypso now. *Ugh. I just need to get up.* I'm going crazy here. I need to move, run, kick someone's ass, do something that makes me feel alive.

I violently roll to my side, smacking my fore-head straight into the side of a primitive bedside table.

"Ouch, Godsdammit!!" I complain to nobody, rubbing my forehead. I deserved that, but what-ever. I'd rather stomp my way over to the crum-bling fireplace and pop a squat on the floor than think about it.

I reach over and threw in some logs and kin-dling. Snapping my fingers. Igniting a spark. Soaking up the warmth my body stopped pro-ducing.

If Deacon were here, he'd tell me to un-fuck myself.

And I'm trying. Pinky swear I am! I just wish I could identify the moment everything went into the shitter; I wish I could have seen it coming. I have the Sight, for Goddess' sake! What's the use if it doesn't work when I need it to?

"Beyond redemption," I mutter to the decaying ceiling with a humph.

Can an Incubus enter your dreams and cause a spontaneous orgasm? I know I took a hard left there with the subject change, but it's nagging at my brain. I do not know how Killian's powers work; I guess I should have paid more attention in class. But I must've skipped class on incubus day, because I have no idea. Dreams. Reality. Some-where between? Only the devil knows.

I'm too embarrassed to ask Willa about the dream orgasms. First, because she hates me, and I can't guarantee that she won't enjoy my pain. Next, because I don't know if she'll make it go away. That's crazy. Of course I should want her to, but I'm fucked up. I'm not even going to make excuses.

The last thing I should think about is hot, nasty dream sex with the devil incarnate.

I hate him.

For not being who I thought he was.

For being *exactly* who I thought he was.

I hate him for so many things, but one sits at the top of the list.

The last thing he said to me... *'I won't let you go, Kitten.'*

Ugh, gag me with a twisted wand. What the fuck is that? Some new method of psychological warfare? I wouldn't put it past him. Those reckless words fester in my gut like the worst poison. Because it's the only thing I've heard him say that I absolutely, undoubtedly, do believe.

He will not let me go.

Not because he actually gives a shit. No, nothing as chivalrous as that. Killian won't let me go because he needs me for something.

For what, I don't know yet. I'm just the basic witch who forgets my intelligence, sometimes my panties, and the whereabouts of my self-respect in his presence. But I will get to the bottom of it, one way or another.

Yeah, I guess you could say I'm slightly resentful.

I used to have a life before Sir Fucks-With-Your-Head showed up. Was it an extraordinary life? No, not really, but at least I kept my inner demons on their respective leashes.

At least I had some semblance of dysfunctional normalcy. I wasn't on Thornfall's Most Wanted List and I wasn't in any real danger of spending the rest of my days shackled to Faustus as his executioner. Or worse, chained to Mordred. I shudder to think of all the morbid possibilities.

In my former life, the Elders weren't a joy to deal with. There was the whole bit about a prophecy that would have caught up with me eventually, and I had some minor complications with forbidden magic. But at least I had music, hot water, and soap. And there was coffee, the sweet nectar of the caffeine gods.

There's no coffee in the abandoned abbey, which officially qualifies this place as the seventh circle of HELL. The Circle of Violence, according to Dante. Which makes sense because a well-known side effect of having no caffeine is violence.

It's not all bad news and apocalyptic future. We're safe, for now. Iris is teaching me to control my gifts, and she is one bad bitch. She knows her shit, her Barrier of Invisibility is flawless. Impeccable. We're hidden in plain sight. It's so brilliant she might be my new hero.

My control is getting better. I can call the flames at will and dismiss them without starting any curtain or carpet fires. Most of the time, anyway.

So, I practice.

Even if we're safe for now, Killian doesn't strike me as a man that fails. Right now, he's too busy gloating at my dazzling stupidity, but it's only a matter of time before he runs out of patience and shows up in the flesh. And when he does? He'll find a way through, and he'll probably try to drag me to the next terror show in the Netherworld.

He'll do it with pretty words first, but I can't fall for it again. Fool me once; shame on you, right? But not twice because a second time means shame on me.

Speaking of shame.

For the first time in my adult life, I have no idea what to do next. I go through the motions, let my rage burn away my splintery parts. I look like a woman, but if you look closely, I'm just a collection of bones and shadows.

The golden embers distract my thoughts and catch my eye. I stare into them while tracing runes in the ash on the hearth.

I envision the flames splitting in two, creating shadows on the wall. They dance, testing the boundaries of my magic. I concentrate on the wood inside the fireplace, sweat beads on my forehead, the embers morph from burnt orange to canary yellow and finally to violet and I can't help but smile.

My life may be falling apart at the rate of several WTFs per hour, but I'm using my magic.

The Sight works differently outside of Thornfall, without my amulet. It still feels wrong sometimes, but I was given the gift for a reason and it's time I figure out why.

Plus, we can use all the 'heads-up' we can get around here. I can't interpret them very well yet: sometimes what looks like a dire warning in my visions is just a caution not to trip down the stairs. But Iris assures me it gets more accurate with practice. I still pick up on people's thoughts when I'm not intending to.

That, I do not recommend!

Here, I'll save you the trouble. Sex. That's what people think about. All day, every day. Sex in every imaginable position, and some even the imagination couldn't do justice. With forbidden partners and zero inhibitions. I've been working on my mental shields to block it out. I just need to adjust to my new level of power.

The sooner the better. Oof, some of those images can't be unseen.

When I'm not working with my magic, I'm sitting crisscrossed at this fireplace, tapping into the bond with Kalliope. Probably more often than I should be, but I'm obsessed. I know we're connected; I know I can reach her, but the little bitch is blocking me out. I don't know if she's older or younger than me. But exasperating asshole sisters come in both sizes. Jokes on her, though. I'm stubborn as fuck, and I'll annoy the shit out of her until I get a response, if that's what it takes.

After arriving at the Abbey, I discovered that the flames I possess aren't entirely controlled by the blood in my veins. They're also tied to my emotions. Which isn't fantastic news, on account of my temper. You remember Dr. Jean Grey, right? Iris says I have some real potential to rival that level of destruction if I don't learn to master my rage.

I still haven't decided if that sounds appealing or not? And I wish that was a joke, but I'm not a liar. So, take it as you please.

I love the feel of my magic coursing through my body. The freedom of nobody threatening me with death for using it. I can cast a blood spell in the middle of the cathedral if I want to. I can tear the mountains down or persuade someone to stop breathing. It's a heady feeling. Addictive. But all magic comes with consequences, and I don't know what mine will be. Every time I use it, I feel the darkness beckoning me closer.

In a way, I miss my amulet. It was a guarantee. A check and balance on the raging storm that brews inside me. It's long gone now, of course. Buried under a mass of decaying corpses or laying in the bottom of a fracture in the earth. One that I made, which still freaks me out.

I'm not convinced I should have this kind of power.

The darkness that lives inside me. The monster they set free. She's out for blood, and I'm presuming the amulet was the key to her cage.

CHAPTER TWO

VIVI

THE TEMPLE OF DUSK was once a bustling estate that housed prominent members of the Darkmoor bloodline and their families. Time has reduced it to cracked foundations with twisting vines peeking through the holes they've torn, broken windowpanes with branches spilling out, and moss adorning the stone walls like a blanket of insulation.

It's as though nature intends to take it all back.

There's a haunting attraction here, a melancholy allure. The pitted steps and worn staircases and areas of the outer wall with faded blast marks give proof to the violence that happened long ago. It evokes the mental image of witches battling their own kind, using the elements as their weapons.

This rotted old remnant has stories.

Voices echo through an open window, unaware that I've snuck out of my chamber and am currently perched in a Mountain Ash tree not far away. This drafty old abbey is great for acoustics, but it doesn't leave much space for privacy. So, when I realize the voices are familiar, I can't help leaning in to eavesdrop...

"She's a loose cannon," Linc grumbles hoarsely.
"She's wrecked, you idiot! Grief makes people
do irrational things. You, of all people, should
know that! Mister runs away to the woods every
time he has feelings. Do you know what else
makes people do irrational things? Sexual harass-
ment." Marlow whisper-shouts back at him.

I know what they're talking about right away.

Yesterday, one of Lincoln's wolves made the
mistake of believing he could rub his junk against
me as I walked past and I had taken it personally.
Before he could get a word out, I tossed him to
the ground with my dagger poised at his throat.
I bared my teeth and silently dared him to keep
going; he would find out that I am not prey.

There was a whole commotion about it afterward, of course. But it seemed like he got the
point, so I respectfully disagree that it was an
irrational thing to do. Now they're all treating me
like I'm a walking time bomb.

Maybe I am. An even better reason to leave me
the fuck alone, right?

"And he will be punished! Nobody touches
Vivi and gets away with it, period. But it doesn't
change that she's different now. She's explosive.
Unpredictable." Linc continues.

"I'm not saying I'm not worried. Of course, I
am! She lost Calypso, her sister tried to kill her,
she met her dad—and he's a prick! The amulet
is gone. Not to mention Deacon, and I know you
choose to ignore it, but Killian broke her heart!
She's got every right to be screwed up, Linc. We
don't abandon our friends when they're going
through the heavy shit," Marlow stands up for me

like they have put my integrity on trial while I wasn't there to defend myself.

Has it been?

"Deacon is off-limits, Lowe. I feel that too, remember? And I'm not so sure Vivi and I *are* friends anymore." Linc retorts, and my chest cracks open.

"Oh, put a sock in it, Lincoln! You're not friends anymore? Give me a break and stop thinking with your dick. You took your shot, and it didn't go as you intended it to. Build a bridge. Buy some hiking boots. And get over it!"

"Shut up, Marlow!"

"You first!" she bites back. "And that's what I thought... Lincoln. Check your ego. Vivi isn't the only one who's changed."

I contemplate climbing down from this tree and barging into the hallway to shut them both the hell up! Broadcasting my personal shit throughout the grounds of this Goddess Forsaken Abbey. Everyone knows it echoes here, like a creepy train tunnel except with collapsed buildings and trees instead. It's nobody's business. But I don't have the mental capacity to deal with this shit again today.

It's exhausting.

Linc really thinks we're somehow fated to be mates, and I don't know what the hell to do with that. I'm not going to pretend to know what the stars do behind their curtains. But I just don't see a scenario where that works?

I'm not a wolf. I'm not certain that I want children, I'm even less sure that I want hybrid puppies, and I know that's critical for the survival of his clan. Everyone knows that! The Alpha has sons, the sons carry on the line, the pack survives, etc., etc. I don't even know if it's possible for me to be their Lady Alpha, and even if I can there's no guarantee they would accept me. It might even be illegal? I don't know.

Not that I care so much about the illegal part. Fuck the Rune Force and the fossils who control them. But do you see what I mean? It's all tangled up and messy. So, avoidance seems like a legitimate course of action, and I've been doing a stellar job of it.

It doesn't help that Lowe is firmly on team Killian. Except I'm pretty sure Killian isn't even on team Killian, but Marlow's got this misplaced romantic notion that he's pining for me. She thinks he has an explanation, and that I should hear him out. I don't think I need to describe the hundreds of reasons that will not happen, but I applaud her optimism. It must be all the dirty fairy tale books she reads.

I don't fit in with the rest of the witches, so I do my best to avoid conversation. Which is why I've had my ass parked up in this tree for the last hour.

When everyone wakes up, they meet in the cathedral-turned cafeteria for breakfast. It's segregated, tense, and I don't care for the energy one bit. So instead, I get up most days and hang out in the trees for a while. It's a far cry from the quirky coffee shop I used to spend my mornings in, but beggars can't be choosers, I guess. Whatever that means.

After I get in a little earth time to soothe my elemental magic, I leave the safety of the tree and check the perimeter. I know that's a job for the shifters, but I need to see for myself that the wards are in one piece. That Mordred isn't standing outside waiting to trap us. You can call it hypervigilance, paranoia, or a healthy respect for breathing. Whatever glitters your wings.

It's not like that's the only thing I do out there. I also gather firewood, pick herbs, and test the boundaries of my magic without an audience. I mentioned that I've been focused on the connection between Kalliope and myself. What I didn't mention are the side effects. Sometimes I focus so hard my nose bleeds, or a bird falls from the sky and breaks its neck and reanimates itself. I feel like that's an invitation for way too many questions.

I just prefer to practice alone; in case something goes funky.

The wind shudders through the trees as they groan and sway. I follow the path that twists along next to the bustling river, heading deeper into the woods—loving the earthy scent of fresh soil and the morning dew covering the grass. I enjoy the scenery. It's very Monteverde Cloud Forest, or maybe it's closer to Terabithia? Whatever. It's the only place I can think straight, without getting every impression of every emotion from every soul inside the Abbey. Being able to *feel* what your friends are thinking around you fucks with your head.

Speaking of...

Linc isn't wrong, you know. Not that I would ever admit that to his face. But I *have* struggled to control my dark side. Rage, revenge, retribution. My inner monster whispers to me, and I do my best to ignore the pull inside my chest, but some things are addictive, and sometimes I fall prey to my worst impulses.

What's that famous TV show quote again? Oh, yeah... *"serenity now."*

"Did you sleep at all last night?" I jump at the sound of Marlow's voice.

"Fucking hell, Lowe!" My heart beats rowdily, she caught me off guard. I need to pay closer attention to my surroundings.

No wonder my ass got snatched up at The Academy.

"I brought you something to eat." She holds out an apple and I suppress a cringe. Immediately, an image of Jagger enters my mind. That ridiculous dragon and his apples. I'd like to steer clear of thinking about Jagger, because if I do I'll spiral down the rabbit hole. And that hole always ends on familiar stormy eyes and the demon penis they're attached to.

"Thanks." I tilt my head and hold out my hand, gesturing for her to hand it over.

"The witches would like to meet; we have some decisions to make. I know you're doing... whatever survivor type shit this is, but we could use your input." Marlow creases her lips tightly.

"Survival skills are underrated, you know. Ugh, fine." I know I'm out of line as soon as it comes out of my mouth, but the madness living inside me is barely contained, and I'm just trying not to drown in it.

I hate when she's mad at me, I really do.

Marlow opens her mouth like she wants to say something more, but quickly closes it and turns to leave instead. Which makes me feel like an asshole friend, but I already know what she's going to say...

The new witches need a leader. They've left their homes and their families; they are risking their lives because they believe in our purpose. We have a duty. Blah, blah. I know all this. That's what I'm here for, too:

One. Release Deacon.

Two. Take Underhill Academy of Magical Bullshit down.

Three. Reinstate the school under new leadership.

Four. Remove Faustus Culpepper's arrogant head.

That one's a personal favorite of mine!

I mean, come on. I walked out of the Netherworld to be here. Isn't that enough? And okay, maybe part of me was trying to run away from a walking problem with a nice ass... but my intentions here are pure.

Murder is pure when it's justified, right? It's no secret I'm out for blood. Academy Blood. It's about time they suffer the consequences of what they created.

Me.

Ironic right? The monster they built to rule over the realm with is the very same monster that brings about their destruction. Now that's beautiful! It's like macabre poetry.

Anyway, the point is that I'm down with the plan. It's the rest of the politics I have no time for. Things like - who's going to devise a way into

Underhill? Who will lead the fight? What are we going to do with the rogue witches afterward? Who is powerful enough to protect the school when we take it over? I sure as hell don't want to be the leader of anything; I can barely manage to lead myself anywhere other than straight-jacket-crazy-town.

Just give me my daggers and a target to annihilate.

That's my lane, and I want to stay in it.

As much as I hate to admit it, Willa and Iris are the obvious choices to lead. I'm not super thrilled about Willa, for obvious reasons. But Iris is a saint. She would be the perfect headmistress. I suppose we could have Willa sit detentions or something. I bet if we did that, the students would be the best behaved in the realm!

Some of the younger witches believe I should be the one to restore order. Which is ridiculous, of course. What kind of Head Mistress does a hot-headed former executioner turned bartender make?

A shitty one.

I mix drinks, kick asses, and don't bother to remember names. Or I used to, at least. I don't know if that will ever be a reality again. But one thing I don't do is supervise baby witches.

Calm down, I don't hate them or anything. It's not personal. I'm under qualified to mentor a houseplant so they wouldn't stand a chance. And the more advanced witches? That's even worse. Imagine every day telling someone twice your age what's best for them. Then close your eyes and visualize the outcome.

I imagine it looks something like my fairy grandmother chasing me through a coffee shop with a rolled-up newspaper, smacking me in the back of the head. Not pretty.

And then we have the Blackwood clan, which is an entirely different situation.

Linc flipped shit when I was relocated (kidnapped) to the Netherworld. He marched into the compound where he was once rejected, ripped his father's throat out, and took his place as Alpha. Honestly? I didn't think he had it in him. He's so warm, silly, and supportive. The picture of what I always thought the fairy tale princes were. But this new broody version of Linc? I don't recognize that guy. Alpha magic is potent as fuck, and from what I'm gathering? It changes your entire chemical make-up.

Historically, witches and wolves don't tolerate each other very well. I guess a nasty sorceress hundreds of years ago got pissed about something or other, and she cursed them to turn furry for eternity.

Surprise, surprise. Witches love themselves some curses, don't they?

If I were a wolf shifter, I'm not sure how I'd feel about going hairy, but I know I'd be pissed that they did not give me a choice. So, I don't really blame them for the distrust. Linc appears to be trying to change the narrative most of the time, anyway. But if the separate camps on each end of this centuries-old estate are any indication, he's got a major struggle on his hands. I don't envy him.

So, current situation...

The witches don't like the *dogs*. The shifters don't trust the *hags*. Nobody knows who the fuck is in charge. Everyone has an unsolicited opinion. And until we can come together? We twiddle our thumbs, and Deacon sits in a dungeon enduring whatever Faustus doles out to him. I imagine whatever it is, it's painful. And if we don't get him out soon? We may miss our opportunity.

Every day this continues, every hour wasted. I wonder if my decision to walk through the portal and out of the Netherworld was the right thing to do. I'm not a total idiot. I know it would be advantageous to have the help of the Night Court, even if it includes the demon fuck boy.

I'm just hoping it doesn't come to that.

———◆———

The Temple is surrounded by a dense forest filled with supernatural creatures of all shapes and sizes, most of them carnivorous. And the back side? That's even more hazardous. Unless cliff diving from the top of a three-thousand-foot waterfall is your thing? Then have at it, I suppose.

And it was nice knowing you...

Not only does the waterfall offer stellar protection, but it's also incredible for showers. Which is what I'm doing now. Standing under the cool, rushing water with my bare feet on the smooth rocks and sandy bottom. Listening to the woodland pixies flitting their little wings like musical notes on the breeze. They remind me of vivid butterflies—if butterflies had sharp teeth and liked the taste of blood and other various bodily fluids.

Anyway, this spot holds the only peace I can carve out for myself these days.

"Genevieve?" a gruff male voice calls out.

So much for that peace I was just imagining.

"Ansel, I'm naked. In most civilized places, when a woman is naked, you give her some privacy. Not every order is so liberal with nudity. And I've asked you repeatedly not to call me that." I speak plainly, but try not to come off too bitchy.

The name thing isn't really his issue, it's mine.

Soon after arriving here, I decided that hearing 'Genevieve' come from Killian's lips was decidedly worse than Kitten. More intimate somehow, and now every time I hear it, I want to vomit.

"Apologies, Princess Genevieve," Ansel continues, completely missing the point I was trying to make. "Alpha Lincoln asked that I give you an update. As you know, the Netherlings have sensed you through the wards. They have not pinpointed our location, but the dragon is here. With your previous bond, he may be more attuned to your magic than the scouts. Shall we prepare to attack?"

"That won't be necessary," I reply, irritated with... I don't know? Everything!

"Very well," he replies in a monotone voice.

Linc's second in command is a total buzzkill, and not just because they have appointed him my nanny. He's easy on the eyes in a rugged mountain man kind of way, with the enormous arms and the auburn tinted Viking beard. He could be mega sexy, but when I say he's a total drag, I mean, this wolf has the personality of soggy cardboard.

"Ansel, if you're going to stand here for my whole shower, you could at the very least hand over my clothes." He stares at the ground as he heads to the pile of clothing I left at the base of a Wallowing Willow tree. "Bring the weapons too, please!"

I stare up at the sky expectantly. Knowing full well I should head for cover instead, but I can't resist a chance to see Jagger—even if he can't see me. It's astonishing how many times a heart can break, isn't it? And just when you think it's cracked all the way through and can't hurt any worse... you're wrong.

Ansel lays my pack on a flat rock next to the bank and nods, looking away. My heart beats wildly. I feel a stirring in my stomach as I spy a red and gold wingtip moving into my vision through the treetops. Tears well up, threatening to erupt. I have this overwhelming urge to call out to the overconfident jackass. I want to tell him I miss his smart-ass mouth. I want to ask if Anise is okay? If Selene hates me now? If Bronwyn is hiding somewhere outside these wards, spying on me?

If Killian had shown even an ounce of remorse for what he's done...

I want so many things I can't have.

My wrist burns as the spiral brand I'd earned from a Night Creature back in Thornfall starts to glow crimson. It hasn't burned since some princely vagabonds smuggled me into the Netherworld via sketchy boat. This is fishy, something doesn't add up. Why would it glow when Jagger was nearby? It's Mordred's magical tracker.

Isn't it?

I replay the distant memory of that night in my head; the creature came in and asked for me by title, which threw me off my game. I was giving him a piece of my mind when he grabbed me. During the struggle is when Mr. Stalks-A-Lot showed up all sex and candy. Standing behind me, fueling a massive lady boner while simultaneously looming over my shoulder like the grim reaper on steroids. I think back to the look the creature gave Killian.

It wasn't fear. Was it? No, I remember it being an odd look. Almost reverent.

The puzzle pieces fit together, and my temper flares. I'm getting the overwhelming impression that I've been well and truly deceived. But on the battlefield Kalliope said, *"You have his mark, he'll find you anywhere, and when he does, you'll wish you were dead."*

I thought she was talking about Mordred. Wasn't she? She couldn't have been talking about Tall, Dark, and Fifty Shades of Fuckhead.

But she was, wasn't she? Godsdammit. That lying sack of shit!

That swaggering asshat set me up in a dangerous situation, so he could swoop in and save the day. And I was too busy trying to keep my clothes on to notice. Killian Prince Charming-ed me...

I'm going to kill him with my bare fucking hands!

Everything happened so fast that last night in the Netherworld. One minute I was having a fantastic time dancing in the Throne Room, foolishly dreaming of the possibilities my future could hold. And the next, I was face to face with Mordred and his legion. It registered that Killian and Mordred had made a deal, but everything went into pandemonium before I had the chance to get the details.

I was distracted by the betrothal bombshell, and an ancestor spewing from my mouth like one of those vintage ghost hunting ectoplasm photos. And then all I could think about was the danger my friends were in and getting to my sister. But something's missing here, something crucial. What am I not seeing? What's the end game in all of this? There must be one.

Killian had to have something in it for himself.

The heat in my wrist grows more intense, dragging me from my thoughts. I realize that if the brand is glowing now... then Jagger isn't alone. Which means my *fiancé* has finally decided to show up, and he's about to cause a scene.

Shit. Think, Vivi. And it better be fast!

"Ansel, dagger please?"

He moves to my pack and hands me one of my moonstone daggers. Somehow doing so without even one glance at my bare tits. See? I told you! Stale bread.

I rub my arms, unexpectedly shaking. I'm not afraid of Killian. I know he won't hurt me physically, but I am nowhere near safe. There's nothing harmless about The Dark Prince of the Netherworld. I can't see him right now. He can't be here! Shit. Shit. Shit! Anxiety grabs a hold of my throat and squeezes. My fingers felt numb; I'm panicking. I have to do something right now!

This is one of the most deranged ideas I've had in my life, which is saying a lot, but I don't have enough time to cultivate something less insane. So, before I can overthink and talk myself out of it, I press the dagger to my wrist.

"Princess Genevieve, NO!!" Ansel shouts, lunging for me. I block him with my leg, not quite aware that it puts me in a 'spread eagle' situation until I feel the cool breeze on my bare vagina. Which makes me close my eyes in irritation for a split second.

Seriously? Come get me, Satan. I hate it here!!

"Ansel, back off. I'm not doing what you think I'm doing, you big shaggy oaf! If I wanted to die, I'd be dead already!" I roll my eyes as I shove the dagger into my skin, rounding the edges of my brand to make this slightly more expedient.

I take a deep breath and steel my nerves.

This is going to fucking hurt...

When my dagger is in perfect placement, I slice down the circular brand on my wrist. Fast and violent. Removing it from my body in one gruesome wedge of flesh. The crimson glow dims to a sickly pink before it dissipates. With the nasty chunk between my fingers and blood flowing down my hand in rivulets into the river, I summon my inner monster. Violet flames rush through my veins, wild and devastating. Incinerating the dismembered flesh, reducing it to ash.

But I'm not done there.

Instinctively, I transfer the flames into my blade. Holy shit! I didn't even know I could do that! When it glows reddish-purple, I press it to my ravaged wound. The hissing stench of burning flesh damn near gags me, and I stumble against the searing pain. Trying my hardest not to scream or pass out face first in a riverbed.

"Just try to find me now, asshole!" I shout at the sky as my voice cracks.

CHAPTER THREE

KILLIAN

"I NEED A LOCATION!" I launch my wine glass through my office, also known as the war room, smashing it into tiny shards of icy shrapnel against the wall.

What a catastrophic mess I've made. To save my realm, I sold my soul to the proverbial devil. Finding the Lost Princess seemed like a small price to pay for harmony in the Netherworld.

In exchange for Genevieve, they would absolve me of the multiple sins of my father, and my kingdom would be safe from further attacks. Why should I care what Mordred did with her afterward? I'd never met the witch; I didn't care for her. All I had to do was sacrifice one girl, and my plans would have fallen into place...

One foul mouthed, disrespectful, and utterly impossible girl.

But the Gods are vicious bastards. I couldn't let her go. She has no clue how vital her role is in this war. So, what was I supposed to do? Give her to the one person who would make sure she never knew? Hand her over to the man who would make her my mortal enemy. Mordred, the man who took a portion of the Netherworld for himself and corrupted it into a land of living nightmares. The Shadowlands. He had no intention of stopping there. He would use her as a tool to get what he wants and then breed her off to some monstrous beast of his choosing.

I'd never harm her. Not like he would. I'm an asshole, but I'm not *that* heartless. And then I walked into a dive bar on the main street of Thornfall, and she enchanted me. It wasn't her body, her face, or even her suggestive clothing. It was her entire being. Everything about Vivi Graves drew me in, and ensnared me. When I looked at her, I felt like I'd found something I didn't know I was missing. It pissed me off, and I fought it hard. But I never meant for this to happen...

Fuck the stars and their designs. I had a plan!

I set the meeting with Mordred, invoked the right of betrothal. I enlisted the help of Selene to extract the Dark Goddess from Genevieve's body. I knew he'd come, and I knew he would bring his forces with him. I was already two steps ahead. Everything was in place. All he had to do was take her from this fortress, and his life would have been forfeited. I was betting on it. But I didn't foresee that her reaction would be so... human. Whether she knows it, she's a Netherling, and I expected her to behave like one. That was my mistake. I knew she wasn't raised here. All I needed her to do was follow my lead. But that infuriating witch doesn't conform to anyone. Not even the future King of the Netherworld.

"Fuck!" I slam my fist on the oversized desk, knocking over a rack of writing utensils and an inkpot.

"We all want her back, bro. We just need time."
Jagger's voice is laced with concern.
"We have no more time." I exhale a shuddered
breath.

———◆———

There's something you need to understand, the
part of Genevieve's past that she doesn't know. It's
for her own safety, but if she ever finds out the
truth? Gods help us all.

Centuries ago, Mordred was cast into the
Netherworld, doomed to repeat our grave history just like the rest of us. But he wasn't who
he claimed to be, or nearly as harmless as he
appeared. Nobody suspected a thing, least of all
my father. He was The High King! All-knowing.
All-powerful. And blind to who his enemies were.
His ego refused to recognize anything other than
his perceived greatness.

I was young in terms of supernaturals, which
isn't saying much. One hundred years old is
young for a demon, a thousand years old is young
for a God. But I digress... I remember Mordred
often visiting the Night Fortress, attending din-
ners, and the countless hedonistic gatherings my
father would host. Mordred's charming magnet-
ism landed him favor with the ladies, despite the
evil he possessed. But behind closed doors, Mordred was mixing alchemy, sex, and dark magic to
sire a new species of supernatural beings. Living
weapons of his making, with unnatural powers
he could breed and replicate. It was sick, twisted,
and disconcerting. Even for the brutal realm we
Netherlings call home.

His first attempts failed. He was careless with his bedmates, which only managed to produce vile, bloodthirsty creatures that either died hours after birth or became part of his warped legion. But it wasn't long before Mordred evolved, recognizing that a more powerful host was the missing ingredient. So, his next conquest was a goddess.

And the next, and the next.

Finally, a daughter was born to the Goddess of Love, with ancient blood and otherworldly strength flowing through her veins. A stunning white-haired harbinger of undiluted chaos. But it wasn't enough, and so Mordred sought the most powerful and fearsome goddess in the realm. He wooed and worshiped her, playing on all the things a divine being such as she craved. And it wasn't long before he would have another daughter on the way. One that the Oracles prophesied would be so beautiful she could bend men to her will, so powerful she could move the earth, a child made of fire and blood. One that would destroy worlds and command legions of the damned.

A true Dark Queen.

The divination of the Oracles overjoyed Mordred. He built an entire wing inside the Bone Keep for his masterpiece. He'd created the perfect child. One that he would mold and bend into his marionette. His darkest, most sinister design. The destroyer of gods, the child with the power to hand him the entire realm. But in his power-hungry madness, he made a grave mistake. He failed to understand that even a formidable bloodthirsty goddess was capable of the purest and most genuine love there is.

The love of a mother for her child.

In the cover of darkness, Genevieve's pregnant mother slipped into the Night Fortress; with an offer my father couldn't refuse. In exchange for safe passage out of the Netherworld, she would return when the time was right. Promising The Dark Princess's hand in marriage to his firstborn son.

Me.

And when my father aided Mordred's former lover (along with two of her trusted confidantes) through the portal out of the Netherworld, she vanished. Using her extraordinary divination to cloak herself and the child. Genevieve's mother double-crossed us all. When Mordred learned what had transpired, he dispatched his Wicked Shadow Sorceress to hex my father, knowing his bloodline would never survive past me. Because I was born with a killing curse, one that activates when passion awakens my heart.

I lay my hands down on the dark oak executive desk, and cerulean hellfire races along the surface. I should have verbalized all of this sooner. I should have left her alone, protected her. I never should have touched her in the first place! But I was weak. Enthralled by lilac eyes, the fire in her veins, and that venomous mouth of hers. Desperate need to possess her, an instinct to call her mine overcame me. And it defeated my good senses. On that final night together, I claimed her, which activated my curse. And I have told no one. I'm too ashamed of myself to say it out loud. Although, mother suspects.

"I HAVE NO MORE TIME!" I roar, anguish and white-hot rage mixing in an explosive cocktail.

"My son," Selene lays her delicate hand upon my shoulder, "All is not lost, you must...."

"I must do what? She is hiding from me!" venom drips from my words.

"You will get her back right now!! Dirt licking, barnacle kissing, poison tongue dimwit!" Anise interrupts, shouting and dragging her chair across my pristine floor, on purpose. Her unique brand of mayhem was on full, stunning display.

I've seen some unbelievable things in my lifetime, but my baby sister is picking a side. And it's not mine? I'm speechless at that.

Dante and Bane sit beside her along the black walls of the war room, doing their telepathic shit. I don't know what they think, and they're choosing not to share. Bronwyn has been unusually quiet. I believe she's employing what the Earthlings call 'the silent treatment' against me. And it's surprisingly effective.

Genevieve has gone to great lengths to avoid discovery, and to my surprise, she's besting me. I think it's time I upped the stakes. "Mother, an update on the familiar?"

"The familiar has emerged from The Immortal Fields intact. But she remains feral. Nasty place, those fields. I'll say it until the end of my days: nothing ever comes back the same." Selene shakes her head; she was never on board with it. But I made the call, thinking if I could just give Genevieve something back... one thing, in all she's lost. It would be enough to make her stay. But when the time came for me to open my mouth and tell her what I'd done, the pain in her eyes, the hatred. It gave me pause, so I said nothing.

"Have our Dark Fae learned how to release her?" I ask.

"No, we still cannot pass Calypso through the portals." Selene tightens her lip, and her usually peaceful demeanor becomes rigid.

"Keep looking. All magic has a loophole, even death."

I was counting on my Plan A - Releasing Calypso and then tracking her straight to her Blood Witch. Feral, changed, or otherwise—a familiar will always find home. It would have been the most straightforward approach, but I'll have to move to Plan B.

This is a dangerous time for me to leave the realm. With Mordred openly attacking, it was a declaration of war. And as such, I have been needed here. I may despise the role I was given, and the man who passed it down to me, but I honor my commitments. It's been the solitary thing preventing me from ripping the Earth Realm apart to find her. Before *fate* does.

"Jagger, it's our turn to go princess hunting. I'm coming with you."

"WHAT?! Did you eat idiot stew for lunch, bro? Because that's the stupidest thing you've ever said to me." He stares incredulously.

And I stare back, unmoving.

My mind is made up.

"What happens when shit goes down, and the ruler of the Netherworld is off chasing a chick who doesn't even want to be found? I dig her too, man. But I don't think risking our home is the answer to your female problems." He runs a hand through his dark waves and lifts his arms above his head.

"Then we better make it quick."

———⋆◦⋆———

I haven't ridden on Jagger's back in dragon form
since we were children, but I remember the feeling. The freedom. I'd always been jealous of my
brother's ability to escape our father, even if only
for an afternoon.

I wasn't so lucky. I'm his heir, and with that
came responsibilities. I was busy being groomed.
A cruel and unforgiving, fearsome future King
who takes no prisoners. That's what I'm supposed
to be.

I will never forget the last ride Jagger and I had
together until father was cursed. We had landed in the killing fields on a warm summer day.
Laughing and wrestling around in the high grass.
Unaware of what was about to befall us both.

Until the anger radiating off our father hit us in
waves.

That day, he dragged us into the Throne Room
and lashed across our backs until we could no
longer stand. Our punishment for being brothers
in public. Unfortunately, that was the first of the
many "punishments" Selene had to heal due to
our brotherly bond.

But after that day, I made sure to be the only
one taking punishment.

*'The Future King of the Netherworld does not consort
with lessers!'* My father would bellow. That included my illegitimate siblings and their mothers.

I never understood how my mother could love
him, the sunshine beauty and the wicked beast.
How she could lie next to him knowing he had a

harem at his disposal, knowing he fathered children outside their marriage? And worse, knowing they were all expendable to him. Allowing it. The Gods do not behave like humans, I understand. But it never sat right in my soul. They say love is blind, I say it's toxic. And I'm expected to do the same?

The 'lessers' may have been expendable to father, but they weren't to me. I care for my siblings, and never minded taking punishment for letting the entire realm know it. Offering my siblings their rightful places beside me after father was hexed? That was poetic justice.

If this foul-mouthed Princess is indeed what my mother believes her to be, then she will bring the King of the Netherworld back from his slumber. He will once again rule over our realm. My father is not a decent man. I hold no love for him. Still, the sense of duty to wake him hangs over my shoulders like a looming guillotine. It is my responsibility, and when the time comes? I will do what I must.

As we soar through the cerulean sky, zeroing in on the rolling waves of the ocean, and then the trees in transition from summer to autumn... I feel her. I tap Jagger's shoulder and point; we bank hard towards a massive waterfall. Jagger drags his claw through the cascading stream, and my senses come alive as the claiming bond solidifies.

"She's here," I call out to Jagger against the whipping wind. Concentrating on the tether I'd created between us. I'm tied to her now; she is part of me. I am a part of her. Soul-tethered by my incubus nature.

Pain bursts through my skull, and I lose my balance as I'm thrown violently into her mind. Where I find her standing naked in a stream with a male watching over her. A possessive bolt of recklessness rams into my chest. If he's touched her, I will disembowel him.

She doesn't know it, is avoiding it, or maybe she's even convinced herself she doesn't want it, but it doesn't change the fact. Genevieve is mine. What we have set in motion cannot be undone. We are destined to be whatever becomes of us now. And only the stars know what our grand finale holds.

I see her in my mind's eye, and it only takes her a moment to feel my presence as she reaches her outstretched hand for her dagger. She holds it for a few tense moments and then raises it to her wrist...

"Don't you fucking dare!" I shout, trying to reach her mind.

CHAPTER FOUR

VIVI

PEELING THE BLOOD-CRUSTED CLOTHES off my sticky body, I grumble to myself about the severe lack of wardrobe options around this gods-forsaken place! I mean, those were my last pair of leggings, for star's sake. I'm down to one pair of questionable pants and two cropped tanks. I already went commando days ago, and my bralette is in tatters. That'll be next to go. And then what? I'm just nipping out in torn up ass huggers around all these hypersexual shifters. Awesome! Because that doesn't sound like a recipe for an absolute disaster or anything.

Willa will not like it. Nobody will, but unless we want to storm the Academy naked, unwashed, and starving, we're going to have to make a supply run.

"Knock, knock," my inner bitching is interrupted by Linc standing in the entryway.

My cheeks flush at the thought of how long he may have been standing there while I was changing. It's no secret things have been... umm... tense between us. There's an underlying current of animosity now, mixed with some weird chemistry. Linc has made his intentions known, and they are not G-Rated. But he also seems like he might want to remove my head and display it as a trophy. It's confusing.

The ways he's changed since becoming Alpha haven't escaped my notice either. There's an assertiveness about him now that I never detected before, something primal. The quirky comedian Linc is still there, but there's no mistaking the smolder in his eyes or the carnal way he watches me. It's not that I'm unaffected by it. I am a hot-blooded witch, after all. But this is Linc we're talking about. The Linc who pulled my hair and called me 'string bean' when we were seven years old. This is the Linc that held me while I cried and helped change my sheets when I set them on fire. So. Many. Times. The Linc who is supposed to be someone's absolute dream husband.

Not mine, but someone's. I love him. That's not a question. But now we're stranded somewhere between 'my best friend got kind of hot' and 'I want to punch your entire face.' So, I guess you could say our relationship status sits firmly at... it's complicated.

Pulled back from my inner monologue, which I hope wasn't broadcasted all over my face just now, I remember to speak. "Sorry, I just don't have many clothes left. Pretty soon, I'll be down to wearing just leaves and mud!" I joke, thinking it would cut the tension. But it only takes a moment to recognize my mistake.

Really, Vivi? Leaves and mud? He's picturing you naked now. Dumbass.

Linc clears his throat and wipes a bead of sweat from his forehead. "Ansel came to me with some disturbing news, Viv. Did you cut a chunk of flesh from your arm and then close the wound with a hot dagger?"

"Okay, well, when you put it like that, it sounds disturbing." I smirk at the thought. Come on! It's kinda funny. "I had my reasons."

"And would you like to share what those reasons are?" he stares.

"Not especially." I don't know why I'm hesitant to tell him that Killian almost found me, but I choose not to mention it. Instead, I shrug and aim for shock value. "I cut the brand off, okay?"

Linc's eyes widen almost comically. Perfect. Surprise! Am I a masochist? That's what it looks like, anyway. They don't need to know that it was mostly out of spite. It doesn't matter. I resolved the issue.

"Do you need medical attention?" he asks. I can see his forehead creasing as he crosses the room. Then, before I can even think about stepping away, he grabs my uninjured arm and drags me into his chest.

"Linc..." I don't know what I'm supposed to say. It's familiar, comfortable even. But my body isn't on fire, begging for him to control the flames. Or swallow me up in them and spit me out in a pile of ash.

Maybe flames are overrated? They're fucking danger-ous, that's for sure.

"Do you remember when I'd run my fingers through your hair and rub your back so you could sleep? Did I ever make you uncomfortable?" He mutters in a gravelly voice.

"Of course, I remember. What a silly question! And no, you didn't," I reply with minor irritation.

"Well, then chill out and let me see your wrist, weirdo. I'm not going to bite." He chuckles and then turns my wrist, running his finger across the angry, puckered skin—sending a wave of something down my spine. I can't place what the something is, but he studies my arm so closely that I wonder if he thinks there will be a pop quiz later? The silence is deafening in here...

"Hey, boss!" a jovial voice calls out as we both startle and move away from each other.

Linc's third, Osric, stands in the doorway with a Cheshire cat grin on his handsome, boyish face. He reminds me of someone's punk kid brother, complete with the skinny jeans and concert tees. All he needs is a beanie and a skateboard. Mischief is his middle name. Not literally, but his talent for stirring the pot and then watching it boil over is unmatched. Bottled Chaos, that's an excellent description. He lifts one brow and licks his lips, appraising the situation and coming to the incorrect conclusion, "Interrupting something? Do you need me to come back later?"

Ugh, puppies!

"No!" I say a little too enthusiastically, "We were just finishing up here."

Osric doesn't move. He doesn't even flinch. How irritating! Damn pups don't know their little corkscrews from a hole in a tree stump. It's not his Alpha he needs to be paying attention to right now. I'm the deadliest monster in this room.

Linc clears his throat, catching my mood change, and he nods. "I should gather the clan anyway. Willa and Iris would like to sit down for a civilized meal. This should be interesting. See you in a few, Viv?"

He thinks I don't notice the lack of correction on what Osric saw, and the new strut in his step on the way out. Mmm hmm. It's complicated alright.

———◁◉▷———

I roll into the cathedral-cafeteria, fashionably late as usual. But if I'm being fair, Willa and Iris should be glad that I showed up at all. My track record hasn't been so great. As I search for a seat, all eyes are on me, which isn't comfortable. Contrary to pretty much everyone's opinion, I do not enjoy the spotlight. I just have a reckless mouth, and a go fuck yourself attitude that clashes with my introversion. It confuses people, but that's not my problem.

Marlow stands and waves me over next to her. I'm flooded with instant relief. She's my emotional support person. I slide into the spot beside her, and she sets a reassuring hand on my thigh. I take a few calming breaths, and I sure am glad I did because Willa is sitting across from me when I lift my head, and she trained her milky eyes right on my face.

"Nice of you to join us, *Daimona*," she sneers.

She used to call me "Abomination" or "This One"... I'm not sure if this is a step up from that. Her disdain for me is a puzzle I could never figure out. Somewhere around mine and Lowe's seventh year, I gave up and decided to just roll with it. I've been collecting derogatory nicknames ever since.

"Hello Priestess Willa," I address her respectfully. It doesn't seem like the time for my witty comebacks. She looks especially wicked-witchy today, and I'm not about to press my luck.

Making eye contact with Iris, I flash a genuine smile. I don't understand for the life of me how these two function in the same marriage. Or how they are more successful at love than I could ever hope to be. They're opposites in every way, a ray of sunshine and the ominous thunder cloud. I'm pretty sure Iris keeps Willa from growing horns and a tail, but I'd never say that out loud. I do have some sense of self preservation, despite what it may look like.

Glancing away from the pair, I take in the room. It's lovely, really. In a discarded house type of way. A home can't live without souls in it. No smoke in the fireplace and laughter echoing off the rafters. This sanctuary was deceased when we arrived, hollowed out and decaying. A sad beauty. It needed a soul. And boy, did it get one!

Seriously, it looks like a middle school dance up in here. Shifters on one side, witches on the other. All we need is a mediocre DJ and some nineties music. I'm guessing by the way some of the ladies are trying their damnedest to avoid eye contact that they have noticed the shifters. And not in the innocent way! There's something to be said about hating a man so much, but also secretly fantasizing about them throwing you up against a wall in a dark corner and ripping your clothes to shreds...

I get it, believe me. I get it! But it's a tricky one. Mixing the Witchling bloodlines is looked down upon in our twisted society. Combining orders, though? I don't even want to know what the punishment is for that. Probably death. Or worse.

"You can cut this tension around here with a knife, sheesh! Everyone in this room needs to get laid," I whisper to Marlow as she tries not to crack a smile.

"No doubt." she whispers back, making a blowjob gesture with her hand, and I giggle.

Iris stands, looking at us with displeasure.

Did she see that? Oh, my goddess, I hope not.

For a moment, I think she's going to call us out, but she moves toward the front of the room and steps up onto a wooden platform. A beam of light shines just right, hitting her face, making her look like a wise and ethereal crone. Are we about to get a sermon or an ass-chewing? It's a toss-up.

"We've asked for you to join us today with a specific intention." Iris's gentle voice raises over the hum of conversation, and the room quiets. "We've come together for a singular purpose: to end the corruption and brutality that lurks behind the doors of Underhill Academy."

All heads nod in unison, mine included.

Iris continues in her grandmotherly tone, "To achieve this goal, we must overcome our prejudice and work as one. So, as of today, you pair up. Witches train with shifters, and shifters learn to protect your witch as they spell cast."

There's a noticeable lack of head nods now. Like, none. But I can't argue, it's a good plan. It would eliminate the need for two witches to focus on the same target. Twice as many witches free to divide and conquer is an advantage. Shifters are the perfect bodyguards. Muscle & magic working together.

It's kind of brilliant! And... it doesn't seem like anyone is listening.

"It's not up for debate." Willa's power spills over the room, and it feels as though thousands of tiny spiders are crawling across my skin.

I hate it when she does that! Gives me the heebie jeebs.

But not even phantom spiders wipe the scowls off their faces. They look like a room full of petulant children, if you ask me. Bunch of babies! And then before I even know what the hell I'm doing, I'm up and moving towards Iris.

We weren't going to do this, Vivi. Not a babysitter. Not a godsdamned girl scout. Not their mother... Ugh.

"She's right." I roll my eyes clear through the back of my skull. "Listen, shitheads. If we can't work together, we're fucking dead. That's as real as it gets. D.E.A.D. Kiss your ass goodbye. Dead. So, kindly get over yourselves and pick your training partner."

I sound like a foul-mouthed hall monitor, but messing around isn't getting us any closer to pulling this off. And I have this feeling, it's an instinct. I can't explain it, but it's telling me we're running out of time.

"Also, while we're all here, do we have any earth elements?" I call out to the room, a few raise their hands, "Good, from here on out, while you're not training, you're in charge of growing food. End of discussion."

Iris nods in affirmation.

"Water elements?" The room is hesitant, and for a second, I wonder if we've got an Abbey full of useless witches?

But after a few moments, some hands slowly rise.

"Oh, good! So, you're not a bunch of chicken shits. Thank the Goddess for that, huh? I need you to figure out how to make electricity from the waterfall. Oh, and reroute some of the water for the earth witches to tend their crops. Bathing would be nice, too, if you can figure that out. Thanks."

The delegating of tasks goes on for a few minutes and ends with Linc commanding the shifters to continue hunting for meat and patrolling the wards. Iris smiles and nods her head at me appreciatively.

Too bad she's not going to appreciate what I have to say next.

"One last thing. We won't survive here without a supply run. We need anything and everything we can get our hands on. Which means we need to go to Thornfall, and I need a team."

"Viv," Linc's voice goes low, a warning, which I do not appreciate at all. He can save the overbearing shit for someone who cares. I mean, damn, he didn't even give Willa a chance to complain! And she's the first to shoot down every idea I've ever had.

"What?" I challenge him.

"It's not safe outside the wards."

"Yeah. Well, dying here without proper supplies seems pretty unsafe too, don't you think?" I snap, "Who's willing to volunteer?"

The seriousness of my face must have struck a chord because Linc moves to the front to stand beside me, followed by Ansel. And then several of the new witches.

"Osric will stay behind with the remaining shifters as acting alpha until I return," Linc adds.

Finally, Marlow stands, but Willa shut that shit down faster than greased lightning! Her argument is that Marlow's vast knowledge of herbs and spells is better employed at the Abbey. I can't argue with that, although Marlow looks like she *really* wants to.

As I turn to Iris, silently asking if we're done here? A witch I'm unfamiliar with stands to join us. Her cascading blonde curls and attractive facial features remind me of someone, but I can't quite place it. She's built stocky, tall. She looks like someone I'd most definitely want on my side of a fight.

Iris's weathered face goes from pleased to panicked in a matter of seconds. "Amethyst Crowe! Can I speak with you privately?" she hisses and damn near drags the poor thing into the hallway. Their hand movements and facial expressions suggest a heated conversation, which only makes me want to eavesdrop more. I allow the Sight to roam over them both. It's still a strange feeling, but useful! I caress it lightly over Iris's mind, hoping to avoid detection—fear, apprehension. She doesn't trust me with Amethyst. Or she doesn't trust Amethyst with me...

Interesting.

As my gaze makes its way to Amethyst, I only get so far into her aura before something smacks into my energy field. Hard. Giving me an instant headache. How the hell did she do that? And which one was it? I rub my forehead and look up in time to see Iris stalking off, as angry as I've ever seen her. Man, I wonder what that was all about?

We waited a respectful amount of time to see if Iris might come back, but when it was clear that she wouldn't be rejoining the conversation any time soon, I figure we better start planning without them. Marlow sits quietly beside me at one of the many tables, her freckled nose buried in a stack of maps we'd found in the lower levels. Doing what she does best, being a godsdamned beautiful genius! I love seeing her in her element. I know she's disappointed about being held back from the danger zone. But this? This is where she shines better than anyone I know.

"First, we should map out your routes." She suggests confidently, "You'll enter through the woodlands here. She points to a spot. There's a path that skirts the edge of the Academy, but it's far enough away to avoid the Rune Force."

She continues, pointing at several areas on the yellowed map. Finally, she gathers loose stones from the floor and placing them on specific routes, demonstrating checkpoints.

"We should leave under cover of night," Linc suggests, and Marlow nods in agreement. "It's just a few hours' walk to Underhill. If we leave at night, we could come out near the mountain's edge and head straight into Thornfall, unseen by the nature trail. However, if we follow that into town, we'd end up coming out in an alley just down the street from Enchanted Brew."

"Could you and Lowe come up with a safe place under the radar? A meetup point in case we get separated?" I ask, enjoying the companionable teamwork, especially with Linc. It's reminiscent of old times.

"Sure thing." He nods and rests his arms on the table.

A sound comes from my right as if someone is quietly clearing their throat, so faint it's barely audible. I turn to investigate as Amethyst blinks at me and then lowers her eyes to the stone tiled floor. It's a genuine surprise that someone who looks so imposing could be so timid.

"Do you have something to add?" I ask.

Indecision tints her face. It's clear that she does have something to say, but she's hesitant for whatever reason. Unfortunately, my tolerance is running on empty. "This isn't the time or the place. There are lives at stake, lives I give a shit about. So, if you know something. Spill it."

"I... um... it's just that I'm not supposed to tell anyone." She nervously searches the room. Then, finally, a look of determination moves across her face. "There's another way."

Amethyst explains that there are a series of underground tunnels, they call them The Catacombs. She and the new witches I haven't paid any attention to have apparently used them their whole lives. Even lived inside them!

Um, what the actual fuck?

So, this is what Iris didn't want her to share with the rest of us? That's suspicious. But I don't ask questions, not yet. Amethyst already has the attention of everyone left in the room, and the looks on their faces range from disbelief to flat-out anger. No. We can't talk about this right now, but I intend to find answers later because something about this new development stinks. And it's not just the cauldrons of agrimony, madwort, and tar in the kitchens.

"Okay." I reply.

"Okay? What do you mean OKAY? I'm not taking my men underground just to have it cave in on us. How do we know it's structurally sound?

Who built it, and for what purpose?" Linc recoils, staring back and forth between Amethyst and me.

Back to bossy alpha-douche, I see!

"Alive underground is better than dead above it, correct?" I tease, trying to change the subject. Anything to avoid yet another testosterone-filled shifter blow-up. I know he's adjusting to changes in his power, but they're seriously getting old.

"You're insane, Viv! You could get us all killed! You don't know the first thing about those tunnels, and you're just going to let this witch you've never met lead us into the unknown? You're not even going to argue it?"

I think the answer to that question is clear, so I don't bother disputing it.

"When are you going to give a shit about... anything? You're so fucking reckless! When are you going to snap out of this 'I'm heartless' routine"? He roars, forgetting that we have an audience.

Snap out of it? Out of losing a soul bond with my familiar, and my shot at getting my sister back. Snap out of having my heart ripped to shreds under a cascade of lies. Not any time soon. He has no idea just how close to the edge I am. Flames glow hot from my palms as the ground shakes.

"When I make every single one of those fuckers pay! That's when."

CHAPTER FIVE

THE CATACOMBS

I GLANCE DOWN AT the stones beneath my feet, noting the geometrical design they're laid out in. There's a sculpted archway at the end of the path, leading to the outer wall of the Abbey. The entire property has a strange smell, like a mixture of chalk and the earthy aroma of soil and decomposed leaves. Something nags at the back of my brain. A memory I can't unlock. It's not the place—it's the smell.

A wave of unbearable heartbreak sweeps through me. I don't understand where it's coming from, but it's got me close to hitting my knees in crybaby sappiness. No, thank you! I would pick bloody knees on jagged glass in front of Satan himself before I feel a damn thing.

Where are these dipshits? I need to get the fuck out of here.

We had agreed to meet on the front steps at dusk. So, I'm sitting here watching the sherbet-colored sunset, and apparently, I'm doing it solo. Because I'm the only one here. For just a moment, my pulse races, and unease blooms in my stomach. What if they're not coming?

"They're coming." Iris's voice startles me. "I've temporarily detained them. But don't worry, they won't remember it. We need to talk."

Well, that sounds ominous.

"Uh, okay?" I'm kind of speechless.

"Amethyst means a great deal to me, Genevieve. She is... unique. She must be protected. It's life or death. Do you understand what I'm saying to you?" she levels her gaze at me.

No, I really don't have any idea what she's trying to say to me. I'm confused as hell, and now I have a thousand questions. Like—how is one witch's *life or death* important? Who's life. Mine? Everyone's? What the hell kind of witch is she? Is she an endangered species or something? Hidden love child. Long-lost daughter. Changeling...

My mind spins off its axis, but then I remember Iris is waiting for a response. I clear my throat. "I get it. Don't get the special witch killed." I make a gesture with my hand as if I'm holding a pencil and a to-do list. "Check!"

Iris shakes her head and flashes the grin that always makes me feel like I'm sitting in front of a warm fire with hot chocolate and Nirvana records. "That mouth of yours, girl. It's something. You've been through so much already, and I fear the worst is yet to come. Stay the course. You have the stars on your side."

Here we go with this again! Iris is obsessed with the stars; you'd think she has an oracle in her pocket or something. I roll my eyes and slap on my best monster-in-your-closet expression. "I'm the worst thing that's yet to come, Iris. They just don't know it yet!"

And with that, the supernaturals that volunteered to come on this possible suicide mission file out of the main door and onto the stone path. I run a hand through my unruly midnight locks. Hmm, ten shifters and eleven witches. I've seen worse odds. If this is what we've got? Then we'll just have to make it work.

"We're going to make this run fast and furious. Sneak into town undetected, do what needs to be done, and get the fuck out of there. We are not ready for a showdown with the Elders just yet. We need medical supplies, magical supplies, and food supplies." I call out to them, making sure we're all on the same page.

Also, I will die if I can't put on some gods damned underwear soon. I don't even care if they're butt floss, and I hate butt floss! But listen. Leather pants, plus bare bits. The. Situation. Is. Dire. But nobody needs to know that part.

"Who's ready to play in the dirt?" I smile.

------◆------

"Are you shitting me?" I exclaim as we stand at the base of a cliff strewn with dead trees and cobalt wildflowers. "You mean to tell me I've been standing naked, not even fifty feet from a network of underground tunnels that span... how many miles again?" I'd lost my train of thought. The idea that I was vulnerable without knowing it irks me.

"It's hard to say, but I've been as far as Rockvale and all the way to the ocean caves," Amethyst replies.

That's a long way. For what, I wonder? A question for another time, I guess.

The first part of the tunnel was dug right into the side of the cliff, the entrance hidden by deep shrubbery. They lined the cave walls with crude lanterns and strange carvings. I run my finger along the edge of one that calls to me. It reminds me of moons mirroring each other. Is this like caveman dinosaur-type shit? What does the symbol mean? A lingering voice in the back of my head whispers *dark magic.*

We walk through this section for maybe thirty minutes. Then the terrain changes from sedimentary rock to a flat earthen path, dotted with odd green jewel-toned stones. Perhaps they're crystals? If Marlow were here, she'd know.

I feel like an earthworm.

At least the tunnel is wide enough in this section to walk two or three side by side. And since Linc wants to pout, I speed up to meet Amethyst and fall in stride next to her. She's tight-lipped. I'm not sure if she's just shy or if it's something deeper than that? But it's worth a shot to see what I can find out.

"So, you're Iris's what... niece?" I throw pure speculation out just to see if I can get a reaction, but nope. Nothing.

"Daughter?"

An almost invisible flinch crosses the bridge of her nose.

Okay, so I'm getting warmer.

Before I can voice my next theory, one of the other new witches is screeching. I really should learn their names, but how do I accomplish that without spending time with them? A problem for later, I guess. The wolves scramble to form tightly around us. I know it's protection – but it feels like

I'm being corralled, and I hate it. I push through to the front, where the noise is coming from. Ready to lay into the screeching witch for broadcasting our location to the entire realm. "What the hell is your fucking probl...."

And my ass hits the ground, and my tailbone is on fire! Ouch! I swear, if I don't stop getting knocked around, I'm going to flip out. The brief sense of movement is the only thing that alerts me to the fact I'm being dragged through the packed dirt like a flopping rag doll.

Whatever has ahold of me is fast. Like, fast-fast!

I try to distinguish what the hell it is, but it's too dark. What happened to the lanterns? This entire situation reeks of fucking magic. Damn, I should have listened to whatever was tugging at my attention when we entered these tunnels.

Dark Magic, it whispered. But I thought I was just going batshit. Like, no big deal. Some of my favorite people are insane. They make the best art! Creativity lives in the murky corners of those magnificent souls. But clearly, it was an *actual* warning, and I'm a numbskull.

Searing pain blossoms in my ankle as I feel warm, slimy moisture pooling into my pant leg. The murder dingo bit me!! And now it's dragging me around as a personal chew toy.

Great, just fuckin' great! Ruin my pants, too, why don't ya? As if I'm not indecent enough as it is!

At this rate I really will be fighting Faustus naked. If I survive that long.

I reach deep in my well of power to access my flames, but I can't get a firm enough grip to call on them. So, I do my best to regroup and make another attempt, calming my breathing and emptying my mind, which is nearly impossible while impersonating a living Milk-Bone.

Shit, shit. It's not working... I'm running out of options, so I do the last thing I can think of. I shove my Sight so violently into its mind that a strangled yelp emits from its jaws, and it drops my foot.

See, that wasn't so hard now, was it?

I crawl over to the snarling mini beast, still having no clue what it is. Demon dog? Cujo's darling brother? It lunges for me, and on instinct, I swing my dagger, slicing upwards, piercing its heart.

I feel terrible for a moment; I hate to take an animal's life unless it's unavoidable. A memory of Calypso rips into me. A flashback of watching her crumpled on the bloody ground, surrounded by chaos and carnage. I never got to say goodbye...

My hand moves to touch the creature instinctively, reaching for its essence and releasing it to wherever it belongs. A lone tear busts loose and travels down my cheek.

Holy shit, did I just? No, I can't command souls. That's ridiculous.

"What the fuck was that!" Linc roars, running towards me like an Olympic hopeful.

"It's a Haunt," Amethyst is right behind him, shaking, "They live in cavernous places and can go for long periods without food or water. But they only hunt when it's a...."

"Let me guess, a full moon?" I interrupt her, holding my ankle, wincing.

"But the full moon isn't for three more days," Linc adds.

I guess he'd know better than I would. I'm a witch, but I've done everything to avoid using magic until recently. Remember? So, I'm kinda iffy in that department.

"They shouldn't be hunting," Amethyst is still shaking, and paired with the I-just- saw- a -ghost expression on her face, she's starting to freak me out.

"Vivi..."

"Yes, Amethyst. What can I help you with?!" I'm the reigning queen of sarcasm right now, but really? I'm bleeding out in a weird-ass dirt tunnel. Kinda busy, ya know.

"Haunts have poisonous saliva," she finally gets to the point, staring down at the bloody mess that used to be my pant leg.

Damn it all to fucking Hades!!

Of course, it has venom. Why can't anything just go smoothly?! Could I have one day, just ONE — when my life isn't in mortal danger? Is that too much to ask for? Apparently so.

"Does anyone happen to have anti-venom hiding in their pockets?"

The somber faces staring back at me answer that question quickly; they're all wearing the look. And I'm feeling a bit like I'm being watched by funeral mourners. What with me bleeding here on the ground and them standing over me with... I don't know. Funeral expressions?

Right about the time I realize I'm going to have to do something drastic, my mind swims, and my limbs feel heavy. My vision blurs, and I wobble...

"Sonofabitch!" Linc cusses and rakes his hands across his face and then he hauls my limp body into his lap. "Viv. Hey! Stay with me here. No night-night for you! Keep those eyes open, sugar tits. We really do have to stop meeting like this."

Sugar tits? Haha. Leave it to Lincoln to make a joke while I'm draped across his lap like a corpse, dialing the grim reaper for an Uber. I hear him, but I can't make my mouth move, come to think of it? I can't make anything move. No. No. No... A memory tears through my mind. Me on a bed in the Night Fortress just steps away from Killian as Lilia slits my throat. Helpless, friendless, alone, bleeding out on designer sheets.

Panic boils up the center of my chest.

Get your shit together, bitch! If you freak out right now, you're going to die.

"Hey! Look at me," Linc is still talking, "You're a blood witch, remember? Just remove the poison. That's all you need to do. Your ankle is torn up, and I'm not sure how to get the poison out through there. So, I'm going to make a cut, and then you push, okay?"

Linc speaks gently, calmly. I forget that after all these years, besides Marlow, he knows me the best. My breathing slows, and he nods in encouragement. Then, pulls out a knife and slices it down my thigh.

When did I become a supernatural carving board? That's what I'd like to know.

When the cut is open and there's a steady stream of liquid oozing onto the packed earth, I calm my mind and look for anomalies. My blood has an energy signature, when I concentrate—I can feel it. It leaves a taste on my tongue like warm honey and nutmeg spice. It tastes like fall. I isolate the wrongness, something that isn't honey and spice, and I command it to evacuate my body.

Black ichor bubbles and hisses at the wound site. This is fucking nasty! It looks like those movies where you stab the bad guy in the chest, and black slime comes out instead of blood. Ew, gross. But I keep pushing, slow and steady; my vision falters as I nearly pass out.

Duh, make fresh blood to replace it, dumbass...

I'll forgive myself for the faux pas this time on account of the actively dying thing. But man, I'm not feeling so great. When I think I've got it all out, my brain clears. I'm sore, kind of pissed off, and I look like an extra from The Walking Dead.

But I'm alive. And then, for the second time in as many days, I'm directing a bluish-purple flame into my dagger and cauterizing my own skin.

Yep, that's going to scar.

I swear I'm not a psychopath, but if I wasn't already viewed as a loose cannon before, this should seal the deal. Pun intended.

CHAPTER SIX

THORNFALL

AFTER SOME CREATIVE WOUND dressing, our trek through the rest of the tunnels is uneventful. The air feels damp and the salty aroma of fishing docks and ocean water hits my nose. We've made it to Thornfall.

Amethyst is still weirdly quiet. She hasn't spoken since she explained, once again, that haunts *only* come out on the full moon. Repeating for emphasis that the creature shouldn't have been there. She is adamant, and although I don't know her very well yet, I believe her. This begs some questions. Did someone know we were in the catacombs and spell a gods damned demon dog to attack me? Because that would royally suck. Or am I just riddled with terrible luck? I don't know how we can prove that one scientifically, but I'm open to suggestions.

Something strange is going on, that much is obvious.

As we come to the end of the tunnel, there's an atmosphere of apprehension. If this goes South? Some, or all of us, might not make it back. I'm sure everyone else is thinking it too, but nobody dares say it out loud. That's just asking for trouble. But as a result, there's an undercurrent of mistrust brewing. It's to be expected. When we're anxious, sometimes it's just easier to fall back into old habits and lash out rather than face what's in front of us. I get it, but I can already see the witch vs. wolf smack down firing back up. And *that* will most definitely earn us front-row tickets to the coffin show.

"Pay attention, assholes!" I direct everyone's awareness to me. "You can fight or fuck it out of each other later. Yeah, don't think I haven't noticed the way you're all sizing each other up!" I flash them all a sarcastic eye. "But right now, we have a job to do, and it's kind of dangerous in case you've forgotten. So, we all need to gather up our shit and keep it away from the fan. Got it?"

Have I mentioned how much I really hate leading people?

"Our targets are just through the alley at the end of the walking path. You need to keep to the shadows; I'm sure they plastered our faces all over the media. Be smart." Linc takes over for a second, and I'm glad of it.

"We should split up." I look from Ansel to Linc and then to Amethyst, who seems to be the 'leader' of these wayward witches.

"Amethyst, take the witches and hit up Enchanted Brew. There's a stockroom in the back full of seeds and herbs. First aid kit is behind the counter, and another one is in the bathroom. Oh, and I think Rowena's office has medical supplies. It's the Pepto Bismol Pink room. Grab what you can and come straight back to the meeting point."

"Got it." She nods, bobbing on her heels.

Hmm, so this seemingly timid witch isn't so shy after all? She looks thrilled to be running head-first into danger. The plot thickens on Amethyst Crowe! I like the enthusiasm.

"Linc, we hit up the Gravestone?" I ask, not wanting to upset his hierarchy by ordering him around. I don't know exactly how that works, and I would hate to undermine him and somehow put his position in danger with the Blackwood Clan.

"I'll send a man with the witches for protection." He motions to Ansel, who just grunts and agrees like the plain bagel he is.

"The rest of you are with us. And remember NO MAGIC in Thornfall. The entire city is mon-itored, and you *will* trip an alarm. I don't think I need to explain what happens if you do that." I end our little pep talk bluntly because there's no sugar-coating it: "If the Academy gets ahold of us? It's game over in the piss and vomit dungeon."

Getting to the Gravestone undetected went nice and easy. Too easy. Thornfall is a ghost town, and I don't trust the energy. It's eerily quiet. I don't even see the Rune Force patrolling the streets. I can't imagine what would cause both humans AND supernaturals to abandon their everyday lives and go into hiding. There are citizens of Thornfall in the bar until closing time on any night of the week. There's always the hustle and bustle on the main square, no matter what day it is.

This doesn't make any sense. Where is every-one?

"Linc, does something seem off to you?" I ask as we pick the lock in the back alley of Gravestone like we have a thousand times before. I can't help but glance down the path to my death traps as Linc works the pin with his fingers, listening for the click.

Is it strange to miss inanimate objects? Because I think I miss my rusted-out murder steps. Or maybe it's just my old life I miss. The second that thought enters my mind, my stomach drops. *Calypso...* my heart is pierced with broken glass, bursting into fragments on the cobblestones. That's the thing about grief. It sneaks up on us in the most random moments. The pain demands to be felt, whether or not it's convenient. I fill my veins with purple flames, letting rage wrap its arms around me—offering comfort. The darkness slithers underneath my skin; a black line races down my arm and into my fingers. That's new. I can't decide if I'm exhilarated by it or if I should be terrified?

Now that I know I am, in fact, a monster. I wonder about all kinds of things. What kind of monster am I? What if I'm not the vigilante kind but I'm the villain kind? It takes a monster to kill a monster. But how far am I willing to go? I'm wondering if that phantom voice is the darkest part of me or something else entirely.

"Yeah, Viv. Something is fucked up. None of the lights are on in any of the businesses. No people on the street. I think the city is on lockdown." He shakes his head like he's trying to make sense of it, too.

Lockdown. That's a possibility; from my time in the Academy, I'd overheard the pompous pricks in casual conversation frequently when they thought I wasn't listening. They'd love nothing more than to have complete control over the entire city, and the realm, too, if they could get away with it. And it hits me. I've given them the perfect excuse to do just that! I stepped out of line, I infiltrated the Academy, I escaped their dungeon, and I fought against them on the side of a Netherworld Prince. Fuck. We have to succeed. This is my fault; I know it in my bones. An entire city paying for my actions...

Godsdammit!

As we gain entrance to The Gravestone, my breath is stolen away. The iconic landmark building has been ruthlessly trashed. Bottles have exploded across the floor, high-top tables are overturned and splintered. There's a stool embedded into the wall. My eyes follow the dried blood streaked across the doorway going down into the offices. Deacon put up a hell of a fight!

'There appears to have been a struggle' is an understatement, and I wouldn't expect anything less. But at what cost? He's injured, no doubt. Is he beaten, starved, or something worse?

And where the fuck is Rowena? Why hasn't anyone heard from her...

Linc and I exchange a loaded glance, both feeling the pang of guilt mixed with rage. This is our home, and those dirty motherfuckers came here and destroyed it. Then they took the closest thing either of us has to a father. Ruined our home. Fucked with the sanctuary for supernaturals we built together. It's a Herculean effort to keep my fury in check. Everything within me is screaming to march straight up to those gates and demand

Deacon delivered safely in my arms. And then I'll bury the entire shithole Academy in a sinkhole. Reveling in their screams like it was the most magnificent symphony. That's better than they deserve. My nerves hum with the need to inflict damage. The air around me thrums with power.

"Not right now, Viv. They'll get theirs, alright? We'll deliver karma to them on a golden platter. But that's not why we're here. Keep your head straight. Revenge comes later." He puts a warm hand on my shoulder and waits for me to snap out of it. "Stay focused, Genevieve."

"Yes, yes, of course." I agree half-heartedly. Mostly out of shock, because he never calls me that, and I'm not sure if I want him to?

As soon as Lincoln and his wolves are out of sight, I enact my plan.

Climbing these creaky old death traps never seemed this noisy before, but with our city reduced to a ghost town, it feels like every step I take is setting off rocket ships. The sound ricochets off every building in this narrow corridor, and paranoia has me ninety-nine percent convinced I'm going to get my ass caught. Wouldn't that be hilarious?! I can see the headlines now.

Vivi Graves, the Earth Realm fugitive, was apprehended while breaking into her own apartment for underwear and a bra...

On second thought? Perhaps I shouldn't joke about it. The stars really seem to have it out for me. I don't think they need any encouragement. As I finally make my way to the top of the steps of calamity, I sense a tingle. A cool breeze raises the hair on my skin, sending waves of suspicion up and down my spine. *Something wicked this way comes.* I can feel it in my bones, and it's making me jumpy. I move to touch my doorknob, and it turns. Unlocked. Shit! Someone's either inside my apartment right now, or they have been recently. I clutch my dagger in one hand and my backpack in the other, ready to swing. Goddess, I wish I could use magic right about now, but that's too risky. I'm back in my old stomping grounds, and I've gotta go about it the old-fashioned way. *Quiet breath. Slow the heartbeat down. Light as a feather. Invisible.*

Deacons' words echo through my mind as my training kicks in naturally, like a second skin. I've been well versed in violence for so long that my body remembers, even when I think I've forgotten. One, two, three. Here goes nothing...

I use the tip of my foot to ease the door forward, silently crouching down, shifting like a shadow toward the entryway. At first glance, nothing seems out of place. My dresser is where I left it, as well as my bed. It's not torn to shreds like the Gravestone was, which confuses me. Downstairs, it almost seemed as if they were looking for something. So why not here? Why not my space? I can still smell the lingering scent of cat and Moonlight Mist perfume. My favorite. I need to remember to stash that in my bag.

When I'm confident that Bridgewater and Faustus aren't hiding under my bed, I move more freely. The uneasy feeling roiling around in my stomach hasn't dissipated though, and I find myself gazing at the door of my bathroom looking for any sign of movement, when I feel a faint breeze, just a subtle indication of air traveling toward my bed. And then Spirit Frank blinks into existence, legs crossed—sitting like he has all the time in the world to hang out so we can paint each other's nails.

"Holy shit, Frank, you scared the curses out of me!" I shriek, holding one hand on my chest and placing my dagger back in its holster with the other. Never in my life have I seen him anywhere but outside in the alley, scaring off the delinquents with his creepy silence, glowing eyes, and menacing presence. Why is he inside my apartment?

"I don't know what you thought you were going to do with that dagger. I'm already dead." A deep voice fills the room.

It takes my brain a second to catch up. "WAIT A FAIRY-FUCKING MINUTE. YOU CAN TALK?!"

He offers me a sly grin. "You never asked."

"Why would I ask you anything if I thought you couldn't talk? That doesn't even make sense!"

But hang on a second...

"Why are you inside my apartment?"

My brutal upbringing has taught me a few things about how the mind works. First, everybody has something to hide. Second, everyone has ulterior motives; they just vary in degree and severity. So, what does he want from me?

"I am a gift," Frank derails my spiraling train of thought.

A *gift*. What does that mean? It sounds like nonsense. Maybe his spirit has lingered past its expiration date? Perhaps he's experiencing the confusion that comes with being separated from your body for too long, trapped in the wrong realm. Nice, now I have a deranged spirit chilling on my bed. Can this day get any more awesome? Or this year.

"I'm not sure I understand correctly. Did you say you're a gift? Like wrap me up in sparkly paper and slap a bow on my ass... gift."

"My name isn't Frank."

Oh, great! So, on top of being utterly clueless that the buffed-up homeless ghost in the alley is lucid as fuck. I've been offending him, too. Way to go all-in, Vivi!

"Okay, not Frank. Let's get back to the gift part... A gift from who? A gift that does what? What is your primary function? And can we be quick about it? I kind of have this life-or-death thing going on right now." I've already started moving around the apartment, looking for some items on my mental supply list.

"I am a gift from the Dark Goddess." He says it nonchalantly, like I'm the odd one for asking.

I have fifteen minutes to pack some essentials and get to the meeting point before I have livid shifters hunting for me. And I don't feel like being thrown over someone's shoulder caveman style unless it's a sexual thing. So, I'm gonna go ahead and load this mess of crazy up in a neat little box and tie it with a bow for later.

"I'm going to level with you here. I need to move my ass. Like yesterday—but I also have a few thousand questions. So how about we make a deal? You do nothing creepy or try to kill me, and you can come back with me to where I'm camped. We can sort this out there."

The Goddess of Night and I are connected. I don't know exactly how, but I know enough to know she's not an enemy. Not *my* enemy, at least. By the way she looked at Mordred in the Night Fortress? He's the one who's got something to fear from her. I don't think 'Not Frank' is here to hurt me. But on the other hand. I'm not all that thrilled with the Goddess at the moment, so I'm not sure I want a gift.

First, she's been MIA. And correct me if I'm wrong, but I feel like when I'm exiled to a decaying Abbey being hunted by Netherlings, a War-lock prick, and a host of strange creatures who seem hell-bent on ending me, she should be here helping. AND my power-hungry psychotic excuse for a sperm donor... that seems like a good time to be reachable. Second, she said in those visions, "Trust him. You must trust. Blah, blah." And I did. I figured out who she was talking about, and I trusted The Dark Prince of the Netherworld.

Look where that got me.

She's not my favorite right now.

Anyway, like I said: time. I'm running low on it. I race back to the door and grab the backpack. Then, rushing back over to my dresser, I rifle through my clothes. I stuff a couple of tanks, band tees, a pair of jeans, some leggings, socks, a bra, my backup leather pants into my bag. And some goddess blessed underwear! Thank the fates. I'd do a happy dance if I wasn't in danger of being dragged out by an irate Alpha like a sack of Witch's Cudweed.

Next, I run to my bathroom and grab the soap, a razor, a first aid kit, and my toothbrush. Then I head back out into my bedroom, past the sheer curtains to dig through my drawers, frantically looking for anything of importance.

Ooh, my ear pods and dock. Score! A funny thought crosses my mind. What if I had background music to my life? I guarantee it would be the kind they play at haunted houses and those old school creepy carnivals.

It strikes me as a little strange that 'Not Frank' watches me as I race through my apartment like a hellcat on fairy dust. It's almost like he's awaiting instructions.

"Frank, what did the Goddess tell you to do, and what is your real name?"

"Atlassian is my name. Pleased to be acquainted."

"And you're not going to divulge what she told you to do? That's just perfect. At this point, I should just buy stock in lies and secrets. Aitlass... Aittl..." I giggle.

All I can think about is the word *ass* in his name. How am I supposed to create a nickname out of that? I can't call him GI Assface. It's funny, but it seems... I don't know, disrespectful of the departed or something.

"I'm just going to call you Frank if that's okay?"

"As you wish, my princess."

"It's Vivi. None of this princess shit, alright? You sound like a Genie. Wait, ARE you a Genie? Never mind. I don't have time for this conversation. I need you to take this backpack. Can you see inside my mind?" He nods, affirming that he knows what I'm thinking.

I remember learning something about ghosts. The memory is hazy, but the mind-reading part stands out. They don't need to hear you speak. It's something about them being on the same frequency as our brainwaves. I'm foggy on the specifics. Is it creepy? Yes. But it can be quite helpful in this circumstance.

I pull up a picture of Deacon's office in my mind and concentrate on the word 'weapons,' and Frank blinks out of existence. Minutes later, he returns with a stockpile of every weapon in the Gravestone. Including the ones in our training room and some I've never even seen before.

This should be fun to explain to Willa! She already thinks I'm an abomination. Just wait until we add necromancer, medium, or whatever the hell this is on my list of talents.

"Can you take this backpack and the weapons to the meetup point and wait? Then, if I don't show up in the next twenty-five minutes, you can look for me. Oh, and make sure Linc gets to the meeting point too. I need him not searching for me, understand?" I need to work on my delivery. I'm aware. But I'm really in a hurry here.

"As you wish my...." He doesn't get to finish the sentence before I immediately shut that shit down.

"Don't say it!"

Not Frank shakes his head in agreement and leaves with my backpack and a shitload of weapons.

I take one last glance over the apartment, and I can't deny the sadness at the back of my mind. Will I ever see this place again? I don't know. But something tells me that when I step out this door that I'm ending a chapter. When I'm satisfied that I have everything I need. I stop and swap out my threadbare boots for a kick ass pair of knee-length, patent leather-heeled zombie stompers. I know what you're thinking—how is she going to run or fight in those? But let me tell you, I can fight better in heels than I can in sneakers. Trust me on that.

As I tiptoe down my former deathtraps, that foreboding feeling grows more compelling. Ice skitters through my nerves, sending shivers up my spine. This is why I sent Frank ahead with the supplies. I need to investigate what my Sight has been screaming at me since we entered Thornfall. I may appear to be alone, but my gut says otherwise.

When my feet touch the cobblestones, the foreboding intensifies. I know I should run, but whatever I'm about to find will not be pleasant, but if I leave it here? What if a citizen gets attacked? A human. A child. I can't have that on my conscience. I need to take care of it before I leave Thornfall.

What would Deacon say?

Assess your surroundings. Look for anything out of place. What do you see? What do you hear? What do you smell?

Daggers ready, I follow the uneasy feeling, hoping to locate the source. A faint gurgling noise echoes off the buildings in the dingy alleyway, making it hard to pinpoint which direction it's coming from. However, it doesn't take long to find out. As I head towards the center of the alley, a humongous man lumbers toward me. I'm using the word *man* liberally here. He is a monstrosity. With rotted teeth, something stringy lodged between them, about five feet taller than me, and one eye smack dab in the middle of his forehead.

A cyclops.

Really? REALLY?! I glare at the sky and give the most enthusiastic one-finger salute I can muster

to the Gods, Goddesses, Sky mamas, Cloud dad-
dies... whatever the fuck they are. All of them can
piss off! Can't I go twenty-four hours without one
of their creations trying to murder me? Fucking
hell.

"Easy there, my guy. We can work this out. I can
make you a burger or something. Way yummier
than me, right?" I call out to the hulking beast,
wondering how the hell one of them is wandering
the streets of Thornfall when they're not even
supposed to be in this realm?

On a positive note, this is a class I actually
paid attention to. The Cyclops order is generally
dumb as rocks. So, I've got a snowball's chance
in hell to fight my way out of this, I think? There
is no way I can overpower this giant on physical
strength, and I can't use magic. So, I'll have to get
creative. I clutch my daggers and creep them just
behind the back of my thighs. If I can draw him
to me—I only need to get close enough to stab
the eye without getting Hulk smashed. It seems
as good a plan as any.

As he draws closer, his odor is potent. Like ran-
cid meat mixed with rotting fruit, my stomach
lurches. Good Goddess, that is appalling!

Just hold it together for one more minute...

When the brute is mere steps from me, I reveal my daggers. Crooking my finger, beckoning
him closer. Smiling fiercely. He smiles back, and
I swear I see the shard of a finger bone lodged
between his decaying teeth.

*Oh, my Goddess. Please let this work. I do not want
to be Cyclops food!*

With a slight crouch, my leg muscles coil, ready
for attack. First, I'll need to jump high enough

to hit the target. Knees don't fail me now! He takes another step, and we're almost there. Just one more step...

A sickening crunch reverberates against the buildings, and something pulpy hits the ground with a moist smack. There are cyclops pieces littered across the stones. In my hair, I think I feel something jelly-like on my face. Ew, nasty! It's like he exploded. But how can that be? I'm flabbergasted at the sheer brutality of what I'm seeing. And then my eyes shift their focus to the sexy, tattooed, and intimately familiar hand protruding from the gaping hole in this creature's chest.

Did he just punch straight through this cyclops's back and shove his heart through the front of his rib cage? What a fucking psycho! And why do I find it disturbingly hot?

Before I can formulate any words out loud, the newly liberated organ still weakly beating, complete with a mangled aorta and dangly arteries, drops to the ground with a repulsing thud. Rolling just far enough to hit the tip of my fancy boot.

The mutilated corpse falls to the cobblestones, shaking the earth.

When I tear my gaze from the bloodbath at my feet, I'm looking up into a pair of stormy turquoise eyes...

"Miss me, Kitten?"

CHAPTER SEVEN

VIVI

"YOU SON OF A bitch!" my voice shakes as I glare at the subject of all my wet dreams and horrific nightmares combined. "Are you fucking crazy?"

Cold fury glows in his swirling galaxy eyes; those aren't his pissed-off eyes. They're his monster eyes, and it's clear that if he could rip its heart out again, he would.

"Did he hurt you?" Killian's gaze trails down my body. Meticulously checking for injuries, caressing my skin without a single touch. And I shudder, leaning into his familiar scent. I have the oddest urge to rub myself against him until I'm covered in that scent and never wash it off.

But I'm not that stupid.

"I'm fine," I reiterate as I stare down at the pool of blood surrounding my feet. "You owe me a pair of boots, asshole!"

His devastating grin knocks me to my knees. "You almost got yourself killed, Kitten. And you're concerned with your boots?"

"Yes, I am! Look at them. They're ruined!" I shriek.

He tilts his head, kind of like a dog does when it hears a weird noise? And with a magician-like sleight of hand, he's covered in spiraling sapphire flames. Maybe covered isn't the right word? It's more like he's made of them.

Flickers of blue lightning race across the ground and up the sides of the buildings, raising the hairs on my arms with the static electricity. His flames spread across the stones, burning away any evidence of the gore-fest that was just on grisly display.

No more blood, no more spare body parts, no more Cyclops.

Then his inferno changes course, traveling toward me. I watch in semi-horrified fascination as it slithers onto my foot and wraps itself around my leg, then continues swirling up the inside of my thigh. Hovering just below my pulsing clit, lingering there.

Oh, he is such an ass!

Just as I'm about to lose control of the moan I've been trying to hold in, the flame travels across my stomach and follows a path all the way to my neck. Instinctively, I lean my head back, exposing my neck to his power. It doesn't burn me. Instead, it tingles in a way I can't explain. In a different setting, this could be so fucking hot. But standing there in the open alley, with a man I should be nowhere near... it feels immoral.

Forbidden.

When the flames are finished exploring, and they burn themselves out. Killian is once again standing in all his arrogant glory. Shirtless, of course. His broad tattooed chest is a work of art.

Too bad it's attached to a manipulative fuckstick.

I didn't even know he was capable of something like that! And he hasn't set off any of Thornfall's magic alarms, either. Umm... Mr. Sex on Wheels has some serious explaining to do!

"Is that better, my feisty Kitten?" he smirks, voice dripping with dark promises.

"For the fifty-hundredth time, don't call me that! I'm not your anything." That's not even a real number, but I'm so godsdamned frustrated I don't care. I don't trust myself around him. And I trust him even less.

When he starts toward me, my skin goes clammy, and sweat beads on my neck. This is dangerous, and I should run for the nearest sanctuary. As if there was a place in the universe I'd be safe from him.

Every step he takes forward, I move back, attempting to create some much-needed space between us. But when the brick building bites into the back of my shoulders, and I groan in frustration.

"I have a proposal for you," he presses his mouth-watering chest into mine, bathing me in his intoxicating scent.

"ABSOLUTELY NOT!" my cheeks turn pink at what I think he's suggesting.

"You have a deliciously dirty mind," Killian chuckles, creating profane chaos in my bare lady bits.

No, I did not have time to put on a pair of undies when I was at the apartment. It's a decision I am regretting now, thank you very much.

"Come back to the Night Fortress." He continues.

Excuse me, what?

This is trickery. Straight-up bullshit. He's an Incubus. Remember? You do not want to power walk your stupid ass back to the Netherworld and rock his world in reverse cowgirl style. He is not here to profess his undying affection for you. These touches come with strings, Vivi. None of it's real.

"That's your proposal? Come back to The Manson Mansion? Are you high?" I'm asking, because this is absurd.

"Not currently, but we could change that if you're so inclined." he moves closer, lowering his sinful lips to my neck, sending waves of intense pleasure down my spine and into my toes.

"I don't know what that means! Do you mean getting high on drugs? Or are you being cryptic about sex? Everything you say is ass-backward and in circles! What do you want, Killian? Seriously, what the fuck do you want from me!?" I'm pleading now, desperate for an actual answer.

A tidal wave of heat floods his turquoise gaze. "What I *want* is you, Genevieve."

My heart splinters at those merciless words, a dagger twisting in my chest.

If only they were true.

"You don't get to call me that either." It comes out as a whimper rather than the roar it was supposed to be. I can't do this; he can't say my name like this. It's cruel, and I've had enough pain to last a lifetime.

"So, you prefer Kitten?" he smirks, pressing his torso against mine, pinning me to the bricks. I glare daggers straight into his wretched soul. If he even has one, the smug bastard.

He grips my hips, fingertips digging in just enough to border on pain but having the opposite effect. Just like in my dreams. Why? WHY does my body betray me like this? I think he can feel the anger rising to the surface, because before I can tell him where to shove it—his lips collide with mine, and I am toast.

He runs the tip of his tongue along my bottom lip, and against all the warning bells going off in my brain, I moan quietly. Killian mirrors me with a low rumble in his chest. Melting my insides. His mouth is over mine again, parting my lips and turning my world blurry. He kisses like he fucks; it's heated and intense, all consuming. With the expert motion of his tongue, he owns me. His embrace grows desperate, his hands move to grip both sides of my face, and then he breaks the kiss long enough to stare into my eyes.

Our breaths are labored, gasping in time with each other.

It's as if I can feel his soul tethered to mine in a complicated maze of lust, fear, hatred, and longing. And I can tell it's overpowering for him as well; I can feel him. Flashes of pain and scars, a young Killian hiding a crimson-haired baby among the servants, a terrifying man with wild, unhinged eyes. Blood, pain, rage.

Are these Killian's memories? My eyes widen in surprise before sorrow settles in, and then he knows I've breached whatever wall he'd built around his darkness, and he shuts me out.

What happened to him? And why do I feel like I could tear someone's spine out for causing him that pain. I don't even like him! I don't...

His mouth dives back into mine, and he consumes every bit of my resolve. Something tickles the back of my mind, a warning, but I'm lost to him now. I'm lust and sensation, ripping and tearing at his shirt like a feral beast. I need this man like I need air. I need him so much it hurts.

Without knowing how I got here, my trembling legs wrap around his slender waist, shuddering against his hardness as I throb for him. He presses himself into me possessively, and I slash my nails across his cheek. I want to rip him to shreds. I want to hurt him and then heal his wounds. I want to destroy him and save him and damn him and be his salvation. But he only looks down at the blood I've drawn and chuckles.

"My savage little enchantress," his voice is husky and filled with a pride that liquifies me.

This is not enough. It will never *be* enough...

I groan as I move my hands to his throat, gripping lightly. Equal parts turned on and enraged. I can't decide if I want to get down and dirty right here in the middle of a back alley or squeeze harder and suffocate the life out of him.

The warning bells are deafening now, filtering through the sex haze. "Killian," a breathy plea escapes me, but the sound of his name on my tongue pushes him over the edge. He lowers his mouth to my chest, lifting my tank top, pressing his heavenly mouth to my breast. I push against his chest, backing his face away so I can see him. "Look at me."

He pauses and turns his molten gaze to my face, searching my eyes intensely. I don't know what he's searching for. But I'm anxious. That stare feels like something raw, primal. It feels like destiny.

Fuck. Destiny.

Fight or flight kicks in, and I need to get away, "I can't think. Stop, Killian, I can't think! STOP!"

The panic in my voice stops him in his tracks.

"What's wrong? Did I hurt you?" His voice is trembling as he searches my eyes, and I can almost believe there's something genuine behind it. But while I was distracted, those warning bells kept going off. Getting louder and more desperate until I listened.

Magic. I tasted magic on my tongue. And there it is! His ulterior motive; there's *always* something in it for him.

"Oh, you've hurt me plenty. Stop acting like you don't already know it! I'm sure it makes you proud. What do my emotions taste like, Killian? Are the messy ones like expensive chocolate? What about anger? I bet that tastes like a juicy filet minion. Sadness, grief, complete and total wreckage?!! I bet you get off on making me feel those things, on getting your fix. What the fuck did you just do to me? And don't you dare tell me nothing!" Anger surges past the arousal and takes a firm hold of my brain.

I search his face, looking for something, a reaction. And this motherfucker grins at me! I shove him with all my might, moving him an inch. Maybe less. So, I push him again. "I'm glad you find this all so amusing. What did you do to me? I want an answer!"

"You're overreacting." He replies, picking at his already pristine fingernails.

Overreacting?! Does this colossal douchebag not understand how to speak female? Its Universal knowledge! You do not tell an angry woman they're overreacting. It's like trying to baptize a cat!

My control snaps, and before he deflects my attack, I've got my daggers crossed at his throat. Pushing them against his skin, shaking with the need to end him. He swallows hard, lifting his hand to my blade and pressing it further into the rough skin at the base of his jaw, drawing blood. Encouraging me!

It's official. He is certifiably insane.

My hands shake with fury, and I see red. I adjust my blades to sever his head from his neck, and just as I'm coiling to strike—his eyes glow neon blue and the daggers fall from my hands, clanging onto the stones beneath us.

Just like that. He's disarmed me *and* played with my emotions at the same damn time.

"Did you put a tracking spell inside in my mouth?" I should lower my voice, but I've misplaced my godsdamned marbles. Stupid, stupid girl! Of course he did. I cut off the last one. What made me think he wouldn't replace it?

"This is a sick game. You need a fucking therapist!"

"Should you ever require my help, you only need to call out my name," he speaks in riddles, of course. That's not even remotely what I meant. Color me surprised. Whatever he did to me? Calling out his name undoes it.

The hallway in The Night Fortress invades my mind and overtakes my senses. *I'm up against a wall, his head between my legs, coming undone for him. "Say it again..."*

"Remove it, Killian."

"I'm afraid I can't do that. Unless you want to go somewhere a little more private?" he flashes an evil grin as he glances towards my death traps. "I recall your appreciation for bathtubs."

"Fuck you!"

"Gladly," he answers seductively, inching toward me as if he's going to snatch me from this alley right here, right now.

"You're going to kidnap me again?" My bravado deflates; all of this is for nothing if I'm just going to end up back in that pretty cage.

Killian's face becomes solemn. "That was a mistake."

Huh? I couldn't be more shocked right now if I had shoved a sword into a lightning bolt. He must notice the deep confusion written on my face because he continues. "I didn't intend to hold you against your will, and I will not do so again. When you come to me, Genevieve, it will be of your own free will. I give my word."

Stop saying my name, you bastard. It hurts.

"Your promises don't mean shit to me! You're not Fae. You can say whatever you want, that doesn't make any of it true. I'm not an idiot, and I'm not your fucking toy!"

Anger, yes! That's what I need. Maybe it'll be enough to ignore my rioting hormones. "I have to get back to the meeting spot before the rest of the crew comes looking for me."

Killian stiffens, "You mean before Alpha Lincoln comes looking for you?"

I can't even believe the audacity. What in the bipolar rollercoaster, spicy stalker fuckery is this? Now he's jealous? Is this a joke? It must be. I don't even have the words. He is the most infuriating creature I have ever encountered in my life!

"We're not talking about him, Killian. It's none of your business." Stepping past him, I make my way toward the end of the alley.

"Oh, it's my business, Kitten. You can bet on that," he smiles, running his hand along his jaw and his stormy eyes over every part of me. Like he's appraising a car or something.

"Doubt it," I call across my shoulder.

I don't want to do it, but it's no use. I turn for one more look at the face I can't stop dreaming about, but he's already gone. A tear breaks free from the corner of my eye, falling onto my cheek as I furiously wipe it away.

"Fucking Incubastard!!" I scream into the emptiness.

Suddenly, surviving Faustus seems like child's play.

How am I going to survive the Dark Prince of the Netherworld?

CHAPTER EIGHT

VIVI

THE WALK OF SHAME back to the meeting spot will go down in history as the dumbest thing I've ever done. I don't know what the hell is wrong with me. It's like the darkness takes over, and I can't stop. He's like any kind of addiction, I suppose. You know it's hazardous to your health; you know it's likely to tear you apart, and your demise is a genuine possibility. But chasing that high makes you feel so alive... until it doesn't. And then everything you love is destroyed and you don't recognize yourself in the mirror. That's what he does to me.

What if I could somehow disable Killian's magic? If I could control his hold over me, if I could somehow take an elixir or have my mind spelled. I could resist him, but if I can't resist him, then I can inflict some damage of my own. I don't feel an ounce of remorse for these dark thoughts. I probably should, but instead I embrace them. Imagining taking my power back and sticking it to him forms a slight grin on the corner of my lips. It's not like he hasn't earned it.

Walking the path back into the mountain, I stumble on a rock and almost face plant, catching myself with the palms of my hands. The rocks

skid along my skin and tear through. Motherfucker that stings! But it brings my thoughts back into
focus. What does it mean now that I have another
tracker in my body? Would Killian follow me and
breach the wards? It doesn't seem like it. He said
when I come to him, it will be of my own free will.

Fat chance of that ever happening! If anything,
he'll send Bronwyn to live in the woods outside
the ward and report back. I can handle that. I
think we're still safe at the Abbey, so I check that
off my worry list.

Heading towards the meeting point, I stick to
the shadows. Not that I'm sure it matters. I haven't
felt a single soul in Thornfall, which is still nagging at the back of my brain. There's something sketchy going on. The silence, the deserted
streets, a Cyclops that doesn't belong here. It's
connected, and it reeks of the Elders.

I don't know what I'm going to do about Frank.
The Dark Goddess has been missing in action
since the ballroom at the Night Fortress. Why?
Did something happen to her? I must admit that
ever since I realized she was an ancestor, I have
questions I think only she can answer. Maybe she
knows about my mother? She knows about the
box. Why was she inside it? Did my mother really
trap her in there, and if so. Why? I'm overthinking now, anxiety brain turned up to eleven out of
ten.

As I round the corner on the dirt path, past the
trees, and into the unassuming shrubbery, I feel
Linc's energy surging like a damn electric plant.
Impatient, angry, confused. Okay. So yeah, I gave
him the slip, which I expected to get reamed for,
but it wasn't like I was throwing myself headfirst

into danger. Not on purpose, anyway. How was I supposed to know the things that go bump in the night were crawling through the alleyway? I just went a few steps off course to get some underwear, for star's sake! I still got the supplies from Gravestone. No harm, no foul.

Can they even see Frank? Or did a pile of weapons float into the cavern seemingly by themselves?

Maybe the sudden appearance of a ghost was startling. But I don't think it warrants such a tizzy. Sheesh.

As I suspected, Linc is standing outside the opening to the tunnel, arms crossed, irritation written on his otherwise handsome face. Before I can finish crossing the last five feet to enter the tunnel, he's already running his big mouth.

"You smell like him." He bites out, disgust peppering his words.

Damn these shifters and the above-average sense of smell! I'm sure I do reek like Mr. Tall, Dark and Dangerous. I was just wrapped around him like a cheap prom date, after all. For one fleeting moment, I let the shame wash over me. I should regret what just happened, and I do, but part of me feels powerful. Whatever he wants from me, he must want it badly. A scheme forms in my head. I think I know how to pay Killian back for all the mental anguish...

"So, you're going to ignore me now?" Linc snips.

Actually, I wasn't listening at all. I have too much on my mind to worry about Linc's hurt pride right now. I haven't explored how I feel about what just happened—let alone having to explain it to someone else. I don't owe him that. Plus, I'm trying to devise a plan here. One that gets me the answers I need and keeps everyone safe.

"You're not even going to deny it?" Linc continues, "You'd rather sneak off to your filthy fucking Prince than help us gain what we need to get Deacon back?"

He did not... because he couldn't be that stupid, right? Tell me that Linc didn't just throw Deacon in my face with the singular purpose of hurting me. Because the Lincoln I know would never dream of doing something so hateful, no matter how angry he was.

I stare at him, expecting his wits to return to his thick skull. Waiting for him to realize what he'd just done and apologize, but the apology doesn't come. Instead, he stares right back at me, dead-set-serious. And with that one judgmental sentence from my best friend's mouth and the balls to stand behind it, something inside me comes unhinged, and the darkness is there to comfort me.

I haven't had a single moment of my life that wasn't already planned for me, whether I knew about it or not. Instead, I've had one overbearing person after another watching my every move. Judging it, controlling the outcome, manipulating me. I'm not sure I've ever been in control of my own decisions. And I am so fucking done!

I march right up to Linc and grab the back of his neck, planting a savage kiss on his slack mouth. It's not romantic in the least. It's a warning. It's a threat—but he immediately sinks into it and wraps his arms around my waist. So, I shift closer. As close as I can get. Within seconds, I've rubbed myself along every angle of his body I can reach.

Then I pull away, and it's over as quickly as it began. His breaths come out in huffs, eyes panicked and confused.

Speechless looks great on him! Wish he'd do it more often.

I chuckle at his reaction. "There, now you smell like him too! Better hope the witches figured out how to get us running water while we were gone. Seems like you might need a doggie bath. And if you ever doubt my loyalty or slut-shame me again, I'll pass out enthusiastic BJs to your entire clan. I'm sure they won't mind. Do. Not. Fuck with me. Lincoln Blackwood."

"You don't mean that! What the fuck, Viv?" he stammers, anger seeping into his voice.

Like he has any right!

"Weird. That is exactly what I was thinking, too, Linc! What about it is any of your business? What makes you think you can degrade me? When did you become my keeper? I must've missed the invitation to that party! So, yeah... Linc. There are all sorts of '*what the fucks*' flying around tonight." I seize him with an accusing glare. "You're not my Alpha, and I don't have to explain myself to you."

I shove past him into the tunnel where the rest of the crew is anxiously waiting. One look at their horrified expressions, and I know they've overheard everything.

Great! Just what we need. More division.

I pull the earbuds out of my pocket and pop them in. Blaring 'Rumors' by Lizzo turned up loud. I don't want to hear anyone's shit right now. Frank trails behind me like a godsforsaken toddler, and judging by the confounded looks he's getting, I answered my earlier question. Yeah, everyone can see him.

Minutes after making it back to the Abbey, Marlow grabs me by the arm and drags me into her chamber. I don't need to read her mind. I can see twenty questions written all over her face. "Girl, you better start talking!" she eagerly crosses the room and sits me down on her matching lumpy straw mattress.

Her space looks so much cozier than mine. She always was better at transforming anything into a haven of relaxation and creativity. Colorful mandala tapestries line the walls. Her makeshift altar has a few hand-dipped candles lit next to some freshly picked moon root. There are tie-dyed strips of fabric hanging from her doorway, creating a curtain of sorts. It all just screams Boho Marlow, and I love it.

"I don't know what you mean," I blush, not entirely sure which part she's asking about.

"Well, first. What the hell did you do to Linc? He's madder than a giant in a limbo contest. And then you can tell me how you came back smelling like the Dark Prince of Sexy Town. I thought it was just a supply run. Did you make plans to meet him and not tell me?" a hint of offense seeps into her tone.

"Of course not, Lowe! I would never keep something like that from you. He just showed up! Rather inconveniently, might I add? And nothing happened. Okay, well, not much happened. I didn't sleep with him or anything. I just got stuck on stupid for a minute before I came to my senses."

Marlow sits patiently, adjusting her glasses and waiting for the rest of the story.

"As far as Linc? He went all caveman on me when I got back. Like, full-on jealous man child. It pissed me off so bad, Lowe. It was either kick his Alpha ass in front of his wolves or go into full bitch mode. So, I gave him a dose of his own medicine and he didn't appreciate it." My eyes lower, and for a fraction of a second, I do feel like a terrible friend. But screw that. This pissing contest between Linc and Killian is on my last available nerve. I'm not a possession to fight over.

"What's happening in that beautiful brain of yours, Vivi?" Marlow asks.

"Nothing. I'm just tired of being their fire hydrant. Fuck 'em both."

She shakes her head in understanding. "You went scorched earth."

"Yeah, kind of. I did keep one thing from you, though. It was dumb. I went on a side quest to get some underwear from my apartment." I giggle at how silly that sounds.

"Girl, you've been free crotching it the whole time? No wonder you've got these horn balls sniffing around your sexy ass all day long." She laughs, an infectious sound that chases away the darkness, at least temporarily.

"Not the whole time! Haha! But yeah." I chuckle.

"You kill me, Vivi. You're an absolute legend! And look, I know you're gonna make him sweat it out, which you should! But don't punish Linc for too long, okay? He's still figuring out how to be an Alpha, and he learned very little about it from his abusive asshole father. He's finding his way, and he's got it bad for you. Your milkshake is strong, my friend! Slide something over my way, would ya?" Her face lights up in a way I've never quite seen before.

"And who am I sliding your way, Lowe? Because that sparkle in your eye says he's got a name." I needle her, hoping it's not Linc, because how messy can it possibly get around here?

"I can have my secrets too," she winks. "Oh yeah!! I came in here for a reason. Your umm... ghost friend? Willa wants to talk to you about that."

Shit!

"I figured she would. Can you run interference for like fifteen minutes? I just need to get myself together."

"Sure thing, babe." Marlow smiles and shakes her head, chuckling to herself.

I waited to hear her feet move down the hallway, making sure nobody was able to eavesdrop. "Frank?" I call out into the empty room, waiting for the chill to cross my skin.

"Yes, princess." He appears from thin air in the corner of the room, looking the same way he's looked for years. Cargo pants, V neck T-shirt, buzz cut. He looks way more like GI Joe than a meddling ghost.

"Okay, remember we discussed this? No - 'yes, princess.' No - 'right away, my princess.' None of it. Just call me Vivi and act normal. Please? Especially in front of Willa, because I have zero idea how she's going to react to you."

CHAPTER NINE

THE TEMPLE OF DUSK

WILLA AND I SIT on opposite sides of one of those antique pinewood writing desks. She has said nothing yet, but I can sense the judgment wafting off her the moment I plant my ass on the chair. The cantankerous old bat. Sheesh.

I let my eyes roam the room for something else to focus on, noticing the damask papered walls. It's odd, so different from the rest of the building. I wonder what the room used to be? I don't know a lot about the Darkmoors. We didn't have many attending the Academy when I was there. The only one I've ever spoken to is Meredith Bridgewater, and we all know how I feel about her. But were all the Darkmoors as wretched as she is? They had an entire Abbey to themselves away from the Academy. Perhaps they were aware of the corruption, or maybe they were just loners. As I'm scanning the surprisingly intact bookshelf behind Willa, the door creaks and Iris glides into the room. Her warm smile and infectious energy are calming.

"Hello dear," she fills the uncomfortable silence.

"Hey," I smile modestly.

Willa cuts in, "You had an encounter with the Dark Prince on your supply run?"

Oh, hell. They did not prepare me to talk about that! I thought we were here to address the dead guy in the building. I was readying myself to field the questions about necromancy or, I don't know, death magic? But Killian. Ugh, I'm so sick of talking about Killian.

"Well, technically, yes. But I didn't plan it that way or anything." My answer comes out more shamefaced than I intended it to sound. "I needed clothes; I can't very well fight in rags. So, I made a pit stop at my apartment."

"Where you picked up a hitchhiking spirit?" Iris asks, and I burst into a giggle-snort.

Worst timing ever! But something about the way she said it has me in hysterics. I did, didn't I? I picked up a hitchhiking ghost, and then I let a demon prince plant a tracker in my mouth because I was too horny to pay attention.

I can't. It's too hilarious!

I'm wiping tears of laughter from my eyes as I feel Willa's empty stare focused on my face. Her lips pressed together so tightly they look like plastic. I guess she doesn't appreciate dark humor the way I do. So, I should probably shut my big mouth now.

"There are things you don't know about your... ancestry." Willa wears an expression on her face like she's smelled something rotten.

Okay? Weird. And if I thought *this* was going to be the most shocking part of our little heart-to-heart? I was in for a rude awakening.

"There is no gentle way to tell you this, Genevieve. You're a Netherling." Iris's eyes are forlorn.

Excuse me, huh? A Netherling. My sperm donor lives there, so I guess I assumed I was half whatever he is. But my mom was a High Priestess here in the Earth Realm. So, tell me how that math works? I mean, granted. I'm not the greatest at math, and the minute they put letters in with the numbers? Forget about it. But by my calculations, it doesn't add up...

"Genevieve?" Iris flashes me a concerned look.

"Chill, I'm not going to freak out or light the damned Abbey on fire. But I think you're mistaken. My mother is a Bloodgood Witch. I remember her, I remember the Manor. You know, where she was attacked by the Shadowfax and died. Or tried to kill me and failed? Those details have always been hazy."

"Your mother is not a Bloodgood Witch, Genevieve. And there's no such thing as a Shadowfax. Evanora was a goddess, and so are you." Iris continues.

"And the other part?" This sounds suspect, but it's as close to an answer as I've ever gotten. So, I'm willing to hear them out.

"Demon. Abomination. Creature of Darkness." Willa spits, literally SPITS on the floor like I've seen mobsters do in the movies. I'm gathering that she dislikes demons.

I'm a demon?

Wait, I hate demons too! I'm going to need so much therapy after the world stops ending. Psychiatrist on speed dial type of therapy. Because we have entered a whole extra dimension of fucked up.

"So, I'm a Demon Goddess Witch?" My mouth goes dry, and I try to disguise the trembling in my hands. I want to deny it, to tell them they're crazy. But it makes sense. The prophecy, the amulet, the visions, the flames, my darkness.

In my heart, I know it's true.

Iris replies, "Your abilities are still manifesting."

"Okay, and what do you mean—no such thing as a Shadowfax? We've been taught our whole lives they started a war. You know, the biggest witchling war in history. The one from every textbook. Ring a bell?"

Iris and Willa glance at each other as if they're trying to decide. Finally, Iris's hands move to her lap, twisting nervously, "The Shadowfax were conjured up as villains because they were mixed orders."

"Wait, what? Mixed order? Like Dragon and Witch. Shifter and Fae. Goblin and Ghoul? Like a Labradoodle, but supernatural?" I ask.

We're not supposed to mix. How is this possible? Why didn't I know this existed? That would mean... holy shit! That would mean not only are supernaturals from different orders shacking up, but different realms too...

"I am mixed order, Genevieve." Iris drops a bomb squarely on my lap. "I am Witch and Fae."

Well, that sure explains some shit, doesn't it? I knew it! I knew she was different, and now I'm even more positive that Iris can, in fact, walk through walls.

"Oh shit, I'm sorry about the Labradoodle thing. I meant nothing by it. I just have diarrhea of the mouth sometimes." That was a shit apology. I need to work on my filter. And my people skills.

"It's okay dear, this is a lot to process, I'm sure," Iris smiles.

That's it. She's an angel. You can't convince me otherwise. I just offended the shit out of her, and she forgave it. Man, I really have to think before I speak.

And then another thought hits me...

Did Deacon know about this? Is THAT what the tunnels are for? Are *all* the witches here mixed order? I don't even know where to start!! Luckily, I didn't have to start anywhere because the biggest mindfuck comes next.

Both Iris and Willa explain that the Gods and Goddesses of old never technically die. Instead, their essence transfers. As in, body-hopping. Because that's not creepy at all!

It gets a little sketchy on *who* receives the essence of the Crème De Body Snatchers. But for a long time, they thought it to be the first-born of each generation, and that's true in most cases. But not all.

So that means my mother transferred her inherited goddess gifts to me when she died. I thought she was trying to kill me. Who knows? Maybe she was. But I finally have the answer to why I ascended so early. Mommy stashed Goddess powers inside me like a secret envelope, and then locked them up. Until my sister broke the key.

So, yeah. Just wrapping my brain around THAT...

"Mordred is a demon or a God?" I have so many questions.

"Both," Iris answers hesitantly.

At first, I'm confused. Still trying to figure out the math, but then it hits me. She said my mother is a goddess, and if my father is a God? I'm not a half- anything, I'm a whole ass goddess. But with some demon witch sprinkled on the side? As a treat.

"What God?" I'm not sure I want the answer, but if I don't ask? I'll kick myself for eternity.

"Your father is a descendant of The God of War, Genevieve."

Awesome! And I'm just spit balling here, but I think we can add fire demon to the checklist on dear old dad. So that would mean it doesn't matter what order you are, the essence transfers through generations, regardless. We get the power of our supernatural order AND whatever God or Goddess in our ancestry?

Whoa. That's deep.

I'm slightly terrified to ask this question, but I'm already tits deep in this shit creek, anyway. "And my mother? What Goddess?"

"We don't know."

Gotcha. So, the mystery is *not* solved. No Scooby snacks for us! Just then, a horrifying realization hits me in the gut. Killian is the child of a God, and I'd bet my nicest ass cheek that Selene is a Goddess too. And I already know he's a demon.

So, does that make us the same? Minus the witch part.

"Who is Killian's father?" I ask Willa.

I'm not sure why I didn't ask Iris instead? I try not to psychoanalyze myself if I can avoid it, but let's call it a hunch and say that I don't want to hear what I think I'm going to hear from sweet Irises mouth.

"Killian's father is the God of the Dead."

———◦———

After excusing myself from the most emotionally scarring 'meeting' I've ever had, the only thing I can think about is telling Marlow and Linc.

Oh, and a soothing dip in the waterfall wouldn't piss me off. My last 'peaceful' moment was rudely interrupted, if you remember. And I could use *all* the peace right now.

But first, Marlow and Linc...

I'm power walking my dumbfounded self through the main corridor when Frank blinks into existence and falls in step beside me. I'm so shell-shocked it doesn't even startle me this time. "Did you know all of this?"

Frank only bobs his head in agreement.

"Are you going to tell me what else you know?"

"All in divine timing," he replies.

Great, he's on this kick again.

I'll tell him where he can stick his divine timing. Right up his asshole! If ghosts even have assholes... I'm sure they do, right? Even if they're not functional? Whatever. He can kick rocks barefoot and lick a cactus.

We round the corner in the cathedral-slash-cafeteria. I find Marlow sitting in a rather uncomfortable-looking chair reading a book. One distraught look in her direction has her up and moving toward me.

"What happened?" Her eyes dart back and forth around the room.

"Not here. We need to talk somewhere isolated. Where's Linc?"

"I'm sure he's in the infirmary building or outside training," she replies.

I nod and turn toward the main corridor, and Marlow automatically follows. We don't get very far before she takes special notice of the handsome ghost trailing me like an un-alive security guard. How do I know that? Because Marlow gets this lopsided smirk on her stunning golden-brown face when she's about to be inappropriate as fuck.

It's the smirk, and the glimmer in her eye that I'm seeing right now...

"So, you're a real deal incorporeal being, huh? It's too bad, Frank. I've always thought you were kind of hot. Waiting in the alley to kick supernatural asses, but the whole—not having a body thing keeps us star-crossed lovers. Tragic, isn't it?" she smiles and plays with her tight curls. "Maybe you could dirty-talk me to sleep? I heard your voice is sexy."

She did not hear that!

She's totally bluffing, but if ghosts could blush...

I can't help but crack a smile; even in the middle of the biggest shit storm we've weathered to date Marlow still has the time to brazenly hit on a fucking ghost. It's almost comforting? Something familiar. My best friend being a filthy mouthed virginal deviant, is my emotional comfort blankie.

Analyze that! On second thought, maybe we should leave well enough alone.

We continue down the path from the main building through the overgrown garden on our way to the infirmary building. Back in the day, this is where they'd house the sick and injured, so we'd searched up and down for leftover medical supplies but unfortunately everything we found was so old it had disintegrated or far surpassed its intended expiration date—but the building itself had the perfect amount of space and a side yard the shifters could build obstacle courses and do training in. So, this is where they've chosen to bunk.

It doesn't take long to find Linc. They're all out front, having what looks to be a game of hacky sack with some improvised gauze and medical tape creation. As if he's got a sixth sense, Linc turns his head and makes eye contact before I can even call out to him. The moment he sees the seriousness in my eyes, he excuses himself from the festivities and meets us halfway.

"What's going on, Viv?" the vertical line in his forehead creases.

"We really need to talk." I glance at the rest of his pack, who have all stopped and taken an interest in our conversation. "Alone."

Linc nods and leads the way to an empty courtyard. None of us speak as we head down the gravel path. Them, because I'm sure I've just scared the pixie dust out of my two best friends. And me? Well, I haven't said anything yet because I don't know what to say, and I'm trying to figure it out before we reach the end of this path.

I can't help but feel a little insecure: demons are wicked. They're evil, murdering foul perversions of nature. That's what we're taught; it's never been questioned. It's kind of like how The Nether-world was supposed to be this intensely abysmal realm, where all the worst creations are damned to spend their eternity in pain and torment. I believed that until I ended up there and found something very different from what we'd all been taught. I witnessed 'evil' beings laugh, cry, and risk it all for each other. Someone capable of that is capable of love. And if they love? They're not all cruel and merciless.

In Thornfall, I'd be publicly punished for shar-ing that observation. They'd call it a betrayal of 'my kind.' For a moment, a soul-crushing thought enters my mind: will Marlow and Linc still love me if they know what I am?

Please say yes. Please. I'll stop making jokes about Willa having horns and a tail. I'll even try to get on her good side. I pinky promise to the sky.

I think I'm in shock. I know what I should feel, but it's all under spiderwebs. Sticky and tough to grasp. It will be better to say what I need to say now, because when this hits me? I have a feeling it's going to knock me on my ass.

The minute we're out of sight in the South Courtyard, Marlow throws an arm into the air, waving it across the garden of stones. A blanket of silence descends upon us as the sounds of the outside world are blocked out. This is one of the most fabulous spells Marlow has learned since arriving at the Abbey. "Y Tawelwr"—*The Silencer.*

"What the hell happened in that room?!" Mar-low shouts. Holding her arms across her chest, tapping her foot.

Linc is unnervingly motionless. Everything about him right now says predator, "I can't control the shift forever, Viv. Too much adrenaline."

Okay, fine. I move over and take a seat on a stone bench, and I tell them everything. Repeating the words to them somehow makes them more real to me. Mordred is a demon with the essence of the God of War inside him. Whether I like it or not, I have inherited abilities from my father. My mother wasn't who she said she was, and I don't know if it's because she loved me so much that she gave up her entire life to keep me hidden or if she was dark and had some other motivation? I don't even know if Evanora was her real name, but her powers were dormant inside me. Or they were? But the amulet set them free.

I'm a fire-wielding demon, blood witch, goddess, earthmover? Which sounds fucking ridiculous. Then I explain to them that there are mixed orders, and they have been hunted down and vilified to the point of going into hiding.

They're nearly extinct.

Let that sink in, almost extinct. Hunted not by Demons and Netherlings but by their own people. Us. Me. I've probably executed them and had no clue what they were being put to death for. My hatred for Faustus increases by the minute.

The floodgates open, and I spill it all. When I'm done with word vomiting all over their feet, Linc stares at me. I can't tell what's happening in his head, and I'm tempted to call the Sight and dig around in his aura, but I'm afraid of what I may find.

I've tried to tell him I'm not what he envisions me to be. When we were back in Thornfall, I told him I'm not the good girl. I'm not the damsel in need of saving. He refuses to acknowledge that I'm not pure or innocent. I'm not a victim. I'm the monster, and I always have been. He just never listened. I bet he's regretting that right about now. It's a good thing he's not a witch, or he'd probably banish me himself.

The awkward silence is driving me nuts; I'm fidgeting.

"Say something," I deadpan, speaking directly to Linc. I need to hear him say it out loud. I need to listen to him tell me I'm an abomination and I don't belong here.

A sideways grin forms on his mouth, and I don't know if that's malice or amusement. "So, you're a Demon Goddess from Hell?"

His face turns red, and I swear he looks as though he's about to burst... and then he laughs with his entire chest. An honest to goddess, I'm-a-comedian, Lincoln Blackwood goofy-ass laugh. And I swear it's the best sound I've ever heard.

"Come on, Viv. That's funny!!" He stands up and crosses over to me. Pulling me up off the bench in an obnoxious bear hug, "We already knew that! Didn't we, Lowe?"

She's stifling her giggles with a hand over her mouth. "I thought she was a diabolical bitch from hell, but I was close enough!"

Now trapped in his ridiculously muscled arms, Linc's laughter shakes my entire body. And I let out the breath I feel like I've been holding forever as a cackle escapes my lips–and before I know it, we're all three holding our stomachs, wiping tears of laughter from our eyes.

Demon Goddess from Hell... it's a good joke!

CHAPTER TEN

THE TEMPLE OF DUSK

I'M IN AN INTRICATELY woven labyrinth made of earth and dark magic. My heart beats through my chest as a grim shadow looms in the distance. I glance up at the sky—terror fills my veins. It's Mordred, no. It's Faustus, no. It's the God of the Dead. His eyes glow crimson, then white, then pitch black. Finally, his face morphs into a snarling beast as he rushes forward, and I run. I take a left, and a right, and another left. Rushing through the tall hedges, but the path only leads me past the same haunting statue. A horned beast sits upon a throne of skulls, every shape, every size. Even made of stone–it watches me. Silence heightens every noise, every sharp inhale of breath I take.

The stone cracks and beastly claws thrust out from the crumbling rock, piercing my skin. The monster is made of flesh now, and its jaws part, revealing a chilling, pointed tongue. It moves and slithers, growing longer as it seeks my flesh. As it finds my wounds, a scream builds in my throat. It wants my soul; it wants to devour my darkness. The tongue spears into the injury the beast's claws have created, forcing more blood to flow as it drinks and drinks. The screams inside my mind are deafening.

Pure terror fills my vision; I don't want to die here.

And then I'm floating. My body explodes in ecstasy as solid arms hold me close, rising higher and higher into the star-filled sky. These arms are safe; they eat my pain and replace it with desire. Burning, hungry, necessary to live. My head spins, and I throb for him; I think I might be pleading. My words are breathy, desperate. They don't sound like words I know. But *he* knows them, and so I beg.

Save me, touch me, devour me, own me. I am his, and he is mine.

I am nothing. I am everything. I am divine. I am sinful. I am immortal.

I shoot up out of fitful sleep, drenched in a cold sweat. What was that? A vision? A nightmare? I pound my fists into the lumpy makeshift sack of straw I've been sleeping in. Rolling over in a state of exhaustion, a stalk of straw pierces my thigh. I could scream my frustration, but I think better of it.

These walls don't absorb shit.

As I make it to the side of my cot, my stomach becomes ill. My heart beats wildly, my body shakes. I can feel my magic brimming to the surface of my skin, prickling and pushing against its confines. And I'm not sure what will happen if it manifests. I need to get out of here.

After I've sneaked out of the Abbey undetected, I make my way to the gravel path just outside the front doors, and I jog. I'm not dumb enough to venture outside the main property into the forest while it's still dark outside, so I settle for running laps around the estate—at least until the sun peeks over the horizon.

After several laps, my mind calms, and my calves ache. I've been having more of them: visions, or nightmares. Whichever they are. Something about them eats at me, sending anxiety straight to the core. Whatever they are, it's a warning. Something is coming, and we're all running out of time.

Where is the Goddess of Night? Do I have to be in mortal danger for her to show herself, or has she moved on to another plane? Goddesses transfer their essence to the bodies of their next of kin?! What does that mean for me...?

A thunderous crack reverberates through the air, startling me half to death. As I whirl around to see where it's coming from, I'm hit by something the feels like a semi-truck. With my face smashed into the earth and what feels like a ton of bricks on top of me, I can't help but wonder what in the absolute hell have I done to deserve *this* much bad luck? Because karma has a tracker on my ass, I swear.

"Are you alright, princess?" Frank's deep voice is full of concern.

That was Frank? How the fuck did a ghost tackle me like a godsdamned linebacker, and here's an even better question... why?

"What the hell, you ass waffle! Get off me!" I groan out at half lung capacity. He moves quickly, extending a hand to help me up off the ground, and the only thing I can think to say is, "But you're a ghost. How, um, how did you turn solid?"

"Are you going to let me help you up? Or are you content with your backside in the dirt?" he replies.

"Ohhh, so you're a sarcastic dead guy! I'll remember to thank your Mistress of the Dark for sending you my way," what an ass.

"Turn around," Frank orders, and I balk at him. Who does he think he is? My dad? "Genevieve. Turn. Around."

So, I do, to find a humongous tree branch mangled and dug into the ground. Right where I was jogging when I heard the noise. What the fuck is going on here? Holy shit, biscuits, I almost died! Again! That massive thing would have smashed me to a pulp. This is some Final Destination type shit.

"I will not apologize if that's what you're waiting for." I smile at Frank, slight remorse exposed in my eyes.

Gah! There are too many mysteries, and I don't have the right amount of brain cells to handle this at the moment. I need a shower, and since I have Captain Kickass, the Warrior Ghost stalking behind me. I guess it doesn't matter if it's still dark outside.

"Well, come on then!" I call to Frank as I hobble into the forest. Scraped knees and bruised spirit in tow.

———— ◆ ————

Staring down at my bare feet in the frothy cascade of water, I lean my head back and close my eyes. The earth witch in me sings with joy, surrounded by Mother Nature. I'm just close enough to the waterfall that the spray bathes me in a cool mist, filling my magical cup to the brim. I suppose I could just spend forever here among the moss-covered rocks and mystical critters. I think I could be something that resembles happy.

Wading over to the large boulder that sits in the middle of the stream, I grab one of my daggers, making a small slice in the pad of my thumb. I let the blood bead until there' are a few drops' worth, and then I smear it across the top of the boulder. The moss stirs, and roots sprout upwards, slowly becoming more solid. Leaves burst from the dark-green stalk as it reaches toward the sky. Pink petals bloom like fireworks. A genuine smile spreads across my lips as I gently stroke the petals, feeling maternal.

I've been practicing Blood Magic. It's not that they don't know I'm a Blood Witch. That's not why I'm concealing myself. It's because of this...

I make a jagged slice across my palm, angry lifeblood pours onto the flower I'd just created, and it withers. Disintegrating into a heap of nothingness. Acrid smoke wafts from the wreckage into the air.

The power to create and the ability to destroy. As if the stars have given me a test.

Light or dark, Vivi. Are you a woman? Or are you a monster?

But what if I've been a monster for so long that's all I know how to be? What if there's only darkness when you open me up and look inside?

A strange swirling warmth wraps itself around my mid-section and up across my collar bone, leaving an uncomfortable but not entirely awful sensation in my bones. I don't feel alone anymore, but there's something 'other' about this energy. Something I can't quite place. I still my movements, scanning the trees as discreetly as possible. If there's someone inside the wards, then I'm sorely unprepared to defend myself. If things keep gravitating in this direction, I am going to end up in a death match with someone while completely nude.

"Frank," I call out, but nothing happens.

Double fuck.

As I turn past the direction of the Abbey and gaze past the wards, I'm met by a pair of haunting gray eyes. A tall, thin, muscular-built Adonis stands across from me. His white-blonde hair lays in a messy pile atop his head. A cross between bedhead and I-did-this-on- purpose. I don't recognize him, and I would remember if I had seen him before. He stirs something inside me, something not quite attraction, but not quite terror either.

Somehow, I just know this man is lethal.

My first instinct is to rush him. It would give me the upper hand, but I realize he's on the other side of the ward. He's not actually looking at me—he's looking through me.

Oh, thank the Goddess and all the baby fireflies! He can't see me! I plop my backside down in the shallow water and release the breath I was holding.

Now that the threat doesn't seem to be as dire, I watch him. It feels strange to sit across from someone who doesn't know they're being watched. So, all those times I joked (sort of) with Killian about being a stalker, and here I am, being a stalker.

I'm fascinated by this... this... man who resembles a fallen angel? But like one who fell because he ripped someone to pieces and feasted on their organs. Or smoked a lot of fae flower and partied too much. Or both? I'm unsure.

Why is he here?

I didn't mean to stare at him for so long, but as the sun peeks over the horizon and bathe the forest in shades of oranges, reds, and greens. I realize I've been naked in a river for a long time, and my skin is all shriveled up like raisins. Plus, there will be wolves roaming the woods soon on patrol. Now would be an excellent time to get dressed and the hell out of here.

I'll tell Linc about this, well... maybe not all of it. But the part about a scary hot guy poking around on the other side of the wards, for sure. He can monitor it, maybe even figure out what the man is doing there.

———◆———

Strolling into the cafeteria, I find Marlow seated at one of the long tables. She's got her hair up in two puffs on each side of her head, and it's cute as hell. I'll have to remind her to do that more often! I make my way over and glance at the book she's got her freckles buried in 'The Society of the Boundless Serpent.'

Interesting! Lowe's reading about dragons...

"Dragons, huh?" I poke fun at her, putting together what, or rather *who* may have my best friend preoccupied.

"Oh! No, no, I just... well, I just wanted to know how the wards could withstand..." she stumbles and trips on her words.

"Uh-huh." I toss her a smug grin. I bet.

I shove over her stack of books, planting myself next to her as I grab a few grapes from her plate and pop them in my mouth. "We have grapes?"

Marlow looks relieved at the change of subject, "Yes! Some of the earth witches figured out how to grow them in jars! And they're infused with extra nutrients and vitamins and stuff, too. Super grapes!"

Her nervous laugh is infectious, and I can't help but join in.

"What's so funny over here?" Linc's comedian voice is music to my ears. He slides in across from us and grabs a handful of grapes from Marlow's plate.

It almost feels normal. A memory of Enchanted Brew invades my mind. Countless mornings spent drinking lattes and people watching. The three of us laughing and swiping food from each other's plates. The nostalgia tugs at my heart, but that was before...

"Super Grapes!" Marlow and I both shout in unison, giggling. Linc unveils his famous lopsided grin, and then all three of us are cracking up over absolutely nothing. It's the best I've felt in a long time.

Eventually, after the laughter dies down, I tell them both about the strange man loitering outside the wards. Of course, Linc wants to rush off

and kill the guy without asking a single question...
eye roll... and he says I'm dramatic!

Obviously, I convinced him what a stupid idea
that would be. Why leave the safety of the wards
and alert him to our location? We agree to keep a
close eye on him and his movements.

"I have something to share as well," Marlow
adds, which garners a look of surprise on both
mine and Linc's faces. The air shimmers, and an
iridescent bubble forms around us.

"The Silencer," Marlow smiles.

*She's getting fantastic at that spell, leaving us with so
many fun possibilities.*

"Willa and Iris gave you some information
about your lineage, right? The essence of the
Gods and Goddess's trickle-down thing. Well,
they also took me aside and filled me in on some
family history of my own." Her joyful face turns
angry.

"Oh shit, that bad?" I ask.

"Worse," she replies, "My father is crueler than
we could have imagined."

Linc and I both settle in, listening intently.

Unfortunately, Marlow was correct. It's worse
than any of us thought.

Willa is more powerful than her brother, but
because of her 'disability' they passed her over for
leadership, her words not Marlow's. So, they sent
her off to 'The Order of the Crimson Eye' where
the High Priestesses go for preparation. Which
is a fancy way of saying "sent away to boarding
school" because she would have ascended to High
Priestess either way.

While attending boarding school, she met Iris,
and they were drawn by fate almost immediately.

During their time together, Iris trusted Willa with her secret. That she was a Spirit Witch and Fae, a mixed order. It didn't change their love. Willa vowed to keep her secret. After boarding school, they found a Priestess and were hand-fasted, also known as married in many Witchling traditions.

After coming back to Thornfall to introduce Iris to the family, something had changed. Their father was dead under mysterious circumstances. Faustus was on the Council of Elders and refused to recognize Willa and Iris's union.

Marlow's mother had always been an excellent friend to Willa, so she went to Judith to plead her case. But something was off about her. She wasn't herself. It was as if nobody was home, and that's when Willa realized Faustus had Judith under mind control.

Judith turned Willa in for attempting to go against the Council. And as punishment, they banished Willa and Iris to Tanglewood Mansion.

It was never their home. It was their prison.

CHAPTER ELEVEN

VIVI

ALTHOUGH IT'S IMPORTANT TO me to check in with Marlow after hearing that someone stole her mother from her, which is complete bullshit, and if I didn't already want to make Faustus pay, this would solidify my convictions. Marlow is the best person I know, and she doesn't deserve any of this. But I know when my presence isn't wanted. When the pain is too much to bear—a little solitude, a good long cry, and a fat nap are better healing than garden sage and rosemary tea. And when she's ready for a friend, I'll be waiting.

Meanwhile, I have some plans of my own.

My legs swing from a tree branch above the walking path, the smell of earth and damp bark, the woodsy scent of fallen leaves clear my brain. This is my happy place, and today it's also my thinking place. I have knots to unravel, big ugly messed-up clusters. Starting with learning a lot more information about mixed orders and ending with one blonde-haired ominous angel, who doesn't strike me as a mountain man, but appears to be living like one? Right outside our ward.

"Amethyst Crowe!" I call out to the elusive mixed order witch as she's traveling towards the

Greenhouse. She looks up at the sky, puzzled, and I jump down, landing sideways and stumbling over myself, "Wait up!"

I fall into step and give her a little shoulder jab. "I suppose we should attempt friendship or something?"

"You know they call you Princess Biatch when you're not around, right?" she lifts the corner of her lip, a mischievous glint in her eye.

"Who does? Do you mean all my besties?! It can't be. I feel so betrayed!" I roll my eyes and laugh. Do they really think I don't know what they say about me? My hearing is fantabulous, and I don't want to lead Amethyst on, but that's not the worst thing I've heard them say.

That elicits a genuine laugh from Miss Amethyst as I follow her into the Greenhouse. Causally watching as she uses her gifts to tend to the plants. We make our way to a corner of the building where it's clear they have separated these pots, their leaves wilting and drooping. Amethyst looks at me and then turns to one of the dismal-looking leaves. She lifts her finger in a swirling motion, muttering words I don't understand. A light dusting of a pink glittery substance settles over it, and I giggle before I can even stop myself.

I did not intend to laugh! It's just that, well, Amethyst is already a dainty name for a six-foot-tall warrior woman who could bench press a Minotaur. And now you're telling me her magic is pink? It's ironic, is all. I wasn't expecting that.

Amethyst gives me the side-eye, but she doesn't commit to a full-on bitch face. So, I think our new friendship is off to a stellar beginning!

"So, you're Fae, huh?" I ask.

"Yep." she replies.

"Light or Dark?"

"That's a stupid question," she smiles as she insults me. Or maybe I offended her? I probably did. Unfortunately, my social radar isn't known for accuracy.

"Well, I hate to tell you this, but my fairy grandmother always said there was no such thing as a stupid question." I tease.

"Sounds like that's a Vivi problem." She's got tits of steel talking to me like this. I love it!

"Do you want to train with me today? You and the other mixed orders, witches, umm? What do you like to be called?"

Amethyst grins and shakes her head. "By our names, weirdo."

———◇———

The makeshift arena takes some time to get used to. It's rough. Linc and his clan can only work with what they have available, but I think they did a decent job. There are some tires laid out on the ground for agility, and they built a wooden 'ninja warrior' type set up with the climbing wall and wooden beams. With their own hands using wood from the forest. Which I think is impressive, and also sort of hot. There's something about a man with rough hands, am I right? I don't even know what it is. Security maybe?

"As far as magic, there's not much to practice on. So, we try to watch where we aim," I
say to a group of not-so enthusiastic-looking
mixed-witches, shrugging my shoulders. What
can you do? Haters gonna hate, and these witches?
Ooh, they're hating. On me, not the shifters. I'm
not sure if I should take that as a compliment?
But I'm choosing to for my sanity. After some
convincing, we paired everyone up in threes. Two
shifters and one witch per group.

"One shifter fights the other off while the witch
casts at a target. If the shifter reaches your witch?
You're out. Then you switch out with someone on
the sidelines. Got it?"

We have uneven numbers. It's the only thing
that makes sense.

Linc, Osric, and I stand up front, ready to
demonstrate. I grin wide and release my flames,
slowly at first, guiding them through my veins
and into my palms. Violet bursts through my skin
as two towers of flame reach high into the sky like
fireworks gone up in flames.

I can hear a whoosh of air exit Linc's lungs as
Osric lands a decent blow to his chest. Shifters
have accelerated healing, so these fuckers are a
little crazy! Breaking bones and drawing blood is
not off the table. Which is a good thing because to
have a pixie's chance in Purgatory at beating The
Academy we're going to hit them with everything
we've got.

I step into the middle of the arena. Screams and
grunts echo around me in stereo, fists meeting
skin, magic flying. Pride swells in my chest; this
is beautiful. This is what we need. Teamwork.

Nobody is paying any attention to me aside from Linc. They're lost in the melee's excitement, which is precisely what I want. I take one mischievous glance in Linc's direction, and he stops moving, curious about what I'm up to.

I put my hand up and lift three fingers–*our sign for it's all good*–and then I whip out the dagger and slash my palm. Blood drenches the dirt and grass, and Linc's eyes go wide, but he doesn't make a move to stop me.

That sign of ours is sacred. We've had it since we were children. It means 'trust me'.

I feel the energy churn and swirl underneath the ground. Giddy excitement blooms in my chest at what's about to happen, and then the dirt trembles. Growing more and more unstable, everyone is stopped now, watching.

Good.

Soil rains from the sky as a twenty-foot-tall plum-colored Arching Belladonna bursts to life, ripping her roots from the ground and turning to me, dropping poisonous berries onto the ground as they explode in tufts of noxious powder.

For a moment, the silence is deafening. All eyes are on the deadly creature I've created. My inner monster stretches and pushes against my insides, and the well deep inside me blazes to life. I turn over my palm. Flames erupt, and then, with a vicious grin, I turn and strike. Incinerating the plant-beast.

"The time for hiding is over," I call out to the whooping crowd. "When we leave the safety of these wards, the Academy won't hold back on us. They have conditioned us to hide what we are. Controlled by the fear of being found out, of the punishment for being born different. But I hope you understand just how vital this is: we can't afford to hide in the shadows any longer. The war isn't just in the Netherworld, it's here in Thornfall too. Everything they have taught us is a lie. The Elders don't care about anything but power. And all of us are pawns in their power games. No more, though. Our lives depend on every one of us embracing who we are." I drive the point home.

For my first actual speech, I think I did okay.

The atmosphere changes to one of apprehension, and I look at Amethyst. I don't know what she can do, but I know she can do more than she lets on. I suspect that's true for just about every witch here, but Amethyst is their leader.

I gesture with my hands to her, hoping that she understands what I'm trying to say. I need her to reveal herself. They need her to reveal herself. If they won't trust me yet, then I need them to trust her.

She strolls forward, making eye contact as more unspoken words pass between us.

If I do this? Help me keep them safe.

I tilt my head in agreement.

Amethyst spins in a wide circle, throwing honest to goddess sparks from her fingertips. She spins and spins until she's nothing but pink sparks and blurred vision. And then suddenly, we're all rendered mute. Unable to make a sound.

Holy shit, she has Fae Magic!

After Amethyst reveals her secret, the rest come one by one. Trusting the people inside these wards with their lives. Some have ice, some have the fire, some have double elements, and one has triple. They can cast illness; they can cast hexes. Light, Dark. Neutral. Chaotic. We have them all. We even have a witch who transforms into a Phoenix! We may have a chance at surviving this after all.

After a long day of training and learning each other's talents, we are all tired, hungry, and covered in a thick layer of sweat-crusted grime.

All of us pile into the cafeteria and descend upon the feast that's laid out for us. Since our supply run, things have been looking up around here. First, we've got enough magic to grow food. Then, with Marlow's help, the extra vitamins and proteins infused into everything strengthen us. We've even got a makeshift bathing room with warm water and soap now.

I don't mean to sound like a joyful jackalope or anything, but it's starting to, I don't know? Not suck around here.

Even Willa has calmed down on the Cruella these last few days. So, I grab a plate and sit next to Marlow as Amethyst and another mixed order witch named Sybil Lovelace settle in on the other side of the table.

"Hey!" Sybil grins. My Sight tells me she's been dying to talk to us, but doesn't do much of anything without Amethyst by her side.

"Hey! Join us; sit." Marlow cheerfully replies, and I nod in agreement.

We eat in companionable silence for a while, soaking in the atmosphere. Then, when I'm done stuffing my face, I let my eyes roam the not-so-segregated cathedral. A few of the shifters are more than accommodating to the pretty witches at their tables, and I can't help but giggle like a schoolgirl.

"I hope your young ladies know the contraception spell." I wiggle my eyebrows suggestively. If I'm right about the vibe in this room? And I am, because I'm a fucking Seer, things are about to get a little frisky around here after the sun goes down.

Amethyst sits up straight, surveying the room. I can't make out her expression as she observes the same thing I'm seeing, but I'm interested in her reaction. Finally, she rests her hands on the table and chuckles, "Oh, Goddess. What have we done?"

"Well, you all just topped every pornographic fantasy these shifter boys could imagine in that training ring today..." Marlow belly laughs, and we all follow her lead.

I wasn't about to wait in line for the new bathhouse, warm water or not. Like I said—now that they have a semi-green light and an excuse to be near each other? I wouldn't be caught walking into any dark corners around this Abbey without announcing myself first.

Nobody likes a surprise face full of shifter schlong. That's like the real-life equivalent to an unsolicited dick pic.

So, I make my way to my chambers instead, ready to grab some clean leggings and an oversized sleep shirt before I make my way to bathe in a bubbling stream beneath the cascade waterfall.

It may be cold, but it's tucked away in an oasis of 'nobody knows where I am' and I'll take that any day over a crowded room full of people doing things I wish I could do, and thoughts of the sexy demon I shouldn't be doing them with.

I thought I was here to stand underneath my favorite waterfall. I thought I was here to wash the filth from my body while surrounded by a mist that carries refreshing rainbow droplets through the air and across my upturned face.

That's what I wanted anyway, but the Universe believes I deserve to be endlessly tormented by criminally hot men with serious psychological issues. Because instead of doing any of those things, I'm sitting crisscross applesauce, soaking wet in the middle of a stream–clothed, this time–watching the strangest man I've ever seen do nothing. And for some reason? It's mesmerizing.

It's not that I want him... not like that. At least I don't think I do. I don't feel the earth-shaking necessity to be near him like I do with Killian. Not exactly. It's more of a fascination, a curiosity.

It's the man-angel from before. He's beautiful and terror-provoking. There is no doubt of his darkness. It's thick in the air and smells of bitter chocolate. But I'm ensnared. Who is this fascinating creature, and what is he doing in the Earth Realm? He must know there's something beyond this ward, but he makes no move to bring it down. I checked with Linc, and he reported the same thing.

He just sits.

"Frank?" I call out into the void, testing it. And just like last time, no response.

Somehow this man... fallen angel... unearthly beast... is blocking Spirit Frank from reaching me.

I don't understand. If he's not here to collect me, and he's not here to hurt me. What the fuck is he here for?

Is he a scout, a spy, an assassin, a singing telegram?

I don't know, but it's been days.

This is stupid, even bigger than stupid. I should not, under any circumstances, try to communicate with him. But here I am, about to do it anyway...

"Can you hear me?" I whisper, waiting for any slight change. A finger twitch. Anything that gives him away. But unless he's got one hell of a poker face... he doesn't seem to know I'm here.

Finally, I yell, "HEY FUCKSTICK! ARE YOU MESSING WITH ME?"

Nothing.

Is he mute? I jump up and down, spraying water over everything in my sopping wet clothes. Waving my arms back and forth, I feel like a total head case. Why am I whipping myself around like the main character in a cheesy music video trying to get the attention of a man-creature that might strike me dead? I don't know.

Maybe I have a death wish.

CHAPTER TWELVE

VIVI

IMAGINE MY SHOCK WHEN I open my eyes to blinding daylight and then realize I'm in my cot. A tip of a piece of straw pokes my inner thigh again! And I twist my body to get away from it.

My head feels blocked and floaty, like there are cotton balls where my brain should be. I look around my chamber room, confused and irritated. Why is my bag sitting against the wall exactly where I left it before I went to bathe last night? I move my feet from under the quilt to find my sheets a mess. The caked dirt from my clothing had flaked off during the night and ruined my bedding.

Wait. A. Minute.

I jump up out of bed, not even bothering to make a pit stop in the potty room, before I take off at a sprint towards the forest path. I run until my legs shake and adrenaline pumps through my veins. Then, when I skid to a halt at the edge of the river, I collapse on the bank. Afraid to look across the stream, but that's what I'm here for. He's real.

He has to be real, or I'm truly insane and cannot be trusted.

I peek over the arm I'd used to shield my face. And there he is. The dark angel... vicious beast... beautiful creature. His blonde hair sticking every which way and gray eyes still haunting everything they look upon.

Now that I know Mr. Mysterious is still here, somehow it makes me feel better. So, I spend a few minutes soaking up the sounds of the forest. The water trickling over rocks and twigs, the humming of dragonflies, wild winged creatures calling back and forth to each other from one branch to another.

My mood slides into melancholy. Calypso would love it here; I can almost imagine her lounging near the bank—lazily hunting for fish. We would have spent so many days here just existing with nature. I always felt guilty for having such a big cat in a tiny apartment; she would have been wild and free here. Hot tears well up and spillover.

I can't think about Lippy without thinking of Kalliope. It's impossible to separate the two. A deep hurt aches in my chest, and I'm racked with violent sobs.

I've tried to reach Kalliope so many times. I meditate, I concentrate on the bond I know must be there; I call out for her. I've even tried some questionable magical methods to reach her mind. But there's still nothing, silence. More tears spill down my cheeks as the realization hits.

I'm alone.

I know I have friends, and I care for them. But they're not bound to me like Calypso was. They don't understand every inch of my muddled soul like she did. And my sister, my blood, the only

family I have. She's abandoned me after trying
to kill me. Aching fills my chest to the brim and
spills over. Now that I know Kalliope exists, I
could never walk away. It doesn't matter what she
did to me. What she tried to do. Or even what
she may do in the future. She's alone, too, and I
intend to change that by any means necessary.

*Alright, alright. That's enough, sad sack. Pull it to-
gether.*

I wipe my eyes dry and inhale the clean, crisp
air. Glancing back over at Mr. Angel of Death. No,
wait. That's not quite it.

He's an angel of... sorrow?

My heart twists. "I'm not sure why I'm saying
this when I know you can't hear me? And maybe
you're super dangerous. I don't know. But I hope
you're here tomorrow, whatever your name is."

———◆———

Heading back towards the Abbey, I notice a commotion. There are voices raised; the energy is
pure chaos. People are losing their shit. Everything was fine when I left, peaceful even. What
on earth realm could have happened in the last
hour?

I take off at a sprint towards the cathedral where
most of the noise is coming from, as I round the
corner—hand on an old pillar. I take in the atmosphere. There are witches everywhere, gathering
books, gathering candles; I can smell food being
made in overtime beside me in the kitchens.

And standing in the middle of the room is Marlow, tears streaming down her face, while Willa
looks after her. A wrinkled hand resting on her

shoulder. Linc is pacing back and forth, wearing a hole in the stones under his feet. He looks up as he feels me enter the room, and I know something terrible has happened by the pure dread swirling in his eyes.

I dash to her side, smoke wafting from my hands, "Marlow, why are you crying? Who hurt you? Who's getting their ass flame broiled?! Point me in his direction; I swear I'll fucking kill him.... Or her. Is it a her?"

She looks up through her tear-soaked lashes and clings to me; and the sobbing starts again. I run my hand across her back. I've never been fantastic at being the consoling friend. I'm more of an emotional support attack witch, but I give it my best.

Looking over her shoulder at Linc, we hold a silent conversation with our eyes.

Why haven't you kicked someone's ass yet, Lincoln?
He shakes his head.
It's not like that.

My eyes go wide as Marlow hyperventilates and rubs her snotty face on my shoulder. What. Is. Happening?

Surprising the ever-loving shit out of me, it's Willa who speaks first, "Faustus has sent word. He knows where we are, and he's given us three days to surrender Marlow to him before he attacks the Abbey."

Shit. Time's up!

"Wait, so he's saying we're all dead. But Marlow doesn't have to be?"

"Pretty much," Linc replies, clenching his jaw.

"Don't even THINK it, Genevieve Graves! I am not going anywhere without you." Marlow screeches, "I know what you're thinking. I won't go! So don't you dare try to trick me, trap me, or find a back door to shove me through while you risk your life for me. Because I'd rather die. Got it?"

Well, there goes that plan...

I look between Willa and Linc. What are we going to do? Shit, we have to do something other than stand here and leak bodily fluids from our faces. Where's Iris? Where's Amethyst and the mixed orders? And where the fuck is Frank?! Because I've got a message for the Goddess of Night, and I'm pretty sure he can deliver it.

Too many cooks, just one kitchen. That's what it feels like inside this claustrophobic room. After the initial shock, the crazy panic, and more than a few tears (not mine) we gathered the 'leader types' in Willa's temporary office. The room seemed much bigger than the last time I was in here. Weren't those bookshelves stacked up to the ceiling? Now, there are too many personalities. It's overwhelming my senses. And none of them are shutting the fuck up.

Pass the ibuprofen.

Yes, I'm a witch, and I can make my pain-relieving tea—but sometimes it's easier to just grab the plastic bottle and pop a godsdamned pill, okay? Judge away. I've got no shame in cutting magical corners.

Speaking of, I hope there are some travel packets in that first aid kit I swiped on the supply run. And while we're at it, I would do unladylike-felonious-immoral things for a latte right about now, and I am not ashamed to admit it.

One catastrophe to another, and then straight into the next, is weighing on me. I need caffeine. How the fuck am I supposed to grieve, heal, or even think in these conditions?

"Let's send her to him, Willa! He won't hurt her. She could take them down from the inside." One of the older witches, whose name I do not recall, speaks up. Her suggestion includes Marlow being used as a bargaining chip.

I growl in disagreement. Yes, *growl*–baring my teeth like a feral bitch. We will not be offering my best friend up as a sacrifice. Period.

I'm not so sure Faustus won't hurt Marlow; he's spent most of her life ignoring her existence. He's far too psychotic not to use her as bait for what he really wants. And he's already proven the lengths he'll go to by what he's done to his wife, and his own sister. Would he hurt his daughter too? Yeah, I think he would.

"We could increase training time, starting now. If we use all the hours in a day, we might be ready for them when they come." Osric adds to the conversation.

Nope. That will not work. We'll be tired, sore, and hungry. Why would we wear down our power before an attack? I applaud his effort; he's trying to contribute. But that is not a plan. And neither are the next several off-the-wall ideas getting thrown out into the room.

Finally, I can't take it anymore...

"It's simple. We attack first." I let my voice carry over the chatter, and everyone drops their jaw like I've stripped naked and did a public pole dance.

"What? It makes the most sense. He thinks we're weakened; he's given us a timeline. He's so full of himself that I'm sure he thinks we're all scattered to the winds. Not only that, but he won't expect us to strike first."

I silently thank Deacon for years and years of combat training and making sure most of it was done while fists and arrows flew past my face. He made sure both Linc and I were prepared from every angle. We think like the bad guys, because that's how you stay a few steps ahead. It's how you stay alive.

"She has a point," Linc co-signs, as I knew he would.

Willa has been staring blankly for the entire conversation, eyes trained on the paint-chipped doorway. If she thinks I haven't noticed, she's mistaken. I know she's crazy like a fox, and I can see her wheels turning. Willa is waiting for something, or rather... someone.

So, when Iris comes barreling through the archway, winded, and beckoning me to go with her? I follow.

Iris takes my hand, and we're off. Fast. Through the winding halls of the Abbey, and then out into the courtyard and through the rock wall into the forest. Yes... THROUGH the rock wall. I fucking told you! I knew it. My inner competitive asshole smiles.

Iris can walk through more than just walls.

In the frenzy, I hadn't thought about asking questions. But now that I'm running blindly deeper and deeper into the forest with no clue why... my radar acts up, "Iris, where are you taking me?"

"No time, child. No time," she retorts as she beckons me to run faster. One minute we're on the path lined with wildflowers, and the next we're inside the cave that houses the catacombs. My senses tingle. Something big is about to happen. Something I'm not sure that I'm on board with.

Iris drags me deeper into the tunnels, and just when I think maybe she's switched teams and is playing for the bad guys? She stops.

She just... stops.

Iris waves a weathered hand over the symbol I'd noticed the first time we'd been down here, in the spiral. Like the one I'd cut off my wrist. We stand in silence, anxiously waiting. For what? I have no idea. And then the earth cracks open, revealing a dark spiraling galaxy-like substance swirling behind it. "Iris, is this a freaking portal?"

"Hurry, child!" and then, without warning, she shoves me in.

CHAPTER THIRTEEN

THE COVE OF MYTHS

"WHAT THE FUCK, IRIS!?" I screech as I land on my ankle at an odd tilt. That shit stings like a bitch.

"Would you shut your mouth, hardheaded, lunatic girl, before you get us both killed? Don't you see where we are?" she hisses.

In my defense, I hadn't been paying much attention to where she was leading me. I'd been more focused on being shoved through a portal by a crazy woman! But now that she's pointed it out, I'm finally seeing what's around me.

The words 'get us killed' will do that to a person.

Taking in my surroundings gives me a sense of foreboding and familiarity at the same time. We're in a cave, but it's one of the most elaborate caves I've ever seen. There are swaths of wispy cream-colored fabric strung throughout the towering space, and candles dripping on every surface. It's dim and haunting. It's alluring, and I can feel the immense power pulsing within the rock walls. It feels like a heartbeat, like this cavern is very much alive.

The air smells of roses, incense, and old magic.

This is an ancient place.

A sacred place.

We should not be here.

I move my disbelieving eyes to Iris, "Are we in the Cove of Myths?"

She confirms with a knowing look, and my palms go clammy.

The Cove of Myths is a theoretically fictional place where the Oracles exist and perform their elusive gifts. I've never known anyone who's been here. The only stories I've heard from unreliable intoxicated bar patrons claiming to have seen it first-hand. It's kind of one of those big fish stories, a tall tale everyone just assumes is bullshit.

"A picture or it didn't happen" kind of thing. But it's real?!

I don't have to wait long for confirmation on that thought, because the moment it crosses my mind an otherworldly woman swathed in thin red cotton voile appears at the top of the carved stone staircase, leisurely making her way towards us.

The air is forced out of my lungs, my heart beats uncontrollably out of my chest. Suddenly, it's stifling in here. Fight or flight kicks in, and my body tenses.

Iris places a subduing hand on my shoulder. "Do not show fear."

Easy for her to say. I'm a godsdamned demon witch in a supposedly fictional place, and one of the old ones is hovering inches off the ground, floating toward the middle of the cavern. Totally normal, nothing to freak out about. My ass!

Iris grabs my arm and guides me toward a rock lined trail that ends in an elaborate fire pit. It also reminds me of the brand I removed from my wrist. Why? The radiant spirals, and the smooth stone seats placed around it in rings.

Three rings, to be exact.

We shift to the seats closest to the flames as the mystifying enchantress kneels.

"Genevieve," her haunting voice beckons from behind the veil she wears over the lower half of her face. Her eyes are endless depths of darkness, as if she carries the void inside her body. Even so, I want to go to her. It doesn't make sense, but regardless of the absurdity, I'm having a hard time staying motionless. I grip my seat for dear life, still not knowing why I'm here. Or how Iris knew how to get inside...

I clear my throat, "Yes, Priestess."

Her eyes go white as she raises her hands into the air, and the smoke from the ritual fire takes shape, bending to her will. It pulses a magical miasma into the air, creating a euphoric effect on all who breathe it in.

I am relaxed, unrestrained, all the stress and anxiety melt away. I've never felt freer. I want to wear gauzy fabric too, and sway to music only I can hear. I could stay here forever. The smoke swirls and dances before us, hypnotizing my soul.

If I have a soul? Do demons have souls? Where am I again?

Oh yeah, I'm with the Oracles. This is an altered realm, a place we don't belong. My eyes glaze over, my body is weightless, and I grin. The captivating cavern is full of haze now, and I bask in it. I feel a stirring low in my belly as I peer into the mist and find a pair of turquoise eyes staring back at me.

Oh, fuck me sideways. Not here too!

I can't even escape Killian in a weird magic-in-duced psychic dream? That's it. He needs a warning label. Or maybe just a shitload of caution tape, the red kind with the symbol for toxic all over it. Yeah! Skulls and the scary triangle with the exclamation point. Something that screams RUN!

That might be enough, but I doubt it. My mind clears enough to have some coherent thought. But the allure of the smoke pulls me back under the euphoric current. My body sags, and my thoughts calm.

Then, another scene unfolds, a battle, a lover's embrace, a flash of blood, eyes on fire, someone screaming, people on a balcony watching over scorched earth, pain, sorrow, and anguish.

Is it past, present, or what's yet to come?

That's the thing about visions; they don't always bring clarity. Sometimes you won't understand until it's happening in front of you. But I recognize one thing in the elusive mist. Daggers... *my* daggers.

And then a melodic voice speaks and I'm lucid again, "When air turns to fire, an act of cruelty shall create a strengthening of bonds."

Okay, then? Not alarming at all.

"The sister becomes the mother, and children of darkness shall emerge."

I open my mouth to ask what the fuck she is talking about? But Iris grabs my thigh and pinches tightly. I guess that's my cue to shut my trap and listen to the unsettling nursery rhymes...

"The second is reborn. The Daughter of Oracles brings about the destruction of two empires. Only one can be saved."

Well, I can tell you this much right now. I am not having any demonic resurrection babies or whatever the hell she's talking about. So, she can scratch that! And only one what... Empire? Child? SISTER? I don't comprehend, but she said something familiar. And despite Irises death stare, I can't stop the words from pouring out of my mouth.

"Excuse me, um... Priestess? Oh, Hallowed One? Mistress of Secrets? I'm sorry if that's disrespectful. I don't know what to call you. I'm pretty sure I'm not supposed to be addressing you at all. And I really hope you don't strike me down or curse me for eternity. Anyway, whew! I'm nervous. Is it hot in here? It's just that someone recently called me Daughter of Oracles. And I don't know what that is. Shit, I'm rambling. I'm sorry. What I mean to ask is... what is a Daughter of Oracles?" I'm mortified by the word soup that just came spewing from my mouth.

"The Lost Heir returns." She replies. At least I think it was a reply? Why are visions, prophecies, whatever this is? Why does it always have to be so cryptic?

Just once can a deity just say—Genevieve, don't go to the dance. Or you should buy a lottery ticket.

That would be helpful! But this is just confusing. Before I can muster the balls to ask for clarification, she morphs into ribbons of red silk, floating through the cavern and out of existence.

Oh, good! Because for a minute there, I thought something logical was going to come out of her mouth.

Iris and I are back in the tunnels in the blink of an eye, and I'm more perplexed than ever. What the hell was that? And why did it have to happen right now, in the middle of complete and utter mayhem?

"Are you going to tell me what that was all about?" I ask.

"We had to know before we made any decisions." she replies.

"Who's we?" I ask, eyebrows knitted together.

But her expression says this conversation is over.

The catacombs are full now. I'd say we're a group of about forty witches and shifters in total. Some stayed back—primarily those with enhanced knowledge in protection spells. They're tasked with reinforcing the wards and keeping Marlow safe.

We made the collective decision to leave Iris behind to look after them. Lowe had no issue this time; she wants to avoid being in the clutches of her fucked up father more than any of us. She knows she's a target. Or worse... bait.

So, she's working on some other options. You might never know what can roll sideways and how fast it can go downhill. But trust me. We do!

In the wise words of Deacon... "If you don't have a Plan B, C, D, and fucking Z. You're an uncommon idiot."

Goddess, I miss him so much! Hold tight, Old Man. We're coming.

"Ready, Viv?" Linc sneaks up behind me, wrapping his arms around my shoulders and resting his stubbled cheek on the back of my neck. It's not a sexual thing, it's a shifter thing. We're both wound tighter than the mighty Zeus's sphincter muscle, and he's just offering reassurance the beastly way.

"Ready as I'll ever be," I nudge him back, happy to have my friend with me regardless of our differences lately.

Leaving the Abbey, we travel in silence for what seems like hours. Willa and some older witches travel closely together near the front, Ansel and Osric march with a handful of shifter warriors bringing up the rear. Amethyst and Sybil have quite a few mixed-order witches trailing behind them. While Linc and I move in perfect sync, years of training together paying off in the way we mirror each other's movements.

I won't lie; there's an excitement building in my bones. The thrill of the fight, a target to release this wrath on, justification for the monster to stretch her legs and roar. I crave it as much as I fear it. But the softer side of me feels responsible for the people in this tunnel. And that girl is petrified.

We have a plan; it's a decent one as far as last-second strategies go. The good old 'creates a distraction while someone sneaks in the back' approach. It's basic, but it works almost every time if the distraction is good enough.

And I am the ultimate distraction.

So, why does my stomach feel queasy? Why is there a touch of hesitation? I should buy a fucking hamster wheel if these dark thoughts insist on running like track stars through my brain at all hours, leaving muddy footprints all over everything.

Catching up to Willa, who has somehow wormed her way into my heart. I think it's the shared loathing that finally broke the animosity between us. She has just as much reason to hate Faustus as I do, and hearing her story helped me understand her unpleasant nature. He stole her life, too. Maybe not in the same way as he stole mine, but they took it from her all the same.

"We're almost there," Willa sneers at me, but it doesn't have the same bite it used to. "Stick to the plan, Abomination."

Somehow, over a few weeks... 'Abomination' has become a term of endearment, and despite our checkered past, it warms my insides.

I smile as I pop in my earbuds and blast Chevelle, ready for the fight I've been begging to have since the first time I took a soul on Faustus's orders.

———◆———

Underhill Academy of Magical Arts looms before us as we congregate at the edge of the muddy bank. We're just under the radar, on the far edge of the wall. Nervous energy skitters through my veins. If we fuck this up, it's going to be bad.

I guess we'd better not fuck it up.

I look at Linc, ready to carry this out. "Take your wolves up the hill behind me. Stay out of sight. Then, when it's time to attack, I'll give the signal."

He nods, no words needed. Linc will protect my back, and if it goes South? He'll get everyone else out.

I task Willa and Sybil with entering the Academy, while I provide the distraction. The rest of the mixed orders will guard the exit with their full powers on display. I wish it were me risking my life. I wish it was my face that Deacon sees as he's being set free. But, as long as he comes out of that hellhole alive and enters the portal? That's all that matters. I'm the real prize.

Faustus wants his executioner back, and he's going to get more than he bargained for. With a deep breath, I exhale my doubts and call on my inner monster.

It's time to come out and play...

I confidently stroll up to the front gate alone. And to my surprise, it's open. No Churchill or Second Churchill. That's strange, but there's no going back now.

So, I enter the grounds. Moving quickly along the side of the fence, inching myself along the edge—I'm almost there. It's a straight sprint down the line of trees to the courtyard. I can't see it from here, but I know the distance by heart.

I look over my shoulder and give two short whistles. That's Lincoln's cue.

Get ready.

"Faustus Culpepper!!" I call out sardonically, "I've come to visit."

And then I run at full speed towards the front door. But as the courtyard comes into view, my heart sinks...

Faustus and the rest of the Elders are standing on the front steps. Culpepper's eyes move to mine, gleaming with satisfaction. And as I skid to a halt in front of them, I don't even have the time to speak before Bridgewater sneers.

Shit. This is a trap.

And then I'm hit squarely in the chest with a pale green mist.

CHAPTER FOURTEEN

KILLIAN

THIS GODSDAMNED SHADOW CAT is a menace. Anise and I circle her within the barrier Bronwyn created to keep her contained. She growls and hisses as she turns and whips her flaming tail toward me, scorching my sleeve.

She's been like this towards me since she emerged from the ground, making it clear that her days of rubbing against my leg in alleyways and sleeping at the foot of my bed are over. If I were a superstitious man, I'd say this cat is holding a grudge. But I don't believe that's possible. It's more likely that she's returned to the Netherworld warped and mindless with savagery.

Anise bobs on her heels, giggling like a maniac. "Here, kitty, kitty!"

Calypso lunges, her powerful jaws snapping dangerously close to my crimson-haired sister's face. Instead of backing away, Anise tilts her head and meows like a domesticated house cat.

"Anise, I don't think this is the appropriate time to goad her." I use the brotherly tone, hoping to dissuade her from any more life endangering theatrics.

"I don't know what that means, but you sound dreadfully boring." She grins, taking another step closer.

When Calypso lunges again, Anise whoops as she grabs the feral Shadow cat by the muzzle without a care in the world that her dress is now on fire. She snares Vivi's newly reanimated familiar in her gaze, using her Siren Call. And the damned beast settles! Moving to her haunches and planting her feline backside on the ground.

"Tell me how you did that."

"She's just hungry, silly. I'll go get her some cakes!!" Anise exclaims, skipping across the courtyard humming one of her tunes, her tea-length dress utterly ruined.

Hedonistic laughter echoes in the distance as Jagger approaches the enclosure. "She's gonna need a lot more than cake! Maybe a couple of gallons of sleeping potion, or perhaps a village of unsuspecting victims?"

I grin despite my frustration.

I desperately need this devil-cat to behave in a civilized manner.

I didn't tell Genevieve that I'd collected her broken body.

I didn't tell her we'd taken her beloved familiar to the Immortal Fields.

At first, it was out of an abundance of caution. We didn't know if it would work. Calypso was in awful shape; her essence was damaged. It's not common to bury familiars in the Immortal Fields, and the soul bond to her witch is a wild card. And mother is right—the creatures that emerge aren't what they were before. I'd banned the practice shortly after father was hexed. Desperate families would bury loved ones, only to have monstrosities born from the soil. Most were unsavable, most had to be eradicated. Putting the families through loss all over again. Most Netherlings wouldn't mind—we thrive on chaos and dark magic, but it never sat right with me.

I broke my own law for this, and to have a Shadow cat emerge? That is as rare as it gets. A Shadow cat is folklore, rumored to stalk the highlands and build dens of bone. The bones of their victims, specifically.

I preferred not to give Genevieve false hope.

And then she left me.

I could have mentioned it in the alleyway, but I didn't. I'm an asshole, through and through. I'm not above playing dirty to get what I want, and ruthlessness is my preferred method. I'm not the good guy, but she makes me want to be something else.

"Jagger, I need the familiar to cooperate, or I'll have to put her down." The thought doesn't please me, but if she's a danger to Genevieve. I won't hesitate.

"Whoa, chill, bro! I know you're stressed, but that's extreme. Go get some wine and feed, for fuck's sake. You haven't fed since... well, you know when you stopped feeding. It's making you irritable."

If he only knew the half of it...

"I claimed her, Jagger." The shame of it cracks my facade.

"You did what! Claimed her? But that means... Killian, that means... the curse." he fumbles for the words, "I know you said Genevieve was going to die and we need to get her back, all that shit about not having time. But I thought you were just being a crybaby about it."

Jagger rubs a hand over his beard, distraught by my confession. With good reason, "You CLAIMED her, bro? Like with the capital C?"

That doesn't dignify a response; my brother knows exactly what I mean.

"Ohhh, shit. Well, that was a stupid move! How are you going to feed now? She's not going to let you feed off her. She won't even talk to you! This is so fucked." Jagger spins around with his back to me, looking far off past the mountain into the Shadowlands. Taking a moment to collect himself.

I'd rather not continue this line of conversation, anyway. When an Incubus claims a mate, they feed from only that source. Forever. Essentially, I'm starving myself. We'll find a solution, but not right now. I change the subject.

"Are you going to help me tame this beast, so she doesn't eat your Little Monster or what?" I grumble.

I hate that they have pet names for each other and it's difficult to keep the spite out of my tone. I wish I could say I was trying to work on it, but that would be false. He gets *Dragon Boy* and a beaming smile. What do I get? Bastard, Asshole, Stalker, twin daggers at my throat...

I've earned them. I've only got myself to blame, but it doesn't rankle any less.

"Oh, I'll make this kitty purr." Jagger chuckles at his adolescent innuendo.

Calypso pins her ears to her head, rears back, and spits red-hot cinders into Jagger's face.

"That was rude!" He exclaims as he extinguishes the flaming projectiles with a shit-eating grin and then reaches for her again like nothing happened.

I'm ready to watch him get deep-fried by the hell beast. But, instead, Calypso leans into him with her giant head and rubs her whiskers on his chest. Smearing flames across his abs.

It's a good thing he's fireproof.

Anise wanders back from the kitchens with a handful of cakes. Swaying and dancing as Jagger and I discuss what sort of Netherbeast would be best to feed Calypso. She's singing to herself, a strange song even for Anise, "Today shall be the day what is false seems real. Two brothers shall mark a reunion of foes!!"

Her song is unsettling, and it instills a sense of foreboding in my chest. This has happened before, with my sisters' nonsensical poems and songs. If I hadn't seen my father drown her mother with my own eyes, I'd wonder about her family tree. Prophetic Sirens aren't unheard of, but they are rare.

I'm about to ask her to repeat herself so I can dissect the words and try to make sense of them, but I'm cut short. Because Calypso is going berserk. Roaring and thrashing about, spewing flames in every direction, throwing her massive blazing body against the barrier repeatedly.

Genevieve.

"Jagger!!" I call out in distress. "It's Genevieve!"

Rage and fear combine in a lethal cocktail. If someone has harmed her, I will rain hellfire upon them, tear their limbs from their bodies and bathe in their blood. I'll hang them from the walls behind my throne and watch them wither in suspended animation. I will deliver them pain unlike anything they've ever known. My body hums with deadly electricity as my demon awakens.

"Let's go, Killian!! You can go nuclear when we get to her," Jagger shouts over the hum in my ears as he bursts into dragon form. His ruby-tinted scales reflect the trees surrounding us. He bellows in fury as I climb on.

"I'm coming with you," Anise snarls, brandishing her row of shiny razor-sharp teeth, "I will make them all pay!"

As the Heir to the Netherworld and the person responsible for her safety, I have always sheltered Anise from the foul deeds required to run a kingdom. But just this once, I can't think of anyone better than my vicious baby sister to help me save my girl.

———◆———

We race through the sky at breakneck speed, barreling toward the veil between realms. Crossing the iridescent barrier with a popping vibration. The moment I enter the Earth Realm, my connection to Genevieve slides into place.

"The Academy!" I alert Jagger.

That infuriating, stubborn, pig-headed woman! She's gone after Faustus without me. Again. As if the last visit to the Halls of Repentance under the Academy never happened. As if I didn't have to send in a Dragon Shifter to prison-break her out! If she needed help, all she had to do was call my name. Does she really hate me so much that she won't save her own life by calling out for me?

Fuck.

The Cosmos are already seeking to assassinate her with the curse; it's like she's taunting fate. She's daring the stars to strike her down. The Daughter of Oracles. My Savage Queen. She is my equal in every way.

I'd throttle her myself for this recklessness if I thought it would do any good.

We soar over the clearing just before the Academy Courtyard, and my breath stills. There's a battle already in progress outside the walls. It looks as though the wolves and some of the liberated witches are in league, and they're fighting together against the Rune Force. My eyes dart across the scene, searching for midnight hair and lavender eyes.

When I don't spot Genevieve, my pulse spikes.

"Anise, do you see her?" I call to her against the wind.

Her eyes are scanning the entire grassy bank, to the outer rock walls of Underhill. Zipping from each bloodied supernatural to the next. Her eyesight is by far the best of us all, so the seconds tick by like hours. The silence is maddening. And then she screeches like a wild banshee, "JAGGER! THERE!!"

Half-shifted into her true Siren form, Anise points her elongated claws towards the courtyard entrance. Where Genevieve is standing eerily still, surrounded by green mist. I can taste the corrosive emotions coming from her in waves.

Wrath. Anguish. Unbearable Pain.

I spot Faustus standing on the concrete steps. The rest of the Elders surround him in procession. There's a figure on the ground at their feet, shrouded in shadow. Faustus waves a dramatic arm to remove the concealment spell, and I'm staring at Deacon.

Genevieve's guardian, the warrior who raised her.

Faustus removes his gloves and then places his hands over the base of Deacon's neck. They're pulsing, glowing, writhing with dark magic. It builds and intensifies as he prepares to strike Deacon down. While Genevieve helplessly watches.

I release a violent shock wave of power as we crash land through a section of the outer wall, and tumble into the courtyard. "NO!!!!"

CHAPTER FIFTEEN

VIVI

I'M FROZEN IN PLACE, immobilized. The people I care about fight for their lives all around me, and there's nothing I can do to assist them. I've been helpless before. It overwhelms me with dread. I focus on my arms, willing them to move, but there's nothing. Nothing! No magic, no Sight, I'm useless. Focusing my energy inward, I reach for my flames, only to find an empty abyss. They're gone. It's all gone.

I've never had a vision like this before.

Screams ring out from all directions, tangled bodies moving so fast I can't make out friend from foe. Then, finally, I spot Amethyst in the fray—it's three on one. She's putting up a hell of a fight, but she's outnumbered. My anger surges and I beg the stars for flames, for anything. I've always resented my magic, but there's nothing like having something stolen from you as a reminder of how being powerless feels...

It feels like shit.

I lose sight of her again, unable to spot any of the mixed order witches. Where the hell are they? There are wolves scattered across the court-yard. Some missing arms, legs... heads. This is a nightmare, a hell on earth realm. No, this can't be happening! Where is Lincoln? Pure terror fills my chest. Oh, my Goddess, where is he? I drag my eyes across the ground, looking for dark gray fur with black paws and glowing forest green eyes. I know his wolf form by heart...

I squeeze my eyes shut. This isn't right. This wasn't part of our plan. Something is amiss; my body feels wrong. This is all wrong! I've never had a vision like this, and then I gasp for air as realization socks me in the temple. I'm not watching a vision. This is not the Sight. It's an ambush.

Fear grips my throat, tightening as I struggle to understand through the green haze of confusion. I concentrate, bringing my mind back from hysterics. But it's nearly impossible to penetrate the mist clinging to my skin. The more I try to move, the tighter it coils around me. Pinning me in place. I've never heard of a spell that freezes elemental magic, let alone blood magic, and whatever else I've got inside me. Goddess only knows the horrors that lurk underneath my skin. What kind of potion am I dealing with?

What did that evil bitch on wheels do to me?

Deacon is going to have a ring-side event to ream my ass when we get through this mess. I'm going to need a new pair of jeans when he's done with me. Because I know better! And he knows I know better. How many times has he said it?...

"A, B, C, D, and fucking E. All the way to plan Z, Vivi Graves! Backups, for the backups, of your backups."

I can hear his voice inside my head even now.

Think, Vivi. Godsdammit!

Where are the witches? Scanning the expansive grounds again, I don't find any of ours. But that doesn't mean they aren't in danger outside these courtyard walls. Hopefully, I don't see them because they've made it inside the Academy. Yes, they and are rescuing Deacon as we speak, bringing him to safety. I need to believe that. I can endure whatever I need to for however long it takes. If they can just get him out...

Torture built me; pain shaped my entire childhood. Bring it, Faustus, you couldn't break me then and you won't break me now.

I'd like to think if my talents were something to boast about, I'd have some serious bragging rights! My track record for getting out of awesomely shitty situations alive is undefeated. And I don't plan on that changing today. If they can just get Deacon into that portal. Everyone else, too, for that matter. I can run my mouth like a pro. I'll make myself the main attraction. Whatever it takes.

Please, just let Deacon be okay. I'm silently begging anyone who will hear me. I don't know what's happened to him in those dungeons, but I know what happened to me. Lying on the ground, busted lungs, broken bones, vomiting my blood. Skirting the edge of death, while rats feasted on my skin and infection set in. I can't picture that for Deacon, I won't. I refuse to see him broken.

They're going to get him out, Vivi. Just shut the fuck up and do what needs to be done.

My pulse races, my vision blurs. And then I feel familiar slick magic pouring itself over me like a corrupted oil spill you can never scrub away. The booming voice that follows makes my stomach turn. "And so, the prodigal child returns! It's a pleasure to see you again, my Blood Seer."

Faustus stands before me with his slicked-back hair and hollow, soulless eyes.

"I wish I could say the same, fuckhead. But I'm underwhelmed by your presence as usual. Do you mind telling me why I can't move?" I fire back with a death glare that would impress a basilisk.

I am not a fan of being restrained, and he knows it. The coward, guess he can't fight me one on one. Always playing dirty. They better hope to the sky above and earth below that what they've done to me holds my magic at bay. Because if I sense even one sliver of an opportunity and break free from this spell? I'll rip the veins from their bodies where they stand. And then I'll dance on top of their worthless skulls. My wrath is never-ending.

"Oh, it's a magnificent invention, my dear!" He mocks, and I can tell by the twitch at the side of his mouth that he's enjoying it. "It's rather new. Malefic Grasp, made by the best sorceress in the Shadowlands...."

Faustus prattles on about the grandeur of this spell like a boisterous peacock.

"Are you going to get to the point soon? This is all so painfully dull and unimaginative." I interrupt him intentionally. His smirk returns, and I'm momentarily disappointed. Something has him in an excellent mood today.

I'll just have to try harder to ruin it.

"Ah, yes! The point. It took us several tries to perfect a spell that could immobilize one such as you. The poor subjects we drained; it was quite the ghastly mess! We could have used your help to put them out of their misery, but alas, they suffered." He 'tsks' and shakes his head, leveling the dissatisfied mentor stare at me. As if I'm the one responsible for their fates.

Front-row seats to thirteen years of my life, folks!

This is what Faustus Culpepper is. A sadist. A raging narcissist. A perverse coward who feeds from your insecurities. Warping them inside your brain until they alter your own fucking memories and you don't know who you are anymore. Faustus knows which of my buttons to push, because he's the one who installed them.

"Salvation or Damnation, Genevieve?" Faustus asks. It's another one of what he likes to call our 'sessions'.

I pick salvation, thinking it would free the injured woman from the cell in the Hall of Repentance. I know I'll take her place in that cell for a few days, but I'm willing to pay the price. Faustus smiles, a cruel mockery of genuine kindness, as he raises his hands and brings his power down upon her. Snuffing out her life.

I chose the wrong answer. I killed her. It's all my fault...

I remember when I used to vomit at the sound of his boots coming down the hall. I'd hide in broom closets and pray to the Goddess for the gift of invisibility. Crying, begging, screaming for him to pick someone else. But nobody ever came to save me, and I'd go back to the Gravestone silent. Ashamed to tell anyone.

As a little girl, I remember myself with the softest of hearts. Every cell in my body wept at the thought of someone else in pain. Once upon a time, I felt compelled to heal them all. He took that from me. When I had to learn to save myself, I learned to fight back in other ways. But with every lethal dose of my blood magic, every life-less body laid at my feet, my heart grew colder. Until one day, it turned to stone, and Faustus couldn't hurt me anymore.

The sound of fists hitting skin and screams of pain draw me out of my spiraling thoughts. When my mind comes back from memory lane, I find Ansel beating the ever-loving shit out of The Elder, Niam Blake. And I smile viciously, bringing my eyes back to Faustus for a moment before I return my attention to the scene unfolding before me.

Ansel isn't in wolf form like the rest of his clan. No, he's in his human form. Using his meaty fists as battering rams, pounding Niam's face with savage ferocity. With blood-splattered lips, he smiles with an expression of pure, unfiltered joy. Damn, that's kinda hot! Talk about a Viking wolf! I think I finally understand why he's Lincoln's second in command. I can't hold back the gratified smirk that blooms across my lips. Ansel is anything but soggy cardboard today...

"Miss Graves," Faustus redirects my attention. He's visibly displeased with my lack of reaction to his taunting, but that's just too bad. Isn't it? His days of controlling me are over. This potion won't last forever.

Plus, I have a solid backup plan cooking in this spell-drunk brain of mine.

"Let them go, Faustus. Let them all go, and I'll stay," I look him in the eye, unwavering. I will one hundred percent give myself up. He'll have what he wants, no reason to keep anyone else. I'll figure out how to escape later. Preferably with his head in my backpack as a souvenir.

"Tempting! Where have you hidden my daughter, Miss Graves? Her mother misses her terribly." He brings his gloved hand to his chin.

"Cut the shit, Faustus. You don't want Marlow. You've never given a shit about her a day in her life! And you don't give a damn about Willa either, so don't even try that next. It's me, right? That's what this commotion is all about. Did my daddy dearest send you to fetch me? Good boy!" I scoff. "Maybe he'll offer you a treat?"

I cannot stop the sarcasm from pouring out of my mouth. It's a lifelong struggle. But I know I've hit my target when Faustus stares at me, one lip curled in restrained fury.

"You may be correct, Miss Graves. We need you for... other purposes. But they gave no such instructions regarding your friends. Isn't that right, Mr. Blackwood?" the satisfaction in his eyes has me screaming on the inside.

Two giant lion shifters drag a battered and bleeding Linc into the courtyard by his arms; they stop near Faustus and the remaining Elders, placing him in my direct line of sight. Linc's olive-tinted face is turning a shade of purple with the strength he's exerting against them, but he's injured. And unfortunately, it doesn't look like he's gaining any leverage.

"Viv!!" his eyes go wide with fear when he notices my current predicament.

Yeah, this is bad. I'm going to be honest, short of Faustus accepting my offer and letting the rest of them go. I have no idea how to get out of this. My heart skips, and my skin sweats. Dread swells through my veins. And when Faustus leans forward, I just know something terrible is about to happen.

"Now that we've got the family together for a reunion, let's proceed to the main event!" He looks to Invidia Tamsin and Meredith Bridgewater with a wide grin, his chin lifted high as he bows dramatically, sweeping his arm across a shadowed figure on the stones at his feet. It was a concealment spell. When I look at who was under the shadowy mist, I don't want to believe my eyes.

It's Deacon, on his knees...

I flash my eyes to Linc, who's wearing the same expression as I am—and my body goes rigid. I hold my breath, not wanting to make any sudden movements. The sound of my heartbeat thrashing in my ears overpowers the urge to scream. Instead, I clench my jaw. This has gone far enough.

"I said. I surrender." I feel it would be better not to blink. If I don't blink, Deacon is right here in front of my eyes. He's bloodied and beaten, and in terrible shape. But I can see him.

I think I may have a heart attack.

"You will not!" Deacon raises his head and speaks, despite the apparent injuries to his face. "No child of mine surrenders, Vivi. Ever."

The look on his face is unyielding, absolute. This is the man who taught me everything I know about survival. The only man I have ever trusted implicitly. And with that, my heart bolsters itself. That is the first time he's acknowledged me as his child. I know I'm not really his daughter, and Linc isn't really his son, but we are a family in all the ways that count. And Deacon's right, we don't give up. We do not surrender.

Okay, old man. All the way to Z...

I take a steadying breath and bite down on my tongue, drawing blood. It's time to test the limits of this immobilization spell. I move my tongue across my lips, smearing a few drops without capturing notice. My lips tingle as I allow a small amount of my blood to trail down my chin, reaching my neck. It tingles there too, so I ever so slightly move my head.

Oh, Faustus... it's wearing off. It befuddled my brain for a few minutes, but I forced it out. My mind is clear, and my limbs won't be frozen much longer. Wait, my mind!!

"Kalliope, can you hear me?" I call out telepathically, "I don't know how this bond works, and I'm pretty sure you've blocked me out, but I'm in trouble, Kalli. That's your nickname, for when we're best friends someday... I'm afraid I'm powerless right now, and I can't find a way out."

Finally, I let my walls down completely, baring my soul. *"I need your help, Kalliope!"*

I've tried for months, and none of my attempts worked. But maybe, just maybe... this time will be different. So, I wait. Moving my eyes across the manicured courtyard. The bushes pruned and plucked into shapes, the fountains, and grand gardens.

"This is a screwed-up situation to happen in such a pretty place. Don't you think?" I do my best to keep stalling him.

"I grow tired of your theatrics, Miss Graves," Faustus grins as he removes his gloves, and what I see underneath them rouses actual horror. His hands are teeming with dark magic, his fingertips stained pitch black.

*What the fuck? That's dark magic, powerful magic...
Mordred's magic.*

He raises his hands into the air, gathering immense power from an unknown source. They pulse and glow. Dark veins slither just under his skin and move to the tips of his fingers—like snakes, winding themselves around branches. And then he lays them on the back of Deacon's neck.

My entire being trembles in fear as Faustus takes that stolen power and directs it into Deacon's skin. Pushing more and more until his body was trembling. Deacon fights the pain as he looks over to me, and then to Lincoln. Locking eyes with us both. So strong, even now. But I see the crack in his armor as a tear slides down his cheek.

"I love you." He mouths, and then Deacon's head falls to the stones in a gut-wrenching smack, and he looks up at me through lifeless eyes...

NOOO!!!!

No!! This isn't real! I refuse to believe this. I think I'm shaking; shudders rack my entire body. My heart plunges itself against my rib cage. I think I'm going to be sick. My vision blurs, narrowing itself down to Deacon's lifeless face. All my surroundings fall away as I stare at the only man I've ever trusted. The only man who's ever shown me unconditional love.

And then I scream.

I scream like my muscles are being separated from the bone. Like a banshee hell bent on destruction. It's a blood-curdling sound that vibrates the earth itself, something wild and untamed. A scream that isn't just my monster, but something else, too. I cry rivers of blood as my power comes rushing back and fills the void inside me with vengeance and unbearable pain.

Bright yellow-green eyes enter my mind. She answered. Kalliope showed up, and she freed me... but it's too late.

As the spell unravels, I drop to my knees on the Academy lawn, and the earth weeps with me. The ground trembles as the water rises between the stones and flows over my hands, mixing with the blood pouring from my eyes. I'm aware of movement and explosions happening all around me, but I don't care.

I scream and scream until my throat hemorrhages and my soul fractures.

CHAPTER SIXTEEN

VIVI

I THRASH, PUNCH, KICK. But it's no use. I'm caught. I can't think straight or see through the haze of murderous wrath coursing through my bones. I am hell on Earth. I am the monster under his bed. I am going to make Faustus pay for this is the way he taught me. Painfully. I am the best executioner there is, and for the first time. I'm going to enjoy it.

It's chaos on all sides, but I have tunnel vision. The only thing I can see is Deacon's lifeless body. My Deacon. He was good; he was A FUCKING HERO!

Was...

Doubling over on myself, I throw up. And suddenly, someone has my hair, holding it to the side, "We have to go now, Kitten."

Killian? It's Killian holding me back from my vengeance? I don't understand. I feel faint, but I'm fighting it. Trying to focus. And then, as my vision comes back, I see the utter destruction of the Academy Courtyard.

It's not as bloody as I was envisioning it to be, but it looks as if a bomb went off. A powerful, uncannily accurate bomb. The part of the Academy that has sustained the most damage just happens to be the steps Faustus and the rest of the Elders were standing on.

This destruction has Killian written all over it.

"Where's Linc?" I fully expected a scowl or a sneer. At least a smart-assed comment, but instead, he looks at me as though I may break.

My pulse spikes. Another wave of nausea hits me like a cannonball, and Killian is right there with a gentle a hand placed on my back.

Not Linc, please. I can't survive that. I can't survive any of this...

"He is with Anise. She's using her Siren gifts to calm him; he's lost control of his bloodlust. Your wolf... I mean, Linc is in expert hands," He replies tenderly.

Who is this man, and what did he do with the Darkest Motherfucker in the Netherworld?

"The witches?" My voice is shaking, and I feel like I'm made of questions. But taking care of my people is distracting me from falling to pieces. I'm a doer, and I'm also terrified that I will have another epic meltdown if I allow any emotion to penetrate the barrier I've just created around my heart.

"You lost four, my love. And six wolves. The rest are safely back at the Abbey with Willa. We arrived as the mayhem was erupting. Like I said, Anise is tending to Lincoln, and Jagger is..."

Did he just say... my love? I don't think he meant to say that. I'm hearing things. My thoughts feel slow, like they're wading through quicksand trying to get to me, but it's a struggle. Everything hurts. Is there something wrong with me? My posture stiffens with the thought.

A powerless Demon Witch from Hell? I'm as good as dead.

Killian was saying something, I think. What was he talking about again? I'm trying to get my brain to cooperate with the rest of my body. It was important... JAGGER!

"Jagger is? You didn't finish your sentence." my stomach does another somersault waiting for Killian's response. But, instead, he stares down at the bloody mess I've made, refusing eye contact.

Why is he taking so long to answer?

Killian finally speaks after what seems like a millennium, which was more realistically only a few seconds. "We came in red-hot and violently, Kitten. I threw my power straight into the front of that building, thinking to take them all out in one fell swoop. But then I saw you, and... well."

Is he stuttering? Mr. Smooth-Talking-Steal-Your-Girl. Stuttering.

Oh my Goddess, his brother is dead.

"I lost him, Vivi," he stammers; the shame rolling off this beautiful man hits me somewhere deep inside. It brings me to my knees. Tears form in the sore recesses of my swollen eyes.

Yes, I still hate him, but nobody deserves this.

I lean in to give him a consoling hug, but he pulls away from me.

He's never pulled away from me...

"I lost Faustus." His shoulders slump, defeat lingering in his aura.

And I slug him straight in his nose!

"Ouch, what the hell Genevieve?" he yells through his fingers as he holds his face.

"I thought Jagger was dead! You asshole! You just did that to me twice. If someone isn't dead, then say that! And say it fast, so people don't think the worst. What the fuck is wrong with you?"

I'm speechless, or the opposite of speechless. I have so many things to say, and none of them are pleasant. But my muscles are screaming, my mouth tastes like someone dumped their compost pile into it, my head hurts, and weirdly—I'm hungry? I must be in shock.

"Vivi, Faustus is free. I didn't get to you in time. Not to save Deacon, and not to kill Faustus and the rest. I didn't protect you. I failed."

Oh, for the love of Hades! I want the asshole Killian back.

"Would you shut up? I'm glad you didn't kill Faustus. That slimy snotling is mine!"

A perplexed expression crosses Killian's face, and just for a moment, the mask drops and I can see him, *really* see him. He's sorry. He wanted to protect me, and he feels responsible for this. And I don't know if it's blood loss, a concussion, or a need for comfort, but my heart swells.

"We really do need to get out of here." Killian pumps the brakes on the sap-fest. Putting his mask firmly back in place, "Can you walk?"

To be transparent, I'm uncertain that I can. But I'd rather be dragged over a bed of baby fire drakes than show any more weakness than I already have. So, I gather all the energy reserves I have left, and I stand, taking a few shaky steps.

Unfortunately, I only make it two feet before I'm doubled over and throwing up what's left in my stomach, which wasn't much in the first place. And then I'm being hoisted off the ground against my will.

"I said I can walk, jackass!"

"I know what you said, and I know what I saw. Sorry to inform you, there seems to be a discrepancy in those two stories. Don't argue, just save up all that sass for later when you can kick my ass," he flashes me that famous smirk I hate and holds me against his chest like precious cargo, my useless legs draped over one of his arms and my head on his shoulder.

I think I like this even less than the sexy mojo. It's disarming.

Killian takes a few more steps towards the vine-covered outer wall. We don't really need to use the front entrance anymore, I suppose. Since (I'm assuming) Jagger created a new 'gate' on his way in. There's an entire section missing. An intrusive thought burst through my exhausted mental haze.

"Deacon!" I squirm in Killian's arms.

We can't leave him lying there like that. He's a Blood Warrior, a good man. He deserves better than this. He deserves the world. He deserves respect! My flames roar to life without warning.

"Whoa there, fire starter! Watch the hair! He's going home to the Netherworld, where he will receive a warrior send-off and eternity with the heroes in Elysium. Everything is taken care of. Rest now, Vivi." Killian reassures me.

"Don't leave his body here, Killian. I'll find out, and I'll kill you." It's not a request. It's a declaration.

"Noted. Now sleep." His voice holds more weight than usual, and it pulls me under.

I'm draped in a blanket of cozy stars.

Spiders, there are spiders on my skin, and it startles me from a blissful sleep. I'm still draped across Killian's arms. And by the sounds of it, here's a hell of disagreement in progress. I want to open my eyes, but I fear they may be swollen shut. I'd also like to move my limbs, but they're currently made of mashed potatoes. So, I take the next best course of action; I relax into Killian's chest and listen.

"That demon is not entering this Abbey!" Willa states.

"He just saved their lives! Willa, you're being unreasonable. Vivi needs medical attention. She needs a healer. Don't do this!" Marlow counters.

"Then he can hand her over, and we'll take it from here." Willa isn't budging. Which I'm not surprised about in the least. She has something serious against demons. It's more than dislike. It's deeper, something that traumatized her. I doubt I'll ever find out what it is.

Killian's chest vibrates across my cheek with a low, menacing growl. "Try to remove her from my arms. I dare you."

"I can fucking take you! Square up, pretty boy." That's Linc. Is he trying to fist fight Killian? Ridiculous.

"Not before I turn you to ashes, bro." Jagger! I missed that voice so much I could cry, but that doesn't mean he can flame broil my friend.

What the fuck is going on?

I'm struggling here, and I want more than anything to take a warm bath and go to bed. It doesn't even have to be a comfortable one. But I need to open my eyes first. If I could just get up, they would stop fighting. But something doesn't feel right; my heart is beating slower than it's supposed to, and the world is spinning. Or Killian is spinning? Someone is spinning. I think I'm going to be sick again.

Whimpering, I turn my head and angle it away from Killian's feet. I guess this is one way to ensure he's no longer attracted to me. I have no clue how many times I've done the stomach Olympics while in his presence today. But it's enough times that as soon as I can move my body? I may join the Witches Protection Program. Mortifying doesn't even come close.

I make another attempt to adjust myself in his arms, and an excruciating pain ricochets throughout every nerve ending. My head falls back, and I convulse.

I think I'm in trouble...

"The potion has a secondary spell. Shit! It's draining her dry! Killian, please. Will you give her to me? You know I won't let anything happen to her. She needs help! Now. You can stand right here, and I'll update you every thirty minutes. Just please! Killian, I'm begging you." Marlow pleads with Tall Dark and Dangerous like my life depends on it.

I'm afraid she might be right.

Marlow's touch warms me from the inside out. I'm safe. Then, as Marlow moves, a sense of overwhelming sadness fills me. And I don't know what I'm thinking? But every instinct is telling me to listen to my gut.

"Let him through," I croak out through my ravaged throat, my voice barely audible.

"Viv! What's the point in wards if we just let the enemy through them?" Linc spouts off at the mouth. Marlow yells something about why he's arguing with his half-dead friend.

It takes all that's left of my energy to say it, and I can't even believe this is about to come out of my mouth. "They're not our enemies. Let them through."

Summoning up the will to move one more time, I drop Linc a weak version of our sign. Three fingers—*Trust me.*

As I feel myself slipping away, I can only hope they'll respect my wishes.

———◦———

The last several days have resembled a bad acid trip. I remember flashes, but it's like someone threw a puzzle on the floor, and I can only see the right-side-up pieces. I can recall Linc brooding next to my bed like an animal guarding its kill. Weird, but whatever. He's got animal instincts he doesn't have control over.

And I remember Marlow's voice, murmuring. I think she was reading a smutty book to me? The words *velvet shaft* and *in my throat* are the only words I remember. But it paints a clear enough picture.

Fucking Marlow, what would I ever do without her? I crack a weak smile at the thought, and someone squeezes my hand. No, not someone. *Him.* I can feel him from miles away, maybe even through other realms and galaxies.

There isn't any mistaking Killian.

Well, I guess they let him in. That, or he destroyed the wards and swaggered through whether they allowed it or not. Either scenario is likely. He's holding my hand though? This is weird.

"Hi," my throat is so sore it comes out as a whisper.

"Hello, Kitten" that silky smooth voice inspires goosebumps everywhere, and awakens my inner vixen. Goddess, I could listen to the sex-on-a-stick voice all day long.

It's too bad I still hate him...

"Turn it off. Stalker," I crack one eye, and try my best to give him the look.

"Genevieve Graves, I have never used my gift of sexual persuasion on you. Not once. So, whatever you feel when you're near me? That's you telling on yourself." He runs a hand through his inky waves and looks at me with a devious grin.

"Bullshit." I scrunch my brows and give him a suspicious glare.

That can't be true. Never? Yeah, fucking right.

Killian leans in close, so close his eyelashes are touching my cheek. For a moment, I think he's going to kiss me, and the tension in this room goes from a five to an eleven. But, instead, he rubs his thumb across my hairline and whispers into my ear, "If I was using my talents, you'd know it, Kitten. I look forward to showing you the difference."

Farewell to another good pair of panties, Godsdammit!

"Why do you call me that?" I'm so tired of telling him not to call me Kitten. He ignores me anyway. So, I might as well find out if he has a reason behind it? Other than irritating the shit out of me.

His eyes light up the most hypnotizing shade of stormy blue. And then he opens his mouth to speak...

"She needs water, you dimwit!" Anise springs on her heels next to me with a glass in her hand, spilling half the contents onto Killian's feet.

Her Siren nature comes in handy sometimes; she may be eccentric, but she's incredibly tuned in to the needs and emotions of others. Come to think of it, if I felt everything all the time, I'd be a little off-center, too. I appreciate her unfiltered nature, though. Nobody could ever be bored near Anise, not in a million years.

Killian's crimson-haired sister elbows him out of the way, and his cheeks turn a charming shade of pink. Then he awkwardly gets up from the chair next to my cot and moves out of her way. Which is the most comical thing I've seen in quite a while! I'm not sure how many people could toss the Dark Prince of the Netherworld and get away with it? But I'm guessing it's a short list.

"Drink," Anise has transferred her attentions to me, and the next thing I know, there's a cup at my lips, and the water is going in. Whether I drink it or breathe, it is my choice, I guess.

Killian snorts in the background, amused.

After I drink an Anise-approved amount of water and eat a few pieces of bread. I'm ready for another round of sleep. But before I can close my eyes, reality creeps up on me. Deacon is gone. Calypso is gone. Rowena is missing and Faustus is still out there, controlling an entire city and using Marlow's mother as his own personal robot. I feel terrible for all the Stepford Wife jokes I've made over the years. If we only knew how close that was to the truth. My emotions begin to surface, and I can feel the depths of sorrow waiting for their turn to rip me apart.

"Where's Jagger?" I change the subject, in the room and in my mind.

Killian bristles at my question, and I cannot for the life of me understand why he acts so bitter when I ask about his brother? I know they're close. Is this just about me? Because that's dumb—I am not attracted to Dragon Boy. Big brother vibes only, even if he has seen my boobs. Twice.

"He's outside training with Alpha Lincoln." the scowl on Killian's face concerns me.

For Linc's safety, I mean. In a way, I understand. Having to see Jagger bond with someone he has a rivalry with? Ouch. But I wish the two of them could knock it off with the pissing contest and just leave each other be.

"Your pretty friend has been watching them all afternoon. Jagger is showing off," Anise adds. "And I've been watching your sexy wolf."

Killian and I exchange a loaded glance.

"I think I'd like to get up now," I say to nobody in particular.

Seconds after I utter the words, Frank winks into existence.

Killian jumps up, ready to kill, and Anise snarls. Grabbing the closest thing to her as a weapon—which is a thermometer. Who am I to judge? If anyone can do some damage with a damn thermometer? It would be Anise.

"Back off," I instruct both Killian and Anise, "He's with me, I'll handle him."

Oh, I'll handle him, alright. I've got a mouth full of unpleasant things I've been dying to set free. And it's Frank's unlucky day.

"Where the fuck have you been?" I can't help myself, and my anger spills over. "I haven't seen you in days. Days! I walked into an ambush. I almost fucking died! Deacon is DEAD. I needed you. Where were you!?"

"She gave me instructions," he says.

"Instructions to abandon me?"

What the fuck is The Dark Goddess playing at?

"No, my Princess. Instructions to locate Kalliope." He says it like he's talking about the weather.

"Why?"

"You know why." Frank replies.

CHAPTER SEVENTEEN

VIVI

AN OVERGROWN GARDEN MADE up of sad-looking grass is where I plant myself, slumped on an old quilt I found in one of the cellars, picking at the ground. I've been here for a while, staring at—I don't know? Nothing, I guess. I can't be inside the Abbey now. Everyone is giving me that 'poor broken Vivi' look. Asking me if I need things. Offering empty condolences. And saying things like... "if you ever need to talk, I'm here."

Ugh, sympathy. Disgusting.

Even Willa! Which is ludicrous and more than a little disappointing. The wicked bitch of Tanglewood Manor hasn't said one rude thing to me since I got back! What kind of crotchety old crone is she if she's gonna go all soft when a tragedy befalls someone? I expected better.

I think I should wander through the stages of grief now. But I don't even know what they are. Denial then acceptance. Some other shit in between? But here's the thing, what good does it do? It won't change anything.

Do you know what gets results? Action.

We need to make a move. Not just any move. A fucking power move! I don't have the time or the emotional capacity to sit around here any longer. I've already wasted too much time and look at what happened. If we had gotten to The Academy sooner. Maybe... maybe... I can't even think of his name without my eyes leaking.

"A penny for your thoughts?" Killian's silky voice holds a hint of taunting.

At least someone can let me be whatever I am right now and not treat me differently. I swear, if he coddles me, too. I'll lose my shit.

"They're not worth that much," I half-heartedly attempt banter.

"I disagree, Kitten."

"Well, it's a good thing I don't give a fuck what you think," I reply. He may have saved my life and possibly Lincoln's, too. But that's not going to make up for all the bullshit he's put me through.

Eventually, we settle into a semi-cordial conversation. I express the urgency of clearing everyone out of the Abbey and coming up with a diabolical plan. I've been thinking. If I'm the chosen one, or whatever the Oracles believe. Then that means they meant me to be what I am. It means I'm an intentional monster. What if the only thing that will get me through this alive is to embrace her?

What if destruction is my destiny?

I don't even realize I'm rambling about all these things out loud until Killian shifts his sitting position. He's been resting here, listening. And part of me wonders if he brain-fucked me again? He says he never has, but I had no intention of telling him a godsdamned thing. This man puts Jedi mind tricks in a whole new category.

Honestly, it feels good to get it out, though. Even if I am spilling my guts to a startlingly attractive liar.

"Anyway, we need to make a power move." I blurt out.

"We?" He grins, and I know something spicy is about to cross those filthy lips of his.

"Don't hassle me about this, Killian! I understand where I messed up, and I know the only path to making them pay is by teaming up. The enemy of my enemy is my friend. Or some shit like that." I stare at him, waiting for I don't know what? Something cocky.

Killian nods as if he's also deep in thought, but he doesn't reply.

"Don't go conjuring any deviant thoughts after I say this, but I have a slightly outlandish idea." his head perks up at that. Maybe demon men aren't so different from the other orders after all?

His famous devilish smirk makes an appearance, revealing a dimple in his left cheek I'd never noticed before. "You've piqued my interest. Go on..."

This is stupid and goes against every one of my instincts, but go big or stay the fuck home, right? What else do I have to lose? Between Faustus and Mordred, they've already taken everything from me.

"What if we pull a 'Can't Buy Me Love' on them?" my cheeks redden at the thought of saying it aloud, giving it life.

"What is this can't buy me love?" he sounds suspicious.

"Seriously? Do you not have access to television in the Addams Family Mansion? It's an old movie I used to watch on repeat. There's this nerdy guy who fake dates the most popular girl in his school."

"You want to go through with the betrothal?" both of his eyebrows raise, and fuck if it's not kind of adorable.

"Slow down, sir! I said they faked it." I roll my eyes and pick at the sad grass. There's no way in hell I'm going to tell him what happens after that. Let's just hope he doesn't decide to find the movie and see for himself.

"You want to fake a marriage?" It isn't a question, it's a statement that I'm pretty sure he's making to himself more than me.

His face is contemplative; I can see the wheels turning in those turquoise eyes. "If Mordred believes you've bonded yourself to me. That our power is combined...."

"He'll be fucking pissed." I finish Killian's sentence, "And when people aren't rational, they do desperate things. Believe me, I know. I'm a professional. An alliance would rattle the Netherworld, and in turn. Faustus. Since he seems to be my sperm donor's rabid pet."

We sit in silence for what seems like forever, both preoccupied with our thoughts about it. For me? I know this is a risky move. It could backfire in a myriad of unpleasant ways. And being fake married to someone I'd rather murder than have breakfast with most days- it's not ideal. And don't even get me started on the pants situation, because keeping them on has been problematic in the past...

But if Faustus thinks I'm the new Demon Queen of the Netherworld? That's an advantage. And if Mordred believes he's lost his chance to enact whatever plan he had in store for me? Even better. It could be a game-changer. All I need to do is put up with this insufferable asshole until they're defeated.

I can do this. Right? I don't trust him, but I don't need to trust him to be fake married. I just have to pretend to be his Queen. How hard can it be?

"You are aware of the Netherling Binding customs?" he eyes me warily.

Um, no. I'm not. I haven't a clue what he's talking about. But it's probably just the usual stand-up, say some vows that we can have Iris or Selene nullify later, and have a ball to introduce the new Queen. Eat, Drink and be Merry type bullshit. No big deal.

Maybe they do like the ancients and watch while the new couple consummate the bonding. That could be an obstacle, but I'm sure there's a way around it. And if there isn't? It's not like he hasn't already screwed me silly. I can take another one for the team, let's be real here. It was mind blowing, and although I'd prefer to keep it PG? I'll do what's necessary.

You know what? I'll have Marlow do some digging into these customs in that fancy Night Fortress library. We'll see what we're dealing with here. And she'll love it! Research is her healthy addiction.

"Yeah, sure. It's fine." I absentmindedly agree with it, and I don't think I've seen his eyes turn quite this shade of an electrical storm before.

I can't tell if he's angry? Horny? Off his meds? But I decide that's not any of my concern. He's a big boy; he can figure out his own shit.

———◦———

Talking about doing something reckless and going through with it are two vastly different things. So, after Killian and I come to an agreement, we thought it was best to call a meeting.

This will go over like crabs in Merlin's beard, but once we explain it, they'll understand. I hope.

Did I just say we again?

Ugh, not even an hour into the fake-it-to-make-it marriage, and it's already we? I question my decision-making skills more and more with each passing day. This is unicorn shit crazy.

Maybe instead of crying and falling into sad girl depression, I grieve by doing the most outlandish thing I can think of? Not that I find this healthy behavior, I'd venture to guess it's a dysfunction of some kind. I'm self-aware! I just don't give a shit anymore. I'd drag my bare ass, *lady bits and all*, across a mountain of firebugs without a lake nearby if it means ending this and having a future with my sister.

Even so, I don't recall ever being as nervous in this office as I am right now. The tension is thick, and I'm feeling smothered by it. Willa sits at the desk; Iris stands next to her. I'm in the chair across from them, and Killian is standing at my back.

This is fucking weird.

And we're waiting on Frank. Go figure.

The anxiety of what we're about to say to everyone is getting the best of me. So, to distract myself, I take in the room. First, by staring at the bookshelf, which doesn't hold my attention for long. Then I made the mistake of observing the inhabitants in the room.

How in the fresh hell did this become my inner circle?

Jagger looks ridiculous trying to fit his hulking frame in the doorway. Marlow is damn near drooling on the decrepit old wooden floor while scandalizing him with her eyeballs. Although, come to think of it, his expression is a mirror of hers. And neither of them has noticed I'm watching...

Holy shit! Dragon Boy and my Bestie Bitch? I mean, I don't *hate* the idea.

Linc has taken up his permanent residence, brooding in corners. It's a thing with him now. Different rooms—same brooding. Except for this time? Anise is sitting on the arm of his chair, sniffing his hair, and asking nonsensical questions.

She's been unpredictable here in the Earth Realm; the sights and sounds overstimulate her, and as a result, we've had a couple of incidents. Nothing too serious, but she tried to bite my pinky off with her razor-sharp teeth while in the cathedral-cafeteria. In her defense, I said pinky swear and held mine out for her to latch on. How was I supposed to know she didn't know what it meant? I'm a Seer, not a mind reader.

But anyway, Marlow and I had to explain that we didn't eat pinky fingers. We twist them together as a sign of a promise. Then she thought I meant to bind her to me! Goddess, it was a whole mess.

But back to the matter at hand. I'm not sure what role Frank is playing in all of this? But it's clear as glass that he's unreliable. Frank may have been 'gifted' to me, but he's loyal to the Dark Goddess, who hasn't shown her cards yet.

Yeah, she's saved my ass a few times and obviously had Frank watching over me for years. So, I don't believe she means me harm. My worry is that she's got her own plans for my future, and I'm done being controlled. By anyone.

"Look, I don't know where the Phantom Wonder is, or if he's even coming. I have this uncanny habit of attracting supernatural creatures who don't listen to a fucking word I say. So, screw it. Let's do this without Frank." I look at Killian, silently asking which one of us is going to light the dynamite?

When he takes too long to give me a sign, my lack of patience kicks in and I blurt it out.

"I'm going to impersonate the next Dark Queen of the Netherworld."

CHAPTER EIGHTEEN

VIVI

THAT WENT OVER AS expected, like a whole dumpster fire! I can't even hear myself think over all the raised voices and arguments breaking out. It's giving me a massive headache. So, I sit in the chair and observe the chaos unfolding.

Linc lost his shit. He didn't even stay to listen; he just got up and shoved his way past Jagger out the door. I guess he's lucky that they've created a bond while I was magic-slapped and unconscious. Because I'm a badass–don't get me wrong, but I don't think I'd be shoving Jagger under any circumstance if I didn't know him. He's a scary-looking sonofabitch.

At least Anise seems excited. She squealed and started bouncing, like she does, talking nonsense about curse breakers and pajamas. I'm not sure where she was going with either of those things, but she's not violently thrashing about and threatening anyone's life with silverware or glass thermometers. So, I think that's a win.

Marlow looks concerned, but not disapproving. She is insisting on coming with me, of course. She doesn't know I already planned on it. I haven't had a moment to get a word in sideways. She's too busy arguing with Willa.

Who is animatedly against the idea? Shocker!! No really, I'm shocked. I kind of thought she'd jump at the chance to be rid of me. Which makes her reaction confusing. I never thought I'd see the day, but I think the old bat might like me a little? Even more bizarrely, I think I like her too.

Ansel and Osric are in a heated debate about whether to follow their alpha outside or stay and listen so they can report back. I'm inner smirking at that because neither of them is going to have the 'honor'...

I plan on hunting the shithead down after this and making him listen to me.

I know he's hurting, too. I'm not the only one who lost Deacon. And I'm not the only one who wants revenge. He's going to need to get the fuck over it, and quickly. Because he's coming with me.

And Ansel too.

I want my personal guard. Not that I don't trust Dante and Bane, or even Jagger, for that matter. But Lilia got to me inside that fortress despite all the precautions. I want MY people in my corner.

And Killian? He's just enjoying the show, aggravating smirk in full effect.

The smug bastard.

"Hey, shitheads!" I interrupt the rumpus room. "You're giving me a headache, and for no reason. It's happening. An alliance is the best course of action, and right now, it's the only option that makes sense and keeps us all alive. So shut the hell up! And let's make some decisions."

Faustus will not wait forever. He knows where we are, and he'll follow through on his threats. Especially now that I've escaped him. Again.

Once everyone stops acting like a lunatic, the planning isn't all that difficult. Only a few scenarios make sense. Either the mixed orders scatter to the winds, and the wolves move. Or we utilize the caves and tunnels that nobody knows about. Amethyst and Sybil have them memorized, as did Iris. And caves are ideally suited for wolves that aren't traveling in search of food. So, it's not a problem.

Not only that, but now that we're all working together and being honest, I've learned that one tunnel comes out into the basement of Tanglewood Mansion.

It may have been Willa and Iris's prison, but the house itself is sentient. It was meant as a means to keep them contained... but the house was willing to listen. It only took a year for Willa and Iris to convince Tanglewood to help them, and it has been repelling Faustus for years.

He won't step foot on the property.

Because, get this, the house has convinced Faustus he'll die inside on the toilet! It sends him mental images of him dead, on the goddess-forsaken shitter!

Mad respect to Willa and Iris. They are way cooler than I thought they were. Sticking it to the man from inside their so-called prison. And smuggling everything from dried herbs to mixed order witches right under his nose too! They'll be fine in the tunnels, and we'll keep in touch.

Marlow is coming with me, Sybil is too. Killian complained when I told him I would not do this without Lincoln, but he didn't say no (he's getting smarter). So, all that's left now is to find Linc and whip his whiny ass into shape! Of course, Ansel will do whatever he's told because he has the personality of an unseasoned crouton. But the way he pounded the absolute shit out of Niam? I want him watching my back. Stale bread or not.

We've got a few hours to pack up, so everyone scatters.

As I'm preparing to do the same, Iris asks me to hang back for a minute. She's looking at the Netherlings in the room now. Jagger is the first to catch on. "I think we're supposed to fuck off for a minute, bro."

Killian looks at me questioningly.

"Iris and I just need to have a little chat, a *private* chat." I urge him to give us a moment. He doesn't look happy, but he nods, and the three of them exit too.

When Iris is sure there's nobody within earshot, she gives me something I didn't even know I needed...

Back before everything went all Nightmare on Elm Street, when I was just a bar tending blood witch slinging drinks and secrets, Deacon was leaving town regularly. Always something secretive, and sometimes he came back home roughed up. I worried he was selling drugs or in an underground fight club. I even thought about following him a time or two. Just to catch him in the act.

Turns out, there was no need.

Deacon is the one who found the mixed orders in whatever city they were hiding in and brought them to safety. To Thornfall. To Iris. He was never a drug dealer or hiding something nefarious. Instead, he was saving lives, and he was so good at it, I never had a clue.

⸺◆⸺

Lincoln Blackwood is a godsdamned toddler! And he's lucky I love him so much because he is a genuine pain in my ass. But, of course, he put up a fight. With every excuse he can find...

Killian is an ass.

I don't disagree.

The Netherworld is dangerous.

I know that.

What about his wolves?

They're already taken care of.

He said everything except what he really wanted to say.

Which is... "I'm jealous, and I don't want to watch you be pretend married to him."

He doesn't have to say it. I don't want to do this either. But it's not about me, or him, or even the Dark Prince of the Netherworld. It's about justice for Deacon and everyone else who's ever been abused by Mordred and his pet psycho, Faustus.

It's bigger than us, and he knows it.

When he finally agrees and leaves to pack his things, I drag my exhausted ass all the way across the estate and into my chamber room where I find Killian sitting on the extremely uncomfortable cot of disaster.

Part of me hopes he got poked right in the balls by a malicious piece of straw, but I'm not surprised to find him here.

"This is where you've been living." Anger seeps through his voice, and I'm once again very confused. I thought we were done with the emotional whiplash. Wasn't he just taking care of me like a nursemaid and acting like a semi-normal person an hour ago? I can't keep up.

"Yep." I don't know what he wants from me, but I don't have the energy to unlock the fucking vault of Mr. Darkside to figure it out.

"You chose this. Over me?" he accuses.

Oh, shit. That is not where I thought he was going with this at all!

But if he wants to go there? Fine.

"No, Killian. YOU chose this. When you lied to me, manipulated me, made me think we were something we are not. Do you want someone to blame? Blame yourself." And then I storm out of my own room.

I was on autopilot, but I ended up here. Again. At the base of a waterfall, staring across the stream. The anticipation of being back at The Night Fortress is wreaking havoc on my insides. I'm excited. I'll never admit it, and I'd call you a liar if you tell anyone, but I am. The Netherworld feels like home, and now I know there's a reason I've been itching to go back. Plus, apart from Prince Dick Fingers, I love the Fortress. And I miss Bronwyn, and Selene. I even miss the Twin Creepers.

But I'm also scared to death.

Again, I'll lie if you tell anyone—but it's true.

The Dark Queen of the Netherworld? Fuck, that's a heavy lie. I know I'll have to say and do things that go against my better nature. I'll become what they meant me to be. A Demon Goddess from Hell in truth. I will if I want to be convincing because the Netherlings aren't like Earthlings. They're a more brutal lot, and if they don't believe us? I'm dead.

That's not the part I'm tense about.

My mind wanders back across the stream, watching this dark angel. He's doing something this time. Those sad gray eyes are staring back, and I know in my gut that he can see me. So, this means the mystery beast-angel guy has been ignoring me. Watching a specific spot in the barrier. Not making any moves to bring it down even though he's hella-full of dark magic.

I can't figure it out, but I guess it doesn't matter. "I'm leaving tonight," I whisper.

That was dumb. But I wanted to say goodbye? He doesn't respond anyway.

Maybe some mysteries are meant to stay unsolved.

Imagine my surprise when I walk back through the doors of the Abbey and find Frank lounging devil-may-care in one of the cathedral window seats. If I thought Lippy was problematic, this is something else entirely. I march past the rows of witches and shifters, stacking their bags, readying to enter the caverns.

"Hello, Princess Genevieve," he smiles.

Oh, for star's sake.

"I imagine you think you're following me to the Netherworld?"

"I don't think I'm following you, Princess. The Goddess demands it." He replies.

"Oh, I just bet she does! You know what I'm going to do there, correct? Does your Dark Goddess know that?"

"The Goddess knows all." He offers another odd smile, and I'm not a hundred percent sure he's working with a full deck of tarot cards today.

Wandering through the corridors for the last time is surreal, not that I'm attached to this place at all. It's just the knowing. A chapter is closing, and whatever comes next is going to alter the course of my life.

After grabbing my bag, which fits everything I own, I make my way back through the corridors and to the cathedral-cafeteria where everyone is gathered. It's on the other side of the Abbey, and my walk kind of resembles a labyrinth. So, I keep turning the wrong way and getting myself lost. When I recognize a tattered painting of, I'm guessing, an old Darkmoor's face. I know I'm close.

I'm rounding the corner, and as I go to take another step, an agonizing screech stops me in my tracks. It's rattling my brain; I think my ears are going to bleed. Pain, so much fucking pain. Whoever said sound can't kill someone is an honest to goddess liar. I can feel it draining my life away. A psychic attack? What in the name of Zeus's community penis is going on!!

Why do random things keep trying to murder me?

"It's the curse, Kitten." Killian's voice cuts through the noise, silencing the brain-piercing screech. "Come on, let's go home."

CHAPTER NINETEEN

BACK TO THE NETHERWORLD

HOME. IT SOUNDS SO foreign in my mind, but it *is* my home. Until I was dragged into the Netherworld by some princely criminals, the closest thing to home I'd ever felt wasn't a place. It was my people. Now two of them are dead, and one is missing. Being here again, a piece of me I didn't know I was missing locks in place. Making me more whole, somehow. Imagine that I find solace in the fucking depths of the most evil realm there is.

My life is a series of fucked up shit, followed by a side of "what the actual hell?" and then washed down with a big gulp of "it can always get worse."

I can't even make this shit up.

Speaking of worse. Color me a dipshit, I guess, but—surprise, the curse is real!

To be fair, it sounded like bullshit. And the possibility of Killian feeling anything of substance for me? Ludicrous. I don't know what triggered the curse, but whatever he felt, I can promise you he doesn't feel it anymore.

The minute we arrive back at The Night Fortress, his mask goes up, and I no longer exist. He avoids me, and when he can't? His ice-cold behavior could freeze out the sun. And I'm supposed to be his Queen, in front of this entire court and somehow make it believable.

There's no way this is going to end well.

So here I am, standing on the balcony of my old rooms. Taking in the smell of apples and... cinnamon bark? Admiring the rust and scarlet-colored leaves on the towering trees. Their oranges, reds, and golds flutter in the breeze. Forests of bursting inferno-colored beauty sprawl before me as far as the eye can see, all the way to the mist-filled Shadowlands.

I'm pretty sure I'm seeing tiny Netherlings pick pumpkins underneath me. My balcony is high up in the Fortress, and from here they look like ants. But I think there's something that resembles a twisted version of a Pumpkin Patch down there. With a concerning petting zoo, and hayrides pulled by Golems? Strange. But there's that soul-deep feeling in the air. It's Fall in the Netherworld. My favorite season.

How in the complete fuck is it Fall in the Netherworld?

My rooms are the same, but also different. I have a television now, and a one cup coffee maker on my bathroom counter. Which makes me wonder about the way magic works in this place? I guess electricity isn't a necessity. Does Killian power the Realm? Or is it someone else? Maybe it's neither. Maybe it's both. I'm not sure that it matters all that much.

The giant four-poster bed is still right where I left it. The deep red walls are the same, although the artwork has changed. Someone painted a rendition of me as a goddess and hung it above my headboard. I can't deny that I'm slightly disturbed by this, and flattered? Unless Killian painted it. In that case, I know just the place to decline his gift.

On fire, in his fancy fucking bathtub...

My closet is a little different now. It's still filled with dresses of every style and color. But the other half of my wardrobe has my jaw dragging on the floor. Leather Pants. Tactical Pants. Tanks. Long sleeve shirts. Boots. And a shitload of weapons! Everything from throwing stars to a bow and arrows.

I don't know whose idea this was, but I could kiss them right now! I bet it was Jagger. And the television in my room with unlimited earth realm channels? I'm gonna say that's a Bronwyn move.

There's an excited bunch of Netherlings downstairs waiting for me to join them (plus two witches and two shifters) for lunch. But I'm exhausted, filthy, and in desperate need of decontamination. Oh, how I missed this tub! And the hot water that's filling it.

After my toe-curling bath, I head to the dresser to unpack my clothes, only to realize there's no room. My entire wardrobe is in these drawers. Like the one from my apartment. I want to be pissed because this is definitely the work of Mr. Stalks-A-Lot, but he can fuck off twice, ask for directions, and then go fornicate himself.

But the clothes!! Ugh, my clothes. I missed them so much! You know what? Screw him. He can think whatever he wants about what me wearing them means. It doesn't mean shit. Except I'm wearing ripped leggings and an oversized Stevie Nicks t-shirt to this lunch. And nobody is going to stop me.

———◆◇◆———

As far as awkward Netherworld meals go, this one is in the top three. They did not prepare me for the absurdity going on underneath this garden terrace.

Jagger and Lincoln mess around and punch each other's shoulders like a pair of high school jocks. Killian is staring at them like he's ready to smite them both where they stand. Marlow is sitting next to Bronwyn but making fuck-me eyes at Jagger. Sybil is watching the Silver Twins, ready to pounce if need be. Anise is drawing disturbing anatomical hearts in a notebook. I end up grabbing the only open seat between Killian and Selene, and when I look up, everyone goes silent.

Way to make it weird, guys! Not embarrassing at all.

"What the hell are you looking at?" I question them.

And it's Selene who speaks, "It's just that... we weren't expecting..."

She glances at Killian; he has nothing to say, so she continues.

"We weren't expecting such an interesting outfit for your first appearance as the future Queen." She's not being judgmental, and I don't take offense.

"Oh. Well, I guess we should come to a compromise. I'll wear the dresses when it's public or formal. And when it's not? I'll wear whatever the fuck I want." I'm not looking at Selene now; I firmly locked my attention on Killian, daring him to tell me no.

Killian levels a glare at me that could peel the feathers off a Griffin, but he doesn't say a word.

"Still being a broody bitch, I see," I say to him.

Linc and Jagger both stifle their chuckles.

"I believe Earthlings use that term for their females. Are you suggesting that I am female, Kitten?" His face is the perfect mask of civility.

Oooh, he's pissed. The more pissed off he is, the more proper he becomes.

I smile, feigning ignorance. And he leans in closer, whispering in my ear. "I can show you how very male I am, *My Queen*. All you have to do is ask."

And then I feel it.

The sleek, erotic effect of Killian's influence. I clamp my knees together, half crossing my legs. I'm going to come right here in front of everyone without him touching me at all! I'm trying to hold back a moan of pleasure and losing the fight when he releases his hold on me.

Well, shit! He really wasn't using Incubus sex magic. Not once.

"Nah, you're definitely a bitch." I shrug, playing it off like I didn't feel a thing.

Jagger straight up snort-laughs, "It's good to have you back, Little Monster!"

"I'm not back."

"Whatever you say," he smiles wide, perfect teeth gleaming. Then he gets up out of his seat and scoops me up in an animated bear hug.

Killian excuses himself from the table and stalks off to eat some small children or torture defenseless animals. Whatever he does in that war room of his.

And the rest of us? We have a decent lunch. A mixture of Earthling and Netherling favorites. So, there were tacos and breaded golden Wapiti. I don't want to know what kind of meat that is, but I also don't want to ask. But there's cheesecake! And something called Mountain Mustard Strudel.

Watching Marlow shamelessly flirt with Jagger is entertaining! I don't think I've ever seen a dragon blush before. Come to think of it? I've never seen a dragon before I met Jagger. But Marlow's filthy mouth is more than he bargained for, I'm sure of it.

It doesn't occur to me that the gardens have changed until we finish eating; hay bales and pumpkins line some fencings. None of the plants are the same, although some of them don't look any less cannibalistic. Now they're just burgundy flowers with fangs and burnt yellow petals that can make you hallucinate.

Interesting. I wonder who did all this?

"How's everything been going?" I ask Bronwyn, just trying to break the ice. It's been a while, and the way I left...

Let's just say I don't know how she feels about me.

"Fine, good!" she answers too fast, and she's acting a bit squirrelly if you ask me.

Jagger's eyes go wide, and he gives her a slight shake of the head, almost like he's saying no. And my suspicion level rises. What's going on here, and why are my Netherling friends acting like weirdos? I look at Dante, who is already staring at me. Probably reading my thoughts.

Are you going to tell me what they're hiding?

He shakes his head...

It's not my information to share, My Queen.

So, who's information, is it? To share.

Bane speaks out loud, "You know who."

Ahh, yet another scheme the Dark Prince doesn't want me privy to. Fantastic! Because we're going to have a conversation about that. The last time I was here, it wasn't willingly. There was a power imbalance, and Killian called all the shots. That will not be happening this time. Fake Queen or no, I will not be blind to what's happening around me. I will not be caught unaware ever again. So, he's just going to have to deal with it.

Happy Pretend *Wife*, Happy Life! Dickface.

After the brief visit with my bizarre inner circle, the exhaustion settles in. I'm still curious, but I am bone tired. It's a tad early to retire for bed, but not so early that it's unreasonable. I need my brain back in full-working mode, and the only thing that's going to reset my body is sleep. So, I excuse myself from the table and make my way back through Castle Grayskull.

It feels liberating to be walking these halls without an escort. Although I better soak it up because when I wake tomorrow morning, I'll have one. And I bet it'll be Ansel, also known as uncooked ramen. No seasonings packet.

Once I make it to my rooms, it doesn't take me long to fall face-first into the illegally soft mattress. I see I've been upgraded, and right now—I'm not going to complain. I didn't hate the Temple of Dusk, and I appreciate the safety it afforded us for the short time it lasted. But they can burn those cots in the fires or Mordor. I won't be sad.

Anyway, I'm already snuggled under a mountain of luxurious blankets when I realize I never got pajamas. Deacon's words echo through my brain, "Never go to bed in the clothes you wore all day, Genevieve. That invites chaos newts into your sheets."

Yeah, Chaos Newts...

I'm pretty sure he was full of shit, but if you hear something all your life? It sticks. Oh, Deacon. I'm not gonna cry. I don't have any saltwater left in me. But I make a silent promise—I'll hunt them down. And they'll never see me coming. I promise.

I'm far too lazy to get up and change my clothes, but I've come up with a compromise. I'll just strip them off from under the covers and pick them up in the morning. I'll have to sleep in the nude, but I'll be asleep. So how would I even notice?

I whip my bra straps off my shoulders, twisting them around, so the clasp is at the front. As the last clutch comes undone, I sigh. There's just something about taking off your bra at the end of the day.

The bra and tank top come off, and I take extra enjoyment whipping them toward the closet. But as they fly through the air, the strap of my bra catches on the handle, and it sways as if to mock me.

You're naked. In the Night Fortress. With you know who, right behind that door.

I decide that I don't care. That's where it stays.

Maybe Killian's like the boogeyman? Because as soon as he enters my thoughts, delicious heat wanders between my toes and twists and strokes up my legs. I whip my eyes to the door between our rooms before he can move his demon heat any further North.

"Are you inside my head?"

"It doesn't take much when you broadcast your thoughts for all to hear." He smirks.

"Well, access denied. I'm tired, Killian. Can we play who's the bigger asshole tomorrow?" I exhale an audible sigh.

Yes, I'm being dramatic. I'm naked under this blanket and he needs to go now.

"I'd like to talk for a moment." He replies. Brandishing his famous... I'm Killian. Look at my sex-on-the-moon face.

Low blow, man. What a dick move.

"Oh, now you want to talk? That's convenient. Is this *the* talk? Am I to be the quiet wifey who does what I'm told and only speaks when I'm spoken to then?" I give him a wide-eyed stare, blinking innocently, "Because I'll scorch my own eyeballs out before that happens."

Killian strides to the edge of my bed, leaning against the frame. He knows what he's doing with his bare-chested abs and low-slung joggers, "Now you're just being facetious, Kitten."

"No shit!"

He leans closer, his hand brushing my hard nipple through the blanket. He's on a mission to unnerve me. "If you're not available this evening, then I'd like to have a meeting in the morning if your schedule is clear. After that, we'll be making plans for The Binding."

He has no business using that fuck-me tone of voice while talking about something as mundane as a stupid meeting. I level my eyes at him, "It's not a real binding. How much planning could you possibly need?"

He thinks I haven't noticed him inching closer, like that's even possible.

"We have a spectacle to create, Kitten. Do try to conceal your obnoxious side from the rest of the court. It's off-putting."

Ouch! That stung.

"Good talk! I'm sure there's a feeder waiting for you somewhere around here. You can fuck off now. Close the door, please." I dismiss him.

Killian continues to bend down, his face centimeters from mine. "I don't have any feeders, Princess."

Huh? Then how does he plan on feeding? How does he feed? Is he going to feed on me?

Just when I think he's about to kiss me. He places his nose on my forehead, only for a moment. Then he stands up and leaves the room. Closing the door behind him.

Wait, what does that mean? He insults me, and then in a minute he's in my personal space giving me the pussy throbs, and then he ghosts me?

Ugh. What a first class assface!

My temper flares, and before I can help myself, I'm launching the bedside vase at his door. Fuck those flowers. I don't even know if they're from him, but I don't doubt it. Flowers and notes are how he bamboozled his way into my panties the last time I was here.

The sound of the crashing glass has him ripping the door open in frantic alarm. He sees broken glass mixed with water and twisted petals spilled across the floor when he looks down. And a growl vibrates low in his chest as he pins me with a furious stare.

"Whoops, it slipped." I smile, rolling over with my back to him.

He slams the door so hard it rattles the wall, and I drift off into a restful sleep.

CHAPTER TWENTY

VIVI

FRANK IS LOITERING ON the end of my bed when I open my eyes, and the only thing keeping me from throttling his spectral ass is the steaming elixir of life he's holding in his hand. Also known as a heavenly-smelling mocha latte, which I could make myself now, I guess. But hand-delivered coffee tastes better.

"Frank, you are *so* lucky you come bearing gifts! But we need to have a chat, mmkay?" I stare, waiting for a sign that he's catching my drift.

"A chat?" he grins.

"I don't expect you to be next to my side every minute. I have no need for a Velcro buddy attached to my asshole all day long. But what I do need... is to know that you're not playing me for a fool. Or working against my interests behind my back. Do you feel me? So, hand me the coffee! But also, explain the disappearing acts." That seems straightforward to me.

He leans toward me, offering the cup of java. "Ah, yes. That chat!"

Is he going to elaborate? Or what?

"I am a citizen of the Netherworld, as is our Night Goddess. Therefore, I go where I am needed." He replies.

At least, I think that's a reply? I never know with Frank.

"So, let me just get this straight. The Goddess calls on you for... whatever, and that's when you wink out of existence. But when you come back, like now, it's because that is where she wants you to be? I'm just trying to understand the dynamic here; I have trust issues."

"Correct."

"I can accept that. Can I just ask you one thing?"

"You may."

"Does the Goddess of Night want to hurt me, use me, exploit me in any way?" I know it's silly to ask. She's shown no sign of ill intent towards me. But neither did Faustus, at first.

"No, Princess."

My Sight says he's telling the truth. So, I take a deep, steadying breath, "Well, alright then! Follow your stars or whatever, but if you're supposed to be my guardian spirit dude, you better show up the next time I'm knee-deep in murder-y trouble."

Frank throws me a crooked smile and winks out of existence.

Next order of business, Killian wants to have a meeting.

Like, a formal meeting with a business partner, or a private one with someone he's already shared several body parts with? Because I feel like that matters while picking an outfit...

Business. Definitely business. I grab some of the leather pants and a black long-sleeved top. Setting them on the bed and then deciding maybe it would be better to put a few outfits next to each other. You know, just to compare.

Why am I being such a girl about this right now?

A knock on the door brings unexpected relief. I'm overthinking hard. A distraction is what I need! "Come in."

"Morning bitch! You missed breakfast," Marlow tosses a muffin in the air, and I fumble across the fancy flooring to catch it, "Is there a reason you're running around topless with someone's bipolar wardrobe strewn across your bed?"

"Shit. I am topless, aren't I? And Frank was just here!" I hide my face with my hands, shaking my head in violent denial.

Kill me now. I need to get my whole life together.

Marlow sits on the Victorian-looking chair next to my dresser and laughs as I explain the valid reasons for both things. When we get to the part where I threw a vase at the door, she raises her brow. So, of course, my eyes follow her line of sight. Low and behold, the floor is clean. No glass shards or twisted stems in sight. I wonder if that means Killian cleaned it up while I was in a sleep coma, or did he have someone else come do it for him?

Why do I even care?

"How is your first day in the Night Fortress going?" I ask, partly out of a need for some Vivi and Marlow standard bonding time. And partly just to get the subject off Mr. Wet Dreams and Night Terrors.

"No complaints here," she replies, and then sadness tinged her features. "Vivi, how are you doing? Not the bullshit you project to everyone who doesn't know you're not indestructible. Like, how are you really feeling?"

Hurt creeps to the surface. "I don't think I'm very good at feelings, Lowe. I'm so sad it makes me livid. I don't want to lie around and cry or look like the people in the movies with all the casseroles overflowing in their arms. I want revenge. Sometimes it feels like vengeance is the only thing that will ease this pain."

Marlow puts her hand to her chin, eyes glistening with unshed tears, "I understand. I miss him too. And it was... my father did this."

I stand up and pull her into an aggressive hug. She doesn't need to say it for me to read it all over her face. Guilt. She's feeling responsible for this, and I can't deal with that. It's too much.

Now seems like a good time to pull a smooth subject change. "Whew, enough about that! Tell me about Jagger!"

Now it's her turn to blush. I can see the faint pink blooming under her light brown cheeks, and it's sickly adorable. I don't have to ask her twice; she damn near skips to the side of the bed with me and then swan dives onto my mattress, just like we used to do...

"Girl, he is like all my favorite book boyfriends come to life! He's so fucking HOT. Does he have... you know. Have you ever seen him with a woman? I'm no home wrecker, but if he's free? I'll toss my v-card right on daddy dragon's lap!" Her eyes light up like its firefly in mating season, and I almost choke on my latte.

"You're just gonna throw it on his lap, huh? You never told me you had a detachable vagina!" I joke, and we both burst and into riotous laughter! Doubling over and holding our stomachs.

The most inappropriate virgin I have ever known, I swear...

We spend a while catching up, and then she gives me the less exciting updates. Amethyst and Sybil seem cool. They don't trust the Netherlings, so neither of them is okay with using their mixed order magic. Which is weird to me. Is it not? I mean, have they seen the creatures who live here? Everyone is mixed with something. I'll have to talk to them.

Linc is surprisingly chipper, according to Marlow. I'm surprised, but not really, though? It seems like Ansel, Linc, and Jagger are getting along famously. Which I'm sure irritates the shit out of Killian, and that itself would be enough to make Linc pretty dang cheerful.

Speaking of Jagger, as we're just wrapping up our girl-talk session—here he comes, barging through my door like he's never had an ounce of home training in his life. "What's up, Little Monster! You're being paged...."

He cuts himself off mid-sentence when he notices Lowe sprawled across my bedding, using one of my pillows for a headrest.

"Oh, sorry! Um, hi Marlow." He stammers. Goddess, he is so awkward right now! I am going to tease him mercilessly about this later.

"Hey sexy," she smiles, "You can just call me Lowe. You can call me anytime."

Oh, for star's sake! She's going to give this poor man a heart attack.

"Tell Killian I'll be there in a few minutes. We were just finishing up here," I smile, and he nods and quickly dips out.

Someone had to save his goofy ass from trying to come up with a reply to Marlow. I was just being a good wingman. That girl is something else! Plus, I needed him gone. There's one more thing we need to talk about.

That big sexy gothic library is waiting with her name written all over it. Wouldn't it be a shame if she did some extracurricular digging around and stumbled across a few juicy Netherworld secrets?

So, I fill her in on our super-stealthy side quest. Which is... find all the dirt.

Mission Incubastard in full effect!

This spacious, square office is just as pretentious as I expected it to be. Too bad I fucking love it! The floor is carpeted black, and he papered the walls with a tasteful damask print in gray. The furniture is old-world elegant with a hint of modern flare. He has a fainting chair in here! A velvety one. The artwork is interesting, but something tells me that Killian didn't pick out a mural of what appears to be a bacchanalia celebration of debauchery to go behind his desk.

But what do I know? Maybe he did?

I'm so tempted to get up and snoop through his drawers before he gets here. I mean, really, who calls a meeting and then shows up late? But I can feel him near, so, unfortunately, the snooping will have to wait.

Just as I predicted, within two minutes, Killian swaggers through the double doors. Closing them behind him, all scorching sex God and swirling thunderstorm eyeballs.

Oh, so this is a private meeting?

I'm relieved that I decided on the I'll-whoop-your-ass-blindfolded outfit from the tactical clothing side of my closet as an alternative to the titties-out tank top and booty shorts combo I was contemplating.

What? If I'm going to be here a while, they might as well get used to my style. I'm not getting stuffed into those itchy dresses every damned day; I can tell you that! Not this time. But today? I'm glad I have options.

"Good morning, Genevieve," he speaks with lascivious undertones, and despite my inner protests, my hormones riot.

"What's this meeting about, then?" I fidget with my hair. Attempting to pull it off as flippant rather than salivating incubus bait, but I don't think I'm fooling anyone.

Instead of taking the seat behind his massive desk where it would be safer for the both of us, the Dark Prince makes his way to the deep purple velvet couch I've got my backside planted on. He takes a seat on the other end, putting maybe a foot between us. But I'd be more comfortable with, say... a mile?

My brain knows that he's a smooth-talking, shit-spewing liar.

But my body? She's a total dumbass.

"I wanted to go over the rules," he answers effortlessly.

"The rules?" I don't understand what he's getting at. "What do we need rules for, Killian?"

"Everything. For instance, if I move in closer and place my lips at the base of your neck. Will you flinch, or will you play along?" his eyes are smoldering now, and my gaze gravitates towards the bulge in his pants.

Yep, still large and in charge...

Shit! He just caught me checking out his junk.

"What are you playing at right now? I don't see how this warrants a meeting."

"It's simple, Kitten." His voice has turned husky, and his proximity much less friend zone. He slips a hand to my thigh, and even in leather pants and a turtleneck (as covered as I could be without wearing a ski jacket), my insides turn to molten lava.

His lips graze my ear lobe as he continues his sentence, "We're going to have an audience at The Bonding, and our performance cannot disappoint. What I'm asking is, are they going to believe us, Genevieve?"

He trails the tip of his tongue across the edge of my ear, and I suck in an intense breath. The things I want to do to this man are immoral, inappropriate, and quite possibly illegal in some realms. How did I ever think I could pull this off?

Stupid, stupid girl!

I give his chest a good shove, breaking contact.

"Okay. The Rules. How about this? Rule one—if we are alone and nobody is watching? Keep your hands to yourself. And your lips too!"

His mouth twists in a wicked grin. "Fair enough. And when they *are* watching?"

I don't like the way his eyes light up speaking that sentence, the mischievous heathen. But I understand the point he's trying to make. The Netherlings will expect to see us amorous toward one another. And since I'm feeling more than a little sassy myself today, why not give him blue balls as a parting gift?

I smile, pure evil shining in the depths of my lavender eyes as I slide over and straddle him, applying a little pressure to his groin with my thighs. I lean in, running my tongue up his neck as he holds my ass in a possessive squeeze.

I rotate my hips and nip his ear lobe. "When they're watching. I'm your insatiable, filthy-mouthed, Dark. Fucking. Queen."

Killian's breath shudders as he grabs the back of my neck in a firm grasp, bringing his lips perilously close to mine, and growls, "Watch yourself, Kitten. Or I'll say fuck the rules and bend you over that desk. No matter who's watching."

Holy. Shit. I'm going to pass out.

We sit like this, tangled up and unmoving, staring into each other's souls with a mixture of desire and hatred for what feels like several lifetimes. It's the most erotic stalemate I've ever experienced. Until the creaking of a door breaks the tension-filled sex enchantment. Killian smiles, and in one motion he lifts me from his lap and deposits me on the couch. Just as Bronwyn pokes her head into the office.

"I apologize, my Prince. I wouldn't interrupt if it wasn't an emergency." She looks rattled; anxiety rides her energy field like a wild Pegasus. She's scared.

"I understand."

They both look at me with an odd expression, and then Killian tries to excuse himself from the room. Leaving me in the dark once again. But hell no! Not this time. I'm not sitting in this overgrown indoor cemetery locked up ever again. If I'm to be believable as his future Queen? Then I'm going to be included in the decisions.

"Where do you think you're going?" I stop him in his tracks.

"I have an urgent matter to attend to. We'll finish this conversation after dinner," Killian replies.

And that's when I lose all my chill.

"THE FUCK YOU WILL! I'm done being dismissed, Killian. I'm here to play a part. If I'm believable when you want to paw all over me, then I'm also going to be believable in matters of this realm. You want rules? Okay. Rule number two—you do not get to lock me in my pretty tower ever again. I am to be your Future Queen! Fake or otherwise, and you're going to stop hiding things from me."

"It's not safe, Vivi." Bronwyn tries to interject.

"Yes. Another time," Killian agrees, and I don't like the way they're both throwing nerves from their auras as they try to shut me out.

"I said, I'm not staying behind!"

A small crowd has gathered in the doorway now, almost certainly because of all my screeching and cursing, like a deranged sailor.

Marlow, Linc, and Ansel look confused. As well as Amethyst and Sybil.

But the Netherlings? They look worried.

"Dante, Bane? Either of you care to elaborate?"

No response.

My anger is growing into something wild and unchecked, a level that I'm not positive I'll be able to control for much longer without incinerating something. My entire body is humming with destructive power. It feels off. I thought I felt something similar yesterday too, but I was so tired I chalked it up to exhaustion.

"Let her see," it's Jagger that finally has some common sense.

Man, I love that overgrown lizard!

"Let me see what?" I ask.

And I keep asking all the way down the hall and into the training arena, past the new sparring zone, past the magic containment dome, and into a clearing further down the trail.

It's surrounded by hedges and briars.

And in the middle...

No. No, this can't be!

In the middle of the clearing is a smaller dome, and inside is a tempestuous inferno. Snarling and bellowing like something from the depths of the deepest, darkest hellscape. And it's shaped like a cat. Like *my* cat.

"What is this?"

Marlow's hand flies over her mouth in shock. Lincoln looks like he's seen an actual ghost. But Bronwyn, Killian, the Silver Twins, even Jagger... their expressions are entirely different.

"You knew. All of you, and you kept her from me?" I can't keep the hurt from my voice. My heart feels like it's being shredded into strips.

"Let me explain," Killian tries to placate me, "We were going to tell you. But she came back changed. I wanted to be sure we could control her before... and then you left. I couldn't risk her hurting anyone."

"Fuck you!" I fall to my knees, tears flowing.

"He's telling the truth. I was working with her myself. It was always the intention to bring her back to you. She's just not ready yet." Jagger's voice calms me, and in that moment, I realize I trust him.

Jagger is my friend.

"Let her out," I whisper through my body-racking sobs.

"Genevieve, I don't know if that's a smart...." Linc tries to reason with me, but I am far beyond reason now.

"I said. Let. Her. Out!" Violet flames explode from my palms as Calypso whips a flaming tail into the barrier with a thunderous crack.

They're all just standing here as Calypso erupts again and again. Yowling and hissing, throwing herself against the magical barrier holding her in. She's in distress. Can't they see that? Why isn't anyone moving?

"I'm sorry I can't do that. A feral Shadow Cat loose in the Netherworld can do untold damage and harm the Netherlings I've sworn to protect." Killian sounds remorseful but remains firm.

Screw him!

"Fine. Then let me in." I spit back, hatred burning in every word.

"Viv, maybe he's right," Linc intervenes.

Goddess, I never thought I'd see the day that these two would be on the same side of *anything!* Let alone against me.

Wiping the tears from my eyes with my long black sleeve, I climb back up off my knees, and

I start towards the enclosure. They can argue all they want, but there is nothing in this realm or any other that will keep me from her. Changed or not, she is my familiar and I feel her pain as deeply as if it were my own.

"Viv..." Linc warns, and I ignore him.

Reaching the edge of the boundary, I use my magic to test the outer edge. Calypso stills, a low rumble in her chest. She's got me pinned in her sights, tracking my movements. When I determine the barrier isn't going to fry my ass like a chicken strip. I step through, and Lippy crouches.

"She's going to attack!" Jagger shouts.

"Oh, shut up! I told you she's just hungry," I hear Anise's voice as she argues with Jagger, and my stomach swoops at the thought of her knowing, too.

Hypocritical of me? Maybe. I've hidden plenty from all of them, but I can't change the way I feel. Right now, I feel betrayed.

A high-pitched yowl startles me out of my thoughts.

"It's okay Lippy, I'm here. Everything is going to be okay now." I speak out loud, holding back more tears as I inch closer. "I'm here."

Smoke billows from her muzzle, she flicks her flaming tail back and forth, and I crouch close to the ground. Putting my hand out for her to sniff. Calypso takes a few predatory steps forward. I can hear the collective intake of breath behind me, but I don't take my eyes off her.

She stalks closer, and my nerves wobble. Only a little, though. I just hope my gut feeling is accurate. Because I don't want to get my tits burned off, or I suppose at this size she could eat my face off?

Please don't eat my face.

And then I hear her beautiful voice inside my mind... *MINE.*

My hands tremble, and I exhale the breath I didn't know I was holding. Silently thanking the Goddess as I lose control of my composure and collapse under the flood of emotion. A strangled cry escapes my lips as I lunge for her, wrapping my arms around her massive neck. Curling my face into her flaming fur and bawling with relief.

Calypso whines, bunts her head into my shoulder, and then rolls onto the dirt packed ground—knocking me flat on my ass with a bone jarring thump. She huffs, and then she's rolling onto her back demanding tummy rubs, and I oblige.

She's alive! My little spoon. She's here, and she's alive. I might burst from the relief.

After everything I've been through these last few weeks. I've lost so much, been on the verge of giving up. But she's really here! I don't care if she's different now. I don't give a single fuck if she's a zombie cat, or an actual minion for the devil. She could be a mass murderer for all I care. She is mine, and nobody will ever take her from me again.

It's not until I hear sniffling that I remember we have an audience, and when I turn my head, it's tough to stay angry. Who knew that all these big bad monsters had such soft hearts? Marlow is sobbing, of course, but she's not the only one wiping tears from her face. I see a little something on Lincoln's cheek, and Ansel's face is ruddy.

Bronwyn is a mess; her aura is all over the place. Amethyst and Sybil just look puzzled but also moved. Even Anise is affected in her own way.

"Well, I'll be damned!" Jagger exclaims, smiling like a jackass. And I grin back.

I can't bring myself to speak just yet, but my gaze moves to Killian. He's still standing imposingly, and most wouldn't notice the subtle reaction he's giving away. But I do. I detect a hint of pride in his satisfied smirk. And underneath that? Desire.

I'm not ready to make nice, not even close. But I flash a quick head dip in his direction.

I don't have to say it. He knows it's a reluctant *thank you.*

CHAPTER TWENTY ONE

The Night Fortress

HAVING CALYPSO BACK IS surreal. I can't stop staring at her just to be sure she isn't a figment of my imagination. After the entire scene that played out in front of everyone, which I'm not especially proud of, Lippy and I go for a walk around the grounds, away from prying eyes. Much to Linc's dismay, might I add.

This new domineering Alpha thing was a little hot at first, I admit it. But with every instance of him trying to control me? It's quickly wearing off. Now he's just getting on my godsdamned nerves.

Anyway, Calypso and I walk, not doing anything exciting, just content to be together. At one point, we lay down near some unthreatening bushes, ones without teeth or anything that appeared poisonous. It was heart wrenching to tell her what had transpired since that night in the field. It feels like a lifetime ago. When I got to the part about Deacon, I lost my shit again and we mourned him together. This time, without an audience.

In my experience, showing my softer side has always been an invitation for someone to exploit it. Use it against me. I learned at a young age that intimidation and fear are much more powerful, so that's what I became. Intimidating. Someone to fear. The child executioner you don't look at sideways, because she may rip the veins from your body. And I like it that way. I suppose that's one thing I can thank Faustus for. Although, I'll be much more satisfied when I can *"thank"* him in person.

After an emotionally draining afternoon, I ended up falling asleep on Calypso's outstretched belly, and when I wake—Anise is sitting across from us holding a mangled creature that resembles a mixture of a rabbit and a deer. The way its neck is sagging at a ninety-degree angle across her lap makes my stomach turn.

"Grim likes jackalopes," she smiles with those charmingly jagged teeth, picking the dead creature up and offering it to Calypso.

Gross.

"They don't listen to me. 'Anise is disturbed, crazy, invisible,'" she protests. "I told them your Shadow Cat was hungry, and they gave her steak. They cooked it! She likes cake better than that!"

Anise gave Lippy the cake. Somehow, I'm not surprised.

"She'll like this more." Anise cocks her head to the side and throws the fresh carcass in our direction. Lippy nudges me off her and swallows it in two grizzly, sickening bites.

Bleh! You know the cartoons where the characters face turns green at their steaming pile of vegetables? I bet that's what I resemble now. That was unpleasant to watch, but Lippy does seem to enjoy it.

I think Anise is right about a lot more than she gets credit for. It bothers me she's treated like an outcast, and I'm beginning to feel awfully protective. Just because her brain is wired differently doesn't mean she's not a valid person. And yeah, she spews nonsense and sings unsettling songs. Sometimes she wigs out for unseen reasons and goes feral too, but if Anise is crazy? Then she's crazy like a fox. I decide right then and there. The next time I hear one of her brothers coddle her with baby gloves while ignoring what she's trying to say? Someone's getting bitch slapped.

"The wolf has kind eyes, but he doesn't like cake, and he smells strange," Anise randomly divulges.

"Oh?" I'm not sure what to say to that. But as quickly as she hopped subjects from Calypso's eating habits to Linc, she was already on a different thought train.

"It's time for you to come back to the Fortress now."

———◦———

Bringing a flaming jungle cat the size of a small house into the Night Fortress is comical. There are more Netherlings milling about than I've ever seen here before, supernaturals of all orders, and even some I can't readily identify. They are all racing around, rearranging and... decorating? I think.

But when I stroll through the front doors with Calypso, their expressions range from utter fascination to piss-your-pants-terror. I guess Shadow

Cats are rare in all the realms, not just this one. I wonder if she can still shift, or if my little spoon is a permanent jumbo spoon now? If that's the case, sleeping arrangements should be interesting.

I'm assuming all this extra racket is about The Bonding? And a shiver of trepidation climbs up my back. I know this is the best course of action to take down Faustus, and possibly Mordred too—but I can't deny the second thoughts I'm having now that I'm here and seeing it for myself.

Am I a spectacular idiot for doing this? I'm not so sure anymore.

A problem for later, I suppose. I want to check on Marlow's progress before dinner, and I'm not totally acclimated here—some clocks would be nice! But by the looks of the auburn sky outside, I don't think I have much time before I'll be enduring yet another awkward meal at the dining table of horrors.

As I make my way to the grand staircase, a shriek of frustration and a loud crash disrupt the festivities, I turn to see what the hell is going on now, only to be knocked sideways by an exuberant volcano. Grim the Hellhound.

Wait, oh shit. Grim!

I look to Calypso, sending a silent plea to the Gods that I'm not about to witness a supernatural shit show, but to my surprise... she's acting playful. What the fuck is going on around this absolute circus of a castle?! A moment later, the most unlikely pair of flaming demon pets are rough housing on the expensive marble floors.

"Out! I said, outside. You wicked bloodworms!" An orange skinned Brownie with pink hair shouts through the hall.

"Maius!"

"Greetings Princess," she smiles, and I swear I could hug her right now! But I'm not well versed in Brownie customs, and I'm not sure if they considered hugs threats? But goddess, I missed her, I didn't even realize...

Grim and Calypso tear off out the door like two old friends on a hellish crusade, and I shake my head.

Waving to Maius, I make my way to the library where I'm certain I'll find Marlow.

———◆———

If I thought the library at Tanglewood Mansion was awe inspiring? The library at the Night Fortress is literal paradise. Weird to say while standing in the Netherworld, but it really is beautiful. And I don't even like books that much.

I take a moment to admire the glass-domed ceiling, at least ten stories high. Each one with its own balcony and posh sitting area. The mesmerizing chandelier hanging in the middle, glittering like black diamonds. Beautiful, just exquisite.

Marlow is where I thought she would be, surrounded by a stack of books. Pouring over them like they hold all the world's mysteries; which, I suppose they do, if you have the right ones.

I'm surprised to find Amethyst and Sybil at a connecting table with a stack of their own.

"Hey Lowe, Amethyst, Sybil. What's going on here?" I ask, glancing at Marlow with questioning eyes.

I thought this was a secret mission.

"I will never forget this library. It's amazing! I'd stay in the Netherworld forever, just for this library. Sit! We have so much to talk about," she replies, oblivious to my silent questioning.

"Okay, but it's almost time for dinner. And those are formal affairs, so we gotta make it quick." I remind her.

She nods absently, "Do you have any idea what The Binding is, Vivi? Look at this here. It says The Binding is a ritual where you merge souls! You'll stand on mirrors facing each other and let your magic barriers down to each other. They mix and mingle, binding your magic to each other."

Her demeanor is much more frantic now, and the other two mixed order witches look just as stricken. Shit. That's not what I want to hear...

"It says here that the two will become one as flesh and bone. If you don't, the Bonding will not be complete. You know, like BONE. As in boning. Pound town. The horizontal mambo. Fucki..."

"I get the picture, Lowe!" I cut her off before it gets any more X-rated in this elegant library.

"You're going to go through with this, Vivi? I mean. This is deep." She questions.

"I don't see how I have much of a choice. We need this alliance, Lowe. We won't get very far without it. Like it or not, it's our best option." I think I'm saying it as much for myself as I am for her.

I don't want to be soul bound to that fucking prick! I can barely stomach his handsome, chiseled, stupid face right now.

Marlow shakes her head in reluctant agreement, "Okay then, wherever you go, I go."

"Into the thick of it... right?" We both nod, but why does it feel like I'm signing over something I may never get back? Can I trust him to undo this when the time comes?

Goddess, what have I done?

"I found something else," Amethyst speaks up.

Fantastic! Because this wasn't enough fuckery for today.

"Incubus demons have something called a Hypnotic Kiss. They plant it inside your mouth with a... well, a passionate kiss? I think." She opens her mouth to continue, but I cut her off.

"That scheming fucker. It's a tracker, right?" I swear, every time I think there may be a little spark between us, I learn something rage inducing and we're right back at square one.

"Actually, Vivi. You're right, it is a tracker! But more importantly, it's a rarely given gift. An Incubus shares the Hypnotic Kiss with someone they wish to cherish and protect. They can only give once it in their lifetime. Which is a very long time if you're wondering about that. Like, thousands of years and then some." Amethyst corrects me.

I feel like I've been shadow smacked.

It's for protection, and not stalking? He gave me something he can only give once in his lifetime... thousands of years?! I don't understand him. Why would he gift something so special to me?

Sure, he wants to fuck me again. That much is obvious, and he's smoking hot—so sue me if I partake here and there. But that man looks at me like he'd rather cut his own heart out than give a shit about me beyond physical attraction. Most days I'm convinced he'd burn me at the stake himself if I wasn't so useful to him.

This bipolar rollercoaster has officially gone off the rails.

CHAPTER TWENTY TWO

VIVI

I HAVE EVERY DRESS known to Baba Yaga sitting out on this absurdly oversized bed. Are all the beds in this fortress made for orgies? Strike that; I don't want to think about orgies at a time like this. I may be having a mental breakdown. Or an existential crisis. Some type of emotional emergency, that's for sure. I have to go to dinner in a pretty dress. Sit across from the man I love to hate, and I'm losing my shit. I wish Amethyst had never told me about this Hypnotic Kiss of his because I know without a doubt that I received one in that alley. And now I can't stop thinking about why...

Why on Earth Realm would he do something like that? Does he... no. He can't care for me like that. He's a manipulative ass. He lies more than he tells the truth, or not even that! Because he doesn't tell me anything. In the time we've known each other, what have I learned about him? Nothing of substance. He hides who he is; he hides what happens in this fortress. He conceals his thoughts, plans, and schemes.

I know nothing about Killian that I haven't as-
certained on my own. But I can't deny I've seen
the other side of him. Those rare glimpses of
tenderness and even a sense of humor. There's
an entirely different man hidden somewhere in
all that cold posturing shit headed-ness. I've experienced a little of it for myself and it is a thing
of wonder. If that's even a portion of Killian's
affection. What would it be like to have his love?

*No. We're not doing this! You absolute dumb fuck.
We've been there already, remember? And what happened? You got burned, Vivi! Fucking incinerated. You
handed him the matches!*

And yet, here I am. Staring at dresses, unable
to decide how much or how little skin to reveal.
Whether my hair should be up or down. If I'm
going to wear goddess-forsaken makeup! I can't
decide if I want to impress him or rip his throat
out.

Ugh. What is *wrong* with me? Forget this.

I rush to my door, flinging it open to find Ansel.
I know he's my nanny for the evening, and there
he is—standing outside my door looking like a
redheaded Ragnar with the disposition of un-
scented hand soap. It's too bad, really. Such a
handsome man, with not a whole lot going on
between his ears. But I like him, I can't explain
it. Maybe it's because he's uncomplicated? I don't
know. The big oaf has grown on me in the short
time I've known him.

When I need someone? He has my back. And if
he's judging me, he's keeping it to himself.

Just the way I like it.

"Ansel, can you find Bronwyn? I'd like her to
visit my rooms before dinner." I ask politely.

"Yes, Princess," he replies. And it goes over his head, yet again.

Princess. Kitten. Genevieve. None of those is my name.

I am Vivi Graves. Deacon gave that name to me when he took me from Bloodgood Manor and raised me as his own. I don't want to be a princess. I don't want to be anything but Vivi.

But you're about to be crowned a Dark Queen. You'll blow your cover, refusing to accept your title... dummy. Ugh.

"Am I interrupting?" Bronwyn pokes her lilac head through my doorway.

"No, sorry! I just have a lot on my mind, is all. Please, come in. I wanted to talk." And distract myself from the spiraling rabbit hole of kinky fuckery daydreams and self-loathing I'm drowning in, but she doesn't need to know that.

"Yeah, I figured this was coming at some point. Look, there's so much I want to say, but I just want you to know that I don't blame you." She looks at me like I should thank her.

She doesn't blame ME... Wait just a fucking minute! Since when is any of this my fault? Wasn't she the one spying on me at the Gravestone? Working for the Prince, regardless of what that meant for me. We have already been through this. She deceived me. Then she saved me from the chopping block. And I forgave her. What could she blame me for?

I have to control my breathing not to smack her into next week. And to think, I called her here to tell her I forgive her for Calypso. To make amends.

What the shit?

"Okay, thanks, I guess. And I forgive you for not telling me about Lippy." I'm just going to bite my tongue. There's enough tension in this fortress as it is. No need to create more.

"Well, I should get ready for dinner. See you down there?" And with that, Bronwyn dismisses herself.

Well, that didn't go anywhere near how I envisioned it!

I decided on a knee-length black dress and some strappy heels. My hair is down in midnight waves, with a jeweled barrette swiped across one side. I went with minimal makeup, just some mascara, and red lipstick. I couldn't help myself with that choice. Red lipstick is enchanting, you know. Powerful. In the Dark Ages, red lips were a sign of courting the devil. That's what I'm doing now, aren't I? Having dinner with The Dark Prince of the Netherworld. Flirting with Hell itself.

The last time I sat at this infernal table, it wasn't the most enjoyable experience. Killian had just returned from what I now know was a meeting with my father. I stuck my foot in my mouth about aces and holes. Killian walked me back to my rooms, got me hotter and more bothered than I've ever been in my life—and then he rejected me. Oh, and Lilia slit my throat on his expensive sheets.

Such fond memories.

"First order of business as your new Dark Queen, we have got to get a new dining table. This one holds too much evil," I mention as I sway my hips into the room, staring into the blue flames that dance in Killian's eyes.

"Agreed." He doesn't smile; he doesn't give me much of anything, but at least he agrees.

I find my seat across from The Dark Prince, taking in the odd change of events. Who could have ever imagined I'd be at this table again, and with my friends by my side?

If Deacon could see us now, I question what he'd think.

I wish I'd known this was his home, too. I wonder if he ever longed for it like I did while I was away. He must have. How couldn't he? There is something here in this realm that doesn't exist in Thornfall. It doesn't have a name, only a feeling. I can sense the land under my feet. The Netherworld is alive, and it knows me.

Grabbing a plate of unidentifiable fruit and a couple of pieces of French bread, I nibble on a few bites. My nerves work backward. They always have. Most people stress eat, but me? I've never been able to do that. Stress murders my appetite, and I've had so much over the last few months that I'm genuinely surprised I'm not made of bones yet. I reach over to the goblet in front of my placemat and allow a brownie to pour me a glass of wine. "Thank you so much."

I remember to smile and bow my head. However, being served still makes me uncomfortable, even if they enjoy helping.

Everyone appears to be tolerating one another. I wouldn't say they're enjoying each other's company. But nobody is threatening to murder anyone with the cutlery, so we've got that going for us.

I'm looking at you Anise...

Amethyst and Sybil are still a bit of a mystery. It's almost like meeting someone who's been home schooled, and then dragging them to endless parties. Except, the parties are sword fights and adventures in the Netherworld. Living in the catacombs and slinking in the shadows has done a number on these witches. They live in constant fight-or-flight mode, it seems like. I suppose that comes from a lifetime of being hunted.

Killian is looking extra sexy this evening, decked out in black on black. A fitted suit that should be banned in all realms and countries. Drool worthy comes to mind. He's shaved the stubble, and his inky black hair is styled haphazardly, one that reminds me of what it looked like the morning after we... you know what? Something tells me that this show is intentional. But why? That's the real question. Killian does nothing without a motive, and the way he's looking at me right now. I can't tell if that motive includes an all-night hate fuck or a dagger in my back.

"Do you have a deformed penis?" Anise blurts out, looking directly at Lincoln. And I choke on the blackberry wine in my mouth. Linc's face is hilarious! I've never seen his olive-tinted skin so red.

Oh. My. Goddess. Alrighty, we're just gonna talk about cocks at the dinner table...

"I've heard that wolves have dicks almost ten inches long!" she continues.

"Anise, darling. That's not an appropriate dinner table discussion," Killian intervenes gently. How can someone so vile be this tender?

"No, it's okay." Linc speaks up, defending Anise, "It's not knotted if that's what you're asking? Not in human form. It's different in wolf form."

Anise beams, her jagged teeth gleaming as she plays with her crimson hair. She's gorgeous, you know, in a rebellious goth teenager way. Except I'd bet my left titty she's three times as old as me. Maybe more.

And Linc, he's always had the gift of making just about anyone feel valid and safe. I'm happy to see that side of him again. The alpha douche is exhausting, but this? This is my friend. I can tell that he understands Anise and her unique mind. The thought gives me all the warm fuzzies. Killian also looks unexpectedly approving.

So maybe these two can get along after all? Wouldn't that be something?

Amethyst and Sybil giggle quietly, and I fire a glare at them that needs no further explanation. Anise is not to be fucked with. On that, Killian and I agree. They quiet themselves immediately, apologies written all over their faces.

"So, what do you do for fun in the Netherworld?" Marlow interrupts the growing tension, and I love her for it.

"Yeah, Killian. What do you do for fun in this place?" I give him a flirtatious grin.

If you can't beat them? Join them, right? I'll poke the demon. He doesn't scare me.

"Killian doesn't know how to have fun," Anise teases.

"Don't I know it!" I reply, daring him to prove me wrong. I'm playing with fire and I know it, but I'm feeling extra reckless this evening. Bring it, sex demon.

"What do we do for fun? We'll show you! Tomorrow night. It'll be a bonfire celebration of our new Dark King and Queen!" Jagger whoops and sloshes his drink onto the white tablecloth. Giving Marlow a scandalous grin.

"Save a dance for me, witch?" he adds.

Someone has been into the wine this evening. Marlow looks as if the heavens have opened and the angels are singing a Kesha tune, "You can have a dance... the panties straight off this nice ass."

Goddess, help us all!

I agree, my Queen.

Dante pushes into my mind, and I detect the hint of playful mocking in his tone.

Just as I'm about to reply with something witty, Grim and Calypso come bounding through the Great Hall. The sounds of Netherlings shouting and glass shattering follow in their wake.

My eyes dart to Killian, and we both share the same expression. Time to wrap it up! Before they tear the damn fortress down around us. I thought dogs and cats were enemies or something! Only in my screwed-up reality would we have a Shadow Cat the size of a horse, and a wiggly, godsdamned volcano teaming up to terrorize the Netherworld.

Killian does the honors.

"We have much to do tomorrow. I believe that's our cue to retire for the evening." He announces, and I nod in agreement. I think we've all had enough crazy for today.

As our awkward dinner concludes, and everyone scatters for their chambers, I ask Selene to hang back. She's been absent since I've arrived, and I think it's about time I had a heart-to-heart with my new fake mother-in-law.

———◆———

I've never been inside Selene's rooms, but they're just as I pictured them inside my head. Everything is decked out in white or gold. The chairs are made of sandalwood, and the cushions are the softest cream-colored linen. I didn't even know sandalwood came in chair form! I've only seen it pieces to burn during ritual. Her bed is piled with soft pillows and luxurious sheets. Even the crown molding is gold! It's as if the sun exploded and glitter was born in here. The stark opposite of every other room inside this fortress.

We both take a seat, and I don't bother wasting any time. "I assume you know why I'd like to speak with you?"

"Sit, Pretty Girl. I imagine we have many things to discuss." I've missed her warm, inviting aura.

"Are you okay with what Killian and I are doing, Selene?"

"Of course, Genevieve. It was written in the stars before you were born." She continues, "You don't believe that, but it's no matter."

"You understand this marriage is false, though. Right?"

"I understand you wish for it to be, and that my son fights against the stars as well."

Great, she is still on this bizarre matchmaking destiny thing.

Selene and I enjoy a more comfortable conversation for several minutes, talking about other events. Even though she is determined to believe that those damned stars created every circumstance that brought us to this moment... it's still lovely to spend a little time just chatting.

There are so many things I want to know, but it's late. And as much as I'd like to learn about Killian as a child, how she ended up being here, and what she really thought of her husband, it's time to wrap things up.

I came here for a purpose.

"I know what you are, Selene. You're a Goddess, in part. If I had to guess, I'd say you carry the essence of the Goddess of Spring? And your husband, your King? He's the God of the Dead. What Killian will be someday." I'm nervous about saying it, but I'm building up to what I need to ask.

"You're partly correct, Genevieve. I am the descendant of the Goddess of Spring, but my son is already what he was born to be." She replies with a kind smile.

I have no idea what that means, and I'm not sure that I want to ask. So, I don't.

"My sister, Kalliope. Her mother carried the of the Goddess of Love. She's not of the darkness, not fully. She's of the light." My eyes well up, but I manage to hold back the flood of tears aching to be set free.

"She may have been once, but there's no telling what's she's become. Her whole life has been inside the Bone Keep with your father." Selene replies.

"He's not my father. My father is dead."

An uneasy silence fills the room. My sister wasn't meant to be in that place. Mordred has taken something bright, someone pure—and he's broken her. I can't help but think, maybe I was meant to be in her place? But the source of my trepidation isn't about that. It's what I'm going to ask next.

"Selene, who is my mother?"

Her face falls, and all my unspoken fears rise to the surface. Was my mother as evil as Mordred? Am I the product of two unspeakable horrors merging? Are destruction and chaos what I bring in my wake?

"Genevieve, there is so much I wish I could tell you. But the stars have an agenda of their own, and it's best not to interfere with our fates. Your mother's story is a twisting tale; she came to the Netherworld as the Goddess of Deceit. A strong and fearsome woman who sowed lies and stirred controversy wherever she went. Her lust for violence was unmatched until she met your father. Together, they were monstrous. She was a powerful woman indeed. But true to her name, and rather ironically—we were deceived. She was not who she claimed to be." She frowns, and it looks foreign on her sunshine face.

"I don't understand." I meant to sound baffled, but it comes out as a whimper.

Because despite my refusal to acknowledge it, I do understand. Without Rowena, the only person who knows who my mother really was is dead.

CHAPTER TWENTY THREE

KILLIAN

BRINGING GENEVIEVE BACK TO the Netherworld, to this fortress, was a mistake. If I were an intelligent man, I'd let the killing curse take her. And then father would wake, and none of this would be my problem. The curse hasn't come for her since we've arrived. I can hold it at bay if I withdraw. If I'm able to reinforce my walls. If I can convince her she's nothing more than a means to an end.

Selene disagrees, but of course she would. According to my mother... *"Fate comes for everyone. You can't run from it, you can't hideaway, and there's no turning back the dial once you've set it in motion."*

I say, make her hate me, and we solve our problem.

"That's your master plan? Treat her like shit until she hates you." Jagger's disapproving tone irks my nerves.

"Do you have any better ideas?"

"Yeah! I do. Tell her everything and break it together. Like a non-psychotic person would do. But instead, you want to deliver her pain. Like she hasn't had her fill already." Jagger shouts, and I detect actual disgust in his tone.

So, the day has finally come. A woman has placed a wedge between my brother and me. I've read about these things. I've stolen away into Genevieve's rooms while she was missing and watched that dreaded acting machine. Anise became obsessed with a vampire program. Brothers at odds over a woman. It seems I'm living it out in real-time.

"Why do you choose her?" I raise my voice, possessiveness taking over.

"All the magic in all the realms, and still, none of it makes you any wiser. She's a witch, bro! They do spells. Remember?"

"You didn't answer my question." My muscles coil.

"I don't CHOOSE HER! I choose you, and if you'd pull your arrogant head out of your asshole, you'd see that." He raises his voice.

I see how he looks at Genevieve's friend, and I'm inclined to believe that statement, but his actions say differently. He takes her side; he undermines my authority when it comes to her. How is that choosing me? If I tell her everything, the truth, I'll deliver more pain than anyone should endure. I'm choosing the humane. If she hates me, it won't hurt. Her fury will make sure of that, and then she'll be safe.

Selene has her maidens seeking an enchantment, one to combat our generational curse. She assures me they'll find it.

Fuck that. It could take years. Decades. If they ever find anything at all. Does my mother believe that nobody else has searched in all the thousands of years my family line has existed? Nobody has done what she's attempting to do now? I'm still cursed, so they've all failed. Genevieve doesn't have decades. She may not have hours; only the stars can tell.

The Daughter of Oracles. We're fated; that may be true. But the only thing I see fate handing us is a disaster. Her destiny lies elsewhere, of that, I'm sure. We'll defeat those who mean to cause her harm; it won't take long with the alliance. And when all the threats have been removed, I'll bow out.

Genevieve will live a long and happy life. First, she'll defeat her enemies with my help. Then, she'll move on to rule the Bone Keep. Finally, it will be restored, and the Shadowlands will be no more. She'll have eternity to live out her days as she sees fit, and she'll spend them hating me.

"You're an idiot." Jagger shakes his head and exits what was my office, but has been turned into a war room.

"I can live with that."

CHAPTER TWENTY FOUR

OBSIDIAN GROVE

IF YOU HAD ASKED me months ago, would I ever go traipsing through a creepy, fog misted forest trail with a water demon? I'd have looked at you like there were far too many fae flowers in your system. Drugs. Because someone would have to be on them to do this, right? Right. That's what I thought.

Anise babbles on, giving me and the girls a rundown on the dos and don'ts of Obsidian Grove. From what I've gathered so far—stay on the path, eat nothing red or purple. The river next to the grove is beautiful, but if you drink the water, you'll lose your memories.

The Netherworld is a uniquely disturbing place. It seems no matter where you go in this realm, there are no less than twenty-five ways to get yourself killed. And this is where they like to party, huh? Okay.

When in Hell, do as the heathens do. I guess.

From our inexplicably long trek through the dark and eerie trails, I've learned many things.

Some I wish I'd never heard, like what happened in Marlow's room last night, for starters! No, she didn't throw her v-card in daddy dragon's lap. But she may as well have. And we've all heard about it in agonizing detail. I'm not sure I can look at Jagger again without the unwanted visuals.

What else have I discovered?

Well, I've learned that Amethyst is not into males, judging by her fingers being intertwined with Sybils at the moment. The rest was implied by the disgusted looks on both of their faces when Marlow went into detail about the.... um... size and shape of a particular dragon's anatomy.

Like I said, agonizing detail.

Anyway, the Night Fortress is in just one of the six regions of the Netherworld. All of which are under Killian's rule. Save for one, the second-largest, which is now the Shadowlands. The Fields of Immortality border the territories. Smack dab in the middle, meaning—to get to the Shadowlands, you'd have to cross them.

Great. That sounds harmless! Not tempting fate at all.

I wonder how Linc is faring with the menfolk. They'd gone ahead of us ladies to prepare the bonfire while we were "gussying ourselves up." Amethyst's words, not mine. I've never gussied a thing in my life that I know of. I put on a dress, though.

In my defense, when I'd gone digging through my closet (which should really be re-named since it's the size of a small bedroom) among all the long, glittering, ridiculously extravagant gowns. I'd found this little rockabilly number, and it begged me to let it out for the evening.

A black vintage party dress with a halter strap and a plunging neckline that makes my titties look ah-mazing! The top is corset tight, and the bottom flares out into a full circle skirt. Not too long, not too short. This beauty hugs every curve I possess. Which isn't many, so I can use all the help I can get. Plus, it's got cherries printed on it!

How was I to say no to that? Paired with some fishnets and Mary Jane flats and a little lip gloss, I'm feeling positively pin-up-worthy. All I need now is a muscle car and a greaser to chase me around singing the oldies and hip thrusting Elvis style.

"Are we going to be in the Blair Witch Woods for much longer, Anise? Or does this trail end somewhere?" I'm no sissy. I've gone up against some of the most terrifying monstrosities in the realms. Still, something is unnerving about the bare, twisted branches and red-tinted moon that just screams horror movie vibes.

A Blood Moon. And you know what the witches say about those.

Blood on the moon, trouble's coming soon...

I've had enough trouble to last several lifetimes, and if there's more on the horizon? Which I don't doubt for a second that there is, I'd like to have a night of fun before it shows up.

As we round another twisted bend, a large clearing comes into view. It's surrounded by endless groves of haunting-looking trees. Enclosed in its own circular barricade of branches and thorns. They cast shadows in the pitch-black night, illuminated only by the auburn glow of the fire and the dim scarlet hue of the moon.

Ah, so this is why it's called Obsidian Grove.

As promised, the men have outdone themselves. There are scattered quilts in various spots surrounding the fire. Each with its own plate of finger foods and decorative pewter goblets. I'm assuming that's for the celebratory wine? And by the looks of it, they've already begun the celebrating.

Linc and Calypso are chasing each other playfully, Grim hot on both of their heels. Jagger is half-shifted with his magnificent wings on display, flying low to the ground, laughing every time Grim nips Lincoln's ass cheek.

I had no idea Jagger could half-shift, and if Marlow hadn't spoiled every innocent thought, I'd ever had about the loud-mouthed frat boy dragon it would be much more awe-inspiring! But alas, it's not in the cards for me this evening. Because all I can think about now is what other body parts may or may not half-shift.

And now I'm picturing dragon dong again. Godsdammit, Marlow!

It only takes a moment before the familiar delicious heat of Killian's stare warms my insides and heads straight to my core; I don't even have to look behind me. I already know that's where he is. The stars are cruel bastards that way, aren't they? I could feel him in a crowd of thousands – blindfolded and spun in circles.

A deep breath and some inner peace-making are in order before I dare turn to face him, but even when I do, none of it improves my defenses.

Killian's eyes flicker with enticing blue flames, the perfect complement to my violet. I might also mention that the blue jeans and white t-shirt combo are working for him. This infuriating man is a tall, dark-haired tattooed bad-boy dream in plain clothes. He looks like trouble, and I am suddenly feeling eager to be punished. Which is why he should never wear anything like it again, but for tonight. Fuck it. We're supposed to be letting loose. I can pretend the ass-faced Prince of Jerks is a fun-loving heartthrob underneath all that brooding. Right?

He looks like someone dragged him here under threat of force, like the thought of engaging in any type of fun sickens him. So why did he even come if he's going to be a dick all night long? He does a fine job of that up at the Fortress.

I shouldn't be so judgmental of him, I know. His realm is basically falling apart. He's at war with my father. I'm sure some casualties weigh on him. Sometimes I forget that there's more going on in Killian's world than a sassy blood witch who likes to push his buttons.

Fine, I can be the bigger person tonight.

"Hello, Mr. Dark Prince. You look nice." I greet him as I make my way to the quilt. He's sitting on it by himself.

"Did you just compliment me, Kitten? Shall I be flattered or alarmed?" He gives me a lopsided sort-of smirk. And there's that dimple again. It only happens when he half-smiles. Good thing, too, because that dimple has supernatural powers.

"What?! I can be well-mannered. I'm not a totally unrefined woman." I reply, pretending to be offended, "I went to boarding school, you know."

"You were an executioner, at a shit school, with even worse advisors."

Ew, why is he such a grouch? If he keeps this shit up, he'll be in Ansel's territory. Although I don't know that I could ever compare him to a plain bagel. There's nothing plain or unseasoned about Killian. Nothing at all. But his attitude sucks, and I'm about to tell him just how much when Anise bounces her way in front of the bonfire and whistles like a charismatic referee.

I guess the show starting...

"Damsels and Dickheads! The celebration is about to begin. On this gloomy night, under the Blood Moon, we gather around the Bonefire to sanctify the Unholy Union of our true Dark King and Queen. Tonight, we sacrifice the...."

"Come on, Anise, let's just skip to the good part!" Jagger interrupts, and she smiles.

"Yes, let's. Raise your bones!!" she exclaims.

I look to Killian, confusion etched across my forehead. "Bones?"

Instead of giving me an answer, he reaches to his side and hands me what looks to be a jawbone. What the fuck is this? And who does it belong to? I thought we were having a party...

Killian takes notice of my horrified expression and chuckles. He leans in close, brushing his arm across my stomach, and whispers, "Bonefire is a bastardized Earthling term. Here, we follow a different custom. The ancients gathered around the bone fire and gave sacrifices. And as you may have already guessed, that meaning is literal."

"We're lighting bones on fire. So, this is what we're doing for fun?" I question.

"Shh, you're interrupting." He smirks.

"Can you at least tell me whose jaw I'm holding?" I screech-whisper.

"Do you really want to know, Kitten?"

Touché dickface.

I turn my attention back to Anise. That's all the kindness he gets from me tonight. The insufferable ass! My cheeks redden in frustration as I toss the jawbone into the flames and cheer with the rest of the people, who aren't fun suckers. I'm about to get up and leave him to his brooding when Maius appears before us. Holding a tray with a decanter of bubbly liquid. Motioning for me to lift my goblet so she can fill it.

"Ruby Gingies!!" Jagger shouts, lifting his goblet to the sky. The rest of the Netherlings join him in the chant, even Killian—although his celebration chant sounds more like a monotone robot than an excited participant.

What's a Ruby Gingy? Sounds like a sexually transmitted disease.

It's a fae cocktail, Princess. Its effects are like what you might call Absinthe. Euphoria hallucinations inhibitions gone nonexistent. So, note how much you consume.

Oh! So, it's like Fae drunk, but also high. Or maybe just the high part? I thank Dante for the mental heads-up. As I take a small sip, an explosion of all my favorite flavors collides inside my mouth. This shit is potent and dangerous. Yum! I look over to where Marlow is seated, raising my brow at her in question. She looks back and winks at me. A wide smile spreads on her mouth. Lincoln wears a parallel expression as he downs his like a shooter at the bar. Even Ansel partakes. But as I return my gaze back to the looming presence beside me, Killian sets his goblet down on the ground. Untouched.

"You're not going to drink?" I ask, disappointed but not applying any pressure. Maybe he doesn't like them, he could have a valid reason.

Before he answers, if he was even going to answer me at all, Anise skips towards us, giggling. With Linc in tow, looking mesmerized by his own freaking hands. He's sooo basic-bitch wasted, and it's pretty funny!

"Told you Killian doesn't know how to have any fun! Always the responsible one. Lonely and moping. He's never shared a Ruby Gingy with a woman before. Boring!" Anise needles her brother.

Oh really? That is a surprise! I had him pegged for a sexed-up playboy. Scandalizing Netherling women across the realm out of boredom. The more I learn about this mysterious Dark Prince, the more baffling he becomes. First, I discover he no longer has feeders. Now, I find out he hasn't ever been in a relationship? How does that even work, a celibate Incubus? No, it can't be that...

Killian gives his sister an irritated glare, grabs his goblet, and drinks it dry in a fashion that leads me to believe it's out of pure spite.

"No shit! I never thought I'd see the day. Your wild abandon is wearing off on him, Little Monster. I like it!" Jagger stumbles toward us, beaming like the sun.

I very much doubt that, but I see no point in arguing my case.

It's about this time when the effects of the Fae drink hit me. A delectable surge of ecstasy rides my nerve endings, and I fall back on the blanket. Staring up at the cloud-shrouded stars. I've never seen anything so beautiful in my life! Tiny drops of light in a sea of darkness, winking with all the secrets of the universe. I could spend forever here, melting into the void. Blissful and electrified. But I also want to dance. And sing! I want to touch and be touched. I want... I want... everything! As I roll to the side, attempting to get up and explore. A pair of turquoise eyes greet me here on the ground.

Killian lies on his side staring at me like I've stolen the moon, and I giggle. "You're fae drunk."

"You're fascinating." He replies, and heat blooms in my stomach, right next to the herd of feral pixies rioting inside my heart.

My cheeks flush, and in a moment of downright insanity, I lean forward, blinking my eyes and fluttering my lashes on his cheek, "Butterfly Kisses. It's an Earthling thing."

"What does it mean?" he asks, and I've never seen something so heartbreakingly exquisite as the vulnerability in Killian's storm-cloud eyes before.

What does it mean? Good question. I'm not sure why I did it or what it means. Affection, maybe. Attraction, definitely. What does it mean? Who gives a shit? The stars are dancing, and I want to dance too!

"We run the Grove!" I hear a voice shout in the distance, and although I have no clue what that means. It sounds like the best idea ever.

I stand in a line, facing the endless aisles of Netherworld trees. Swaying back and forth, trying to pay attention to the instructions Selene is giving us.

"Obsidian Grove is the home of the Dryads. Divine spirits who inhabit the trees. They are the protectors of our crops and punishers of those who would harm what The Goddess has charged them to defend. Tree Nymphs," she explains.

To me, it sounds like gibberish. I'm a shitty witch. We've established that. I feel like I should know these words, but the only one I recognize is a nymph. I know that word! Nympho. Sex trees? No. That makes little sense.

I look at Killian, taking another sip of the sinfully delicious Ruby Gingy. "You have sex with trees?"

His booming laughter sounds like tantalizing magic.

"No, Kitten. We run the Grove! Slap a tree. And try not to get caught!" he looks thrilled.

As a Blood Witch who carries an earth element, I can't figure out why anyone would want to slap a tree. But as the fresh supply of euphoria hits my stomach, I'm inquisitive.

"On your marks!" Selene shouts, and now I wish I'd been paying attention.

"Ready?" Killian flashes me the brightest of smiles.

I don't know what I'm supposed to be ready for. But I'd follow that smile into a woodchipper at the moment, so I nod. "Ready."

"GO!" Jagger beats Selene to the punch, and then everyone is running down the lanes into the moonlit grove.

I run like the wind is guiding my limbs full force into the chaos. Anise flies past me and slaps a towering oak. The branches are alive! They groan and swipe at Anise as she dodges the blows. Linc isn't so fast on his toes. The branch stretches its twisted finger-like appendages and snatches him into the air. whipping him through the sky as he shouts and laughs. Anise jumps and grabs ahold of his arm, yanking him from the branches as he falls flat on his ass.

Within moments he's back up, running and hollering with glee. "That was awesome!!"

I double over with laughter, trying to catch my breath.

Who knew the Netherworld could be such a blast!

"Oh, Kitten!" Killian calls to me, and I follow the musical sound of his intoxicating voice. It's getting further and further away, but I can feel him. When his voice stops, I find him in a clearing, leaning against a tree that doesn't look the same as the one Linc is in.

"Gotcha!" I call out to him, taunting playfully.

"You most certainly do," he replies, and my heart intends to burst. And then Killian levels a violently sexy grin in my direction, one that makes my knees tremble and my pussy drenched... and then he slaps the massive tree.

What the fuck?

The ground trembles and I can physically *see* the gigantic tree stretch its twisted branches. Oh, my goddess. This one is warming up before it tries to wallop our stupid asses! I burst into a fit of giggles and started dodging.

"You play dirty!" I yell out as I fall to the ground and roll out of the way.

"You have no idea," Killian calls back suggestively, jumping high and narrowly missing a thick branch to the face.

My lady cave is rebelling like never before. Just the sound of his voice is doing it for me. And then, as quickly as the thought crosses my mind. I'm caught. Riotous laughter ensues as I'm tossed this way and that. The branches do indeed have fingers. Because this one has a firm hold on the waistline of my dress! Before I know it, I'm dangling upside down. Black panties and a fishnet-covered ass waving hello for all to see. But as the tree quiets, I realize Killian and I are alone. The shouts and whoops of our friends' sound miles away.

"Genevieve, meet Dindellis." He grins as I continue to hang upside down.

"You dirty cheat!" I giggle. "You didn't tell me they have names or that they listen to you!"

"I'm the Dark Prince of the Netherworld, Kitten. I rule over every living thing in this realm," He replies as Dindellis guides me to the ground.

Killian grabs me by my waist, flipping me right side up. His very skilled fingers brush the outside of my panties, and I shudder. He guides me the rest of the way to the ground, tight against his hard body.

When my feet touch the leaves, we're face to face.

Someone tossed my heart inside a clothes dryer. It tumbles end over end inside my chest. Rampaging with every emotion I could ever feel, all at once. Killian's smoke and jasmine scent envelop me, and it's the most intoxicating thing I've ever experienced. And when he brings his fingers up to trace the edge of my cheek, I melt into him.

This isn't like the other times. There's no raging inferno. No magnet to fight against. Instead, it's just me, him, and the pounding in our chests in time with one another.

"You wreck me," he breathes into my hair as his face nudges closer.

I inhale sharply. I've never felt anything like this. If this is what drugs are like? I wouldn't have spent my life avoiding them.

"So beautiful," he whispers, and his lips move over mine. Slowly, tenderly, like I am the most precious thing in his world. His hands move to the sides of my face, and I kiss him back, letting my walls down, pouring my soul into his.

It's not urgent or rough like we've done before. This is different. This is paradise. His tongue is like velvet, and his touch is ecstasy. His powerful hands move along the base of my neck and land on the back of my head. Holding me in place as he worships my mouth.

I am part of him, and he is part of me. How could I ever believe we weren't written in the stars? We are Night Eternal, a symphony of the divine. They made me for him, just as surely as he waited for me. We're lost in each other, and I don't know how long we've been this way. How we found ourselves on the ground–tangled up, covered in leaves. He holds himself above me as he grazes my breast with his soft lips, and I'm falling into nirvana.

"I want to worship you until I can feel that sweet little pussy clenching around me," Killian breathes into my neck, and I'm in wholehearted agreement with that plan.

But before I can encourage him, the Fae drink retakes hold of me, and I want to dance. I must dance! I'm up and running back to the fire, Killian chasing after me. Where we meet everyone else, joy and harmony ride the air. I look back to Killian, smiling, and he smiles back.

"Frank!" I call out to my ghostly friend, and he winks into existence.

"Hello, Princess," he smiles conspiratorially.

"We need music! May I have my portable stereo?" I steeple my fingers in anticipation.

Within seconds he's gone and back with my music. I grab the pod, sprinkle a little witchcraft, and 'Hot Mess' by Cobra Starship fills the air.

Marlow squeals and runs toward me, shaking her ass and singing along.

The Netherlings showed us their tree slapping party. Now it's our turn. Song after song plays, and we dance like there's no tomorrow. Dua Lipa, Prince, Knee High Fox. All of our booty-shaking favorites. By this time, all the ladies and even Lincoln and Jagger have joined in and made a dancefloor of the clearing.

I'm acutely aware of Killian's eyes on my swaying body. He sits on the quilt—sipping his Gingy. Watching the show with rapt interest it makes me feel powerful. And seen. As the beat drops to Britney's 'Breathe On Me', my body heats up. I move my hips to the beat as I look into his eyes. I rock my hips and run my hands along my chest, down my sides and onto my thighs. Throwing my head back as I sway to the erotic lyrics. Imagining Killian's hands in place of my own as he watches...

When the beat changes again, it's Marlow's time to shine. 'The Twerkulator' is her jam, and she's going off! Bouncing her perfect ass with the beat, mesmerizing Jagger to the point of stupidity. Amethyst and Sybil are dirty dancing with each other like nobody else exists. Even Anise is rocking it, and I can't be sure? But I think I saw Linc take a few extra glances.

This might be the best night of my life!

The music slows, and my favorite track plays... 'Fade into You' by Mazzy Star. My body moves of its own accord, twirling and swaying. Undulating with the stars and the earth, I'm in blissful ecstasy and my soul sings along with the haunting melody.

Warm hands find my hips, and I lean back into a muscled chest. And just like that, Killian and I were sharing a dance. His face is buried in the bend of my neck. I arch my back across the front of his body, and my arms wrap around the back of his neck. It feels like I'm living in a dream with this version of him. The Prince Charming he claimed to be so long ago. In this moment, he's all of that and more...

When my body gives in to exhaustion, I find myself lounging on the quilt. Snacking on fruit and feeling the effects of the Ruby Gingies wearing off. My feet hurt, my legs are sore, and dreams of my bed are the only thing dancing now.

The party is winding down. Several of our friends have retired for the evening, but when I look up—I find Killian stumbling. still under the influence, and I take that as my cue to wrap it up for the evening. I call out to Calypso and Grim, and they both come bounding out of the trees, ready to follow. As I make my way to Killian, he's in worse shape than I thought. I don't know how much more he drank after we came back from the Grove? But by the looks of him, it was a lot.

I maneuver myself under his arm, propping him up.

"Alright, the party's over for you, Sir! Let's get you to bed." I tease.

"Yeahhh for the mmmh bed," he mumbles incoherently.

This should be a hell of a walk...

It took a lot of convincing and even a few pit stops to get back to the Night Fortress, but we make it as the sun comes up. As Killian stumbles through the halls, his incoherent rambling gets more and more bizarre.

"You came to the mph my pa-place and changed my liii- my life!" he hiccups and stumbles as I grab his arm and position myself under it to bolster him up.

"You've had quite the impact on my life too, Killian," I giggle at the ridiculousness of this situation. The Dark Prince, the Ruler of the Freaking Netherworld. Drunk as a skunk on Fae magic and mumbling sweet nothings to the girl he can barely stand.

I did not have this on my BINGO card. Just saying.

When we make it to the doors of his rooms, I'm trying to hold him upright and get the heavy door open simultaneously. Grim and Calypso are at my heels, and I'm kind of on the struggle bus.

Killian grins, and continues with the nonsensical mumbling, "Poison, you... yooooooou're Princess mine... poisonous. My chest."

Okay, then.

When I get the doors opened, and he stumbles in, I realize the doors between our rooms are open. Calypso makes her way to my bed, jumping up and curling around herself. Grim follows—and I know that even with my orgy-sized bed, there's no way I'll fit on it with these two hulking beasts taking up all the available space. Shit. That's gonna be a problem.

Killian is trying to take off his shirt and failing. He's leaned up against his bookshelf, half inside the t-shirt, half out. His arm is at an interesting angle, and it looks to me like he's started a game of Twister and forgotten to invite me.

"Oh, for star's sake! Just sit on the edge of your bed, and I'll help you!" I sigh.

He plops, leaning sideways, and I have to yank him upright to get the shirt up over his head. Then, as I'm lifting his arms, he pins me with that turquoise eyeball magic. "I can't wait to be bound to you. You're beautiful darkness."

Great balls of Jupiter. He does not know what he's saying right now.

"Killian, when is the last time you fed?" I have a sinking feeling it's been too long, and that might be the cause of the predicament he's in.

"I don't feed for annyonne but yooush," he slurs his words again.

Huh? But he hasn't ever fed on me. Does he mean... wait, has he not fed since I left this fortress?! Jagger wouldn't allow that. Right? I don't know how he feeds. But starving himself isn't the answer.

What an absolute dumbass!

I finally have his shirt off, and I attempted his pants—but he's just too wobbly on his feet, and

I've head-butted his dick twice now attempting to pull them down. Plus, I'd already caught a glimpse, and The Dark prince of the Netherworld is not wearing underwear.

Screw it. I put him in bed shirtless, but the pants are staying put. As I lean over him to get his blankets around his left arm, he opens his eyes and smiles at me.

Goddess, this has been a crazy night. And now that I'm sober as can be, my brain is spinning. We crossed a barrier tonight that not even sex could touch. Something far beyond the physical. And I'm not so sure how that happened or why. I'm discombobulated, turned all the way the fuck on, exhausted, and quite frankly about to fall on my face. But my heart, ohh how it's beating for him and only him. I never imagined we'd be in this place, but maybe bonding myself to this charming dark prince isn't the worst fate I can imagine.

When I've got drunky-pants all tucked in, I turn to find somewhere to pass out. Maybe Marlow's rooms? I'll listen at the door first because dragon balls are not on my list of things to see today. But as I blow out the candle at his bedside, Killian grabs my arm. Not hard, but firmly. And he begs, "Don't leave me, Genevieve. Please don't leave me again."

There it goes, what was left of my resolve. You can find it on the floor, in a pile of fucking jelly. This is a bad idea. Killian pulls me into his over-sized bed with and wraps himself around me, as if he expects me to run. Flopping his heavy arm across my mid-section, he nuzzles into my hair. This is top tier strange, and exhilarating, and absolutely terrifying. But how can I deny him now? I relax my muscles and sink into bed with my enemy.

CHAPTER TWENTY FIVE

THE MORNING AFTER

WAKING UP IN THIS enormous bed, covered in the scent of night-blooming jasmine and smoke, under Killian's familiar dark-green bedding feels like a dream. Until an overwhelming sense of dread snakes across my spine, and opening my eyes seems like an awful idea. I can sense it, sense *him*. I don't know why he's angry, but his aura reeks of it.

All aboard the bipolar-express, it was fun while it lasted.

It's hard to crack your eyes open when it feels like you went six rounds with a minotaur. Hungover isn't the correct word. I think I got Fae Punched. In the Earth Realm, this would be hashtag-worthy. Which makes rolling over and facing Sir Pissy-Pants even less appealing, but I can't lay here forever.

Fine.

Let's see what's crawled up Killian's bleached asshole before anyone in the Fortress has even gotten their coffee. I roll to face him, sitting in his sophisticated antique black chair with brass nail head trim. And the wrath in his galaxy eyes knocks the breath out of my throat.

The galaxy eyes. Is it that serious,? Drama King.

"Good morning, Starshine," my scratchy voice is somewhere between fifty-year smoker and prepubescent. "Who pissed in your breakfast smoothie?"

"What are you doing in my bed, Genevieve?" His jaw is clenched, and so are his fists.

"Oh, you know. I thought I'd play Goldilocks and check out your mattress situation? What do you mean, why am I in your bed?"

Umm, maybe because you grabbed me like a caveman and yanked me into it...

"Get out of my bed," He snarls.

My eyebrows spike in genuine surprise. Oh, he's serious? I'm lying here in yesterday's dress, in total shock—just staring at him. Trying to figure out who hurt this man so badly that he's turned himself into an emotionally bankrupt Yo-Yo? I mean, what the actual fuck.

Someone screwed this guy up badly, and I'm paying for it. Fuck that. I'm not his emotional kickboxing ring, or his verbal punching bag, and I'm tiring of being fucked around.

"Is this how little you think of me? What am I to you, Killian? The woman you shared your soul with last night, or just some whore you can drag to your bed and dismiss when it suits you?"

You will not cry, Vivi Graves. Not one fucking tear, do you hear me?

"You're a means to an end." He replies, and my heart shatters.

You stupid bitch, you thought it would be different this time...

One night of Prince Dickface showing basic courtesy, and I think there's something inside him that simply doesn't exist. So, when will I learn that he's rotten all the way through? What's it going to take?

Fuming, I jump up out of his precious orgy bed and stomp past his stupid, dark cherry dresser toward my rooms. There's smoke wafting from my hands, and I think it may come from my nose as well. And when I look down, I realize I've burned my footprints on his precious floor.

Good.

I can't help myself as I hit the threshold to my room, and I spin around—pinning him in *my* stare for once, "No matter how powerful you become, or how many worshippers you have. It will never fill that hole inside you, Killian. You're half a man, barely. And I don't give a fuck what the stars say. You don't deserve me. You never did."

And with that, I close my door and rush into my gigantic bathroom. Shutting that door, too. I pull the dress up over my head like it's burning my skin, and when I can't get the halter untied—I rip it. Tossing it into the marble tiles.

"Frank!!!"

He winks in and doesn't seem the least bit affected by my second-day hair and smudged makeup or the fact that I'm standing in my bra and panties with smoke billowing out of my skin.

"Music, please," my voice cracks.

He nods and produces my pod in his hand out of thin air.

"Leave." I'm holding myself together by one bobby pin and sheer willpower.

As soon as he exits the room, I turn on the water and blast 'Short Dick Man' as loud as it can go. Yeah, you can call me Petty Betty. But the rage and pettiness only get me so far. By the time the song changes, I'm like the leading actress in one of those pathetic movie scenes. The girl sitting on the floor of her shower, trying to keep the sobs quiet with my hands over my mouth.

My official decision is to be a badass tomorrow. Today though, I haven't left my bed. Instead, I've been watching sappy movies and using potato chips as ice cream spoons. A few hours ago, Marlow was worried that I hadn't emerged from my rooms, so she came to check on me. Now she's curled up in the blankets with some sour straws and a bottle of soda. They really can get anything in the Netherworld, and I've decided I don't care to know-how. Only that I appreciate Maius, and as soon as I'm the fake Queen, she's getting a real raise.

Not long after Marlow crashed my pity party, Amethyst and Sybil poked their heads in, saw the dismal scene, and without question—jumped in the bed, grabbed pillows, and started watching Legally Blonde.

It's a girl code thing. When you see a sister in emotional crisis mode, you don't ask questions. Just show up with the junk food and chick flicks. It's called moral support and despite my hard outer shell. I needed it today.

We'd scrounged up two humongous pet beds for Grim and Calypso. Double trouble. They've been chilling on them all day. Well, the opposite of chill, but you know what I mean. I still wonder how fire-based supernaturals can lie on fabrics and not have them go up in a blaze of glory. But I don't know how microwaves work either. They just do. And that seems like a good enough answer.

It wasn't long before the movie credits were rolling across the screen, and the silence was getting to be uncomfortable. Marlow was the first to break the silence.

"You want to talk about it?"

"Not really."

"You want me to shove a hot poker up his ass?" she smiles like a cartoon villain, and I crack a smile.

"Maybe."

"Just say the word," Amethyst and Sybil respond in unison and then look at each other and laugh. I feel that finishing each other's sentences is a common occurrence for those two.

And with that, my thoughts drift to the prick who lives on the other side of the door. Of course, that could be us if he wasn't the Dark Prick of Doucheworld. But he is, and I should consider any hope of that changing self-harm from this point on.

Ugh. How am I going to see this through? Maybe I can be Fae Punched at all hours of the day and night. It would certainly help! Is there a potion that can make me look at a pompous bag of dicks like he's my entire world? Sign me up. Because I will be floored if Killian and I can make it to the finish line of this agreement without my breaking his perfectly sloped nose.

I knew it was only a matter of time before the illusion was shattered, but I still cringed on the inside when a soft knock hits my door.

"Come in," I answer.

"Good afternoon, Princess. The Dark Prince would like to meet with you." It's Ansel.

"The Dark Prince can play hide-and-go-fuck-himself."

"I don't think it was a request, Prin... Vivi." He corrects himself.

Nice save, Ansel! Look who found a little seasoning. I'm proud of him.

Ah, fuck. As far as meeting him. I mean, it's bound to happen, right? I can't gain Netherling backing and lead a badass evil/immortal legion straight up Faustus's asshole if I don't pretend to be Killian's arm candy. And I can't accomplish *that* if I refuse to be in the same room with him.

I guess that means it's time for my big girl panties. But if he thinks I've been a pain in his ass up until this point? He's never met a woman with a broken heart, hell-bent on taking karma into her own hands.

Game on, Killian.

———◇———

I marched my fantastic ass into Killian's office slash-war room with bad bitch energy. Dressed to the nines, hair, makeup, legs for days, and cleavage like whoa. I may be hurting, but the last thing I'll do is let him see it. The Dark Prince is about to meet a whole different side of Vivi Graves, and this one is fluent in Bitchcraft.

"You summoned, my Prince?" I say as I walk through the doors, adding something extra murdery to that last word.

"From now on, you represent The Night Court, and you will dress accordingly," He bites out.

"What's the matter? Is my skirt too short? I thought that's what a pet whore to an Incubus Dickhead... sorry... demon was supposed to look like. My bad." I sneer.

He ignores the jab.

"The Binding will take place in three days."

Great. Three more days until they cuff me to the biggest asshole in the Netherworld.

"Is that all?" I ask, poker face in full effect.

"It isn't." he doesn't even bother to look up while he's speaking to me. "You are to keep your flirtatious interactions with Alpha Lincoln to a minimum while in mixed company. I have a reputation to uphold, and I'll not have allegations leveled against my betrothed days before our binding. You will not embarrass me, Genevieve."

"Are you fucking kidding me? Jealous much. No worries, *Your Highness*, the only filthy hands all over my perfectly mannered ass will be yours."

I whisper the word, *unfortunately,* under my breath.

"What was that?" Killian looks up, flames crackling in his eyes.

"I'm pretty sure you heard me." I retort.

He makes his way across the office in record time, grabbing me by the throat and slamming me into the wall. It's not hard, and it doesn't hurt. But it pisses me off and turns me on a little. I stare him down, not giving an inch. A cruel smile forms on my lips when I say, "Nice try, but I prefer it a little rougher than what you can give me."

Killian growls under his breath. The veins in his neck look like they're about to burst.

I did my job here, so I smile like a gracious hostess and rip myself out of his grip, swaying my hips all the way to the exit. As I'm entering the hallway, I hear a crash and something breakable shattering against the wall.

"You will attend dinner! We have guests arriving!" Killian roars as I stride down the hall.

Oh, I'll be there.

These hallways always get me turned around. It's easy to get lost in this gothic labyrinth. But since I don't seem to have a guard following me around, I take my sweet ass time finding my way back. Wandering through corridors, peeking around doorways. I've always been curious about what goes on around here—now that the Binding is only three days away, why not get acquainted with the Fortress? I'm guessing I'll be here a while.

In all my wandering, I've taken a few too many wrong turns. I know this because the hallway I'm walking down now looks far different from the others. Darker somehow, more sinister. Is this the way to the cellars? I've never been this far into the lower levels.

The smell of incense and something musky permeates the air. I can hear voices and rhythmic music. It's not like the kind I have in my pod. It's haunting, alluring. I round the corner and find myself in a dimly lit den. They draped the walls in cerise velvet. There are hookahs on the tables and mirrors on the ceilings. Women and men in various stages of undress, dancing, grinding, and performing. Some watch, some are doing much more than watching.

As I take a few steps further into a carnal haze, a gorgeous blonde woman in latex shorts approaches, "Your Highness, would you like something to drink? To eat, or... to smoke?"

Your Highness? Goddess, that just sounds all kinds of wrong.

"No, thank you. I'm just..." What am I doing here again?

"I'm only curious about what the Fortress offers."

I think I played that off well. I wonder what she is. I think maybe she's a succubus. Does Killian come here? Is this his type? She's exquisite, and the opposite of me in every way. It makes sense, a succubus could anticipate his needs and satisfy them. Or so I would assume?

I'm not sure I like that idea, judging by the tightness in my chest.

Why do I give a shit again? Oh right, I don't.

There are peculiar statues scattered throughout the room. Their facial expressions intrigue me. Some look to be mid-orgasm, some in the grips of terror. It's as if they were alive at one point, and then I remember Dante and Bane are Gorgons, so the probability of that is high. Weirdly, I'm not bothered by it.

The opulent couches line the room's outer edge, and there's a makeshift stage in the middle, with a foursome? Fivesome? I'm not sure what I'm seeing, other than a spectacular blowjob in progress that I cannot look away from. I feel like I should take notes. Wow! Just holy hotness.

I decide to wander a little further to another set of wrap-around couches. This reminds me of a goth strip club. Or maybe a nightclub that has no rules. A hybrid of both? It's sensory overload, that's what it is. And I'm feeling faint with all the blood rushing to places other than my head, and the all-around atmosphere. So, I find a seat, content to observe. As another stunning topless woman moves from the spot a few seats down from me, I realize she was straddling of one twin.

I'll admit, it's a little awkward.

Killian won't be pleased to see you here, my Queen.

"Like I give a shit, Dante. What is this place? Is this the harem?"

No, darling. It's our playroom, where we feed.

"And what is it you feed on?"

Lust, debauchery... blood.

So, this is what a Gorgon's lair looks like. Hm.

You're not afraid?

That's Bane.

"Why would I be afraid? This is what you need to survive, correct? Just like I need water and sunlight. I'm like a house plant with more complicated emotions, and you're kinda like vampires? But more serpentine?" I reply.

We are not vampires.

Oops, I guess Bane took offense to that. I didn't mean to upset him; I just have a lot to learn about the Netherworld and the supernaturals that reside here.

"I'm sorry, not like a vampire. Like a Gorgon." I smile and scoot down next to them, intrigued.

We sit in rapt silence for a few moments. I suspect they're waiting for me to lose my shit and run out of the room shrieking, but I'm not as fragile as I appear. The public sex isn't as shocking to me as they're assuming. I did work in a supernatural bar for many years! It's not like I haven't seen men going down on each other in the hallway, bathrooms, the alley. Or women.

I'm well versed in depravity, and I have no issue with it. They should give me more credit; I don't know where all these Netherlings got the impression of my innocence and purity? But that is *not* the case. I'm much darker than any of them fancy me to be.

Anyway, I'm here now. I'd been meaning to talk to the twins alone. I didn't picture it to be in a setting like this—but it works just as well as any.

"I didn't search you out on purpose. I think I was drawn here? But I have a few questions if you're not... busy." Okay, so that came out sounding more uneasy than intended. It's not the surroundings, or that Dante has leftover blood on the corner of his mouth. It's what I'm about to ask them that has my nerves on edge.

And so you do.

Bane answers.

"Yeah, um. When I was in the Cove of Myths, I saw an Oracle." Dante's brows raise at the mention of the cavern, "she said all kinds of things that made little sense. Some of them have come to pass in their own way. Some haven't. But in the smoke, I saw an image I'm curious about."

Go on... Dante and Bane both nod with their yellow snakelike eyes trained on me.

"I saw my daggers in the mist, which tell me they're important somehow. I remember Dante telling me they had immense power, made by an ancestor. I was wondering—do you know who?" My eyes move away from the fascinating strip show in front of me and I bring my focus to the silver twins.

Ahh, the daggers. Do you have them both?

Bane questions.

"I do. The Dark Goddess gave me the second dagger back in Thornfall. I didn't recognize her, but now I'm sure it was her." I answer.

"Mordred created the daggers. They're imbued with Dark Magic, Alchemy, Power. If one knows how to unlock them." Dante answers aloud.

Okay, this sounds promising.

"And how do I unlock them?"

"Your magic knows the way."

CHAPTER TWENTY SIX

VIVI

I HAVE NO RESPECT or appreciation for the way Killian told me it was mandatory to be at dinner this evening. But hearing 'we have guests' piqued my interest. Plus, if my friends are down there with these new so-called guests? There's no way in Hades I'm not going to be there with them. Especially after some of the things I've seen in the past twenty-four hours.

Not that the Den of Sexual Diversion that the Silver Twins inhabit upset me. It didn't. But that mixed with Obsidian Grove. The Fields of Immortality. Cannibalistic plants. I can't help but think if those things are a reality here in this idyllic Victorian Goth Paradise. Then what else exists?

I'm not willing to let my friends find out without me.

I've chosen an appropriate number for this evening. It's an off-shoulder, split-thigh evening dress in dark cherry red satin. Guaranteed to knock some socks off and leave some laps feeling a tad 'uncomfortable' under the dining table. One in particular, of course. That's my goal, anyway. The Dark Prince wants to fuck with me? I'll make him wish he'd made better choices.

After this morning and the subsequent afternoon of wallowing in ice cream-filled self-pity, I profoundly realized. I am a whole ass goddess. I am an actual demon. I'm a Blood Witch and a powerful fucking Seer with the gifts of earth, fire, and spirit. I'm trained to fight. I've spent my life as an executioner. I am an assassin! And all I've done is try to hide, change, or deny it. For what? What has that ever gotten me? Kicked around and screwed over. I throw the people I love into endless danger. Or worse, they end up like Deacon. Rowena too.

I always thought I was one tough cookie, you know. A real badass, dangerous girl. But a genuine badass doesn't let anyone play her for a fool. Make her feel small and weak.

I am Vivi Mother Fucking Graves, and I am done being less.

My door cracks open, and Selene glides through, looking like a million dollars and a pocket full of sunbeams. Her golden dress sparkles in the dim light, hugging her curves. As she makes her way into the rooms, she flashes me an approving smile.

"I was wondering when you'd decide to fight back," she muses as she takes a seat next to my vanity. "This is a wild place, as beautiful as it is brutal. I always knew you would be a thing of beauty, Genevieve. Even before you were born, you were destined to rule. To be the true Dark

Queen, this realm needs. I'm pleased to see you've found her."

"Yeah, well. It wasn't any thanks to your jackass of a son. No offense." I don't want to anger her; I only want to be honest.

"None was taken, pretty girl. But I disagree, it seems to me he is precisely the reason," she smiles encouragingly.

I guess she has a point. It's because of Killian that I've hit my bullshit threshold. I mean, not solely because of him. Calypso, Deacon, and a whole host of really fucked up shit brought me to this place mentally, but it was Killian that saw me on the edge of a cliff and shoved me from it.

"My son is a complicated man of little faith. As a child, he was thoughtful. Always doting on his siblings, on me. My King tried to beat that out of him. And he did so, mercilessly. I know every lash that ever marred his skin because I healed them. When that approach didn't work, his father found more persuasive means. He twisted my son, molded him into something sinister." She trails off, lost in her own thoughts...

She moves from the chair and pats it, gesturing for me to sit, and I oblige. She brushes through my long midnight hair, arranging it in soft waves, and I can't deny I've missed this. I imagine this is what it might feel like to have a mother.

"Last night, I saw it. The side of him you're talking about." I whisper, not willing to speak too loudly, letting the silence smother my rage.

Selene nods, listening.

"But this morning, when I woke up. Killian was horrid, cold, devoid of anything redeeming Selene. He was a heartless beast of a man."

I don't know why I confess that to her, but she nods like she understands firsthand what I'm talking about, and an odd grin forms across her coral lips, "You have so much to learn about the males of the Netherworld, Genevieve. There's hope for him yet. But first? Give him hell."

Selene smiles wickedly, a hint of Goddess in her own right peeking through.

"Come, let's show the Dark Prince what he's up against."

Wandering this hallway with Selene brings back some bittersweet memories. The moving pictures on the walls make more sense to me now than they ever have.

The beautiful maiden who loved to be among the flowers, her evil mother always watching, forbidding her from what she loved. And the man with the Dark magic who was obsessed with her, as much as she was with him. I understand how she got so desperate, even desperate enough to find a sorceress and beg to be set free. She's the one who changed the seasons in the Netherworld. Killian's distant ancestor, she chased away the darkness. Just as I suspect, while Selene was in power, the Netherworld was eternal spring. And now? Well, now it's Fall.

I have to believe that has something to do with me. It's my favorite season. It's when I'm the happiest. It's an aesthetic I've always held close to my heart. The jack-o'-lanterns and ghost stories. Black cats and full moons, spell craft, and conjuring. It's the crisp smell of falling leaves and bonfires. But, if I stay here, will it really be eternal fall?

The maiden on the walls paid the price, a terrible one. The very curse that still pulses through Killian's veins. Fall in love, and she dies. Have a child, and it's cursed. Not that I want children. My entire life has been one long horror movie with plot twists-o-plenty. So why would someone like me who murdered on command, tends to be selfish, and is a danger magnet? Why would I want to be a mother?

Anyway, now that I know the curse is real. With every step I take down this impossibly long hallway rings with Selene's words. Curses are made to be broken. Haven't you ever read a fairytale? Terrible price. Made to be broken...

Oh, my goddess. MEANT to be broken!

Selene was trying to tell me something without saying it out loud. An idea forms in my head. What if they can't explain it out loud? What if that's part of it? Which fairytales have curses? Snow White, Cinderella, Sleeping Beauty...

If it could be broken, would I try?

Would I do it for Killian?

Before I could go any further down that rabbit hole and ask Selene any cleverly worded questions, we both heard a commotion. A heated one. We make our way to the dining room to find the beautifully decorated table empty.

The shouting is coming from the Throne Room. We pick up the pace and make our way to the jet-black rug that runs from Killian's onyx throne down the center, under the embellished quilting that swings from the walls, and into the glass-domed center. The room is more full than usual; I guess we really have guests, and I suppose this is what you'd call 'making a scene.' I'm just glad I'm not taking part, wouldn't want to *embarrass my betrothed.*

"She's not fucking going out there by herself!" Linc is roaring, his eyes glow forest green, and claws elongate on his fingers.

"Don't you dare shift inside this throne room, Lincoln!" Marlow threatens, hands up like she's prepared to blast his ass with her water element.

"You're too young to be Alpha, bro. Control your shit!" Jagger isn't helping, but I think he's trying.

What in the fuck-knuckles is happening in crazy town?

"Whoa, whoa! Simmer down. What is going on in here? Why isn't anyone having dinner?" Then, I look to Killian, "I thought it was this whole formal thing."

But they're all ignoring me. As their voices become louder, the apprehension grows more palpable. Something happened, something terrible... The Blood Moon. I knew it!

"HEY, FUCKERS!" I yell, and the echoing hall goes silent as all eyes land on me. It seems more like a 'mouth hung open' because of my dress and titties combo than respect for what I said. But whatever, I'll take it.

"Can someone tell me what's going on? *One* of you. Not everyone at the same time, this place sounds like an open mic night at the Asylum." I add before they all go batshit again.

It's Linc who speaks first. "The guards say there's a man at the gate. He's asking for you, Viv. And only you."

"Well, what does he want? Did anyone ask him?" I reply, not seeing an issue worth screaming at each other about.

"His name is Sylas. He's Dark Fae, with ties to Mordred," Killian responds matter-of-factly. "He did not give my men an explanation, only that he needed to speak to you in private."

"Yeah, also known as ALONE. She's not going out there with a Dark Fae!" Linc starts in again, shaking with rage.

Good, Goddess. Not this again!

"I think she can handle herself," Killian snaps back.

Wait. He does? I can't deny the dip in my stomach at hearing him say those words.

He's a colossal prick; that hasn't changed. But he finds me capable of handling something by myself. Without some knight in shining armor waiting to rescue me? It warms my heart. Lincoln has never given me that. Not even Deacon could give me that. I know it was out of love, but it was also suffocating.

Killian thinks I'm powerful and intelligent enough to do this alone? Sure, it could be for show. There are a few important-looking Netherlings here that I've never seen before. But somehow, it still adds a stitch to my ruined heart.

"I'll go."

"No, you fucking won't!" Linc bites out. "What if he strikes you dead the minute you leave these gates? All because you want to be reckless and stubborn."

I'm tired of this fragile-male-ego-bullshit, and I want my friend back.

"Lincoln Blackwood, I love you. You know I do! But if you don't shut the fuck up, I'm going to punch you in the godsdamned jaw. I'm not reckless or stubborn. I'm not a fucking victim. I am a powerful Demon Goddess from Hell! Your words, remember? And this Dark Fae can do his worst. I'll bet you my precious record collection I come out on top." I lift my dress to an indecent angle, baring my creamy thighs for everyone to see—and the twin moonstone daggers attached to them.

I turn to Killian, whose expression has transformed. His eyes crackle with blue flame, and his body language says something else. He's roving those electric eyes along the fold of my dress, appreciating every inch. Looking at me with pride, possessiveness, and lust mingled together.

Someone must've flipped his switch again!

"How do I get out there?" I tap my foot, waiting for Killian to stop eye fucking me and use his damned words.

"He's waiting outside the North Gate, near the portal." He replies.

"Did you hear him say portal, Vivi? Don't get too close. And don't look at me like that! I know you can kick ass with the greatest of them. I'm just doing my best-friendly duty and telling you to be safe, bitch." Marlow smiles.

If tonight was my big debut, these Netherlings are getting a helluva show. I chuckle to myself as I head for the main doors.

Screw the curse. Screw the rules. Screw all of it.

Meet your new Dark Queen.

———◆———

I'll admit it, walking the grounds of the Night Fortress in the dark, completely alone. It's a little fucking creepy. But the paths I can handle, they're somewhat familiar—although now I know that the curse is live and in living color. So, I'm on the lookout for a rogue asteroid or a malevolent toaster racing toward my head. What a curse, huh? Not knowing what freak-random thing is barreling down the proverbial freeway determined to end your life.

It's maddening.

And the sounds! Why have I never noticed them before? I mean, I guess the only times I've been outdoors at night were a full-on battle and a fae-drunk romp through an enchanted grove. So, there's that. But tonight, it feels more ominous.

Did you really have to pick this moment to assert your feminist badassery?

Yes. Yes, I did.

As soon as my body passes the gates, I feel it. Sorrow, despair. I'm drawn to it, like a silly moth looking for a source of light. Guess I didn't need directions after all. My feet propel me forward, and then suddenly I'm standing in front of a handsome fallen angel... beast... or I guess I know now that he's a Dark Fae. That messy blonde hair, his slate-gray eyes, and the glowing symbols on his arms. Not to mention his mesmerizing presence.

Yeah, there's no mistaking him at all.

"Sylas," I address the beautiful man who sat across the waterfall, "So you do have a name?"

"Princess," his voice is sensuous, overwhelming.

"Actually. It's Queen. But anyway. Here I am, alone. Just like you've requested. Care to tell me why I'm out here in Nightmare on Elm Street meets Sleepy Hollow? When we could have done this at the waterfall. Goddess knows you had the time." I feel like snark is better than trembling in my fancy heels, so we're going with that.

"Follow me." That voice. Whew, it does something to me.

He turns, and my feet automatically follow. We're nowhere near the portal now, so I guess that's a good sign. Of course, there's always the possibility we're headed into a Vivi snare, but I have my plan Z for that.

Too bad I couldn't bring Calypso along, but alone is alone.

Sylas moves just to the side of a mist-covered footbridge. It's hard to tell in the darkness with the clouds overshadowing the moon, but I think we're at the edge of The Shadowlands?

"Hey Casanova, I'll admit you're sexy in that tortured soul kind of way. But if you think I'm going to cross over into The Shadowlands with you? I don't know how to tell you this, but you're seven shades of fucking crazy. Plus, I'd prefer if we keep it casual, you know? It's too early to bring me home to meet your mom."

Humor in the face of scary-ass shit is always the answer. We'll trademark that later.

"I cannot bring her through, Genevieve. I cannot break the treaty." He explains.

And my entire world goes red.

"Her?"

"Your sister needs you now."

CHAPTER TWENTY SEVEN

FOREST OF SHADOWS

FULL DISCLOSURE, I HEARD Sylas say the word *sister,* and everything else was a blur. The fear, the uncertainty, all of it disappeared, and that one word is all that mattered. I crossed that footbridge like a track star with no second thoughts. Mordred could have been waiting for me at the other end, and I would have welcomed it.

As I come skidding to a halt in a vastly different part of the Netherworld. It finally catches up with me, maybe... I should have asked some questions? Because this looks like a scene straight out of Silent Hill. Like the land itself is poisoned and trying to purge itself of the evil that lies beneath it. There are fissures everywhere, leaking a black substance that bubbles up and smells like sulfur.

"You said my sister was here. WHERE? And I swear to the Goddess if you're fucking with me, Sylas. I'll cut your dick off and feed it to my Shadow Cat." I snarl in a clear-cut warning.

"This way," he bristles with dark magic at my threat, but I don't give a shit. I meant every word.

Sylas moves forward into the Land of the Lost, beckoning me to follow, and I take his lead. We only walk for about twenty feet, and he stops. We're standing in front of nothing. Just the edge of a malevolent forest. I look down to see a twisted bramble, full of thorns, and although there should be leaves, flowers, berries—it's just a dead, tangled, prickly heap of thorns. My patience is hanging by a thread, and I'm about to unleash my fury on this shadowed asshole when Sylas waves his hand.

I feel the terrifying power he possesses down to the marrow of my bones. This dude is dangerous with a capital D. Why was I so mesmerized and obsessed with him again? Because right now, that seems a bit psychotic in retrospect.

When he's done rearranging the cosmos, or whatever it is he's just done with that pulsating magic, I spot a compact figure curled in on itself—lying on the ground. He disguised her as part of the scenery to keep her hidden.

Okay, I'll let him keep his dick, I guess.

I almost don't recognize my sister. She's covered in blood, muck, and sweat. The once vibrant girl who gave me the whooping of my life on that battlefield is no longer there. Instead, she's emaciated. Her arms look like they've been broken. One of her legs is mangled. Her stark white hair is full of mud, and her eyes are closed. She isn't moving. Panic seizes my limbs.

"Is she... is she dead?" I'm fighting bile and tears at the same time.

"No, but she is close. You must take her away from here. Move her into Killian's territory. I cannot." He responds. A dapple of worry surrounds his aura.

"Why?"

"Because if I carry Mordred's child across that bridge, it's a declaration of war against him. And I'm here for a different purpose." He replies. "I have other plans for the Bastard of the Shadow Court."

Bastard of the Shadow Court, that has a ring to it.

The rage lurking just underneath the surface of Sylas's power tells me everything I need to know. We're on the same team, and whatever he's come here to do to my father? I won't stand in his way.

We have a moment of understanding between us, and then I remove my heels. Because there's just no way I'm carrying Kalli and getting through the mud with spikes on my feet.

Taking a deep breath, I lean down, putting my hands on my sister's chest, feeling for movement. It's there, but it's faint. Relief overwhelms me, and it takes everything I've got to control the emotions barreling through me.

Hold your shit together Vivi, you can meltdown later! First, you need to get Kalliope the fuck out of here.

Someone hurt her badly, beaten and tortured her nearly to death. We need Selene, and we need her right now. I can feel the clock ticking, the time running out on my sister's life. Fuck that. Fuck the fates, the stars, and anything else that means to take her from me.

Over my dead body...

Crouching down in my beautiful silky dress, I swoop her up and start awkwardly, running back to the mist-covered bridge. I make it only a few steps when I hear a spine-chilling growl, and it

stops me in my tracks. I do not know what kind
of creature that is? But it sounds big. That snarl
promises death.

Sylas doesn't look concerned in the least. Umm,
what kind of monster isn't afraid of death incarnate? He looks at me with those haunting gray
eyes and says, "You must go, Genevieve. I'll hold
them off."

I don't know the connection between us or what
kind of relationship he has with Kalli, and I may
never find out, but right now I am more grateful
for this tortured soul than anyone else in all the
realms combined.

"I don't know how to thank you," I admit as my
eyes well up with unshed tears.

"Save her. That will be thanks enough. Now, go!"
Sylas shouts and smacks my ass.

What the...?

But I don't have time to process the 'good game'
butt slap. I have to run. And so I do. I run like hell
is chasing me and I've been bathing in gasoline.
I pump my legs until my chest burns, and I can
barely drag a breath through my ravaged lungs.
It's the most important race of my life, so I don't
stop until I finally see a smattering of red leaves
and the outline of a massive fortress.

As soon as I cross the bridge, I take one more
look behind me to be sure I'm not being followed.
Then, when the coast looks clear, I lay my sister
down in the Netherworld grass and scream, "KIL-
LIAN!!"

His name shouldn't have been the first in my
mind or even on my lips, considering the state
of our relationship. But I don't care about any
of it right now. My only concern is Kalliope's

safety. Even though he's the bane of my existence and possibly the devil himself. Who's been there every time my ass was getting handed to me? Every time they backed me into a corner. Every time my mouth writes a check, I'm not sure my ass can cash. So, who is the biggest, baddest motherfucker this side of that footbridge? Killian.

As I wait for someone to come, I have a moment to look at my broken sister. She seems so small, fragile. Nothing like she did on that battlefield while kicking my ass from Venus to Mars. There's so much blood I can hardly make out her face. Is her nose broken? Her skin is bluish-purple. I put my hand on her chest again, just to be sure she was breathing. Her breaths are shallow, but they're there.

My flames inch toward the surface, ready and begging to destroy someone. *Who did this to her?*

Calypso comes racing into sight like a blazing predator, ready to do some serious fucking damage. And I exhale, instantly feeling safer. Looking past my familiar, I spy Killian and the whole crew not far behind.

"Just hang on, Kalli, do you hear me? You hang on. Don't you fucking die on me! I'll travel to the spirit realm and drag your ass back myself! You hear me? Help is coming." I whisper into her ear.

The adrenaline is wearing off, and fear takes hold. I have tried for so long to reach her. She was there when I needed her the most. But this is not how our story ends. I won't allow it!

"Killian, HURRY!!" The pure terror in my voice startles me. He's coming, I can see him, but he's still so far away.

I don't know what comes over me, but my hands warm to the point of itching. And I know in my gut I can heal with them.

A childhood memory resurfaces, and I remember laying my hands on a cottontail once. A dire wolf had attacked it, and it was in awful shape. My hands itched to touch it, and when I did? The wounds closed.

I don't know how to wield this gift. I've only just remembered I am capable of it. It won't be enough to save Kalliope, but it has to be enough to get her to a more skilled healer. I lay my hands on the sides of her face, pulsing my violet essence into her. I'm trying to stay calm, but I can feel the edge of hysterics peeking at me.

And then Killian is next to me, with a steadying hand on my shoulder.

"I don't know what happened to her! I don't know who did this. I don't know anything except Sylas is a friend to The Night Court, and he's given us a chance to save her life." Of course, I'm rambling, but he understands me.

"I can carry her, but you'll have to let her go." He replies.

Shit.

"I can't move my hands. I think my magic is keeping her heart beating." I stare up at him, willing an answer to fall from the sky.

And in a way? It does. In the form of Calypso and Grim. I take one look at them, and an idea takes shape. "Can you help me lift her onto their backs?"

Kalliope is in the air and gently placed between the two beasts before I can even finish my sentence.

"Let's go," my voice fills with urgency as I prepare to use the last of my energy, keeping up with the double-trouble of nether beasts. "Calypso, Grim... Run!"

And just like that, the four of us are racing to the gates. As soon as we are in earshot of the rest of the crew. Killian calls out orders like a true King, "Jagger! Aerial search. Any threats in the vicinity? Toast them!"

"Bronwyn, find Selene and tell her to get ready. We've got major damage incoming!"

"Anise, where is Anise?" he bellows.

"I'm right here," she calls out from a distance away.

"Ready your gifts. It's time to feed." He looks deadly serious, and she nods.

Feed? On my sister. I think the fuck not.

"No!" I deliver a glare that could melt him to nothing but steam and regret.

"She feeds on pain, Kitten. I'm asking her to be ready to take away Kalliope's pain." He clarifies, as if he can read my mind.

Oh, well... that's fine then.

After what seems like an eternity, we make it to the gates of the Fortress, where chaos ensues. Selene is waiting at the door with a mattress that floats, like in the air, and four women are standing by her side that I've never seen before. All of them radiate light, and instinctively I know they're healers, too.

Killian is barking orders. I hear a dragon's screech outside. Linc is hollering. Calypso is growling. Grim was licking her ear and waving flaming chunks of magma off the back of his tail. Anise is shrieking. Even the twins are standing side by side with looks of horror on their terrifying faces.

When Selene's hands glow white and she places them on Kalli's chest, I feel comfortable enough to remove mine, but not enough to leave her side. So, when they move, I move too. All the way through the dark halls, around every labyrinth corner in this gothic maze, and finally into an infirmary-type bedroom.

And then I watch as they race to her, giving directions, using this herb and that. I watch as they straighten her body to full length, as the horrific state she's in unfolds, as bile rises up my throat at the sight of what they have done to her torso. I watch every horrifying second unfold. I observe what a monster has done to Kalliope, committing it all to memory. Every last scratch.

My beautiful sister, mutilated.

I don't believe my spirit is inside my body now. I can see myself standing at the edge of the mayhem. Unmoving, unblinking. I feel nothing. I hear nothing. The only thing in this room is her limp, broken body, and I cannot. I will not. Look away.

"Vivi...?" a voice breaks through my trance, "You're bleeding."

I don't understand these words.

"Genevieve, we got you a chair. At least sit in it! You're going to fall over and crack your skull."

This noise irritates me.

"She's flown the nest, bro. Nobody's home. Just let her work through this, and I wouldn't touch her if I were you. That bomb is live and ticking."

I watch Kalliope's chest moving in timed intervals. And then a sensation presses into my skin, an essence that pushes against my mind—beckoning me to reconnect.

The room turns a burnt reddish hue, and the scent of lemon verbena tickles my senses. I can feel her now, The Dark Goddess.

"Daughter of Oracles, you've done well, child. She's in safe hands. Kalliope will live. But you must pull your demon back; you are not in control."

I'm not in control...

"That's right. It's time to come back now, Genevieve. The threat has passed."

The threat has passed.

My senses begin to resurface, and as I blink my dry eyes, the room focuses into a better view. It's sterile and plain. There's a pile of bloodied sheets in the far corner, nothing on the Green-tinted walls. Kalliope is on a bed; her clothes have been discarded. Her skin is being washed of filth, careful not to disturb poultices on her wounds. Her breaths are slow and even.

She's okay.

I turn towards the voices behind me, and my eyes are met with stormy turquoise as the pain in my body comes rushing back, and I double over. Then I'm faltering on my feet and headed toward the stone-covered floor.

"Whoa, I got you. Just lean in. You're injured, not badly, but you need to sit and let Selene tend to you." Killian sounds hesitant.

"Okay," I reply.

And a collective sigh fills the room. Linc, Marlow, Ansel, Sybil, Anise, Amethyst, The Twins, Jagger, Calypso, Grim. They're all here.

"I want to sit next to my sister," I hear a chair moving, and I'm placed next to an unconscious Kalliope.

I grab her hand and intertwine our fingers.

CHAPTER TWENTY EIGHT

VIVI

I'M TOLERATING SELENE FUSSING over me, and I don't make a sound when she pulls out the needle and thread—closing the deep wound in my forehead. To be honest, I don't remember how I was injured. It must have been while I was running through the Shadowlands, or possibly when I made it back to the Night Court? Maybe it was a vicious branch? I don't remember much of anything except flashes of pure instinct and adrenaline.

I remember Kalliope's broken body, though, every inch. And what Sylas sacrificed for us. I don't know if I'll ever see him again. But if I do, I am in his debt. I recall Killian catching me as I was about to fall. And my fingers intertwined with my sisters because I'm looking down at them now.

The Dark Goddess was here, and I think she saved me again. I suspect that she had a hand in saving us both. I don't understand why or how. But she's an ancient being; only the stars know why they do the things they do. And maybe the

Oracles? They might, but decoding their riddles is brain-scrambling.

I can't muster the curiosity right now, anyway. If I wasn't holding my sister's hand in the flesh, I'd be face first in a pile of overly expensive pillows and blankets. She showed up when she was needed, and that's enough for me. For now, anyway.

I've dreamt of this. I fought for it. Even before I knew I had a sister, I felt her absence in my life, and ever since I found out she exists—I've done everything in my power to get to her. Sitting in this uncomfortable chair for an unknown number of hours, feeling her warm skin on mine, it's like a dream come true.

If it wasn't such a nightmare, I mean.

She hasn't moved, and her condition hasn't improved much. But her eyes flutter, and every time they do? I tense, gripping her fingers tightly, believing she's about to wake up. And when she doesn't, the hollow chasm in my chest grows.

Maybe if she hears my voice...

"Kalli, I hope you know you can always rely on me. No matter what you've done or what kind of monster he's turned you into, I'll fight for you. I will always be here with arms wide open. You have a home with me. I am your home, Kalliope. Please wake up. You're the only family I have left." I allow one tear to trace its way down my cheek and then lock it up.

Selene is still in the room, and I don't mind that she heard what I said. But I can't do any more weakness in front of her. Or anyone. I'm so close to breaking, and I'm terrified of what that might entail.

"I brought you some hot bean water and a little something to eat," Marlow's voice breaks the silent vigil. I turn my head to look at her, and the emotion painted all over her face cracks my foundation.

"Thank you," is all I can muster without allowing the dam to break.

It's a tricky maneuver, and my muscles feel like they've been through a marathon they hadn't signed up for, but I sip the coffee one-handed. And when it hits my soul, the world looks a little less dismal. My stomach growls loudly, and Selene gives me the look. Guilting me into taking a bite of my muffin.

Moms, they have superpowers.

I'm assuming the rest of our misfit crew has been instructed to stay out of the room since my Sight can feel them on the other side of the wall. But I haven't seen them enter, or at least I don't recall anyone entering until now. Marlow doesn't linger. She only gives me a brief pat on the shoulder and some words of... consoling... or encouragement? I'm not sure. But then she takes her leave.

Kalliope jerks her muscles, and I sit up ramrod straight, looking toward Selene.

"She's experienced major trauma to her physical body. It's a natural reaction while she heals. And I can't say what's happening in her mind. She may have dreams of her torment. It will pass."

"Tell me." It sounds like an order, but it's a question. And Selene understands what I'm asking for.

She takes a deep breath and lets it out. "There was damage to her right leg, a fracture in three of her ribs, her right wrist is broken. I suspect some internal damage because of her state of consciousness. After that, I would say a head injury. And then there are the external lacerations...."

"That's enough." I already know about those. I've categorized and committed them all to memory. The deep cuts on her torso were made with a serrated blade, and they didn't happen all at once. My sister endured this torture for at least a couple of days.

My magic flares to life, and violet flames erupt in my palm. The thought of what they did to her, how she must have felt, the fear of death. The pain. It stokes a fire inside me I've never experienced before. I'm not angry. I'm so far past it that anger doesn't even register on the emotional Richter scale.

Wrath. That's a good word, a fitting term. Fury, rage, a burning desire to annihilate anyone and everyone who had a hand in this loathsome display of impotence. Because that's what this is. The actions of a coward, a bully. Someone devoid of compassion and basic decency. A real deal fucking monster and I have a strong suspicion about which monster it was.

In a few minutes, I'd gone from utterly devastated to seething with unchecked rage. I take one more look at my beaten and mutilated sister. Something inside me ignites. Leaning over, I give Kalliope a kiss on her forehead and a quiet promise. "I'll be back."

I let go of her hand.

I don't bother changing my torn dress. I have already put it through the shredder. So, I walk through the medieval yet modern hallways of the Night Fortress, following the path down past the expansive library and then through the outdoor path with the view of the gardens. When I reach the door to my rooms, I don't stop. My feet are on autopilot, so I continue past Killian's door as well. Down the hall with the moving wallpaper and past the entrance to the dining room.

When I hit the throne room, there are a few Netherlings milling about, and Killian stands with an advisor. I assume they're discussing strategy or approach. Something war-related.

Killian and I make eye contact, and my heart flutters, but I don't stop. I don't ruminate over what his presence does to my body or even the hatred I carry in my heart for him. Instead, I continue straight past his shocked face and out the front doors.

Headed for the gate.

Breaching the gate got the attention of Jagger's guards, of course. So now I am marching through them to the tune of shouting voices behind me. And yet, I keep going. I know fully that I have ripped my clothing to the point of being nothing more than scraps of fabric, exposing pretty much everything I have to offer. I can only imagine what's running through everyone's mind, but I don't have the time to give a fuck. I'm sure I look like a feral hellcat. Covered in grime, barefoot, with Goddess only knows crusted in my hair.

Again, no fucks.

I didn't know where I was headed when I stood up from that chair, and I had no destination as

I walked the halls of the Fortress. But when I bypassed my rooms, a killing calm washed over me. I look like some sort of psychotic pied piper, in the remnants of my red dress, with a crew of Netherling (and Earthling) misfits falling into step behind me. I make my way to the field where I fought my sister, where Calypso lost her first life, where Mordred declared war on my people.

I know exactly where I'm headed.

When I make it to the chasm I'd created, I'm surprised at the ingenuity of the Night Forces. There's no way to undo what I'd done to the field that day, but they'd built a bridge across the crack in the world. And then I cross it. The shouts of everyone behind me sound like hums, buzzing. It means nothing. I'm not phased. My feet propel me forward as if they're being guided by something not wholly me. But I don't fight it. I'm merging with my monster, accepting her, allowing her in.

Past the killing fields, there's a forest. It's still part of the outskirts of Netherworld territory, Killian's territory. My territory. But I can see the glowing lights in the distance. Campfires. I continue walking, with no words, no reaction to anyone following me. I have my destination in my sights.

The forest is modest, murky, and archaic. A variation of beastly uproars surrounds us as I continue down the path through the trees. Vines embrace the saplings on the otherwise brown forest floor, and plant life grows scarcely dispersed throughout. I carry on, barefoot and half-naked, until we come to a clearing.

I observe the Shadow Camp for a few moments, watching our enemies laugh and cajole each other around their fires. I've always heard that the creatures from the Shadow Court were grotesque, but these men — if you can categorize them as that — must be the best of Mordred's legion. One has vivid yellow skin, and a body shaped like a goat, another is a humanoid, but its back is hunched, and a pair of bat-like wings protrude from its shoulders. Another has a scaly green hide and the eyes of a basilisk. Several simple tents surround the clearing in a circle, and I glide through the trees, straight into the middle of their camp.

I must have caught them by surprise because there are roughly fifteen of them here. And none of them rushes me. They're too busy staring in awe, horror, confusion? But I don't give a fuck what they think or feel. I lift my hands to my sides, and violet flames burst from my palms. I allow the fire to rage higher and higher until they're touching the treetops. But I don't want to burn the forest. No, I just want to send a message.

"Hello, boys! I'm assuming you know who I am?" I smile.

It's a rhetorical question, of course. They know who I am, but they don't know what I'm capable of. None of them do. I can feel Killian behind me now, that warm sensation prickling up my legs, but he's keeping his distance. And he must have ordered the others to keep theirs, too.

Good, they can observe the show.

I'm not here to waste time, so when the first man comes barreling at me, I let the flames go out and pull my dagger from the leg tie it's always attached to. Slicing across the pad of my hand—I let my blood flow. And then, with a flick of my wrist, I yank the veins from his body, and he explodes in a shower of gruesome mist. Splattering my face with his blood. My wicked smile intensifies.

The next creature who thinks he can take me steps up, and I wait. No need for movement, no need to say a word. When he rushes towards me, ax in hand, I use my magic to clasp around his neck. He's dangling in the air, struggling for breath before he can ever reach me. I snap his neck with a twist of my finger and then bathe him in a violet inferno.

Shit, I should have bathed him first, so I could listen to his screams.

They scatter, and I hear Calypso hiss at my side. I call to her, using our telepathic bond, which is still firmly in place despite what the Netherlings thought. *Go get 'em, Lippy!* And she tears off like a creature from the depths of hell, although I suppose that's what she is now. The screams I'm craving ring out like the most magnificent symphony of the depraved. It's pure chaos. I'm rushed from every angle, and I revel in it, thrusting my dagger into an eyeball, listening to the pop, and watching liquid ooze from the socket before I drown him in his own blood. Ripping the skin free from muscle with my thoughts and watching it flow from his twisted mouth. My eyes go hazy, and I know they're glowing with the power of my she-demon.

She's hungry, rabid, fiendish. Bodies fly. Some burst into ash. Others leave heaps of gore lying on the forest floor as I balk barefoot through them.

This is for Kalliope. This is retribution, but it's just a taste of what I'm capable of.

This? Oh, this is just a message.

As the last body falls and the entire camp is silent, I take my leisurely stroll through the carnage I've created, admiring my work. Finally, I spy a flash of lilac hidden inside the flap of a tent.

Curious...

Bending down, I snatch Bronwyn from her attempted escape. Holding her by the throat as she struggles to break free. Only now does it occur that I still have an audience, but there's only one person I turn my head to look at. Killian. Searching his face, I find what I'm looking for. He did not order her to be here. She isn't working on his authority. I turn my head back to the dark fae I used to call my friend.

"Bronwyn, I'm disappointed." I suck air through my teeth, making a 'tsk,' sound. "Once a spy, always a spy?"

Her eyes grow wide. "Vivi, I... it's not...."

"Shh. You aren't listening if you're speaking." I whisper. She struggles in my grasp, letting loose her magic. She thinks she can hurt me.

That's cute.

"I'm not going to kill you, Bronwyn. You're going to be a messenger. When I let you down, I'll need you to report back to my *father*. Understand? You're going to tell him that Kalliope is with me now. AND THIS IS HIS FUCKING WEDDING INVITATION! Won't that be nice? Now run along." I put her down, and she scrambles across the bloody ground, gets to her feet, and runs.

"Oh, and Bronwyn... if I ever see you here again? What you've seen here today will be the equivalent of a children's birthday party." I turn on my heel and whistle for Calypso, who lumbers to my side as I lay a hand on her fiery head, rubbing her ears.

Good Girl, I communicate through our bond.

It occurs to me that Marlow, Linc, Ansel, Jagger, and the twins are now staring at me in equal parts fascination and horror. Anise is smiling from ear to ear, bouncing on her toes like she's just witnessed a fireworks display. And Killian...

Killian's eyes are swirling with flames and heat. I give him a feral grin and begin my unhurried hike back to the Fortress.

During the silent journey back, I realize that The Dark Prince is at my side, walking in sync next to me. I wish I could say that he consumed my thoughts, but my mind is elsewhere. I just want to wash myself clean and get back to Kalliope. I want my face to be what she sees when she wakes up.

The silence as we make our way back into the Fortress is unnerving; now that my inner demon has had her fill, she's retreated into the recesses of wherever she lives inside me. And my mind is my own again. I want to say something, to assure them somehow that what I've done was a necessary evil, but I can't find the words, and I don't even know if that's a legitimate concern for them or if I'm just overthinking.

So, instead, I make my way to my rooms.

As I open my door, Killian follows. Closing it behind us. The sheer force of his power radiates behind me, and I shudder at the heady feeling. Walking into my bathroom, I shed what's left of my dress and underthings. Standing fully nude before him, covered in my enemy's blood.

He takes a step forward. His inky black hair has fallen into one eye, and the expression on his pretty face is one of shock and bewilderment. "You are savagely fucking beautiful, my poison princess."

He moves to my tub and turns on the water. Running me a bath, as his eyes roam my blood-crusted curves. And I give him my most wicked grin as I rush to him, grabbing the back of his neck as I devour his mouth. Kissing him deeply, seductively, fiercely. Not caring that I'm covered in gore or that I've taken him by surprise. When I release him from my soul-shaking kiss, I lean in close and whisper. "Make me your fucking Queen."

CHAPTER TWENTY NINE

BINDING DAY

MY ROOMS MIGHT AS well be an animal sanctuary at this point. Calypso and Grim have officially taken over my bed, which isn't the worst thing, I guess. It's not like I've been sleeping there, anyway. I find it amusing that I was so pissed off at the lumpy, straw-filled mattress at The Temple of Dusk, but now? I sleep in a chair.

Someone in this fortress has taken it upon themselves to move a rather comfy recliner next to Kalliope's bed. I have suspicions about who that may be, but I can't be positive. It's a gracious gesture, but it's no giant soft orgy bed. Not that I'm complaining. You couldn't drag me from this chair for all the chocolate in the world. Coffee, however? I can be bribed for short periods. Which is what Jagger is doing.

"You become a Queen today, Little Monster. Don't you want to do it looking less like a bog witch?" he pokes fun at me.

"You have to go to a Binding looking like lizard roadkill, so..." I jab right back.

"She's feisty today! What's the matter? Pick the wrong brother?" He laughs, mock concern written on his bearded face.

"I didn't pick *anyone*; you know what this is. Hey! Speaking of picking someone, Dragon Boy... What are your intentions with my best friend? I've been meaning to ask. Because you know if you hurt Lowe. I'll shove a broomstick straight up your lizard ass." I smirk at my own words.

"Ooh, Kinky!" Jagger waggles his brows and grins.

"Goddess, you really are perfect for each other. Aren't you?" I sigh. "Treat her right, loudmouth. You get one warning. Now get out, it's my wedding day. Remember? A blushing bride needs her alone time." My smile is sweet. The sarcasm is strong today.

Jagger belly laughs as he hands me the coffee and backs away, pretending I'm some sort of feral beast who needs to be appeased by the caffeine gods.

Smart man.

Oh, life. I've spent the morning contemplating how everything got to this point. Like, what hard left did my path take that I'm about to bind myself to a pompous, deceiving, cranky, albeit incredibly sexy Incubus Demon Prince?

I never had a life plan like many people do. You know the five-year plan. Ten-year plan. I never saw the point. As ruthless as the Elders are, and as disrespectfully sassy as I am? I didn't think I'd live to see eighteen. And when I made it out of the Academy, I was just content to sling drinks and help Deacon run his business. Okay, maybe I had one tiny little plan. Not even a plan, really, just a pipe dream. I wanted to live in a pretty countryside away from the Elders.

I guess I sort of got what I asked for? I mean, it's the Netherworld. So, there's that. But it is pretty countryside if you're on the darker side of the Universe. Which I am.

I sigh as I look down at my sister's still form, "Kalli, if you're in there somewhere and hearing me? It's my Binding Day. I mean, it's fake, but the nerves are real. I wish you were here to do this with me. I can picture you being a pesky brat, fussing over details that don't matter because... well, because I think you're just as big of an ass-hole as I am. Who knows, I could sit vigil over you this whole time just for you to wake up and try to kill me again. Don't... if you can help it, okay? I just need you to wake up."

It's funny. My unconscious sister, who hates me as far as I know, has become my personal sounding board. Oh, how the mighty Vivi has turned into a soft ass bitch.

Anise pokes her head into the doorway. I can see frosting on the side of her cheek, and she's exceptionally bouncy today. "I tried your binding cake."

It certainly looks like it.

"Was it good? What flavor?" I ask her.

"Chocolate! Earthlings are vile creatures, so destructive. But they did something right with chocolate. There's no blood ivy it in, though." She makes a disgusted face, and I'm not sure what blood ivy is? But I'm thankful it's not on the cake.

"You're supposed to come to get dressed." Anise changes subjects like a hyperactive squirrel. Others may find it taxing, but I find it endearing.

"Okay, friend! Let's go see what kind of frilly monstrosity they're going to stuff me into today." I squeeze Kalliope's unmoving hand and follow Anise into the fray.

I had no idea what an ordeal this was going to be when I agreed to it. Okay, fine—it was my freaking idea! But I didn't expect all this extra shit. Apparently, getting ready in my own rooms is a bad omen.

So, myself and twenty of my closest friends (sarcasm) are better off packed into a ritual room like sardines? Netherworld logic doesn't seem to operate on the same wavelength as earthling logic. I didn't even know the Fortress had ritual spaces! There's so much about Maleficent's Evil Lair that I don't know. I'm half convinced rooms just appear as you have use for them. It wouldn't shock me.

Kinda like my television, the coffee maker, a more comfortable bed, earthling-friendly bathroom and beauty products, the clothes, umm... the falling leaves and crisp fall air outside these walls?!

I still don't have straightforward answers about that, and my first guess was way off. Bronwyn didn't put those things in my rooms before I arrived. The twins wouldn't. Jagger is too clueless. This leaves two options: Selene or The Demon fuckboy himself.

Here's the thing, though, if he's been presenting all these meaningful gifts to me. Something that he knows I would appreciate. Then why hasn't his pompous ass taken credit for it? Does Mr. Selfish have a selfless bone in his body? I think he might. Either that or I'm romanticizing a complete shithead who could not care less about anyone's happiness, minus his own. Which I *have* done in the past, more than once. So, it's not out of the question.

What can I say? I'm drawn to the fucked up broken ones. There's something addictive about a bad boy who only melts for you. Until you realize the melting part was more about getting laid or stealing your cash than undying love. It's the toxic ones with the pretty faces that fuck us up good.

Anyway. Ladies are moving around so haphazardly it's making me a tad dizzy. No rhyme or reason. One yanking on my hair, another screwing with my eyelids, and yet another one gluing eyelashes to the ones I already have. *Weird.*

I feel like I've been here all day, with people fussing about. Feeding me snacks, drinks, buffing and polishing every part of me. And I mean *every* part. Did you know dark fae can give you a vagina wax with just a few words and a little fairy dust?

While we sit over on the other side of the portal, having our pubes ripped out. I feel kind of cheated. Like, they could have shared that information with the rest of the world. What happened to the sisterhood? When Selene enters with her ladies, my nerves spike. It's time for the dress. And although I've been poked, prodded, buffed, polished, and ritualized for whatever Killian and my Binding Night entails... it's the dress that makes this real.

Don't get me wrong, it's simple and beautiful. And not at all what I had envisioned. It's a revealing gown, but it reminds me of ancient Greek aesthetics. It's jet black with a flowing skirt, a corset waist, and a single strap sleeve. Not monstrous at all. Before they can stuff me into it, a familiar head of wavy brown hair cracks through the door. Linc looks at me and smiles. He says, "May I have a moment with the soon-to-be Queen?"

And that freaks me right the fuck out. What is he going to say? Goddess only knows. He probably came here to talk me out of it or drag me kicking and screaming through a portal somewhere...

But I can't very well tell him no, can I?

"Sure. Would you all excuse us for a moment?" I ask.

And the room clears. It's just Linc and me.

He doesn't waste much time in getting to the point. "You look stunning, Viv. Really. Look, I don't want to take up too much of your time today, but there's something I need to say before you do this. So please don't interrupt, just hear me out, okay? Vivi Graves, I love you."

"Linc, please don't," I interrupt.

"You can't even follow simple directions, can you? I said, don't interrupt!... I love you, and part of that love means letting you go. I see the way you look at him. And you may not see it, but he looks at you that way when you're not paying attention. I don't know about all this shit with the stars and fated mates or whatever the oracles say. But it's hard to miss. And I know you're fighting it because you fight everything! But you're in love, Genevieve. And it's time I accept it."

"What the fuck are you talking about, Blackwood? No, I am not! This isn't even real. It's a power move. That's all." I reply. Although I'll admit

I'm a little shaken by that confession. Is this Linc giving me his blessing?

Just as quickly as he came in, he readies himself to leave. Coming to my side to grab my cheeks and press a kiss into my forehead, "Love doesn't care about our plans, Viv. It shows up when you least expect it. And none of us are powerful enough to fight it."

The way he says it with so much conviction has me wondering if that love speech was about me? Or him? I look up to ask, but instead of opening my mouth. I widen my eyes. Killian is standing in the doorway, and from where he's standing? This looks bad. Like fucking *bad*. His eyes swirl galaxies, and the wave of anger hits me square in the chest. Fuck.

CHAPTER THIRTY

THE BINDING

I ASK LINC TO leave the room with an apologetic frown because I can see it in Killian's murder-y eyes. Shit's about to go down. And today is not the day for physical violence. As soon as he's in the hallway, I march over and shut the door. Something tells me we don't want an audience for this.

"Killian, chill out. That wasn't what it looked like." I try to reason with him, but he's already in the red zone.

"It wasn't? I didn't just see you wrapped in his arms with his lips on your skin. Hours before you bind yourself TO ME!" he shouts.

"Well, yes. You did..."

"I told you not to embarrass me, Genevieve." He bites out through clenched teeth, not even giving me a chance to explain. His jaw is clenched, and he's opening and closing his fists like he needs something to destroy. He grabs the chair and whips it through the room. Shattering an expensive-looking vase and knocking a gigantic picture clean off the wall.

Oh, hell no! What is it with these men in my life and their godsdamned outbursts? I finally, FINALLY get Lincoln to stop acting like a com-

plete tool and even accept that we're not meant
for each other beyond platonic love. Which is a
miracle. And now this? Nope. We are not doing
this toxic bullshit.

*Okay, fine. It's not lost on me that I recently threw a
vase myself... but Goddess, help me. Killian is acting like
a jealous boyfriend.*

"He was giving us his blessing, you fuckwit!
Everyone in this Goddess Forsaken place thinks
we belong together. Your mother, Jagger, Marlow, even Lincoln, is a true believer now! Throwing around the LOVE word like a stupid jackass." I take a breath, not done yelling at him. "But
you don't love me, Killian. Because if you did?
You wouldn't hurt me like you do!! You're a
cold-hearted bastard, and I doubt you're capable
of something as selfless as love. Maybe I'm inca-
pable too. Let's just get this farce over with."

He stands silently, his glare less menacing but
still there. Finally, he speaks, "Are you done?"

You've got to be fucking kidding me. How can
someone so hot be so infuriating? I'm as close to
pouring my heart out as I can get. And that's all
he has to say? Another barb for my skin, another
arrow to my stupid heart.

"Why do you hate me so much?" there's a tremble in my voice now.

"You think this is hate?" he looks at me like a
predator and sweat beads across my top lip. And
the next thing I know, Killian has crossed the
room. He grabs me by the waist, pushing me up
against the wall.

His hands are shaking; he looks unhinged.

"I don't hate you, Kitten; I want you so bad it
drives me insane. Knowing I could bend you to

my will with only a touch, a word, and not being able to use it to the fullest makes me crazy. Don't tell me what I'm capable of feeling, little girl. You don't know shit about me."

"Little girl? I'll fucking show you, little girl!" Rage fills me, and my flames come to life. Then, before I can think, I hurl a fireball straight at his perfect fucking face.

Let's see how you enjoy our fake ass wedding with no eyebrows, dickhead!

But he lifts a crackling blue hand and deflects it. The fireball diverts like a pinball and strikes the curtains, lighting them on fire. Ugh! A life with this sexed-up psycho would never work. We'll burn the whole Netherworld down, starting with this fortress.

"Yeah, you want my body, Killian. I get it. But I need more than that," I cast my eyes to the ground, "Just get out, so I can finish getting dressed for our *performance*."

Standing in front of this full-length mirror, in an exquisite dress, looking like a whole sacrifice to A Demon Prince. My nerves are inciting a riot, and ground zero is in my stomach. They're not the butterflies I thought I'd have on my wedding day. Or the white dress and adoring groom to match, for that matter. But, whatever.

Maybe next time.

Who am I kidding? I never wanted to be any-one's wife. Not in a million years. So, maybe this is as good as it gets for a Demon Goddess from hell? A fake binding to a real asshole. That sounds about right.

I took a few acting classes in the first six months after graduating from the Academy. I don't know why. Just wanting to experience something mundane, something that wasn't bloody or violent. Something an everyday woman would try. I took a yoga class too and walked familiars at the shelter. That was when I thought I wanted to fit in. Who knew one of those things would come in handy? I look back at myself in the mirror, practicing my facial expressions.

I am the fearsome Dark Queen. I am a powerful, insatiable, sexy woman. My King worships me, and I satisfy him. He has no need for any other. I am the baddest bitch in the Netherworld.

I lift my chin, throw my shoulders back, pop my booty, and adjust my tits. Then I pop on some red lipstick and the last of my ensemble—thigh-high lace-up gladiator sandals. They're my personal contribution to the evening. Sexy and practical, I place my daggers under the dress, between the leather straps and my skin.

What, you thought I wouldn't be armed?

Marlow opens the door and invites herself in, "Damn bitch! You put the fuck in fuckable. Whew, that man is going to lose his mind."

"Too late for that. He's already fifty shades of fucking insane." I can't help but smirk.

"So, we're doing this? Because it's about fifteen minutes to showtime, and you know I gotta ask. Plus, I think it's customary for your bestie to offer a getaway car for a runaway bride montage. If that's the route we're going." She raises her brow in question.

"It's not real, Lowe. It doesn't even count." I shake my head in exasperation.

"Whatever you say, Vivi. Well, I guess we better get to making that *alliance* then!" she laughs.

And... I'm on the highway to hell.

Marlow and I take our time passing through the winding hallways. We're taking a different route this time. I guess this one brings me out at the top of a fancy staircase above all my new subjects. Spotlight on Vivi! My favorite. I imagine it's going to be like a 'Cinderella enters the ball' thing. Except I'm a lot more Morticia than fairy princess, and the ball is a viper pit.

My heart is beating way too fast, and my palms feel like an oil slick. I may appear calm on the outside, but on the inside? I am freaking the fuck out. I need to think about something else—like right now. Before I really do pull a Julia Roberts.

Linc met with Willa and Iris. The mixed orders are all doing well. The caverns don't suck that much, and Faustus has made no moves. This concerns me, but we've made plans for every plausible scenario. This Binding has more security than fucking Alcatraz.

Binding... whew. Speaking of, we're rounding the last corner, and I can see Selene and Anise waiting, both with radiant smiles on their beautiful faces.

In the famous words of Beetlejuice. It's Showtime!

I plaster a grin on my lips and some confidence in my step. Meeting them near a billowing red silk curtain that covers the entrance to an Imperial staircase. Glancing through the cracks, I check out the decorating scenario. Since I left it all up to Killian and his minions.

The Shittiest fiancé award goes to... me.

They bathed the throne hall in a soft red light. There are twinkle lights draped in more billowing silk curtains spread throughout the hall. There are tables with pomegranates and poppies in clear, crystal spheres adorning the middle. They have swapped the furniture out for black leather, and the throne platform looks like something out of a sex club. Come to think of it? The whole hall looks like a Boom Boom Room. Netherling weddings are not at all what I thought they were.

"Are you nervous? Pretty girl." Selene's calming voice is much welcomed.

"To be honest, yes. I am awfully nervous," I reply. "There are so many people down there! I don't know what to expect. That reminds me, I had one question for you. Before we were... interrupted this morning."

"Of course, dear. Ask anything you please." She lays a gentle hand on my open shoulder.

"If Killian is a Prince. How does binding to me make him into a King? I thought if the King isn't dead... well, would he just be a married Prince?" Maybe that's a dumb question, but it's been puzzling me.

"It's you, Genevieve. Your title will make him a King." She replies.

My heart sinks. Always something in it for him, I should've known. I should laugh, brush it off, acknowledge that is all fake anyway, so why does it matter? But the piercing pain in my chest tells a different story. All he had to do was tell me, and this wouldn't feel like entrapment. Just a few sentences, to show me that he respects me for me and not my title. But I guess he can't do that, can he? Because my title is what he needed all along.

Before I can muster the righteous anger at being deceived once again, I hear the music fill the Throne Hall. Anise takes my hand, the curtains open, and hundreds of netherlings turn to face me at the top of the staircase. Their eyes rove over me; some are leering at my body; others are nodding in approval. There are a few who look disgusted...

I take a few more steps and find myself on the first landing. That's when the heat builds on my skin. It starts at my toes and moves up my body all the way to the top of my head. When he reaches my face, I turn to look him in the eye. I intend to let it be known that I'm livid. I intend to burn a hole through his forehead with my scathing death glare. But when I'm hit with the full force of Killian's otherworldly masculine perfection, my breath leaves my body. He stands on the platform, wearing a tailored-to-every-sexy-angle black-on-black suit. His inky dark hair is styled back, exposing so much more of his face than I'm used to. He's clean-shaven, tattoos peeking out from the collar of his dress shirt.

He looks like a fucking God.

He looks like my ruin.

Walking towards the base of the staircase, he holds out his hand. Oh! I'm supposed to meet him down there. Shit. I put a little pep in my step and end up tripping on my own feet. Stumbling sideways, I just know I'm about to live out every girl's worst nightmare and face plant in front of a crowd, but before I can make a total ass of myself,

Killian is by my side. Walking me the rest of the way down and onto the platform.

My ruin, and my savior. Fuck me in reverse. I am so reckless!

When we reach our spots, we stop. Facing a priest? No, in the Netherworld, it would be a Dark Warlock or something, right? Anyway, he's about eight feet tall with a face that could traumatize small children.

"All you have to do is listen and follow directions. Can you manage that today, Kitten?" Killian whispers under his breath, a slight lift in the corner of his lip.

Now he's using aggravating smirk lite? But I nod, like a good Dark Queen.

Step on to the mirror, Daughter of Oracles. Princess of Death.

I want to give Killian the eyes, like the... what the fuck did he just call you? Eyes. But once again, I've been swindled into a situation where having a reaction can ruin everything. Not just for him, but for myself, too. Damn, damn, damn! I have to let it go. I'm in too deep now, and there is no turning back.

I step into the mirror, and he steps into his.

Turn to face one another, join hands.

Ugh, this is taking place. It's really fucking happening. I turn to Sir-Sexy-Liar-Face and give him a sensual grin, biting the bottom of my lip, and then I take his hands in mine.

We're going down together, baby...

The Warlock Giant turns to the crowd, looks up to the glass-domed ceiling, and speaks.

"In ancient society, the Harlequin Occidental-is constellation represents the God of Fortune and The Goddess of Power. The old ones blessed those who submit to the Starbound ritual under it. Their power multiplied; souls attached. And upon completion of the ritual, power will flow through all in their domain."

Okay, then. That was NOT in the instruction manual to the dark side.

I wish I could see Marlow or Linc right now, something familiar to ground me. Because I am well and freaked out. Freddy Krueger freaked out. Five alarm. Chucky, the horror doll freaking the fuck out!!! But unfortunately, all I have is this semi-charming spicy rollercoaster who's staring at me like I hung the moon or something.

"Are you ready, Kitten?" he flashes a brilliant grin.

Everything in me wants to tell him to sit on a hot griddle and burn his own asshole to a crisp, but then I remember this is a performance, and I'm supposed to be playing the main character.

"Yes, my King." I give him a smoldering glance, eye-fucking him until I see a touch of pink near his cheekbones. If I can't fight him the old-fashioned way, then I'll make him beg for mercy.

The Not So Friendly Giant grunts, indicating that we're holding up the process. And I fall back in line, ready for the next step. Which is a doozy, come to find out. Now is the part where we drop our walls, lower every defense, and freely share our powers.

Listen, I've been through the relationship ringer. I've got man trauma for days, trust issues for life, and a lot of walking mistakes I wish I could burn from my mind. And this is all from *before* I met the King of all Douches. I am a wall-building professional, never knocked one down a day in my life. And I'm gonna be honest here. I don't know if I'm capable of this kind of intimacy. And with that thought, I start to sweat. Because I already know there's no shortcut, we checked. Meticulously. Obsessively. If I don't do this, everything is fucked.

I look at Killian, allowing him to see my panic. Letting him know this shindig might be headed South, that my feet are getting mighty cold. His brow creases. For a moment, I think he's going to break character and rip my tits off, but then his eyes go clear blue skies, not a storm in sight.

He's found a solution.

His walls drop. And I am overcome with the most intense emotions I've ever felt. All of them at once. It's almost too much to bear. My heart feels like it's breaking and being remade and breaking again. And then I hear his voice in my head, like I hear Calypso.

"Can you do this, Kitten?"

"I don't know, I don't think so. I'm sorry, I can't let you have this much of me."

"Okay." he sounds so wounded. No, worse. Rejected.

Why does that affect me so viscerally? I don't want this any more than he does, and if we weren't in a predicament of Godzilla proportions, this moment wouldn't be happening at all. But the way he just deflates, it guts me. Maybe it's because his walls are down right now. Perhaps it's the loneliness I detect in his voice or the fact that he just said 'okay.'

Like, no resistance. He's willing to let it all fall apart right here in front of his subjects, his family, his enemies. And I know what's at stake. I know more than I should. I now know that I'm the answer to him taking over whether his father is alive or dead. He's got so much to lose. So why isn't he fighting for it? I don't know what makes me do what I'm about to do next. But before I can overthink, I stop him.

"Killian, wait. Can you make me?" I question.

"What are you asking, Genevieve?"

"I'm asking you to use your incubus seduction to take down my walls."

This is for Deacon. It's for Kalliope and Calypso. I'm doing this for Thornfall and anywhere else the Elders have been able to reach. It's bigger than me or him. And I may be a monster, but I won't watch the world burn to save myself.

Killian stares. I think he's waiting for me to change my mind. But the crowd is becoming restless; voices are whispering his failure. My failure. I look him deeply in the eye and nod.

Ecstasy rips through my limbs, drowning me in pleasure. Killian's eyes go hypnotic, and I've never seen a more beautiful creature anywhere, in any realm, not even in my dreams. His darkness arouses me. Calls to me.

"You want to be mine, Genevieve. You want me inside every part of you. There's not a corner of your succulent body I won't touch, and you're going to let me have it all. Aren't you? Let me in. Let me make you burn for me." His voice is like velvet and whiskey mixed in a seductive cocktail.

"Yes, Killian. I want to burn for you." And my walls plummet.

Power overtakes us both. It flows between our intertwined hands, and we turn into freaking supernatural glow-worms! The energy radiating from our skin. It lasts under two minutes, and then an indigo light rises over our heads. A mixture of violet and stormy blue. And then it disperses. Filling the room with the magic Killian and I had just created with one another.

"It is done." Giant Warlock proclaims, and the Hall erupts in celebration.

CHAPTER THIRTY ONE

VIVI

I'D SAY THE ENTIRE ordeal was painless, but that would be a lie. It was anything but. Sure, it only lasted a few moments, but my insides are messy. I told Killian to do it; I have nobody to blame but myself. But we've crossed a line now, one that can't be uncrossed. Even if we somehow find a way out of this bond, I can feel his heat inside me. Every unclean thought he's had about us—together. I feel them. And as much as I'd love to say, they were all depraved and dirty, not all of them were. There was something else, something I couldn't identify, but it was affectionate. And that scares the absolute shit out of me.

We ladies have retreated to my rooms for an outfit to change. I guess this is half-time before the party? But when Selene turns toward me, holding honest to Goddess lingerie. I'm speechless and slightly embarrassed. First, this is Killian's mother! Why she's handing me under-things to wear in public is lost on me. Second, when I say lingerie—what I mean is butt floss and nipple warmers. This leather and lacy number barely qualifies as clothing.

I'm going back out there with all my goodies on display?

"Holy fuckable-hellcat! That's hot, Vivi. Scorching!" of course, Marlow's mischievous ass would have something to say.

My cheeks go rosy. "I... umm... is this customary?"

"Yes, dear. This is to be expected. It won't be shocking. Not in the way you mean." Selene smiles; a hint of amusement sparkles in her eyes.

Deacon, if you're watching this go down from somewhere on the other side? Look away.

I reinforce my lady balls and exhale a determined breath. "Okay. So, where do all these straps go? Is this one... does it cover the top? Or the bottom parts?"

With that, Anise bursts into thunderous laughter, and Marlow follows her lead. I can admit, it's contagious and I giggle too.

"Your pussy, Vivi." Anise barely gets the words out through her uproarious laughter, grabbing the contraption and turning it right side up.

Ah, I see...

And so, while I'm being laced up like a holiday ham, understanding why the magical bikini wax was necessary. I take the opportunity to ask a few more questions about this celebration. As it turns out, it's a sex-fest. The power of the binding temporarily binds all the netherworld subjects in the Fortress to Killian and me. What we feel, they feel. Whatever we do... if you know what I mean. Most of the Night Court will also be doing. This also means whatever we *don't* do, they will also feel. The entire court will know if we don't consummate this binding.

Fucking hell, I am in a situation. I need some liquid courage, stat.

———◆———

The first thing I noticed upon descending the staircase for the second time today is that while I was 'freshening up,' the hall was being transformed. It's like they found the volume control to sex-club-vibes and turned it all the way up. We're now in the Netherworld version of the red-light district.

Titties and ass, everywhere.

On the bright side, Selene was correct. My nudity isn't at all alarming when you consider that my nips and chuckie are mostly covered. Unfortunately, I cannot say the same for many of our guests. These motherfuckers are nude. Let it all hang out, say hello to my disco stick... naked.

As I make my way down the steps, I glance at the platform. Killian's throne has been swapped out for an oversized, extravagant, imposing black chair. It looks like they made it in medieval times as a torture device, and then someone upholstered it. And where is my throne? Chair? Stool? Like, what am I supposed to be sitting on? When the realization hits me, I can't help the soft sequel that escapes my lips. Surely, I'm not supposed to spend this evening on Killian's lap. Wearing the remnants of someone's fancy shoelaces across my nipples?

Fucking hell.

Whatever I did to anger the gods, I'm sorry, okay? And I never say that to anyone, although I should. I'll start! I'll repent starting right now, I swear it. Why did I tell him I understood and agreed to the Binding Rituals of the Netherworld? Knowing full well, I had no fucking clue. But, oh, Goddess, this is more than I'm prepared to handle.

Vivi, you absolute moron.

Killian catches my eye, motioning for me to meet him at the bottom of the landing, and my heart goes full racehorse. He looks delicious, a shirtless and tattooed God. Mmm, mmm. Yum! As Marlow would say, but why does he get to keep his pants? That seems unfair, given my current state of undress.

When I make it to him, he grabs my hand, and I find my inner vixen once again. I have a brutalized sister lying upstairs, a mentor who was murdered while I watched, and so many more reasons to exact vengeance on those who think to underestimate me. I am their Dark Queen, for however long that lasts. And I'll be damned if they see me as anything other than the monster I need to be. If I have to follow this manipulating demon to the platform and play the Enchantress? Then that's what I'll do.

"Like what you see?" I smart mouth my way through my lingering nerves.

Killian's lip curls, "Why don't you come sit on my lap and find out?"

"This is a one-night pass, *King of Death.*" I put a little extra venom on that last part. As a reminder that I know yet another one of his never-ending secrets, and there's no chance of me forgetting it.

He can have me tonight, but tomorrow there will be hell to pay.

"I love it when you try to fight me, Kitten." He whispers into my ear as we take our rightful place. And I smile, piling on the sex-goddess-charm for the room to see.

We're approached on either side by two eager-looking Brownies, each holding a tray with a goblet. Killian takes his and raises it into the air. The mass of Netherlings mirror him, raising their glasses. And then they look at me. Guess it's my turn? So, I mimic Killian's actions. First, grabbing my goblet, lifting it into the air. And then I one-up him, draining it dry as I thrust it out to my side, waiting for a refill.

Shouts of approval ring out through the hall, the lights dim, and music fills the air.

"Welcome to a Netherworld party, my Queen," Killian nuzzles his chin into the crook of my neck as a devious smile spreads across his lips.

———◇———

I'm on my third goblet when movement in the corner of the hall catches my eye. At first, it's difficult to tell what I'm watching with the only source of light being shed on the Throne Killian and I share, but as my eyes adjust, I'm taken by surprise at what I'm witnessing.

They're silhouettes, but as their bodies press together and I make out a hand clenching long hair, I realize they're guests. As the woman drops to her knees, I see the outline of a curvy breast. And on the man standing before her, an outline of an impressive penis. I know what's going to happen next, but I can't bring myself to look away.

She lowers her head, and my thighs clench. I watch as she moves slowly up and down his shaft, and heat blooms across my skin. Of course, they're only shadows, but somehow it adds to the allure. My imagination fills in the blanks, mesmerized by the lustful show playing out before me. The shadow couple switches positions, and suddenly I'm incredibly appreciative of the slope of the chair they're using. It forms to her body as she lies on her stomach, the man on his knees behind her thrusting.

My body heats, and I suppress the urge to squirm.

"Like what you see?" Killian's silken voice echoes in my ear. A hint of mockery trails his words. I asked him that question on the way up to our stage, didn't I?

"I don't know."

"I can smell your need." he replies, and though he's behind me, I know that aggravating smirk is gracing his lips.

He moves underneath me. The motion is subtle, but so not helping my current situation. All I can think about now is the way he moves his hips when he's inside me, and my eyes roll back to the couple in the corner. I imagine myself in her place...

"Uh, uh, uh. Kitten," he scolds. "You will not think of another man in the state you're in. Not while I'm alive and breathing. You will think of me, and only me."

"Was that a threat?" I sass back.

"That is a promise."

And then he unleashes his incubus talents upon me. I can feel his hands cupping my sex, but they're planted on the armrests.

What the fuck? Killian has phantom hands.

He continues to move invisible hands between my thighs, working me into a dripping frenzy, and I moan. Then I rolled my hips in time with his touch and spread my legs to give him better access. Leaning my head back against his chest. His warm lips move across my mid-section, and my eyes widen. His sinful mouth can't be on my stomach because I'm looking at his handsome face above mine right now. Killian smirks and continues the assault on my senses. Dragging a phantom tongue past my navel and lower.

Oh, Goddess of everything unholy. He's not actually touching me at all.

When an invisible finger trails over the thin material of my bottoms, and I feel the sensation of fullness, I freeze. Then, realizing I'm on display, and everyone has stopped moving.

They're all watching. Panic tinges in my throat; I've never done anything like this before. Suddenly, I'm self-conscious and hesitant. Phantom sex in public wasn't on my list of 'things I may have to do' when I'm Queen. I was prepared to strut and sway, make a spectacle of myself pawing at the Dark King when people were paying attention. Even been seen entering his rooms and then walking straight into my own where nobody could see. But this? It never even crossed my mind.

I feel a heady rush of power overtake me. I am a lethal woman. Sexual, compelling, and deadly. And these are my subjects. They will covet and fear me. I shake my head at the thoughts. They aren't mine.

"You are revealing your exquisite body, the way you respond to my touch, and when you come for me—everyone in this room will feel it, Kitten. They worship you, as I am now." Killian says softly.

I can feel an invisible tongue moving along my slit as Killian sits dangerously still. The only sign of his arousal is pressed into my back. Hard as stone and pulsing. I move my eyes to the crowd, watching with intense interest. And then the sensation heightens to a boiling point, and I don't hate this as much as I thought.

A devious smile spreads across my crimson lips as I allow Killian to take the reins. His astute phantom tongue has me rolling my hips in agony, writhing against him as I make eye contact with my new subjects. Who are now engaged in all manner of fornication with each other while they watch us keenly.

Can I put on a show? Fuck yeah, I can.

I move my hand behind my back to stroke Killian's perfect cock, craving it, letting myself fall into this charade. Fuck it, right? I'm only getting this one chance, and I'm not feeling inclined to waste it.

"Later, my Dark Queen." Killian groans huskily.

I resist the urge to stomp my feet and demand what I want, but Killian ramps up the heat before I have the opportunity. And a storm builds deep inside; my body pulses with need as he continues his merciless assault on my dripping sex. My body weeps at the thought of there being more than this; his hand snakes up into my hair, and he pulls tightly—bordering on pain but delivering delectable pleasure. An explosive orgasm builds pressure in my core. My cries are audible now. Fevered. Desperate. Until I fear I may die of anticipation. I move in time with the rhythm, grinding against him as he increases the pace, stroking me to earth-shattering oblivion. After several realm-shaking orgasms, I am nearly hysterical with the need for a private room. In the meantime, I play the part of the voyeur. Eyes glued to some fae women licking, kissing, sucking, fucking while a small gathering surrounds them. Doing the same as I am, watching. Wishing. Ready to beg my Dark Prince. Damn tomorrow and its consequences.

"They'll be at it all night, love. So, what do you say we take this party upstairs?" he smirks with that maddening dimple on full display.

I'm beyond words now, so I only nod in fervent agreement. We bid our goodnights and slink off into the shadows, wandering the halls in anticipatory silence. As we near the infirmary room, I look to Killian. An unspoken question.

"Check in on her, Kitten. It's okay." and at that moment, my heart warms to the vicious bastard I know I'll despise again later, but can't bring myself hate at the moment.

How can someone so vile and devious show such warmth and compassion? Killian is a paradox. A real-life mystery to be solved, but not tonight. Tonight? I raise my white flag, my desire for him overpowering my good senses.

We stop in front of Kalliope's room, and at a glance, I can already surmise there's been no change. But it warms my heart to watch Killian's Netherlings dote on her. I guess, for a time—they're my Netherlings too? They care for my sister as though she's a precious guest, as if her history in the Bone Keep is of no consequence to them. And in a bizarre turn of events, I soften towards them.

There's hope for this Kingdom yet.

I briefly stand by Kalliope's side, holding her hand in mine. And then I kiss her alabaster forehead as Killian guides me from the infirmary to his suite. When we're behind closed doors, I have questions. A flurry in my stomach has me momentarily stumbling over my words. "Does... does someone have to watch us do this? To make it, you know, official?"

"You've been doing your research. And here I thought you wanted nothing to do with me." He chuckles devilishly. "No, wicked Enchantress. There is magic afoot this evening. The realm will share our pleasure with all who we rule over. Everyone will feel what I do to you."

"And what about what I do to you, Killian? I'm not as submissive as you think." I tease. Leading him to the balcony as I drop to my knees.

CHAPTER THIRTY TWO

VIVI

WAKING UP WITH A naked incubus wrapped around me wasn't something I ever thought would happen in my life. But here we are! I'm hesitant to move because I either enjoy this or... I don't? I haven't decided. So, for now, seeing as I'm trapped between tattooed arms and he's way less of a douche when he's asleep—studying him seems like an okay plan.

I'm pissed about his eyelashes; I can tell you that much! I've tried every mascara on the Earth Realm to get mine to look like that, and he just gets them for nothing? I'm calling total bullshit. Beyond that, nobody should get to be *this* attractive. I mean, really, it's gratuitous. Bordering on obscene. I'd ask what it's like to be one of gods favorites, but we all know that's not where he's from.

Fucker.

Laying here trapped under two hundred pounds of man-candy has given me too much time to think, and thinking leads to questions. Of course, this doesn't bode well for anyone because now I have a lot of questions. Starting with 'why the fuck didn't you tell me you needed my title to become a King' and ending with 'how am I supposed to scrub last night from my memory' both are important questions. But one of them scares the shit out of me more than the other, and (shocker) it's the wrong one.

Why does all the good dick insist on being attached to huge assholes? The Universe doesn't play fair. It really doesn't. I gaze back over at the walking headache waiting to happen, and I'm startled to see stormy blue looking back at me.

"Good morning, my Queen," he smiles and nuzzles my shoulder. I can almost feel my ovaries preparing to riot.

I don't like this. No, nope, no thank you. Been there, done that, have the emotional scars instead of a cool touristy t-shirt! Hurricane Killian destroys lives, hearts, panties.

"Killian, how do you feed?"

Avoidance, yes. The golden answer to everything! Plus, I do want to know. I've been thinking about it a lot, but what I want to know is... has he fed on me? Is there another bag of secrets in his fucked-up closet? Why am I not worthy of the truth? Because the only reason I can think of is that the truth would require him to stop manipulating me.

Therefore, blowing his master plan. Whatever that is. And if his master plan requires me not knowing the truth? Well, that's not even a red flag. That's a flag that's already on fire, and I'm the one who's about to get burned.

"I can go for many months without feeding, Kitten." He uses that irritating fucking smirk.

"That's not what I asked you. I said HOW do you feed?"

Killian sighs, "It varies. I can feed on arousal, dreams, creating intense emotion. It's not always physical, but it can be."

Don't look at me like that, you scorching hot swindler. "And you didn't feed on me last night?"

"No, Genevieve. I did not, and I wouldn't without your permission." His smile fades.

I think I may have done it on purpose. This intimacy, the affection, the binding of our souls (and then our bodies) last night needs to be what we intended it to be. Fake. False. A means to an end. Isn't that what he called me? A means to an end. That's fine, he's right. I am quite literally a means to end Faustus and my father.

I can already feel the water getting muddy. My emotions getting twisted up. And I can't do it because I know the moment I let myself fall, I'll drown in him. I don't trust Killian not to throw me into the water without a lifejacket. I don't even trust him not to be the one pushing me off the cliff. I'm here to avenge Deacon, my sister, everyone who's been fucked over by these psychotic motherfuckers. That is my purpose for all of this, and The Dark Prince King of the Netherworld is a monumental distraction.

Lock it down, Vivi.

Killian unrolls himself from my body, and I think I'm colder than I've ever been. The absence of his heat is painful. Not physically, but inside my chest, in my soul. I feel barren without his touch. This is what suffering feels like. As he walks to his closet and grabs a pair of black pants, my heart flip-flops. I don't know if he's showing me his sculpted ass on purpose or if I'm drawn to it like a dumbass moth to a burning candle.

Goddess on a fucking stick! This is just unnecessary.

Time to shake the sex demon...

"I want to be included, Killian. Whatever this is, and for however long it lasts until we dissolve this farce of a binding. I will be treated as the Queen, and I will perform the duties of a Queen. I will not be shooed away with the other women or tricked into my rooms while you run the show without me. It's a deal breaker."

Killian rounds on me, beautiful cock and all, and glares at me like I've just murdered a Brownie or something. But he doesn't speak a word. I guess he doesn't have to. His face is saying it all. I really did it this time. I offended him with a capital O. All I did was ask how he eats and if he's ever done it to me? He acts as if he's this honorable man with a sterling reputation for honesty or something. He really expected me to trust him? Well, that's just too bad. He broke me, and he doesn't get to pretend that one mind-blowing night together fixes it.

Get over it, fuckboy.

"This farce of a binding." Killian says flatly.

"Umm, yeah. That was the deal, right?"

Instead of giving me an answer, he turns to enter his bathroom and slams the door, dismissing me. But was that a flash of pain I saw in his stormy depths?

—◦—

I took the abrupt dismissal as an invitation to go back to my rooms and clean myself up. You know—bathing the depravity off of me from last night, using the bathroom in peace, food, coffee! And Calypso. I hadn't seen her at all last night, and I miss her like crazy right about now. She balances my world, makes it right side up again. Plus, I think both Killian and I need a breather. Especially Killian! I'm not even sure what that was all about, but it was strange behavior—even for him. Maybe because he has such intense gifts, the connection affects him differently? I have no idea. But either way, I'll be showing up in his war room today. And his throne hall. Whether he gives me 'permission' or not. So, let's just hope his attitude is adjusted before then.

Right now, I'm just dying to get some real clothes and, of course, sit with my sister. But as I'm grabbing my ripped leggings and Stevie Nicks off-the-shoulder tee. Anise strolls in, followed by Amethyst and Sybil.

"Hey!" they all seem to utter at once.

I guess I hadn't thought about what it might feel like to face everyone today, knowing they had front seat tickets to the sexual deviant show. But, I'll admit, it's a tad uncomfortable. I'm no prude, but these people saw all my goodies and a literal fuck show. ON A STAGE, no less.

Oh, Goddess, Lincoln saw it too. Kill. Me. Now.

Suddenly, staying in this gorgeous room indefinitely seems like a legitimate plan. I wonder if I could get Killian to figure out Wi-Fi here? I mean, he did gain a television. It's not unreasonable to think he can do just about anything he wants.

"Uh, hey?" my cheeks redden, and the awkward-ness is strong.

"I fucked the wolf." Anise blurts out, and I'm so glad I hadn't taken a drink of my coffee yet, because it would be sprayed across the room.

"Oh! Umm, okay." I don't know what to say, and it's rare that I'm speechless.

The pang in my chest startles me. Is it pain? Surprise? Dare I say jealousy? I know that's wrong, jealousy, I mean. But no matter how I try to mask it or stuff it away somewhere in the far corner of my mind, I think I'm a little hurt.

That's not fair, Vivi. Hypocrite much?

I mean, it's not like he's never slept around. For hell's sake, that was his regularly scheduled weekend activity before the world went to shit. I couldn't count the sheer number of times he stumbled in half-hungover smelling of perfume and poor decisions for our training sessions. And I never cared. I made fun of him.

But Anise is different somehow. I love Anise, and it's more than just on the surface. It's a... well, I guess it's a sisterly kind of love. Maybe even motherly at times? Let's just say I wouldn't hesi-tate to incinerate anyone to fucks with her. In my world, that's the purest love there is.

"Are you mad at me?" I've never seen Anise wear this kind of apprehensive expression. And with those five words from the feisty, savage, eccentric crimson-haired Siren I truly love. My jealousy fades.

"No, Anise. I'm not mad, I'm sorry, I just... I was just surprised, is all." I muster the best smile I can at the moment.

"I can feel it." She looks to the floor, dejected.

Shit! Son of a sea cock! I forgot Sirens can feel emotions. Stupid, stupid!

I glance at Amethyst and Sybil, expecting to find judging eyes. But they've got their backs turned to us, inspecting the movie on the television like it's one of the seven wonders of the world. Trying all their best to mind their business, given the situation and close quarters. And I can't thank them enough.

The gang of cringe-worthy moments over the last twenty-four hours is impressive.

"Come sit," I invite Anise to the adjoining reading chair.

Yes, Killian put two in here. I'm not going to presume why he would do that. The mental picture of him and me sitting next to each other, reading in comfortable silence. It seems light years away from ever happening. Anise drags her feet to the burgundy chair, looking like a child who's about to be punished. And my heart cracks in half.

"I love Lincoln, Anise. And I'm sure you can feel that, but I love him like I love... you. Not as a mate, but as a friend. Like you're my friend. I only want him to be happy, and I'm sorry you had to feel that just now. That was about me, not you."

"You love me?" Her eyes perk up, and she flashes that endearing sharp-toothed smile.

"I do." I give her a genuine smile back and let down some of my defenses for her to feel my truth.

And that's as good a blessing as any, right?

Killian warned me that the entire realm would feel it. I just didn't foresee this specific outcome. Which is kind of ridiculous, being that I'm a fucking Seer! I forget myself around this fortress, around *him*. And that's just another reason to create some space between us.

After the uncomfortable girl chat, Amethyst and Sybil join us. I feel awful that I haven't made time for them while we've been here. Not that I had much to spare, but I don't even know anything about them.

"So, tell me about yourselves," I grin, and we all pile on the bed.

It turns out Sybil was born to a large wealthy family of Trolls. Which blew my mind because when I think of Trolls, I picture the grotesque beastly things we see on television. Not pretty girls, with emerald eyes and rosy lips. It turns out that her mother wasn't immune to the charms of the Dark Fae. And that's how she came about. Her intended father wasn't having the bastard of a mixed breed under his roof, and she found her way to Deacon. And then to Willa and Iris, who've been caring for her for a few years. And Amethyst? Well, it turns out I was right all along. She is Iris's niece, cast out for not only being a mixed breed like her aunt. But also for her sexual orientation.

Their stories are so similar that they trigger my cut-a-bitch reflex, and suddenly wiping out their parents seems perfectly reasonable.

The time with the girls was a much-needed distraction, although I'm missing Marlow. With the news Anise blurted into the room, I'm just assuming she's shacked up somewhere with a loudmouthed dragon, and I'll hear all the sordid details later.

Right now? It's time to pay Mr. Moody Pants an unscheduled visit.

CHAPTER THIRTY THREE

VIVI

BEFORE I CAN LOSE my nerve, I navigate the dark hallways of the Night Fortress. Decked out head to toe in true Vivi fashion. I haven't encountered many netherlings on my way to Killian's war room, but the few I have? I don't know if they're looking at me like I'm a strange new Queen or a shameless harlot. Possibly both? But I pay it no mind.

Calypso trails behind me, whipping her tail into the bricks—knocking over plants. Silly me, I thought, coming back as a Shadow Cat would change her. And although it may have changed her appearance, her rebellious attitude problem is intact.

Bloody Fudge puppies, I never thought I'd be thankful for that!

As I swagger into the room like I belong there, all eyes twist in my direction. And wouldn't you know it? Linc and Ansel have been officially invited to this asshole meeting, but I wasn't? Plain bagel can be in here, but not me? What the fuck is this? Sexist much, my Dark King?

No matter, though. I'm here now, and I'm not leaving this room. I'd like to see him try! I've been dying to stir a little shit, maybe start some fires? All I need is a reason. But to my disappointing surprise—Killian only flashes me a look of irritation and then continues on about Netherling Forces at the borders and something about supply chains.

"What have you heard of Faustus and the Academy?" I interrupt his riveting speech.

He looks like he wants to throttle me, and my lady bits are in wholehearted agreement with that plan! The insatiable traitors. But I burn the xxx-rated brain distraction away and stare right back. I asked a question, and I expect an answer.

After several intense seconds, our battle of wills dissolves, and Killian sighs in defeat. "Faustus was seen traveling to The Bone Keep three days ago. Presumably to meet with Mordred. The security around Underhill Academy has increased over the last week and doubled that since his departure. They are Shadowlings."

I bring one hand to my chin and rest the other on his fancy desk. "So, they're gearing up for their next move."

"We can't know that." He chastises.

"Why not? Extra security, leaving to meet with the Prick of the North, and it coincides with our binding. Sounds pretty dastardly-plan to me." I fire back.

Linc 'accidentally' clears his throat, and I don't want to look at him right now. I mean, I said I was fine with it, and I am. But right now? Really?!

I reluctantly turn my head in his direction, and just as I thought, he's got guilty written all over his face. Ugh! I'm not having this conversation twice. Once with Anise was humiliating enough.

"Maybe we need to increase surveillance? That way, you're both covered." Linc suggests.

I'd love nothing more than to argue, but I'm supposed to be a Queen now. Not a tyrant. I'll have to add the word compromise to my vocabulary. Ew.

"Yeah, okay. I guess that makes sense." I respond, tilting my lip in a half-smile. It's a peace offering of sorts, one of those yeah-I'm-surprised-but-I'm-not-angry looks.

"No." Killian answers.

What a dickbag.

"We need that security here, my *Queen.*" he says the word Queen so sarcastically that I'd like to slap the shit right out of him.

I work my jaw, using all my might to hold the crazy in. "I'd love to hear your superior idea, my Dark *King.*"

Dante and Bane are watching us like a reality tv show. I can only imagine what they're picking up on our thoughts. I lock eyes with Dante, and for a moment, visions invade my mind. Bane, Dante, and several Netherlings (male and female) making good use of their Den of Debauchery together. And they're equal opportunity, which is rad, but I didn't need a play-by-play. Especially when it triggers vivid memories of my very own sexual fantasy come true.

It must've been a helluva night for just about everyone! I shake off the thoughts of Killian sans clothing, face buried in my you-know-where, and focus on the situation at hand. We're at an impasse and we need to not be on opposing sides right now.

"Thanks a lot, Dante." I whip a thought in his direction.

"You're welcome, my Queen." he replies, a hint of mirth in the thought he lobs back.

Turning back to Killian, it seems a subject change is in order. "We bound ourselves last night, and you say the entire Netherworld feels the effects. Does that include the Shadowlands? My father. Would he know too?"

"Yes, he would."

Well, alright! So, we set the stage, the trap is sprung. It shouldn't be long now, and dear old absentee daddy will make his move. We'll be ready and waiting. This is a good thing!

"Okay, Killian, we'll wait." I give up a little ground.

I can be reasonable. Sometimes.

We've been at this all afternoon, and when food is brought into us, I make an audible noise, one that I didn't mean to sound so lusty—but I'm hungry! And food can be downright orgasmic when your stomach has been growling for an hour. It doesn't catch my attention that the meal is for two until the rest exit the room.

How the fuck did he orchestrate that? I've been here the whole time!

Killian and I eat in awkward silence, and at first, I was so focused on my fried chicken and mashed potatoes that Killian was the last thing on my mind. Until the heat crawls up my spine, and I notice him staring at me.

Weirdo, who watches another person eat? But when I give in and make eye contact... holy buckets! He's watching my mouth like he knows what kind of talent it holds. Double fuck.

"Aren't you going to eat? And I'm pretty sure Selene taught you that staring is rude." I smirk.

Instead of giving me the smart-assed reply I was expecting, he grabs my hand. Intertwining our fingers. Killian gives me the most open, vulnerable, tender look. Like he's found a precious jewel, and it's a dream come true.

All aboard the crazy train! Keep your hands and feet inside the car; the climate is unpredictable around here.

He scoots his chair as close to mine as he can get, not letting go of my hand while he does it. And suddenly, I'm rethinking every choice I've ever made. Then, finally, he moves his thumb along my hand, leaning closer and says. "I'm sorry."

UGH! His full, soft lips are coming in for a crash landing. I just know it. And I'm torn about whether I should knee him in the junk or just let it happen? Luckily for him, Selene chooses this very moment to intrude.

"It's time to hold Court." she gives her son a very 'mom' look, and his shoulders slump.

But for me? I might as well be painting a Pegasus ass with rainbows. The excitement plastered on my face is unmistakable. Finally, I'm going to get a peek behind the curtain! Yeah, Killian looks like he's sitting on a crown of thorns, but he can say whatever he wants. I barged into this room, and I'll bully my way into the next if need be.

"Fine, let's go get you changed. And I'll show you the 'real' Netherworld, my Savage Queen."

And there's that smirk again.

―――――◄○►―――――

When I am the true Dark Queen of my own fortress, I'm abolishing these ridiculous dresses. It's first on the list! Sure, they're pretty. But they're neither comfortable nor practical.

Why are my tits pushed up into my godsdamned chin? That's all I'm saying.

I'm not even going to lie; it's a trip being in this room. But at least it's all switched back to the regular goth club motif and not so much a sex dungeon. Also, I have a throne now? It's a smaller version of Killian's with a little more flare. Does he just conjure things out of air? I'm starting to wonder.

Anyway, beyond the self-consciousness of what we all know went down here last night, so far—holding Court is a tad boring. Not quite the pinnacle of insider information and mayhem I was picturing in my head. Which irks me because why is it again that I had to be locked up in my rooms for this?

They packed the room with onlookers; it's hard to even tell them apart in the crowd. And so far, we've had one Minotaur come to complain about the Shadowling camp stealing their food on the outskirts of Killian's territory. Which I know is bullshit (pun intended) because I ripped them all to pieces only a few nights ago. So, it surprised me when Killian agreed to have a few of his men send out that way to patrol and a boatload of food sent, too. Because I know he knows the same thing I do! That guy was lying out of his ass.

The Dark Prince King has mercy. Guess that's good to know.

Killian whispers in my ear. "They're hungry."

He doesn't need to say any more than that. I understand, people will do anything to feed their families. Even lie to a King.

Next, a female harpy (I think) approaches the throne and bows low. I mean, low-low. Right before she tells Killian and me, but mostly Killian—that The Night Fortress having a 'party' while the Kingdom is at war is in poor taste, and just how much she doesn't appreciate it. I detect her bullshit just as quickly as the man before her. It's not the 'party' she's upset about. It's not being invited. Which makes me curious why she wasn't? But about ten more minutes of her prattling on and pushing her breasts out while giving me the stank eye paints a better picture.

"Miss Orinya, the 'party' you're referring to was a binding ceremony. To this lovely woman here, who is your Queen. I suggest you treat her that way! And that binding has given us more protection from this war than anyone in this hall could ever provide. Is that all?" Killian has a little bite behind his back on this one, thank the Goddess. I was wondering if the Dark Prince King just lets everyone off with a warning no matter what they do.

She bows again, titties-on-display low. While looking at me, like I'm going to let her into Killian's bed or something? Sorry lady, but that's not in my job description. And even if it was, I wouldn't be clamoring to choose this whack-a-doodle to fill the position. When she re-

alizes it's not gonna fly with me either, she re-
treats into the crowd.

*Maybe Killian kept me in a gilded cage because he
didn't want my mind to melt from the nonsense...*

Just then, I hear heavy footsteps behind me.
I'm not sure if I'm supposed to turn and look? If
that's not Queenly? But I glance down at some
big ole boots and know it's Jagger. Good! Then
Marlow should be around here somewhere now
too, swallowed up by the crowd. I'll find her after
the circus leaves the hall.

By this point, the crowd is growing louder and
a bit more restless. They're whispering, fidgeting.
The energy has changed considerably.

Great, what next on the screwball agenda?

When the crowd parts, bodies moving as if they
want to be as far away from whoever is coming,
my heart rate picks up. Something feels off; I look
at Killian, who shows no sign of being rattled—except for his knuckles. They're white as a ghost
from gripping the side of his throne.

Okay, what the fuck?

And then I see it, the short figure with lavender
hair moving towards the front. Bronwyn steps
forward, and my flames surge to life. I should've
killed this traitorous bitch when I had the chance.
She was never my friend, and there must be
something wrong with my Sight, because I cared
about her. I believed her. I fucking told her things
I've only told a handful of people in my whole
life!

I'm seething now. Coiled tight and ready to
strike, when Killian lays his hand on mine. I want
to pull away. I want to tell him to fuck himself
with a rusty spike! But noooo, we're in front of the

entire Court, and I have to sit here looking like a dipshit who got bamboozled by a lying bitch! I can feel Jagger tensing at our backs, and when I look towards Lincoln and Ansel, they're doing the same.

"I should hope you would know better than to show your face in this Court, Bronwyn. You better have a good reason to be standing before me." Killian has no mercy in his eyes now; he's gone cold. Ice fucking cold.

"I do," she smiles. FUCKING SMILES! And then she continues. "I have a message from the Shadowlands."

Also known as Mordred...

I can't control the audible gasp that escapes my lips. My heart hitches, and something feels wrong. There are too many people in this room. I can't get a good read on it, but for the love of baby Cerberus, this feels a lot like déjà vu. Killian doesn't make a sound. Instead, he sits preternaturally still. Waiting on the message, I imagine.

"Faustus sends his most sincere thanks to the newlyweds." Bronwyn looks so pleased with herself it makes me sick. And that's it, that's where my sit-still-and-stay-Queenly runs out.

"For what?" I speak up, letting the hatred drip from my words.

"For returning his daughter to him, of course." she replies.

WHAT?! No. She's bluffing, right? Lincoln clenches, weapons drawn, not taking his eyes from her.

Meanwhile, I whirl on Jagger and whisper. "Marlow wasn't with you?"

His face is ashen, and I don't recall ever seeing a dragon look like he may vomit, but there's a first time for everything. "I thought she was with you!"

"I haven't seen her since some time yesterday! You weren't with her last night?" My mind won't accept this, and I know we're bickering in front of a crowd, but all my fucks have flown the coop. My best friend was taken, someone took her!

Motherfucker. That wasn't preparing for their next move; it was their next move! A diversion. Faustus has Marlow. It sinks in deeper and deeper until my body is made of molten lava. Until I am made of only blood and flames. Calypso moves from her perch on the side of the throne and stands at my side. A menacing snarl escapes her jaws as her tail whips with fury.

My vision goes blurry, and I don't have to look at Lincoln to know my eyes are glowing. I see the rage in him, the swirling galaxies in Killian's, the devastation in Jagger's. And I stand.

"Who took her?" I ask calmly.

Bronwyn replies with a cunning grin. And nothing else.

"I SAID WHO FUCKING TOOK HER!" my anger shakes the room, and Netherlings scramble to find their footing under shaky ground.

So, they wanted a Dark Queen? They're all about to get one. My rage is palpable. Vengeance lines every part of my face. Vivi is gone. My monster is in the driver's seat now. And finally, Bronwyn has the good sense to look afraid.

Who's a cocky bitch now?

It feels like hours before she answers. "I did."

And with that, I am down the steps and striding towards her. Flames blazing in my palms, I take one last look at Bronwyn and then let them fly. Burning her to death right where she stands, listening as she screams in agony until she collapses. Enjoying every moment without a hint of remorse. And then I turn to the stunned Night Court.

"Let this serve as a lesson. I have no problem killing the messenger, and I will not hesitate to execute anyone who means to harm the ones I love. You will let her lay where she fell and rot like the traitor she is. Do not touch that body! That is your one and only warning."

Calypso and Lincoln are hot on my heels as I'm leaving. I have to get out of this room, and this dress before I lose my shit and ugly cry in front of all these Netherlings I just shocked and horrified. I glance toward Killian to judge what kind of shit I just got myself in? But he nods his approval. Those stormy eyes overflowing with pride.

CHAPTER THIRTY FOUR

Underhill Academy

I DON'T KNOW IF it's customary or not? But I'm assuming after the public execution I'd just performed, Killian shut down Court proceedings. Because everyone is in my rooms. Everyone. The dull hum of several conversations happening at once is almost like white noise. Which is fine by me because I think I might be freaking out? Not about killing Bronwyn, because I'd do it a hundred times over again. Marlow is just as much my sister as Kalliope, and for longer. I would burn the world down to get to her, and I just might.

No, it's not that I killed her. It's just that I've never executed someone on my own authority before. It's always been a direct order from Faustus, under extreme threat of punishment if I did not obey. I've never executed a friend, well, someone who I thought was a friend, someone I had a relationship with. I don't regret it, but I think I startled myself.

"We're leaving. Now." I call out to the room.

It's the first time I've spoken since they arrived. And clearly, I'm into startling people today because everyone shuts their mouths at once, and an awkward silence ensues.

"I'm going to the Academy. Now." I repeat, for emphasis—because maybe they didn't understand me?

I'm waiting for the outbursts, the arguments, something. But after several silent moments, I realize it's not that they're stunned. They were just waiting for me to stop freaking out. Nobody is standing in my way, quite the opposite.

Jagger is murderous, Anise looks feral, Lincoln is ten seconds from wolfing the fuck out, even the Twins look menacing. And Killian, he is the scariest of all. They want to go just as badly as I do. And I know it's fucked up and even a little morbid, but my heart swells anyway.

Somewhere along the way, these beasts, monsters, and assholes became my family.

"I'll get into the Academy. I know a secret entrance; Marlow and I used to skip class, and we were very good at hidey holes." I divulge. I didn't give this secret way on our last visit because only one person can go through it at a time.

Okay, okay. Marlow and I might have dug a prison-style tunnel using earth and air.

This time, I only need it to get in. After that, I intend to be violently seen and heard on my way back out. Faustus dies today, whether he takes me with him or not.

"What's the plan?" Killian says. And I nearly choke on my tongue. So, he's... he's just going to let me take point on this, and we're not going to argue about it? Sweet!

"It's a simple one. The rest of you, just guard my back and kill anyone who gets in your way. I'll be exiting through the front doors." I smirk. Obviously, I've lost my mind. But I have no hesitation or doubt. This ends today.

"I'll get her back," I reassure Jagger and Linc, looking into their eyes and letting them see the truth of it.

———◆———

With a quick change of clothes (black pants, black shirt) And every weapon I could fit on my body. I meet my ragtag pack of weirdos in the throne hall. It's me, Killian, Anise, The Twins, Jagger, Linc. Even Amethyst, Sybil, and Ansel look ready to fuck shit up.

"We can't fit everyone on Jagger's back."

"We'll portal." Killian offers.

And then we're headed towards the back of the gardens, and it feels like déjà vu all over again. Except for the last time, I was devastated and walking away from the man I had thought I could have a future with.

This time? We're all going as one. Same team, same goal.

I'm saddened that Calypso still cannot cross the portal, that she won't be by my side. But seeing as the last time I did this, she was dead. I'm just thankful to scratch behind her ear and get a sassy huff of indignation before I go.

Selene waits for us by the opening, activating the pretty tornado. And one by one, we enter the jellylike swirling vortex. Landing on our asses from somewhere in the air. This is anything but a funny situation, but I can't stop myself—I snort, because I think we just made 'out of thin air' an actual thing.

I ushered the troops over to a small crack in the outer wall. When I remove a sizeable chunk, they're all flabbergasted at what's behind it. It really looks like a rabbit hole, only wide enough for some silly teenage girls to climb through and run off into the mountain's edge, playing hooky. I smile at the memory of Marlow and me; we really caused some chaos inside these halls. But, on the other hand, it was my favorite part of being stuck in this shithole.

I'm coming bitch, you're not dying with that v-card still intact! Not on my watch.

Turning toward Linc specifically because she's his sister just as much as mine. I give a few simple instructions, "If you go to the far side of the courtyard, around the wall to the opposite side of the Academy, the student side. There's a metal gate. It's probably covered in vines and overgrown weeds because nobody ever uses it for anything. So, wait out there until you hear my smart mouth or see a lot of fire, okay?"

Linc nods and then crushes my ribcage with a wolfish hug. "Go get our girl, Viv."

"See you on the other side!" Anise bounces, excitement bubbling in her very essence. My little fiery-haired ball of chaos and mayhem. I just love her to pieces.

I don't want to look at Killian. I know what I'll see there, and it's a distraction I don't want.

"See you on the other side." And then I'm crawling into the dirt-filled hole.

A moment of complete transparency. I've always hated this tunnel. With the creepy crawlies and the 'buried alive' feeling as I shimmy my way through. Can we say claustrophobic with a side of nyctophobia? But it had to be small enough to escape the attention of our professors and the elders. Plus, I was smaller back then. Now? It's tight quarters, and I'm doing all I can to keep my nerves at bay.

When I sense a minuscule amount of light, my breathing calms.

Almost there.

When I make it to the metal grate, I still myself and listen. Footsteps echo in this part of the Academy; you can hear them from rooms away. Which is why we picked it, of course. Who says you can't get a quality education among a bunch of elitist fucks with golden sticks up their asses?

As soon as I'm sure there are no moving bodies in this section, I pop the grate and emerge from the rabbit hole into a defunct ladies' bathroom.

Yep, you heard me. A bathroom. It's on the lower level, where there are only two classrooms. Both with loud machinery and frequent potion explosions. Like I said, smart cookies! But there are no students here now. I'm guessing their parents yanked them home when I pulled a Houdini. Or it could be the Shadowlings prowling about that had them squirrelly about keeping their pampered brats in the dorms. Either way, there are no innocents here. Everyone left in this building is fair game. My only real dilemma is getting from this corridor to the administration side; that's where Faustus has his office. And it's also where the dungeons are.

Think, Vivi. Think.

And then I've got it! I grab a few rolls of toilet paper (bear with me here) and reduce them to ash using my flames on the 'low setting.' It's nighttime, which means the halls are dark. And my clothing is dark, so if I cover my exposed skin in ash mixed with a bit of water. I'll blend right in!

Keeping low and with my back tight up against the walls, I make my way through the corridors. Slow and steady. Quiet as the Angel of Death. When I reach Faustus's office, I hear muffled voices behind the door. Which is great! Because that means he's indisposed, and by the sounds of it, he will be for at least as long as it'll take for me to get to the dungeon.

How do I know Marlow is in this dungeon? Simple. She disobeyed a psychotic narcissist and made him look like a fool, daughter or not. His ego wouldn't allow that. And we all know that when a narcissistic prick loses control of their intended victim, rage takes over. So, he's punishing her; I know it in my soul. And in Underhill Academy, punishments are in the Halls of Repentance.

Getting from his office to the dungeon is a breeze. It's actually an offshoot of the main building. Some of the corridor is open air, and then it leads down the crumbly stone steps into the bowels of this godsforsaken hellscape.

The smell hits me before I take the first step. Goddess, I forgot the stench. I don't know how? Because it's pretty unforgettable. A mixture of shit, piss, vomit, and decay. My anger spikes just thinking about Marlow in this cesspool. Iron torches line the rock walls, the clammy walls shimmer with condensation, the grimy floors covered in dead vermin, small bones, and broken stone. There will be two guards. There always are. All I need to do is separate them.

I lean down, clutching a slimy stone, and while trying not to gag, I toss it. Making an echoing sound off the opposite wall. And sure enough, footsteps are coming my way.

Excellent.

When one of Faustus's lackies peeks around the corner, I know I have seconds to get this right. Or we're going to be in for a hell of a ride. The mountain of a man takes a moment to locate me, crouched low to the ground. And the second he does, I spring up as fast as I can. Grabbing him by the throat. My blood magic surges to life, and I won't deny it. I take great pleasure in forcing the blood from his veins to exit through all of his orifices. I watch as his eyes, nose, and mouth spew rivers of blood until there's nothing left. And he drops to the ground.

Contestant number two realizes his partner in perversion is incapacitated, and he shouts, "Hey there!"

Shit, shit, shit.

We're going to have to speed this along.

I run into the dungeon proper with my flames already lit. If I throw a fireball, there will be screaming. We don't need screaming, at least not yet. I opt for the throat grab once again, but this time, I burn his vocal cords. And THEN I throw the fireball. He'll be bone and ash in no time.

"Vivi?" a weak voice calls out, and I nearly pass out with relief. Following that voice, I make it to the gate of a grimy cell. Imagine my surprise when I find not one but two occupants.

"Genevieve," Marlow's mother gives me a warm smile, a genuine smile.

"I removed his influence, Vivi. She's back. I got my mom back!" Marlow cries, and although that *is* an occasion worth crying over, we don't have much time.

I assess their injuries as I'm trying to figure out how to get past the lock. They roughed Marlow up. She's got a big scratch across her cheek, and her hair is matted with blood. Which stokes my wrath, but I'll get to that soon. The good news is, other than scrapes and some rage-inducing bruises, Marlow looks okay. Judith is a different story. Her arm is bent at an angle that cannot be natural. One of her eyes is swollen shut and purple. She's been worked over pretty well.

My anger flares and my hands heat. And not like the usual heat up. There aren't any flames, but they are glowing crimson. I wonder...

I take hold of the bars and concentrate on my rage. At first, I think we're gonna have to go old school with a bobby pin and a prayer because this isn't working, but then the metal groans and gives way.

Holy motherfucker of hell. I'm bending iron!

"Can you walk?" I whisper as I bend an opening big enough for them to squeeze through.

"I can," Marlow limps over to Judith and lifts her under her shoulder, "But I'm not sure if mom can."

Judith tries to stand and falters. Ahh, fuck! This isn't going according to plan in the least. And you can just call me a spectacular Seer because I'm positive we're about to get company. Angry and undoubtedly violent company.

"Alright. Lowe, you good enough to drag her to the courtyard? I'll do the fighting. You just stay right behind me and keep up? Backup is outside."

Her sunken eyes light up at my admission.

"Can you carry her weight long enough to get to Jagger?"

She lifts her shoulders and nods. "You know I'd commit felonies to get to Daddy Dragon."

At least she hasn't lost her sense of humor.

"I was counting on it," I wink.

And then we're on the move. But just as I thought, when we hit the open-air corridor, there's a line of Rune Force and Shadlowlings waiting.

Hey, um. Dark Goddess... if you're seeing this? I'm gonna need you to show the fuck up.

Fear creeps up from my stomach and into my chest, "Lowe, I'm going to need you to dig deep, alright? Daddy Dragon is just on the other side of that obstacle. You need to surround yourself and mama Judith with water, and don't let it fall."

I sure hope Iris was right when she said I could pull a Dr. Jean Grey because I think our lives depend on it. I clear my mind, slow my breaths, and drop the walls. Igniting my entire body in a raging violet bonfire. I can't stop to check if Marlow did what I asked. I just have to trust that she did. Because we're about to run.

Like a bullet on a mission, I launch myself forward. Pumping my legs and headed straight on bull-in-a-China-shop into the line of guards. Incinerating them on the spot.

Fuck. Yes!

But I know I won't be able to sustain this for long, so we run. After the first batch of guards, I glance back, hoping I didn't barbeque my bestie. And by the grace of the Goddess, she's got that water shield up, and she's struggling, but she's determined.

Just a few more hallways.

I realize I'm burning the building itself, and anything else in my wake on my way through. And it squeezes on my heart. We'll have to rebuild. But when the front doors come into view, I use that adrenaline spike to stumble through the finish line.

Bursting through the doors in a blaze of glory, I let out a muffled cry at the sight of my people. Waiting with Faustus surrounded. Well, that *is* convenient, isn't it? I let the flames sputter out and turn to Marlow and Judith as she collapses under the weight and clear exhaustion.

"Jagger! Assistance, please." He rushes to my side. "Meet Marlow's mom, Judith. And then get them the fuck out of harm's way. Cool?"

"You got it, Little Monster." He replies. If he's intimidated by meeting the parents, he's not showing it.

Now that I know Marlow is good, I whirl on Faustus. Anise, Killian, Linc, the entire crew moves to the side. Allowing me to approach him.

"So here we are." I muse.

"So here we are." He replies smugly.

Even surrounded by some of the strongest the Netherworld has to offer, he's cocky. Too full of himself to understand when he's well and truly fucked. Faustus isn't leaving this courtyard alive. He's just too stupid to realize it yet. But that's okay, I have a few words for him before we... what was it again? 'Get to the main event,' I think that's what he said right before he killed the only father I've ever loved in this exact spot.

The Universe must be female because the level of fantastical pettiness is off the charts. I love it.

"It's time to stop talking for once in your miserable life. But I have a few things to say." My smile is all teeth and zero mercy. "You are not a man; you're a coward and a failure. I hope you never know a moment's peace in the afterlife, but we will. Because a world without you in it is a better one. I'll sleep soundly tonight, knowing that you'll never hurt anyone again. This is for the little girl I could have been, for every innocent soul you condemned, for Marlow and Judith. For Deacon." I raise my palms and call my flames. He will not go painlessly; he'll burn for what he's done.

My power surges, and I aim for his chest. But as I'm about to exact the vengeance I've been waiting for all my life; I spot Marlow in the corner of my vision. She's shaking. The hatred in her eyes is intense and wrought with pain. And that's when I realize, as much as I've dreamt of this moment, this isn't my kill. Marlow and I lock eyes. No words are needed. I'd walk through hell for her. I'd give my life for her. So, I step back.

She limps her way into my spot, pure loathing written all over her face. "You will never touch my mother again. You will never hurt another one of my friends. Nobody will mourn you. You'll simply cease to exist."

And then she grabs the sides of his head. Faustus screams and convulses, his face twists in horror, and somehow, I just know that Marlow is delivering his memories back to him. From his victim's point of view. He's feeling everything he's ever done. He shakes and seizes until there's blood dripping from his nose, and then he falls. Staring wide-eyed and unmoving at the daughter he never loved. Marlow sinks to the ground and sobs. Within seconds, I'm on the ground with her, along with Linc and Judith.

"It's over?" She managed to get out between ragged breaths.

"It's over, Lowe." I grab her as she melts into my shoulder.

Faustus is dead. The rest of the Elders are dead or scattered to the winds.

Thornfall is safe. The Academy is ours.

CHAPTER THIRTY FIVE

THE NIGHT FORTRESS

SEEING JUDITH AND MARLOW embrace each other in the safety of the Night Fortress warms my stony heart. Of course, there's a lot of healing to do here, but the fact that they have the chance now? It's priceless. As a side note, it's also pretty dang priceless to watch the awe in a human's face when they experience the Netherworld for the first time.

Marlow and I hold each other on my big old bed fit for twenty bodies, listening to Judith recount her memories, "Oh girls, I never wanted to do what I've done, I was aware the entire time—but I couldn't stop it. I love you both, and I'm so sorry."

Marlow and I look at each other, tears in our eyes. And then we drag her in with us for a good old-fashioned group hug.

"You have nothing to be sorry for, mom." Marlow sniffles as she wipes her eyes dry. And I shake my head in agreement.

"You're safe now." I add to what Marlow's already said.

Even Calypso purrs her agreement, with Grim sitting beside her.

A Shadow Cat and a Hellhound. Unlikely besties, indeed.

We spend some time just catching up, and it feels like we're meeting her for the first time. When a knock at the connecting door interrupts, I already know it's Killian, and my heart drops. Since we got back, I've been avoiding him, not ready to have the discussion I know is coming.

He cracks the door and asks, "Everybody decent?"

I can't help but laugh, "I've never been decent a day in my life but we're wearing pants, if that's what you're asking?"

He cracks the door further as he peeks in his inky black head of hair and impossibly blue eyes. "Could we speak privately?"

Ugh, I guess you can't avoid the freight train forever.

I climb off the black four-poster bed, straightening my tank top and adjusting my leggings as I follow him into his rooms, and he closes the door behind him.

"While you were getting reacquainted with Judith and tending to your friend. I received some unsettling news." His eyes look troubled.

He knows how to start a conversation with a bang!

"And you've come here to fill me in? I'm surprised." I retort.

Killian looks as though he's got a mouthful for me, but continues. "The body in the throne hall isn't Bronwyn. Your flames broke some kind of identity spell. Unfortunately, there's not much left of the remains, but Genevieve... she has red hair."

No fucking way. Am I being Punk'd? What does he mean? It's not Bronwyn. Who would trade places and impersonate her for weeks? All the pieces move into place in my mind. She's been acting strangely ever since I came back. Barely speaking, that weird-ass conversation in my rooms, and I swore I saw a look in her eye a few times that wasn't quite right. Who would...?

"Lilia." I gasp.

Killian's answering stare confirms my suspicion.

Well, now I don't feel any remorse for playing judge, jury, and executioner. She's been on my I'll-kill-you-on-sight list since she attempted to cut my head off.

"So, where is Bronwyn?" Oh no, I believed she would betray us. I condemned her without a thought. My friend. In my anger, I lost sight of reason. And all this time, she's been in trouble?

Goddess, I suck... just a real fucking asshole I am.

"I don't know, Genevieve," Killian responds to my question, taking a few steps forward until we're too close for my comfort. He attempts to embrace me, and my heart falters—but my brain doesn't. I gently put out my hand and touch it to his chest. Not letting him come any closer.

And that's when he releases that mouthful he's been holding in. "I've been a fool. I pushed you away to keep you safe. I didn't think you were strong enough to survive my curse. But watching you today? You were a lethal thing of beauty. I was wrong, and I'm sorry. You are strong enough, Genevieve. A Queen in your own right. I apologize for not recognizing it sooner." He pauses, and I'm too speechless to say a damn word. Killian looks like he may be sick, and it's jarring. I've never seen him this nervous before.

"We can fight this curse together. We can rule together. I don't think I can live without you." His voice is raw and exposed.

And he pulverizes my heart with one sentence.

"No, Killian. We can't. Because I feel something for you, maybe even too much. But I'll never trust you. How could I? Every day a new skeleton falls from your closet and cleaves me open. Every moment I think I've broken through your outer shell and found the good man inside you, show me the worst of you right after. We will fight for this realm, and we'll take back the Shadowlands. Together. Because despite it all, we are more powerful when we're bound. But when we're done, *we're* done."

Every word feels like the slice of a razor blade leaving my lips, but I have a duty here. I don't know what the prophecy means or how to fight off a killing curse. But I was wrong about destiny. It's real, and it's undeniable. I was born to restore my realm, and I'm destined to do it with my sister. Kalliope and I will take back our true home and destroy the monster who created us.

As I peer into Killian's face, it's as if I'm being stabbed. He broke my heart, standing in front of that portal before I left him. And now, I've broken his.

CHAPTER THIRTY SIX

VIVI

OUR FINGERS INTERTWINE, AND the frail bones leave scars on my heart. My sister is wasting away, and I can't fix it.

"Kalli, we killed Faustus and took the Academy. I know you've never lived in Thornfall, but I think you'd like it there. I'm a Queen now, for a while anyway. I went through a lot to get here, and I'll tell you all about it when you wake up... Kalliope, please wake up... I need you for what comes next. I need you by my side when we take back what's ours and stop Mordred for good. I can't do this alone; I can't do it without you," tears drip from my eyes to her nightgown. Leaving tiny puddles in the material.

Pulling my fingers from hers, I lay my head in my hands and whisper to myself, "I just need you, Kalliope."

Almost as if on cue, Not Frank winks into existence. The G.I. Jackass smile in full effect.

"What are you doing here?" I give him the side-eye.

"What I was commanded, of course." He winks at me as he moves toward my sister.

I ready myself to pounce on his ass if he means her any harm; I'll punch the Dark Goddess right in her sloped nose if she thinks to come after my sister. Deity or not!

Frank brings his hands to Kalliope's temples, and the dull room fills with murky shadows. I can see the outline of his hands on her face, but then a light breaks through the haze. Clearing the room of shadows, and I am staring into my sister's yellow-green eyes.

To be continued...

Did you enjoy your reading experience? Please help a girl get the word out and leave a review!

For exclusive content, hilarious memes, the first look at new releases, and fellow bookworms doing bookworm things.

Come to the dark side! Join my author group on Facebook – Darwin's Darklings.

Stay tuned for the conclusion of The Gravestone Trilogy.
The Daughter of Oracles.
Spring 2022

STAY CONNECTED

About the Author

An author by day and a Werewolf by night. Amber is a former college professor of Paranormal Investigation.
A lover of coffee, cats, reading, naps, and all things witchy. Not necessarily in that order.
She currently resides in Wisconsin with her rock star husband, three children, and a house full of familiars.

Made in United States
Troutdale, OR
09/10/2023

12798084R00219